Book 2 of the Seeds of Civilization series

I0681294

Tsubute

R.J. Archer

NWIDI Press ~ Portland, OR

Tsubute

This book is a work of fiction.
All names, characters and incidents are either
the product of the author's imagination or are used fictitiously
and any resemblance to any persons, living or dead,
is entirely coincidental.

For more information on the Seeds of Civilization series, visit:
www.SeedsOfCivilization.com.

Library of Congress
Cataloging-in-Publication Data

"Tsubute" by R.J. Archer

p. cm.
ISBN-10: 0-9779109-1-1 (softcover)
ISBN-13: 978-0-9779109-1-5
Science Fiction, general

823.0876   2006902502

Published 2006 by NWIDI Press, P.O. 230154, Portland, OR 97281, US.
©2006 R.J. Archer

Cover art: tsubute illustration by Pierre Loranger, Montreal, Canada.
Cover design by Diseño International, Portland, Oregon.

Manufactured in the United States of America.

"The long anticipated sequel to *Tractrix* is finally here, and once again, R.J. Archer lays a foundation of rich detail that subtly builds into a runaway train of action, treachery and discovery. *Tractrix* offered a glimpse at a vision of history ignored by contemporary scholars; *Tsubute* rips down the curtain and sets it on fire."

Sean Ellis, author of *Magic Mirror* and *The Clive Cussler Code*

"Settle in and fasten your seat belt. You're about to take off on an adventure of action and international intrigue. Your host, R.J. Archer, will be your diving guide and your local expert on Japanese culture. His pulse-pounding plot suggests an island's incredible secret. Most amazing of all, this tale is based on a real island and stunning recent archeological findings."

Richard Jones, feature writer for *El Hispanic News*, Portland, OR

Tsubute

Introduction

The *Seeds of Civilization* series is loosely based on the theories of Graham Hancock and others who believe that highly developed civilizations existed on Earth thousands of years before the time currently put forth by mainstream Anthropology.

If Hancock's theory that an advanced civilization existed on Earth 9,000 years ago is correct, one has to wonder whether or not there were even earlier civilizations, each lost to some global cataclysmic event. These "lost civilizations" may have been totally destroyed by volcanoes, earthquakes or by changes in the global climate.

My series accepts Hancock's theory, in principal, but goes on to explore the question of how and where these ancient civilizations might have acquired their advanced knowledge of mathematics, astronomy and architecture and how they were "jump started" again after each catastrophe.

Tsubute, Book 2 of the series, is set on the tiny Japanese island of Yonaguni where a real underwater "monument" was discovered less than twenty years ago. Some experts believe that the structure is at least 9,000 years old and was well above the water line prior to the end of the last Ice Age, when the Earth's oceans rose more than three hundred feet. Since the discovery of Yonaguni, numerous other submerged sites have been discovered around the world, giving further credence to Hancock's theory.

One of the most exciting of these underwater discoveries is right in our own back yard – just off the northwestern tip of Cuba. There, in more than 2,100 feet of water, an underwater research team has discovered what they think are the remains of an entire city! The megalithic structures appear to be made of granite, which would have had to come from at least 1,000 miles away and initial estimates place the age of the complex at from 15,000 to 50,000 years old. But I'm getting ahead of myself – there will be lots more about MEGA in Book 3. For now, join the team from NWIDI as they explore Yonaguni and discover the mystery of the *tsubute*.

Tsubute

Chapter 1

(January 19, 2002)

The ground shook for the third time in as many minutes and Akimoto looked up from his work in anger. The single light suspended over his workbench was swaying again and the motion made it difficult for him to concentrate on the delicate task at hand. There had been so many of these small aftershocks in the two months since the earthquake that he no longer feared being trapped underground, but the interruption annoyed him anyway.

Akimoto steadied the fixture and returned to his work. Using a tiny brush, he continued copying ancient symbols onto the small eight-sided disk before him. Several minutes later he leaned back and smiled. This was his finest – and deadliest – *tsubute* so far!

***

Half a world away, Dr. Frank Morton heard a car door slam and glanced up from the book he was reading to see his friends, Tony Nicoletti, Jim Barnes and Linda McBride, getting out of Linda's car. As he opened the hangar's office door to greet the trio, he realized that it had been more than five months since he had last seen Tony, his old Viet Nam buddy. Linda lived next door to Frank in a downtown Seattle high-rise and Jim was a professor of anthropology across town at the University of Washington, but Tony had been bouncing back and forth between his home in Atlanta and a friend's place in the Caribbean ever since the four had met here last August.

A lot had happened since that meeting. The tragic events of September 11 had changed the world forever, of course. Today, four months after the attacks on New York and Washington D.C., air travel was just getting back to normal. Temporary airport closures due to security breaches were still frequent occurrences and Frank often reminded himself of just how fortunate he was to have acquired the Learjet 60 aircraft currently parked out in the hangar, just on the other side of the office wall.

Frank opened the door and greeted his friends with hugs and warm handshakes.

"Come on in, guys! Tony, you look like a walking advertisement for a tanning salon. I take it you've been back to the Caribbean since we last met?"

"Several times! In fact, I just flew in from there this morning. I got stuck down there for two weeks after the 9-11 attacks but fortunately Jill let me hang out at her place. She sends her best, by the way. Those attacks were something, weren't they? Can you believe the nerve of those bastards?" Tony huffed. Shaking his head, he crossed the threshold and entered the well-appointed office. "Man, this place sure looks different."

When the four had first met in this building, it had been in a serious state of disrepair. It had been vacant for several years before Frank bought it and it had cost him a fortune to have it cleaned and renovated. In the reception office where they were now standing, for instance, an old wooden desk and the smell of grease had been replaced by high-tech black furniture and the soft fragrance of fresh cut flowers on a filing cabinet in the corner.

"I'm glad you like it," smiled Frank, "but I think you're going to like the changes I made out in the main part of the hangar even more. The renovations were delayed more then a month due to the terrorist attacks, but the last of the office furniture finally arrived yesterday, so we timed this meeting perfectly. Let me show you what I've done to that dirty old airplane hangar you saw the last time you were here."

The meeting back in August had been called by Frank one month to the day after the termination of an impromptu investigation that had started with a mysterious black sphere and ended with some startling discoveries about the origin of Mexico's Maya natives and their predecessors, the Olmec. Since the spheres could potentially rewrite anthropology, Frank had taken to calling that investigation the Tractrix Project because a tractrix is the mathematical equivalent of a sphere that's been turned inside out.

During the course of that short, three-week investigation, Frank and Jim had crawled through ancient caves in the Yucatan Peninsula and Tony had traveled to the bottom of a thousand foot deep tunnel built by the U.S. government on the edge of the infamous Nevada Test Site, northwest of Las Vegas.

Before being run off by agents of the Department of Energy, Frank, Tony, Jim and Linda had managed to decipher ancient Mayan hieroglyphs, solve an international murder and learn some startling facts about a recovered flying saucer – from a Department of Defense researcher who had actually examined it!

But that was then, and this is now. Back then, Frank had proposed that the four join together and form a nonprofit research organization to investigate other mysteries of history and science. Today he had invited his three friends to the hangar to show off the new headquarters of the Northwest Institute of Discovery and Investigation (NWIDI) and to convince the trio to abandon their current jobs and join him.

Since winning an $86-million lottery jackpot last June, Frank had completely transformed his life. Just before Tony acquired the mysterious sphere, Frank had retired from his position at Boeing Aerospace, where he had been a senior team leader for the International Space Station. Since the conclusion of the Tractrix Project, Frank had devoted all his energies to the creation of NWIDI. Frank's wife, Donna, had been killed in a freak automobile-pedestrian accident a little over a year earlier and the total immersion in NWIDI had been good therapy for him.

Frank indicated a door in the back corner of the office and waved everybody through into the main part of the hangar, where the Learjet was parked.

Linda was the first to enter the gleaming white-and-stainless-steel hangar. "Wow, Frank!" she shouted. "This place is incredible. And what's all that up there? I don't remember a second floor when we were here the last time."

Linda was pointing to the glassed-in catwalk that ran down the near side and across the entire back of the large, sixty-six-foot-deep by ninety-eight-foot-wide building.

"We'll get to that in a minute, Linda, but let me show you around down here first. There's a room over here that I think you may be interested in."

Frank opened the door to a room directly behind the front office and Linda's eyes lit up. Tall equipment racks packed full of computers and related communications gear covered two sides of the room.

"I sank almost $100,000 into this room, but I wanted to be sure you'd have everything you might need," smiled Frank as he waved his arm at the equipment.

He led the group around the expansive first floor of the hangar, pointing out several other rooms. In each back corner there were large storage rooms and the area between them contained a well-equipped shop area and an office.

"This is the flight crew's office," indicated Frank. "I managed to steal a husband and wife team away from a local charter company. Their names are Don and Susan Fitzgerald and you'll have a chance to meet them tomorrow. They have a lot of experience with the Learjet 60 and they're really nice folks.

"And now for the fun part of the tour. As Linda already knows, I've been moving out of my condo for the past week. Let me show you why!"

A glass-enclosed flight of stairs connected to the second-story catwalk that ran along the back of the building. As they started up the stairs, Tony noticed a silver BMW Z3 Roadster parked just inside the main hangar door at the other end of the building.

"Looks like you got yourself some new wheels," commented Tony as he nodded toward the sports car.

"Yes, the Durango is more vehicle than I need most of the time, although I've been driving it the last week or so while I've been moving. But the Roadster is a lot more fun to drive, especially in this Seattle traffic."

After climbing the stairs, they came to a set of ornate double doors two-thirds of the way down the rear catwalk. Frank placed his thumb onto a pad and a tiny green light illuminated. He turned the doorknob and motioned the others through ahead of him, into a large living room furnished with tan leather couches and dark wooden tables. In the back right corner of the room was a round, freestanding gas fireplace and a door in the opposite wall opened into a large office.

"Welcome to my humble abode," beamed Frank as the other three fanned out to explore. Eventually they all rejoined Frank in the living room.

"I assume you hired an interior decorator to do all of this," said Tony, nodding his approval.

"Yes, and thanks for implying that my own tastes are crappy," laughed Frank. "I'm going to leave most of my old furniture in the condo and try to rent it out as an executive suite. Boeing often brings in engineers from their larger clients for long periods of time and they're always on the lookout for quality housing."

"Well, this will certainly cut down on the commute to work," laughed Jim, who had been very quiet since arriving. "It's very nice, though. Very nice."

"Yes, it's beautiful, Frank!" added Linda. "It's a little smaller than your condo, but I love the furnishings and you'll probably spend most of your time in your office anyway, if I know you."

"I'm glad you all approve. Speaking of offices, maybe it's time to show you yours. This way, please."

Frank gestured his three friends back out through the apartment's double doors and onto the catwalk.

Continuing on, they came to the point where the catwalk made a 90-degree turn to the left and continued down the side of the building parallel to the main runway of the King County Airport. Before making the turn, Frank opened a door in the corner.

"This is obviously our conference room and library. I've moved most of my reference materials and old files in here, and I invite you all to do the same."

Immediately adjacent to the conference room was an open office door.

"This will be Jim's office," said Frank, "because it's next to the library and he'll probably be in there the most.

"This next office is Linda's. It's directly over the computer room you saw earlier and it has a super-fast workstation connected to the servers downstairs via fiber-optic cable."

At the end of the catwalk they came to a third office. Like the previous two, this one had a large window in the side of the building that looked out toward Boeing's airplane facilities across the runway. In addition, this office had a window in the front of the building that looked south, out onto the apron in front of the hangar. Directly below this window was the front door through which they had originally entered the building.

"I thought we'd put Tony up front here where he can keep an eye on who's coming and going," grinned Frank. "Sort of like the company watchdog, you know."

Jim and Linda chuckled at Frank's insinuation, but Tony just grunted, crossed to the desk and sat down. With his back to the runway, he put his feet up on the desk, clasped his hands behind his head, and said, "I like it. Somebody get me a beer."

Directly across the catwalk from Tony's office was a door that opened into a second enclosed stairway that led back down to the hangar floor. As they exited the bottom of the stairway and walked toward the gleaming white Learjet 60 that occupied most of the main hangar, Frank turned to them with a questioning look on his face.

"Well, how did I do?" he asked. "Is everybody ready to go to work?"

Never one to be shy, Tony was the first to answer. "Except for the fact that your office is bigger than everybody else's this is a pretty cool set-up, Frank. I'm still not sure what we're going to do here, but you can count me in on whatever the plan is."

Casting a glance back over her shoulder toward the computer room, Linda smiled and added, "Yes, me, too. And I don't even care that my office is smaller than yours, Frank. This is a researcher's dream."

"What about you, Jim?" asked Frank. "We're really going to need your knowledge around here. In fact, I don't think we can take on our next project without your help."

Frank, Tony and Linda all looked to Jim for his response.

"Uh, well, gee, guys, I don't know what to say," stammered Jim. "As intriguing as this all sounds, I don't want to give up my position at the University. I have tenure now and I really enjoy teaching. It's an incredible offer, Frank, but I don't know ..."

"Jim, I know your situation is different from these two. Tony was ready to give up long haul trucking anyway, and Linda feels stifled by the routine assignments she gets at the newspaper, so they're both ready for a change. But you're on sabbatical until next fall and you're still searching for some publishable research, right?"

"Yes, that's true," nodded Jim. "I had hoped to do a series of papers on what we learned in the Yucatan last summer but the Department of Defense tied my hands when they classified everything Top Secret. And that's exactly the problem, Frank. I don't know what new mystery you plan to investigate, but if I sink several months into it and end up not being able to publish anything, I will have lost my whole year of sabbatical leave. The University takes a pretty dim view of professors who don't produce, you know."

Frank put his hand on Jim's shoulder and said, "What if I told you our next project is directly related to anthropology and archeology and what if I could guarantee you that this time there would be no interference from the U.S. government? Would you be interested then?"

Jim thought for a second, and then said, "Well, sure, but how can you make a guarantee like that? Ben Kingston promised to help me salvage some of the Yucatan work, but then his superiors overruled him. Our government has a way of making its own rules and breaking promises when it suits their needs."

"I can assure you that there will be no interference by the U.S. government because they have no jurisdiction where we'll be going. If the three of you agree to help me on this project, our investigations will take place completely outside the United States and any discoveries we make will belong solely to us. And unless Tony or Linda objects, I hereby assign all publication rights to you, Jim."

"Come on, Jimmy-boy, at least listen to what our whacked out friend has in mind," encouraged Tony. "Give it a few days and then you can back out if you're not interested."

"Knowing Frank and some of his theories, I'm not worried about any lack of interest," replied Jim, "I'm just worried about the lack of publishable material."

Jim stared down at his shoes thoughtfully for a moment and then slowly raised his head. "I'll tell you what. I'll sign on for this project with the understanding that I <u>must</u> get some publishable work done, either here or somewhere else, and that I'm going back to my teaching duties in the fall, no matter what. If you guys can live with that, I can, too."

Relieved that Jim had agreed to join the team, Frank smiled broadly. Amidst the backslapping and hand shaking, Jim finally asked, "So what strange and mysterious thing have you found for us to investigate this time?"

Frank answered Jim's question with a question of his own. "Would you be interested in a 75-foot tall underwater pyramid that predates everything in Egypt by at least 8,000 years?"

Chapter 2

Frank led the three new members of NWIDI back up to the conference room to brief them on his proposed investigation. When they were all seated around the large table, Frank handed Tony, Jim and Linda each a stapled packet of papers.

"I put this material together in a hurry, so it's probably not complete, but I think it covers the basics. Let me give you a quick overview and you can study the packets later.

"The underwater pyramid I mentioned was first discovered in the mid-80s by a local scuba diver named Kihachiro Aratake. Aratake is an experienced scuba guide and he ran across the monument by accident one day while searching for some new spots to take his clients."

"You mean this thing had never been seen until just a few years ago?" interrupted Tony. "It must be in a really remote spot."

"Actually, it's not, Tony. It sits a mere 500 feet off the coast of tiny Yonaguni Island, at the very southern tip of the Japanese chain. The top of the so-called Yonaguni Monument is only 15 feet below the surface and the structure itself is about 75 feet tall.

"In archeological terms, Yonaguni is a very recent discovery and it didn't come to the attention of the scientific community until even later – not until the mid-90s. But this is only one of the things about this site that caught my attention. The real grabber for me is that most of the geologists who have studied Yonaguni and five other sites near Okinawa all agree that these structures are about 12,000 years old – 8,000 years older than the pyramids of Egypt."

Frank looked to Jim, expecting the anthropologist and archeologist to challenge the dating of Yonaguni, but instead Jim was nodding.

"I've been following some of this work," agreed Jim. "There are a growing number of maverick geologists and archeologists who are challenging the establishment's theories that the early civilizations of Egypt, which only date to about 3,000 B.C., were really the first. As you can imagine, classic Egyptologists are fighting these new theories tooth and nail."

"But haven't they found human remains that are millions of years old?" asked a confused Linda.

"Of course," explained Jim as his teacher personality took over. "In fact, scientists believe that very early humans, called *Homo erectus,* inhabited parts of Asia as early as two million years ago, and may have inhabited Africa even earlier than that. But in my business, *civilization* refers to an evolutionary stage in which there is an advanced state of intellectual, cultural, and material development, an extensive use of record-keeping, including writing, the appearance of complex political and social institutions and a specialization of labor. It is generally accepted that the earliest civilizations appeared in the Mid-east – specifically Egypt and Mesopotamia – about 3,000 BC. The first Asian civilizations in India and China probably occurred slightly later."

"So who built this pyramid in Japan, if it's really 12,000 years old?" asked Tony. "It couldn't have been done by a bunch of nomads. Something like this would have required a lot of laborers and some serious project management."

"And therein lies the mystery!" announced Frank. "A number of scientists, like Schoch and West and a guy named Graham Hancock, believe that a civilization flourished prior to 10,500 B.C. and that this civilization was wiped out at the end of the last ice age by a sudden melting of the earth's ice caps that resulted in a 300-foot rise in the oceans. Their theories have been laughed at for years, but then along came Yonaguni, and not long afterwards underwater structures were discovered just off both the eastern and western coasts of India.

"So here's what I propose," continued Frank. "We'll fly from here to Japan, check out this Yonaguni thing and then maybe we'll fly on to India and check out the two sites there. There hasn't been much real investigative work done at any of these sites, and no single team has ever explored all of them, so we'd be breaking some new ground. Our objective will be to get to the bottom of who built the structures and why. Perhaps we can even link them together. What do you think?"

"It sounds to me like it's going to be one hell of a dive trip," smiled Tony, "and you can definitely count me in."

"Well, I don't dive, but there are certainly some interesting research possibilities," said Jim. "As I said earlier, I want to be back before the beginning of the next school year, but this sounds fascinating – I'm in, too"

"I don't dive, either," added Linda, "but I've always wanted to. I just never had the nerve to do it by myself. If you guys are willing to show me the ropes, I'd love to see these places first hand. But I have another problem. As much as I dislike my job at the newspaper, I feel like I need to give them some notice – at least a couple of weeks. When were you planning to leave for Japan, Frank?"

"Oh, it'll take us at least two weeks to get all the necessary gear together," replied Frank. "And in the meantime, I'll hook you up with an instructor I know. The dives in Japan certainly aren't for beginners but the sites in India should be much more accessible. I'd like you to get a legitimate dive card because some shops won't even fill your tanks unless you can prove you are certified. Are you sure you don't want to do this, too, Jim?"

"Quite sure!" replied Jim with no hesitation. "I'll stay on the boat and analyze any samples you retrieve. I have absolutely no interest in becoming fish food."

"Okay, then I guess we have a preliminary plan. We'll leave for Japan as soon as we can get ready, but no sooner than two weeks from today. Linda, you can give your notice on Monday and I'll set up your dive training with this friend of mine. You should be able to get through the course in four or five evenings if you work at it and you can do your certification dives before we leave.

"Jim, you should probably cram your head full of as much information as you can about these sites, although there hasn't been much written yet. I have books by both Schoch and Hancock here, so be sure to grab them before you leave today. I guess it wouldn't hurt if you brushed up on early Asian cultures, too."

"I'll do that, and I'll try to build a reference library on computer CDs to reduce the weight. I assume we'll be taking the Learjet, right?"

"Well, I think so. I mentioned the possibility of this trip to Fitz the other day and he said Susan would try to work out a flight plan. There are refueling issues on long trips like this because the Learjet only has a 2,800-mile range. The CD library is a good idea, though. As soon as the new computers arrive, I'll bring one over to the University for you. I expect them to be here Monday or Tuesday."

"Tony, we'll need you to be in charge of equipment, especially the dive gear," continued Frank. "My stuff is in a box somewhere downstairs but we'll need a whole new setup for Linda."

"And for me, too," said Tony. "I left my gear in the Caribbean because it's such a hassle to get it through security these days. Jill and I have been doing quite a bit of diving lately, so fortunately I'm back in pretty good shape."

After going over a number of other details, the meeting finally adjourned about 4:00 p.m. Linda had tickets for a concert later in the evening and Jim was eager to get back to the University and start his research. Linda offered to drop Jim off on her way back downtown but she promised Frank that she would be back the next day to check out the computer equipment.

Frank and Tony moved from the conference room into Frank's living room to kick back and enjoy a beer. Frank turned on the gas fireplace to take off the January chill and settled into one of the leather couches.

"So have you thought about what part of town you want to live in?" asked Frank.

"No, but I stayed at the Marriott Courtyard on the south end of Lake Union last night, and I'm thinking that I might like to be near the water. I noticed a lot of apartment complexes up on the hill on both sides of the lake, so maybe I'll check out some of them tomorrow. I appreciate your offer to let me stay at your condo, but the 15th floor of a high-rise in downtown Seattle just isn't my style. I'll need to make a trip back to Atlanta before we take off for Japan, too. I'll probably store most of my stuff back there, but I'll need to ship my clothes and some other things out here."

"Ship your stuff here to the hangar and we can have it stashed in one of the storerooms downstairs until we get back from overseas. I've got a girl who's going to hang out down in the front office while we're gone, so there will be somebody here to sign for it. She's a real character, but she's the daughter of my old boss at Boeing and she's reliable. And if you're serious about the lake, I know a guy who's got a furnished houseboat he wants to rent for about six months. He's being temporarily transferred to Europe and he doesn't want to move all his stuff over there for such a short time. I think it even comes with a 24-foot boat."

Tony's eyes lit up. "Cool! Yeah, I'd definitely like to take a look at it. Maybe you could run me by there tomorrow, since I don't have any wheels yet."

"Sure, we can check it out together, but why don't you take the Durango until you get your rig out here? I'm done moving and I'd rather drive the Roadster anyway. The Durango is in the parking lot back at the condo, so how about if we grab some dinner at our usual hangout on the waterfront and then swing by the condo? I'll pick up a few last odds and ends and you can take the Durango back to your hotel."

"Dinner at Fisherman's sounds great," replied Tony. "And it's fitting, too, since that's where this whole NWIDI thing first started back in July when I gave you the original sphere."

"Good point! Let me show you how to operate the security system here and then we can take off."

Twenty minutes later, they pulled away from the hangar in the BMW Roadster.

"Man, that's some burglar alarm system you've got there," commented Tony. "It does everything except make coffee."

"Well, that hangar and its contents represent a lot of money, and there's not much traffic down at this end of the runway at night. I had it custom-engineered by the same company that does a lot of the Boeing facilities, including the plant where I used to work. We always had a lot of classified stuff lying around, and our security system had to meet some pretty tough government specs."

"Well this system is a real dandy! I especially like the fingerprint scanners. Can each lock be programmed individually?"

"Yes, it's all computerized, so I can grant or deny access to any fingerprint/lock combination. And it's pretty easy to change, too, so if I come home with a date I can quickly lock you guys out of my apartment," laughed Frank. "I'll get Jim's and Linda's prints scanned and stored the next time they're on site."

"And what happens if the computer crashes or the power goes off? Do you have some kind of secret decoder ring to let you in?" asked the eternally pessimistic Tony. "Or do you just have a big crowbar hidden in the bushes out back?"

"No decoder rings or crowbars, but there are a couple of backup systems, so don't worry. I'll go over the whole thing with you the next time you're at the hangar."

At the restaurant, Frank and Tony spent the first few minutes catching up on the past four months. Frank had been closely involved in the hangar remodel, of course, and Tony had sold his big rig in Atlanta and resigned his contract to haul "special commodities" for the U.S. government. The two friends had met Jill Harris in Las Vegas while investigating the sphere that kicked off the Tractrix Project, and Jill had latched on to Tony right away. When Jill's stepfather was killed to protect the truth about the spheres, the government had encouraged her to disappear until the murderer was apprehended. Fortunately, Jill's stepfather had left behind nearly a half-million in cash, so her life in exile was quite comfortable and even after her stepfather's murder had been solved, she had elected to stay "in hiding." Only Tony had ever learned where Jill had actually gone.

"So I've already guessed that she's in the Caribbean somewhere," said Frank. "Exactly where did Jill end up?"

"I guess she wouldn't mind if I told you, Frank, but she's still keeping a pretty low profile because she's always been afraid the feds might have a change of heart and want the cash back. She has an incredible place on St. John, the smallest of the U.S. Virgin Islands. Her front porch looks out across the Sir Francis Drake Channel toward the British Virgin Islands and the constant easterlies keep it quite comfortable, even in the summer."

"Good for her!" smiled Frank. "And I don't blame her for staying out of sight. Look what they did to poor Jim and his research. Maybe we'll take the Learjet down there one of these days and pay her a surprise visit."

"I think she'd like that. I've found some amazing dive sites that I'd like to show you. You could dive every day for the rest of your life down there and never visit the same site twice."

Frank leaned back in his chair and clasped his hands behind his head. "Speaking of diving, what are your thoughts about this trip to Japan?"

"Like I said earlier, it sounds like one hell of a dive trip, at the very least. Beyond that, who knows? One has to wonder why the pyramid wasn't discovered centuries ago, and why it hasn't been overrun with archeologists and National Geographic photography teams now that it has been discovered."

"Well, there are several factors that contribute to the relative obscurity of the Yonaguni Monument, as the pyramid is called. The island itself is small and somewhat isolated and there are no Western-style hotels or restaurants on the island. More significant, though, are the dive conditions. There are really strong currents in the area around the monument and a lot of scientists have traveled all the way to Yonaguni only to be denied the opportunity to see the pyramid because the dive conditions were so bad. And I suspect that the sharks may have something to do with the relatively small number of visitors to Yonaguni," smiled Frank. "Did I mention the schools of Hammerhead sharks that hang out around the monument?"

"All of a sudden, this isn't sounding like such a great dive trip after all," said Tony. "You're not actually going to let a newbie like Linda get into the water over there, are you?"

"No, not unless we get some unusually good dive conditions. But there will be other opportunities for her to dive and getting certified will be a good experience for her."

"And what's the deal with the Hammerheads?"

"I've read that during the cooler winter months – December, January and February – several hundred Hammerheads migrate to the monument area and school near the surface. Apparently they stop eating during this period, so they aren't too dangerous until the end of the winter – and by then they are really hungry. We'll be there during the fasting period so we should be okay."

"So far we have impossible currents and man-eating sharks. Is there anything else you forgot to tell us about this spot, Frank?"

"No, I don't think so … well, not unless you count the fissures in the ocean floor that unexpectedly burp sulfurous gases."

"Perfect! This is destined to be another typical Frank Morton misadventure. The last time I let you talk me into something I ended up 1,000 feet below ground in the largest radioactive waste storage facility in the world. I can only imagine where I'll find myself this time," laughed Tony. "But what the hell, you only live once, right?"

It was nearly 10:00 p.m. when Frank and Tony finally left the restaurant. They made a quick stop at Frank's condo, a few blocks away, and then went their separate ways – Frank headed back to his new apartment in the hangar and Tony climbed into the Durango and headed for his hotel. Even though his hotel was only about a half-mile north of the condo, the streets in the north end of Seattle's downtown area were a mess, intersecting at odd angles, and Tony soon found himself disoriented. An unfortunate choice of turns put him on the Alaskan Way Viaduct, an elevated, limited access expressway, headed south, away from the hotel. Tony got trapped in the left lane and missed the first exit and by the time he came to the next exit, he was near Safeco Field, forty blocks south of where he wanted to be.

Tony had noticed a car following him at a distance not long after he pulled out of the condo's underground parking lot. Saturday evening traffic had made it hard to tell up on the viaduct, but as he eased to a stop at the end of the exit ramp he was sure the same set of headlights had pulled up behind him. It was difficult to be sure, but it looked like the driver was the only occupant of the car. Tony took a few extra seconds to make sure there were no other vehicles around and then he turned right onto First Avenue South and floored the Durango. As soon as he was sure the other car was matching his speed, he slowed down to the speed limit and began looking for an appropriate place to confront his new "friend."

Ahead on the right, Tony spotted a small, abandoned gas station. The windows were boarded up and the pumps had long since been removed, but the concrete pump island was still in place, as were the steel poles on each end that had once held large lights. Tony made a split-second decision and yanked the steering wheel to the right, forcing the Durango into the station's gravel lot. He smashed the accelerator to the floor and raced through the space between the small station building and the pump island. A quick glance told him the space was just barely two cars wide. His action caught the driver off guard but he tried his best to follow the Durango. As soon as Tony cleared the building, he spun the wheel and slammed on the brakes, spinning the Durango around 180 degrees. With skills rivaling an Indy car driver, Tony headed the SUV back through the space between the building and the island, directly toward the other car. The terrified driver steered to the right as far as he could, almost scraping the building, and slid to a halt. Tony brought the Durango to a stop inches from the side of the car, effectively pinning the other driver in his vehicle. He lowered the Durango's smoked glass side window, smiled broadly at the driver and motioned for the thin young man with uncombed hair to lower his own window. The man looked both terrified and confused.

"You've been following me for a while now, so I assume you want to talk to me. Why don't you tell me what you want before I come around there and rip your head off?" threatened Tony.

The man shook his head violently and stammered, "No, no, I wasn't following you! I don't even know who you are. Leave me alone, mister."

"Okay, pal, we can do this the hard way if you want to – it doesn't matter to me." Tony moved to crawl over the console but the other driver finally realized that the only thing keeping his car from moving forward was his own fear. He put the older model tan Ford sedan in gear and spun the tires as he shot forward and back out onto First Avenue South, barely missing a passing car. As the car left the lot, Tony noticed that the trunk lid had been severely damaged and was tied down with a piece of rope. Tony put his window up and smiled to himself as he pulled out onto the street and headed north in the opposite direction of the fleeing car.

"Punk!" he said out loud. "Just a punk kid."

Tony drove slowly north on First Avenue, keeping his eye on the rear view mirror to make sure he wasn't being followed again. He turned right at Broad Street and pulled into a Starbucks coffee shop a few blocks up the street. Tony turned off the lights and sat in the Durango for a couple of minutes but there was no sign of the tan Ford so he went inside and ordered a double tall mocha.

As Tony continued up Broad Street, toward the Marriott Courtyard where he was staying, it occurred to him that it was probably the Durango, and not him, that had been followed. Frank's name had been in all the local papers not long after he had won the $86 million lottery jackpot last June, and the punk kid was probably just a tabloid reporter trying to get an interview with Frank. That would explain why he looked so surprised when he saw Tony's face behind the tinted window back at the gas station. It might also explain why Frank had bought the BMW and stopped driving the Durango around town!

As Tony turned into the hotel parking lot, his eye caught something across the street and he slammed on the brakes. To his disbelief, the empty tan Ford with the smashed trunk was parked across the street from the hotel entrance in front of an all-night coffee shop.

Chapter 3

When Tony arrived at the hangar the next morning, he was surprised to see the 60-foot wide main door standing wide open. He parked the Durango in front of the office next to a burgundy minivan and walked back toward the huge door to see what was up. Just as he crossed the threshold into the hangar, he caught a glimpse of a ball of fur headed his way at a high rate of speed. Tony was caught off guard and didn't hear the high-pitched barking until the dog was almost to him.

From somewhere in the back of the hangar, a voice yelled, "Sandstrom, be quiet!"

Tony's muscles tensed and he mentally prepared to defend himself from the approaching animal, but the small, furry dog slid to a stop less than a yard from Tony's foot.

"Sandstrom! Sit!" the voice said. The dog promptly sat, but he watched Tony intensely, as if on guard duty.

A thin, middle-aged man with a graying beard and dressed in white coveralls appeared from the far side of the Learjet and smiled broadly.

"You must be Tony. I've heard a lot about you," the man said as he extended his hand to shake. "My name is Don Fitzgerald but my friends call me Fitz. And you've already met Sandstrom, here, I'm afraid."

As they shook hands, the man continued. "My wife, Susan, is back in our office working up a flight plan for Frank. Can I get you some freshly brewed coffee?"

The mention of coffee brought a smile to Tony's face. His encounter with the strange man the night before had resulted in a fitful sleep.

"Yeah, coffee sounds great. What kind of dog is that, anyway?" he asked as the animal fell into step with its owner as they headed toward the back of the hangar.

"Sandstrom is what's called a Havanese. The breed was originally developed on Cuba and in spite of their relatively long hair they do quite well in the tropics. Sorry he ran up on you like that – I think he imagines himself to be a German Shepherd or some ferocious guard dog. He's actually quite friendly, once you get to know him."

"I've never been much of a dog person, myself," said Tony, mostly to himself. "But if he's going to be a guard dog, he's got some serious growing to do." Tony shot a look of contempt at the ten-inch-high hairy dog that resembled a trimmed Shih Tzu or a Lhasa Apso.

"You'll be surprised how fast Sandstrom grows on you, Tony," smiled the other man as he opened the door to the crew office. "By the time we get to Japan you two will be best buddies."

"You mean he's going with us?" exclaimed Tony, as the two men and the dog disappeared through the door and into the aroma of fresh, strong coffee.

Meanwhile, in his own office, located directly above the flight crew's office, Frank was in the middle of a heated telephone conversation.

"What the hell do you mean we can't explore the site on our own? Dozens of people have been out to see that monument and we're better equipped and probably more experienced than most of them."

Frank had been on the phone for nearly an hour arranging lodging and a dive boat for his team. He was frustrated by the fact that very few people on Yonaguni spoke English and it now appeared that he was going to have to bring a dive guide in from Okinawa, more than 300 miles away.

"Okay, okay, I give up, lady! We'll use the dive service you recommend, but this guy had better be a damn good diver and he'd better know his way around out there."

"Or she," he repeated, after the woman corrected him. "Can you please have someone contact me as soon as possible?"

Downstairs, Tony entered the crew's office to find a petite, dark-haired woman sitting at one of the two desks. When she saw Tony enter the room along with her husband and the couple's dog, she stood up to greet him as her husband made the introductions.

"Honey, this is the infamous Tony Nicoletti. Tony, this is my wife and flying partner, Susan. Obviously, she's the brains of the operation," he said, indicating the pile of papers in front of her on the desk.

Tony stepped to the desk and shook hands awkwardly. He always felt odd shaking hands with a woman, especially one with hands so small.

"So I hear you're putting together a flight plan for our trip to Japan," he said, stating the obvious.

"That's right," smiled Susan warmly as she returned to her chair and picked up a piece of paper to show Tony. "The Learjet 60 wasn't really designed for intercontinental travel, but I think I can get us there – and back, of course. Right now I'm researching a number of alternate destinations from each of our refueling points in case Frank decides to change our course once we're underway.

"What do you mean," asked Tony. "We're just going over to Japan and back, right?"

"Well, that's the plan, but Frank mentioned something about India, too, so I've located a number of alternate airports in all directions from Yonaguni in case he decides to divert elsewhere – it's just part of the job when you're a charter pilot," explained Susan. "We always have to know where that next tank of fuel is going to come from."

Fitz handed Tony a steaming cup of coffee and invited him to have a seat on one of the two couches in the corner.

"I'll be right back. I need to close the hangar door before somebody runs off with our beautiful bird out there," said Fitz, referring to the Learjet that occupied most of the hangar.

Tony noticed that Sandstrom was sitting in an oval-shaped pet bed on the floor at the end of the other couch.

"Does the dog really fly?" asked Tony, mostly to make conversation.

"Oh, yes," replied Susan. "He's been flying with us since he was a puppy. Even turbulence doesn't bother Sandy, which is more than I can say for a lot of our passengers. Sometimes we even let him take the controls."

"You what?" coughed Tony, choking on his coffee before he noticed the grin on Susan's face and realized he'd been had.

"Sorry," she said, offering Tony a tissue from the box on her desk, "but I couldn't resist. You're obviously not a dog person – at least not yet. But we'll change that, I'm sure."

"Don't bet on it," said Tony quietly.

Sandstrom jerked his head toward the office door an instant before it opened to admit Fitz, followed closely by Frank. The dog greeted Frank with a wildly wagging tail and when Frank reached out his hand, Sandstrom extended a paw to shake.

"Good dog," laughed Frank, as he gently shook the animal's paw and stood back up.

"And good morning to you, Tony. How was your evening?"

"A little weird, actually, but I'll tell you about it later. Susan was just saying that we might go on to India after we check out this place in Japan. What's in India?"

"I'm sure I mentioned it yesterday, Tony. Underwater structures similar to those at Yonaguni have recently been discovered off both the eastern and western coasts of India and I thought we might do a little comparative analysis if we have the chance. It's all in that packet I gave you yesterday."

"Sorry, guess I missed that," Tony lied. The truth of the matter was that he didn't even know what he'd done with the packet and he certainly hadn't read any of it.

"Well, you'll have plenty of time to catch up on your reading during the next couple of weeks. In the mean time, why don't we let the Fitzgeralds get back to work? I'd like to go over a list of supplies I think we should take and then maybe we can run out and look at that houseboat I mentioned. Apparently Dave West, the guy who owns it, has already left for Germany, but his neighbor has the key and she's a lady I used to work with at Boeing, so she's agreed to show it to you today. If you like the place, I'll contact Dave through Boeing and work out a deal."

"Sounds good to me. Nice to meet you both," said Tony as he started for the door.

"We probably won't be back until after you guys take off for the day, so we can go over your flight plans tomorrow, Susan. I'll see you guys then. And you too, Sandy," added Frank.

Sandstrom answered Frank with a small, friendly yip and a wagging tail.

"Yeah, see ya, mutt," added Tony as he pulled the door closed.

"Grrrr," replied the dog.

Frank and Tony crossed the hangar and went up the front stairs to Tony's office. Tony pressed his right thumb into the small receptacle next to the door handle and waited for the green light indicating that the lock had disengaged. As Tony entered the room he noticed a stapled packet of papers positioned exactly in the center of his otherwise bare desktop.

"Ah, that's where I left your packet," he said out loud before realizing that he had given himself away.

"Actually, you never even got it out of the conference room," laughed Frank. "I brought it down here last night. Let's hope we don't get to Japan and find that all our supplies are securely stored back here, huh? So what happened last night? Something weird, I think you said?"

Tony sat down behind his desk and rummaged through the drawers until he located a yellow ruled pad and a pen. Frank took a seat on the couch that faced the desk and watched a new Boeing 747 race past on the runway visible over Tony's right shoulder.

"Well, it's no big deal, really – just a little strange. After I left your condo in the Durango I had the feeling I was being followed but I couldn't be sure in the downtown traffic. Unfortunately, or maybe fortunately, I made a wrong turn and got headed south on that damned expressway. When I finally came to an exit, there wasn't much traffic around and my somewhat stupid "shadow" stuck out like a signal flare.

"I just assumed that the guy following the Durango was a reporter or private eye on the trail of all the money you won. Anyway, we eventually had a little talk and he took off like a scared jackrabbit when he realized who was driving your rig. He peeled out and headed south as fast as his beat-up old Ford could go and I headed north. I kept my eyes open all the way back to the hotel and I'm sure nobody followed me. The weird thing is that when I finally got back to the hotel, there was that damned Ford, parked right across the street from the parking lot."

"Was this car a tan Ford escort with a smashed in trunk?"

"Yes! I take it you know this guy, then?"

"I guess I should have warned you about my old buddy Larry. He followed me all over town for a couple of months after I got back from our last adventure, but I haven't seen him for quite a while, so I assumed he had gotten tired of bugging me and gone back to Las Vegas. I guess he's back."

"Las Vegas?" questioned Tony, suddenly leaning forward in his chair. "And how do you know his name is Larry?"

"Oh, I had him checked out as soon as I spotted him tailing me back in August. His name is Larry Schultz and he's a small-time private investigator from Las Vegas. I considered contacting the police but all he ever did was follow me around and I was trying not to call any additional attention to myself, so I just ignored him. He never approached me personally and he never interfered with any of my property, so I let him do his thing. As far as I could tell, he was just monitoring where I went and what I did."

"Or who you met with," said Tony, deep in thought. "What if he's trying to locate one of us and hoping that whoever it is will eventually turn up here with you? And how do you explain the fact that he arrived at my hotel before I did last night? If he didn't expect me to be driving the Durango, how did he know where I was staying?"

"That was probably just a coincidence, Tony. I think you're reading too much into this, but I'll give you the information I put together on this guy and you can check him out for yourself. Let's walk down to my office for that file and then head out to the houseboat. I need to be back here by 1:00 p.m. because Linda's going to stop by to drool over the computers and since she isn't registered in the security system yet, I need to be here to let her in."

The houseboat, which was located on the Portage Bay portion of Lake Union, across from the University of Washington campus, turned out to be Tony's dream home. The furnishings reminded Frank of something from a Goodwill catalog, but Tony insisted they felt "homey" and he was sold on the place the minute he saw it. Frank was pretty sure that the 24-foot day cruiser tied up beside the houseboat was probably causing Tony's brain to malfunction, but he didn't mention it.

As luck would have it, Karen Davis, the next-door neighbor with the key, had spoken to the owner that same morning. He was desperate to get the place leased and when he heard that it was a friend of Frank Morton's who was interested, he had authorized her to turn over the keys immediately as long as the monthly rent was acceptable and as long as Frank would vouch for his friend. By noon Tony had a new home – at least for the next six months – and Karen had offered to drop off a lasagna casserole that evening so Tony would have something to eat until he could get to a grocery store.

With houseboat keys in hand, Frank and Tony headed back to the hangar. As Frank eased the BMW into the southbound I-5 traffic, he glanced into the mirror and said, "Damn it! Our friend Larry is on our tail again. Maybe this time I <u>will</u> call the police."

Tony turned and looked out the back window. Sure enough, the tan Ford was weaving in and out of traffic trying to keep up with the accelerating Roadster.

"Well, at least we can figure out which one of us he's following," said Tony. "As soon as we get back to the hangar, I'll take off in the Durango and we'll see whether he follows me or sticks with you."

"Okay, but if he tails you, circle around and bring him back to the hangar. I have an idea," smiled Frank as he glanced into the mirror again.

Frank exited the Interstate and headed north on Airport Way. The normally busy access road was nearly deserted this Sunday afternoon, and Frank floored the Roadster, leaving the tan Ford far behind. He made a quick left and then a right onto Perimeter Road and screeched to a stop in front of the hangar. As soon as Tony was out of the car, Frank zipped around the hangar and parked out of sight. He ran back around to the side door, stuck his thumb into the reader and snatched the door open as soon as the green light indicated the lock had released.

Frank ran up the stairs to the catwalk, across the width of the hangar and down the far side to Tony's office. He closed the blinds in the front window so he could just barely see down onto the parking lot just as Tony pulled slowly away in the Durango. Just a few seconds after Tony disappeared around the corner, the tan Ford zipped onto the tarmac in front of the hangar, made a quick U-turn and headed off in pursuit of the Durango.

"Perfect," said Frank out loud. He unclipped his cell phone from his belt and dialed Lt. Sam Snyder, the one member of the Seattle Police Department that he knew. Sam had been in charge of the investigation into the accidental death of Frank's wife a little over a year ago.

"Sam, this is Frank Morton. Fine, thanks. Hey, I need a big favor. Can you send a marked car over to my hangar at the south end of Perimeter Road?"

Frank described the problem he was having with the private investigator and explained that he just wanted to scare the man into leaving him alone. Frank hoped that the presence of uniformed police officers would help get the message across to the persistent man.

Frank described the plan he and Tony had cooked up and Sam agreed to send a patrol car right over. He even offered to stop by himself to add a little supervisory muscle to the plan.

Frank ended his call with the police lieutenant and reattached the phone to his belt clip just as it rang again.

"It's Tony. We're on our way back to the hangar and he's still on my tail. Did you get in touch with the cops?" said the voice on the other end.

"It's all set up. Try to put some distance between the two of you and park right in front. I'll open the office door and you can jump inside. We'll leave our friend outside to deal with the cops."

Frank ran down the stairs across the catwalk from Tony's office and into the computer room, where he made several adjustments on a console. Satisfied with what he saw on the monitor, he went to the front office and waited. A couple of minutes later, he spotted the Durango turning the corner onto the tarmac. Frank opened the door and waited for Tony to dash inside. He had already closed all the blinds in the office, and as soon as the door was closed and locked he motioned Tony into the computer room. On a rack-mounted monitor, a surveillance camera showed a clear picture of the tarmac.

Frank and Tony both noticed the car come into the camera's view at the same time, but it was Frank who spoke first.

"That's Linda's car! Damn it, she'll scare our guy off."

Tony was already heading for the office. "I'll get her," he called from the door.

Frank noticed more movement on the display and turned his attention back to it. The tan Ford was just pulling up out front. Frank watched as the vehicle stopped and the driver's door slowly opened. The man Frank recognized as the Las Vegas private investigator got out of the car, took off the baseball cap he was wearing and wiped his brow with his sleeve. Half way through the motion of putting the cap back on his head, the man's body jerked away from the door and crumpled to the ground beside his car. At the same instant, Frank heard two sharp "pops", the sound of breaking glass and a woman's scream from outside.

"Linda!" he yelled at the top of his lungs as he raced toward the office door.

Chapter 4

Frank yanked open the front door of the hangar's office and spotted Tony and Linda lying in a heap beside Linda's car. They were both face down on the ground surrounded by small chunks of broken auto glass and Tony was using his arm to protect Linda's head.

Tony looked up and saw Frank in the doorway. "Get back," he yelled, "there's some crazy bastard out here with a gun!"

"Are you two all right?" called Frank as he crouched down inside the office and closed the door down to a small crack.

"Yes, but I think your private eye friend has been hit," replied Tony, nodding toward the other side of the car. "Where the hell are those cops you called?"

As if on cue, a Seattle patrol car rounded the corner and stopped at the far edge of the tarmac. From their position, the police officers could see Tony and Linda on the driver's side of Linda's car as well as the fallen investigator on the ground between Linda's car and the tan Ford. As a large pool of blood formed around the investigator's body, the two officers crouched behind open car doors with weapons drawn.

"The cops are here, Tony, so don't either of you move until they figure out who's who."

Frank snatched the cell phone off his belt and dialed 911. Soon he was in contact with the patrol car and explaining what he knew about what had happened. An initial assessment seemed to indicate that the two shots Frank had heard had come from some bushes on the far side of the tarmac. One had apparently hit the investigator and the other had taken out both the passenger- and driver-side windows on Linda's car. With the approval of the officers in the car, Frank opened the door a little wider and signaled for Tony and Linda to stay low and make a run for the office, using Linda's car as cover. As soon as they were safely inside the hangar, Frank locked the office door and used a small keypad next to the door to enable the building's perimeter alarm. Keeping low, the three friends made their way out the back door of the office, through the hangar and into a break room located just behind the computer room. Frank called the patrol car to give them an update and then turned to Tony and Linda, who were seated at a table. Linda was sobbing and Tony was trying to calm her down.

"It's over, Linda," said Tony. "You're okay, I'm okay and the cops will catch the bad guys. Try to calm down and tell us what you saw out there."

Frank took a bottle of water out of the refrigerator and opened it for Linda. Still holding her face in one hand, she waved her other index finger in the air, indicating, "Give me a minute."

Frank and Tony walked out into the hangar to let Linda compose herself.

"What the hell just happened out there, Tony?" asked Frank.

"Well, by the time I got to the door it was pretty much over. I heard two shots just before I opened the door and they seemed to come from across the tarmac, but I can't be sure. Linda was just standing there next to her car in shock, so I dashed out and got her down on the ground but I didn't realize anybody had been hit until I looked over under her car and saw your friend from Las Vegas bleeding all over the ground."

"Did you hear anything? Anybody fleeing, or anything like that?"

"Not a thing, and, of course, I couldn't see anything from where I was behind the car. I was more concerned about Linda than spotting bad guys."

"Of course. I was just hoping you might have heard footsteps or a car or something," said Frank.

"Nope, nothing. In fact, as I was lying there on the ground I remember hearing a plane, probably at the far end of the runway, and thinking to myself that it was unusually quiet. If anybody saw or heard anything, it would be Linda. Let's see how she's doing, shall we?"

As the two men reentered the break room Linda looked up and forced a smile. "Sorry about that, guys. It's just that I've never actually been shot at before." Linda tried to laugh but a sob choked it off.

Frank and Tony sat down, one on either side of her. Frank put his arm around her shoulder and Tony patted her folded hands as they rested on the table in front of her.

"You'll get used to it," returned Tony with a smile. Linda's grim glare told him this was not the time for joking. "Sorry, kid, just a poor attempt at humor. We're obviously both concerned and very glad that you're all right. You are all right, aren't you?"

Linda nodded and took a sip of the water. Just as she was putting the bottle to her lips, Frank's cell phone rang and the sound startled her so bad she spilled water down the front of her jacket.

Tony went into the men's room to get some paper towels and when he returned Frank was gone.

"Where is …" Tony started to ask as he handed her the towels.

"He's letting the police in. They want to ask us all some questions," replied Linda before he was able to finish.

Two hours later the police finally left. Schultz' body had been removed by the coroner and most of the blood had been cleaned up by a fire crew. The area had been searched with a fine-tooth comb – Frank and Tony had even taken part in the search – but nothing was found. No footprints, no shell casings, nothing.

Tony and Linda slumped onto a couch in Frank's living room while he retrieved beers for each of them.

"Well, it's certainly been an interesting afternoon," remarked Tony as Frank handed him a bottle. "And that Lt. Snyder friend of yours is a real piece of work, Frank. I'm still not sure he doesn't suspect one of us."

"He's just doing his job, Tony. It's obvious from the entry wound in Larry Schultz' back and the bullet that hit Linda's car windows that the shooter was on the east side of the property. What I don't understand is why anybody would want Schultz dead in the first place. He was just a no-name private eye."

"And you're positive the shooter wasn't after me, right?" asked a still shaken Linda. "I told the police that the first bullet hit my windows and the second one hit the man, but what if I remember it wrong? What if this detective was hit by mistake on the first shot and the second shot was intended for me? I'm really scared, guys."

"The shots weren't intended for you, Linda. First of all, that would make the shooter a really bad shot – to have missed you twice – and nobody knew you were going to be here except Tony and me," explained Frank patiently. "Even if somebody wanted you dead – and we all agree that isn't likely – how would they have known to wait for you here? No, I think Schultz was the intended target, all right."

"I agree with Frank," nodded Tony. "In fact, somebody wanted him dead really bad."

"What do you mean?" asked Frank.

"I didn't want to mention it in front of your Lieutenant friend, but there's a couple of facts about this thing that fascinate me. First of all they think the bullet that killed Schultz was from a high-powered, small caliber gun, right?"

"That's what they said," nodded Frank. "The coroner said the shot that hit Schultz went completely through the body and I don't think the police found either of the slugs."

"That would make it similar to the gun that killed old man Thompson in Beatty last summer, right – something like a varmint rifle?" Tony was referring to the death of Jill Harris' father in a small town north of Las Vegas during the *Tractrix Project* investigation.

"And another thing," continued Tony, "we all heard two shots and we all think they were no more than a second apart. But most varmint rifles are bolt-action. Even a pro couldn't cycle a bolt-action weapon in a second."

"But that would mean ..." started Frank.

"That there were two shooters," finished Tony. "One hit the target and the other missed and hit Linda's car windows. Whoever wanted this guy dead was serious about it."

"I left that file on Schultz in the Roadster," said Tony. "Why don't I go get it so we can see if anything makes more sense in light of today's events?"

"Crap!" exclaimed Frank, slapping his knee. "I left the Roadster around in back of the hangar. I'll go get it and you can open the big door when I bring it around. Stay back as far as you can and keep an eye out. I don't want any bad guys dashing in here. Linda, please stay up here – we'll be right back."

Five minutes later Frank and Tony rejoined Linda in Frank's apartment. There had been no sign of anyone outside the hangar, but the sun was starting to go down across the runway and the angle of the light cast long shadows that could have hidden a freight train.

Tony tossed the Schultz file on the coffee table in front of Linda and helped himself to another beer from Frank's refrigerator.

"Anybody else want one?" he called from the kitchen.

Linda was already poring over the file and Frank was closing the drapes that covered the back of the living room. Both mumbled, "Yes, please" almost in unison.

Tony returned with the three bottles and set them on the table next to Linda.

"Thanks," she said. "Frank, maybe it's time I tried out some of that fancy computer gear you're so proud of. I'm going down to my office for a little while."

"Okay, but close the blinds and don't wander downstairs unless you let me know. I've set the perimeter security system and armed all the sensors downstairs just in case our friend – or friends – come back."

While Linda went to expand the research on the now-deceased Larry Schultz, Frank and Tony moved into Frank's office to work on the list of supplies that would be needed for the upcoming trip to Japan. An hour later they had worked their way down to the last item on Frank's list.

"Why do you have a question mark next to security?" asked Tony with a yawn and a stretch.

"Well, when I scribbled this out, I wasn't sure what, if any, security we would need. After today, I guess we'd better come up with something, but I don't know what we can legally take into Japan, even on a private aircraft."

"I've heard that Japan has the strictest weapons laws in the world. The Japs not only control firearms, but the average citizen can't even own an ancestral samurai sword unless he or she has a government-issued collector's license. How important to you is it that we do this legally?" smiled Tony.

"Let's try to stay within the law," frowned Frank. "There must be some provisions for personal security, even in Japan."

"I'll see what I can do," smiled Tony again.

A few minutes later Linda entered the office from Frank's apartment. "I had to use the bathroom and you said not to go down stairs," she said, answering the questioning look on Frank's face.

"Have you turned up anything yet?" he asked.

"Well, yes and no. The information you collected on Larry Schultz was pretty accurate. He was a small-time private investigator most recently licensed in Nevada. He lived in a lower-middle class area of North Las Vegas, had the normal number of run-ins with the local police and no spectacular accomplishments.

"Before moving to Nevada in 1998, Schultz lived in New Jersey, where he was born and raised. That's where his ex-wife still lives."

"Yes, I knew all of that, but you said 'yes and no'. What part did I get wrong?"

"Just one minor item, Frank. The Larry Schultz described in your files died of an apparent drug overdose almost two years ago."

"Are you sure?" asked a surprised Frank.

"Quite sure. I followed an alimony trail back to the ex-wife and she stopped receiving court-ordered payments at the time of Schultz' death. The tan Ford the police hauled out of here earlier was purchased and licensed about six months after the real Schultz died. That's probably about the time your corpse assumed Schultz' identity, because I couldn't find any traceable transactions between the date of death and the licensing of the Ford. No credit card use, no phone records, nothing."

"So who the hell got shot in front of the hangar today?" asked Tony. "And why?"

"I expect the police will be wondering the same thing when they discover that the corpse's fingerprints don't match those on file with the Las Vegas Police Department," nodded Linda.

Tony glanced at his watch and exclaimed, "Oh, crap! I forgot that my new neighbor had promised to drop by with a casserole tonight. I've gotta run - I'll see you guys in the morning, okay?"

After they saw Tony off, Frank recorded Linda's right thumbprint into the security system and then reset the building alarm.

As they were climbing the stairs to the catwalk, Linda asked, "Frank, do you mind if I stay here tonight? I'd rather sleep on the couch in my office than drive home alone after dark in a car without any side windows."

"You'll do nothing of the sort! You can take my bed and I'll sleep on one of the big couches in my living room. We'll get your car to a glass shop first thing in the morning and then you can head home before it gets too late. In the mean time, please make yourself at home."

Linda tried to argue, but Frank would have none of it. She finally agreed to his plan but insisted on preparing a light supper for the two of them to "pay for her room and board." After the meal and a glass of wine, Frank and Linda each went back to their offices and worked until nearly 11:00 p.m. Exhausted and confused about the events of the day, they retired to opposite ends of Frank's apartment and crashed for the night.

The next morning Frank awoke to the smell of fresh coffee and the sound of sizzling bacon. Throwing off the comforter, he ran his fingers through his hair and padded off to the kitchen. Except for the towel wrapped around her head, Linda appeared to be ready for work. She smiled when she saw Frank and said, "Morning, sunshine!"

Frank looked at his watch – it was only 6:30 a.m. – and replied sleepily, "My god, woman, do you always get up this early?"

"I'm usually up about 5:00 a.m., yes. Besides, we need to figure out the car thing early so I can get to work – I'm supposed to give my notice today, remember? I'm finished in the bathroom, except for drying my hair, but don't disappear in there because breakfast is almost ready. You really need to stock up on food, you know. Everything except for Spaghetti-Os – you seem to have plenty of that."

"Hey, I happen to like Italian food," grinned Frank as he poured a cup of coffee and leaned against the counter. "Why don't you just take the BMW to work? I'll take your car to a shop when Tony gets here and we can trade back this evening."

"Really? The BMW? Are you sure?" beamed Linda.

Tony arrived about 9:00 a.m. and Frank brought him up to date over a cup of coffee. Before dropping Linda's car at the glass shop, the two friends made another search of the area immediately around the hangar employing some skills they hadn't used in years.

Frank and Tony had both been members of military Special Ops units – Frank an Air Force Air Commando and Tony an Army Ranger – and they had met during the closing months of the Viet Nam war as members of a joint Army/Air Force search and destroy unit operating behind enemy lines deep inside Laos. Their friendship had survived through the post-war years in spite of divergent career paths and life styles. Frank returned to college immediately after his discharge and eventually became a senior engineer at Boeing Aerospace, working on components for the International Space Station. Tony, on the other hand, had returned to his pre-war job as a long haul trucker based in Los Angeles. Less than a year after his discharge from the Army Tony was offered a unique opportunity to do contract hauling for the U.S. Government. Although he was never sure what type of cargo was actually in the sealed trailers he shuttled between obscure military installations, his contract with the government had required that he have a Top Secret security clearance.

The January air was cold but the morning sun was bright and after nearly an hour of intense searching, Tony finally spotted the first real piece of evidence that pointed to the unusual activities of the day before.

"Frank, over here," he called to his friend who was a dozen yards away.

Using a small twig, Tony gently dug in the bark dust under some bushes on the eastern edge of the property, adjacent to the road that ran north and south along the side of the airport. Soon he had exposed a small, eight-sided disc, which he lifted by inserting the twig through a hole in the center of the disc.

"Whatcha sniffin', big dog?" laughed Frank as he approached Tony, who was now on his hands and knees with the disc close to his face.

"Very funny, smart ass," returned Tony as he stood to show Frank what he had found. "Look at this. It was pushed down into the bark chips as if it had been stepped on."

"Good eye, Fido. The edges look sharp, almost like it's some kind of throwing weapon. I suppose we should turn this over to the police for a finger print check, huh?"

"Yes, but I want to do a little investigating of my own before we do. I'm convinced that our shooter, or shooters, is a pro and wouldn't have left behind any fingerprints. I'll bet the only reason this was missed was because Linda showed up just as the hit was going down. I didn't want to tell her this, but that second bullet very well might have been intended for her – to eliminate an unexpected witness."

"I thought of that, too," nodded Frank, "and I'm glad you didn't say anything to her. Let's mark this spot and check the line of sight later with a spotting scope. If the shooter dropped this gizmo, we might be able to determine whether both shots were fired from this single location or from two separate ones. That would tell whether we are dealing with one or two shooters."

Frank and Tony secured the disc in a small plastic bag and marked the location with a piece of ribbon attached to a short section of coat hangar wire similar to a tiny flag and flagpole. They searched the area for another thirty minutes but no new clues turned up so they turned their attentions to the matter of Linda's car.

Frank drove the car to a nearby auto glass shop and Tony followed in the Durango. The manager promised to have the windows replaced by 5:00 p.m., so they left the vehicle and headed to a martial arts shop south of Seattle's SEATAC airport that Tony had located in the yellow pages before leaving the hangar.

The shop's only employee, a short, elderly, balding Japanese man with wire-rimmed glasses, was busy at the counter with a customer so Frank and Tony gradually made their way down an aisle of training weapons and martial arts clothing. On the far wall they discovered a locked glass case that displayed what appeared to be some very authentic martial arts weapons.

"This must be the good stuff," commented Tony. "Look at those throwing stars – they look mighty lethal."

"Yes, they <u>are</u> very lethal," commented a soft voice from behind Tony. "How may I help you, gentlemen?"

Frank and Tony turned to face the smiling shopkeeper. He was neatly dressed in black slacks and a black knit collarless shirt. As the two larger men made eye contact, he bowed slightly. Due to their time in the Far East, both Frank and Tony instinctively returned the bow, causing the shopkeeper to raise his eyebrows slightly.

"Good morning," greeted Frank. And then, indicating the glass case, he said, "This is an impressive collection of weapons. Is it yours?"

"Yes, but I'm afraid nothing in that case is for sale. Perhaps I could show you some other items that might interest you?"

"We're not really here to buy, but thank you anyway," replied Tony. "We were hoping you could help us identify an object we found this morning."

Tony pulled the plastic bag containing the octagonal disc out of his jacket pocket and handed it to the old man.

Before the bag had even settled in the shopkeeper's hand, he shot a cold look back at Tony and said, "Where did you get this?"

"Like I said, we found it. If you'll tell us what it is, maybe we'll tell you where we found it," countered Tony.

Looking around to make sure nobody else was in the shop, the old man signaled for Frank and Tony to follow him behind the counter and into a small room that served as an office. He slumped into a chair at a small round table and indicated that Frank and Tony should take the chairs opposite him. The man who had appeared so pleasant and friendly out in the shop now took on a hard, serious, almost frightened demeanor.

Placing the bag containing the disc in the center of the table, the old man repeated his question. "Where did you get this?"

Tony started to speak again, but Frank interrupted him and said, "We found it at the scene of a murder. We believe the person or persons who committed the crime accidentally dropped it and we were hoping you could help us identify it – and possibly where it came from."

The old man sat up in his chair and slowly turned the bagged disc over and over in his hand several times.

Finally, he said softly, "This is called a *tsubute*. It's a Ninja throwing weapon, but *tsubutes* haven't been used for centuries. And this one, based on these markings, ..." The man's voice trailed off as he seemed to be in deep thought.

"What about the markings?" asked Tony impatiently.

"This one bears the markings of a super-secret Ninja group that terrorized southern Japan for a hundred years before it was finally eradicated by a group of samurai warriors loyal to the emperor."

"Did you say 'emperor'?" questioned Frank. "How long ago did this take place?"

"During the latter part of the 12th century. I recognize the markings because I was born on the island that the secret Ninja group once called home," replied the old man. "I'm from the small, south Japan island of Yonaguni."

Chapter 5

"Yonaguni?" asked Tony. "Isn't that the place ..."

"Yes it is," interrupted Frank with a light kick under the table to Tony's shin. "Can you tell us more about this secret Ninja group? Are they still in existence?"

Tony winced from the kick and shot Frank a glare but quickly realized that Frank didn't want to let the old man in on the fact that the NWIDI team would be heading to that exact island in just a couple of weeks.

The old man, whose name turned out to be Koji Yamato, noticed the exchange between Frank and Tony.

"Do you know of Yonaguni?" he asked, suddenly very interested in the two men sitting across from him.

"Only vaguely," covered Frank. "Please go on, Mr. Yamato. What about this Ninja group you mentioned?"

Over the course of the half- hour, interrupted by only a couple of customers, the old man related a detailed, and sometimes very animated, account of the rise and fall of the *Genji* warrior clan. Like other Ninja, the *Genji* had been professional spies during the age of the samurai classes from the twelfth to the seventeenth centuries. They were often called upon to gather information, plunder their enemy's resources and lead the way in nighttime attacks. According to Yamato, Ninja received specialized and secret training and the *tsubute* that Tony had found was only one example of the many lethal and stealthy killing weapons they had developed.

At the end of his story, the old man took a sip from his cup of tea and asked, "Now why don't you gentlemen tell me where you found this *tsubute* and what interest you have in my tiny island homeland."

Frank started to deny any interest, but Yamato stopped him.

"Please don't insult me with a lie," he said, eyes locked with Frank's. "I have answered your questions, now please return the favor."

Frank looked at Tony, who just shrugged. Frank looked back to the old man and decided they had nothing to hide so he described the prior day's murder outside the hangar and the team's upcoming trip to Yonaguni to explore the mysterious underwater pyramid.

The old man listened, expressionless, until Frank finished. After an awkward silence, Koji Yamato spoke.

"Well, first of all, gentlemen, the person, or persons, who committed the murder yesterday definitely weren't modern-day *Genji*. No self-respecting Ninja would use a noisy rifle when so many silent methods of killing are available."

Holding up the plastic bag containing the *tsubute*, Yamato continued.

"This is authentic, there's no doubt about that, but I don't believe it was lost by your gunman. Perhaps you have had more than one visitor lately. Who else knows about your trip to Yonaguni?"

As the three men continued to talk, a mutual friendship began to develop. The old man was born and lived on the island of Yonaguni until he was 11, when his parents immigrated to the United States to escape the oppressive military regime in Tokyo. Yamato explained that his family arrived in San Francisco in early November of 1941, just weeks before the bombing of Pearl Harbor. By mid-April of 1942 the family had been "relocated" to the infamous Manzanar Internment Camp in the Owens Valley area of California, west of Death Valley. Yamato, along with his mother, two brothers and a sister were released from the Camp in June of 1945 but Yamato's father had died in the camp during the winter of 1944.

According to Yamato, his experiences in the Internment camp produced a teenager with an intense interest in his native culture and heritage. This life-long interest eventually landed him the position as Curator of the Japanese Cultural Museum in Seattle.

At this statement, Tony glanced around the small, cramped office of the martial arts shop and thought to himself, "How does a museum curator end up here?"

Apparently reading Tony's question in the expression on his face, Yamato laughed. "Oh, this is just an old man's hobby. My daughter runs the martial arts school next door and this store is really for the benefit of the students. It just barely breaks even, and it only does that because I don't take a salary. I retired last year, at 70, and I just work here to help out."

"Were you active in the martial arts, yourself, Mr. Yamato?" asked Frank. "You seem to have quite a collection in that glass case out there."

Yamato bowed slightly and said, "I have had some training, yes. Before my family left Japan my father insisted that I take the normal classes offered in the local school. In the internment camp all boys and young men were secretly trained by some of the more militant detainees and after we were released my mother sent me back to Japan to live with my uncle for three years. He was a Grand Master and he taught me much."

Impressed with the old man's credentials, Frank laughed as he described his own limited martial arts training as an Air Commando prior to his service in Viet Nam.

"And yet you survived the experience," smiled the old man. "Often the victor is not the best fighter but rather the one most prepared to fight."

"Getting back to the disk," interjected Tony, "do you have any idea who might have lost it – besides this *Genji* group, I mean?"

Pushing the plastic bag across the table, Yamato shook his head slowly and said, "No, I'm afraid not but let me make some inquiries. Where can I reach you if I learn something?"

Frank produced a business card from his shirt pocket, put it on top of the bag and slid it back across the table.

"I think this would be safer with you, *Sensei* – perhaps in that display case we saw earlier. And my telephone numbers are on the card."

The old man's eyes widened at the prospect of acquiring a 900-year-old artifact from his birthplace.

"Oh, I couldn't accept …"

"Please, I insist," said Frank firmly. "You've been very helpful and if the owner of this disk really isn't our shooter, there's no point in giving it to the police."

Standing up, Frank and Tony bowed briefly and Frank said, "We appreciate your time today and I hope we'll have the opportunity to speak again before Tony and I leave for Yonaguni."

The old man returned the bow, holding his slightly longer to express his gratitude for the unexpected gift.

"I look forward to it," he said softly as the other two men turned to leave. "And thank you again for the generous gift of the *tsubute*. I will treasure this forever."

Outside, Tony slapped Frank on the back and laughed. "Congratulations! You probably just gave away a fortune in there. I assume your accountant will write that off to 'blatant bribery', right?"

"I'd prefer to think of it as an 'investment'," smiled Frank. "At the very least, he's now in our debt. I'm counting on his cultural sense of fairness to result in some information for us – either something he knows but didn't want to share or something he will find out on his own and bring to us."

"I also noticed you called him *Sensei* just before we left," said Tony, as they climbed into the Durango. "What was that all about?"

"Then you also noticed that he didn't correct me. I probably caught him off guard and he didn't object to the title because it's one he's used to hearing. I think our Mr. Yamato is a *Sensei* – a teacher of martial arts."

"So the school ..." began Tony.

"Is, or at least was, his. He probably doesn't even have a daughter."

Frank backed the Durango out of the parking space in front of the shop and before he could move the gear selector from reverse to drive, a bright blue Mazda Miata convertible zipped into their spot. A tall, athletic-looking Asian woman, possibly in her thirties, climbed out of the car and dashed into the shop.

"That would be the daughter," smiled Tony, as they pulled out onto the highway and headed north toward the hangar.

Frank and Tony stopped for lunch at a restaurant not far from the airport and while they were eating Frank's cell phone rang.

"Ten to one it's the old man," said Tony, as Frank unclipped his phone.

The call turned out to be from the auto glass shop. Linda's car wouldn't be done that day after all because they couldn't locate a driver's side window anywhere in the Seattle area. They were having one air freighted in from San Francisco but they would need at least one more day with the car. Frank called Linda at work and suggested she keep the Roadster another day. He also brought her up to date on the discovery of the *tsubute* and the meeting with Yamato.

"Since I don't need to bring your car out to the hangar tonight, I'll spend some time digging into your Mr. Yamato and this group called the *Genji*," offered Linda. "I also need to start getting things in order for our trip – I assume we're still going, right?"

"Oh, absolutely," replied Frank, "especially in light of this Ninja connection. I'll call about your scuba lessons this afternoon and try to get you into a private class beginning Wednesday, so make good use of your time tonight – you're going to be pretty busy until we leave."

After lunch Frank and Tony returned to the hangar to begin rounding up the supplies they would need for the trip to Japan. When they arrived, the flight crew, Don and Susan Fitzgerald, were already hard at work. Susan was putting the finishing touches on the flight plan and Fitz was checking out the Learjet's navigational electronics. Frank went up to his office and Tony started up the steps into the aircraft. As he crossed the threshold, he heard the unmistakable growl of the Fitzgerald's dog, Sandstrom.

"I can hear you, you little mutt, and if you bite me I'm going to bite you right back."

Sticking his head out the cockpit door and lifting one side of the headphones away from his ear, Fitz said, "Hi, Tony! What was that you said? I was checking out the radio."

"Ah, nothing Fitz. Just saying hello to your sidekick, that's all. Where is Sandstrom, anyway?" Tony asked, scanning the plane's interior for the animal.

At the sound of Tony's voice, the small, light brown longhaired dog bounded off the other seat in the cockpit and raced back toward the door. When he saw Tony he stopped short and growled, as if protecting his owner from an intruder.

"Sandstrom, be quiet! It's just Tony – he's a friend," scolded Fitz. "Now get back in here and behave."

Without taking his eyes off the dog, Tony said to Fitz, "You look busy. I'll come back later."

"No, no that's all right. I've got two weeks to finish this up. Is there something I can help you with?"

"Well, actually, yes, there is. Frank and I are putting together equipment for the trip and I have no idea how much storage space one of these things has. I was hoping you could show me around a bit," replied Tony.

"I'd be happy to. Come on in – we'll start here in the cabin," said Fitz, as he led Tony to the back of the luxurious cabin and opened the lavatory door. "Back here is a luggage and garment compartment that straddles the full width of the aircraft. It's about 25 cubic feet in size and accessible while in flight."

Backing out of the lavatory, Fitz pointed to several built-in cupboards in the forward galley area.

"Those are generally used for snacks and beverages, but I suppose you could store anything you wanted in them. Altogether, they probably represent another 5 or 6 cubic feet. Let's go outside and I'll show you the other compartments."

Fitz showed Tony the two external baggage compartments.

"Another 33 cubic feet, between them," commented Fitz as Tony pulled his head out of the last compartment. "But the real problem usually isn't volume, it's the weight."

"How's that?" Tony asked.

"Well, even with a stop in Alaska we'll have to push the aircraft close to its maximum range in order to get to Japan. With a full fuel load, we can only accommodate about 1,500 pounds of payload, and that includes the six of us. I weigh 165 and Susan is a scant 105. By adding the weights of each of your team members you can figure out how much will be left for baggage and gear, but I'd be surprised if it's much more than 500 pounds."

"Ouch!" said Tony. "That's less than 100 pounds per person, including clothes and personal items. That's not going to work!"

"I suggest you ship as much ahead as you can," said Fitz, as he latched the external baggage compartment door shut. "And don't bring anything onboard that you don't absolutely need."

"How much does that dog weigh?" thought Tony as he cast a glance at Sandstrom standing in the aircraft doorway.

Tony knocked on Frank's office door and opened it when he heard Frank call, "Come in."

"Bad news, boss," he said as he settled onto the couch in Frank's office. "We're going to have a serious cargo limit on this trip. It looks like we'll have to ship a lot of our stuff over ahead of time, especially the dive gear. That means we have even less time to get it rounded up and packed."

"Hell, we don't even have Linda's gear yet and didn't you say you needed new equipment, too?" frowned Frank as he leaned back in his high-back desk chair and folded his hands behind his head.

"Yup! I left my stuff in the Caribbean the last time I went down to see Jill. I'll get a line on an airfreight service and see what the schedules are. I think I still have a contact at Evergreen that may be able to help us out. They used to do a lot of contract work for the government."

"Okay, see what you can do. And then why don't you start tracking down the other things on our list. Open accounts where you can and put the rest on this VISA card," said Frank, tossing Tony a credit card.

During the course of the next two weeks Tony secured, packed and shipped most of the items that he and Frank had agreed they would need. Frank worked on permits and legal documents for the team's travel inside Japan and the Fitzgeralds readied the Learjet for the trip. They made several checkout flights, including one to Montana that Frank and Tony accompanied them on.

Early in the second week, Lt. Snyder dropped by to bring Frank up to date on his investigation into the murder of the private eye from Las Vegas. The police had finally discovered what Linda had learned the day after the murder – that the real Larry Schultz had died nearly two years ago. The police were still trying to identify the body they had recovered in front of the NWIDI hangar. Reluctantly, Snyder agreed to let the team leave the country in the midst of the investigation but only after Frank gave him his satellite phone number and his word that any or all of them would return immediately if the police asked them to.

Linda managed to get her scuba certification, but just barely. She lacked the stamina necessary to struggle with the cold water wet suit for any length of time, but Frank assured her that she would be much more comfortable in a warm water "shorty" wet suit.

As the second week wound down, Linda learned that her fellow employees at the newspaper were planning a big going away party for her Friday night after work. When Frank heard about the party he decided to change the team's departure day from Saturday to Sunday to give Linda a day to recover from the festivities. The delay turned out to be a fortunate turn of events for the NWIDI team.

After a hectic week, everybody had decided to take Saturday as a day of down time before the early morning departure the next day. It was about 10:00 a.m. and Frank was alone in the hangar when his cell phone rang.

"Frank Morton here," he said as he crossed the cement floor toward the Learjet.

"Mr. Morton, this is Koji Yamato. We met a couple of weeks ago. Do you have a moment?" replied the voice on the phone.

Yamato had promised to see what he could find out about the ancient *tsubute* Tony had found outside the hangar, but, after two weeks, Frank had nearly given up on him.

Linda had done some checking up on Yamato and his history seemed to match his story exactly. Linda had even found documents authorizing the release of Yamato's family from the internment camp.

"Of course, Mr. Yamato. How can I help you?"

"Actually, I'd prefer to talk to you in person, Mr. Morton. Can we meet somewhere?"

"You name it. I'm at the south end of the King County airport. Just tell me where and when you'd like to meet."

After a short pause, Yamato replied, "Maybe it would be best if I came there. Can you give me instructions on how to find your facility?"

Less than an hour later a sensor alerted Frank to the arrival of an automobile in the hangar's front parking area. On a monitor in his office, Frank watched Koji Yamato get out of a late model Mercedes and approach the door. Frank picked up his telephone handset and pushed a button that connected him to the intercom box mounted outside the front door.

"Good morning, Mr. Yamato. I'll be right down to open the door."

Frank hurried along the catwalk, down the front stairs and into the hangar's reception office. He opened the office door and greeted the elderly man.

"Sorry to keep you waiting," apologized Frank, "but I'm here alone today and I like to keep the place locked up when there's nobody else around."

"That's quite all right," replied the old man. "This building looks big enough to be a hangar. Do you have an ... oh, wow!"

The old man's jaw dropped as they passed from the front office into the hangar proper and the gleaming white Learjet came into view.

Frank smiled at the other's reaction. "If you were going to ask if I have an airplane, the answer is yes. Would you like to come aboard? I was just loading some supplies for our trip to Japan tomorrow."

The two men sat down facing each other in the forward club area and Frank offered Yamato a beverage, which he declined.

"What was it you wanted to discuss?" asked Frank.

"I'm afraid I have some bad news for you, Mr. Morton," sighed Yamato. "Several nights ago there was a burglary at the martial arts shop. The thieves broke into my collection case and stole the beautiful *tsubute* that you had honored me with."

"I'm sorry to hear that. Did you lose your whole collection?"

"Well, that's just it. It took some time to inventory the entire shop and determine exactly what was taken, but it now appears that your *tsubute* is the only item missing from the shop."

"No cash, nothing else from your collection … just the *tsubute*?" asked Frank.

"We never leave cash in the shop overnight, but no, nothing else seems to be missing," confirmed Yamato. "Just the *tsubute*."

"Did you have any luck finding out who might have dropped it here at the hangar in the first place?" asked Frank.

"No, I'm afraid not," frowned Yamato. "I made a number of inquires but no one seemed to know anything about the *tsubute* or its origin. In fact, my daughter is the only person I know of, beside myself, of course, who would recognize it for what it really is. That's actually why I wanted to talk to you, Mr. Morton."

Frank stared at Yamato's bowed head and said, "I'm afraid you've lost me. What has the *tsubute* got to do with your daughter?"

"The day after the *tsubute* was stolen, my daughter, Aya, suddenly announced that she was going to take a vacation and she left this morning – for Yonaguni."

Chapter 6

The members of the NWIDI team met at the hanger early Sunday morning. After the unexpected "down day" on Saturday, everybody was anxious to get the trip to Japan underway. Even Linda, who had partied until almost sunrise Saturday morning, was eager to get going.

Everything had been checked and double-checked and there was a feeling of electricity in the air as Frank assembled the group in the hangar.

"Does everyone have his or her passport?" Frank asked, as he scanned the faces.

One by one, Tony, Jim, Linda, Fitz and Susan acknowledged the question with either a nod or an audible "Yes!"

Frank looked at the small, furry dog sitting quietly between the two members of the flight crew and asked, "How about you, Sandstrom?"

The dog sensed that he was about to go flying and responded with a happy bark and a wagging tail. Fitz pulled several folded pages out of his inside jacket pocket and answered on behalf of his dog.

"I have his medical papers right here, Frank. Sandy's all ready to go!"

Susan climbed aboard the Learjet and Fitz hitched a converted lawn tractor to the front strut. While the husband and wife flight crew positioned the aircraft on the apron in front of the hangar, Frank and Tony secured the building. Frank had made arrangements for a friend's daughter to spend her afternoons in the hangar's front office while the team was gone. In exchange, Frank agreed to have the Fitzgeralds fly her to Cancun for spring break in April and Linda had moved a PC and printer into the office so the college student could work on her term papers while baby sitting the hangar. Frank had assigned her an access code that only opened the two office doors – the front door so she could enter the building and the door into the hangar so she could get to the bathroom and the break room. All other areas would be off limits to the girl.

As Fitz closed and latched the cabin door, Susan's voice came over the intercom.

"Folks, we have just been cleared for takeoff, so please find a seat and fasten your safety belts. I'll let you know when we've reached our cruising altitude and it's safe to move about the cabin."

The Learjet's interior was finished in luxurious gray leather with burly maple wood trim and cabinets. The cabin's six high back seats were arranged three along each side of the aircraft with an aisle down the center. The front row of seats faced the back of the plane and formed what Lear called a "club" configuration with the middle two seats. Small tables pulled up and out between the two sets of facing seats for meals or meetings and the NWIDI team settled into the club area for the trip.

"Well, boys and girl, here we go! Welcome to the first official flight of 'Explorer One'!"

Tony, Jim and Linda each had their own suggestions for airplane names and soon the four friends were laughing so hard they missed the actual lift-off. As the nose of the Learjet pitched up for the climb out of Seattle, the cabin became very quiet. All four adventurers were lost in their own thoughts about what lay ahead in Japan.

For the next few minutes the conversation focused on Yamato's daughter, Aya, and the missing *tsubute* throwing disk. Frank described his meeting with the old man the previous morning and how Yamato had seemed concerned about his daughter's sudden departure.

"You don't think she had anything to do with the disappearance of the disk, do you?" asked Linda.

"I'm not sure what to think," replied Frank. "Yamato told me that his daughter was the only other person he knew of who would have recognized the disk for what it really is and her timing with this trip seems a little suspicious, but it could all be just a coincidence."

"Maybe she was just upset about the break-in and decided she needed some time away," offered Jim.

"Right!" exclaimed Tony. "Somehow I have a hard time believing that the owner of a martial arts school would turn tail and run just because of a second-rate burglary. I'd be willing to bet we haven't seen the last of Ninja Woman."

"I guess I agree with Tony," nodded Frank. "And I just thought of something the old man told us the other day. Tony, do you remember where Yamato said he had studied martial arts?"

"Uh, no. Wait – didn't he say something about an uncle who was a Grand Master?"

"Correct! And do you remember where this uncle lived?"

Tony thought for a moment before the answer came to him. "Of course! The old man told us his mother sent him back to Yonaguni to study with his uncle! Maybe that's where Aya went, too."

"Well, Yamato told us he was 71, so that would make his uncle close to 100 but there might be other family connections on the island. Suddenly, this *tsubute* is almost as intriguing as the underwater pyramid we're going to explore."

"Well, I wouldn't go quite that far," smiled Jim, the anthropologist and team expert on ancient studies. "I don't think the *tsubute* and a 12,500 year-old pyramid have that much in common."

"They have at least one thing in common," said Tony. "We don't know where either one came from. We don't know who built the pyramid, of course, but we also don't know who dropped the *tsubute* near our hangar. Our list of unsolved mysteries is growing already, and we're just barely off the ground."

About twenty minutes into the flight Susan announced that they had reached their cruising altitude and that it was safe to move about the cabin. Fitz opened the cockpit door and a very happy Sandstrom bounded down the plane's center aisle. The dog stopped at the rear of the aircraft, in front of the closed lavatory door.

"Don't tell me that the mutt uses the toilet, too," said Tony sarcastically.

"No, that's just his way of saying that he's hungry. We keep his dish and food in a cupboard under the lav sink rather than in the galley with the passengers' supplies," replied Fitz. "You see, not all our clients love dogs as much as you do, Tony."

Frank chuckled and elbowed Tony as Fitz walked toward the back of the cabin. Fitz soon returned from the lav carrying a metal pet dish and a bag of dry dog food. He was followed closely by the excited little dog. Fitz stopped at the club area of the plane, much to the chagrin of Sandstrom.

"There are a variety of soft drinks and alcoholic beverages forward in the galley. Susan also brought along a supply of sandwiches and snack food, so please help your selves. I'll start a fresh pot of coffee on my way forward.

"I should also point out that there's a pretty nice array of entertainment systems onboard. The built-in Airshow system will provide you with an up-to-the minute display of our location, relative to a map of the ground, along with flight data such as air speed, altitude and ETA. There's also a DVD player and a CD player, each on separate audio channels and there are headphones up front that plug into your armrest. The Airshow and the DVD player share a flat panel display located behind a door just above the galley.

"After I get Sandstrom fed, Susan is going to come back and brief you on the route we'll be taking to Japan and what to expect along the way. Is everybody having a good time so far?"

After receiving three nods and a thumbs-up (from Tony, of course), Fitz and Sandstrom returned to the cockpit.

"Wow," exclaimed Linda, "this plane is the coolest! You did good, Frank."

"I can't really take much of the credit," replied Frank, as he stood up and stretched in the aisle. "The plane was last used by a guy from Central America named Rafael. I don't know if that was his first name or his last name but, in any event, he ran afoul of some ATF agents and the plane ended up in the hands of the U.S. Government. Buzz Edwards, one of the DOE guys we met in Las Vegas last summer, called me one day and asked if I was interested in it. I guess he remembered how impressed I was with the Learjet he flew Jim and me back from the Yucatan in. Anyway, he told me that big-ticket items like this were normally sold at special silent auctions but, given the special circumstances surrounding this plane, he thought he could swing something for me if I were interested. To make a long story short, I flew to a military airfield in New Mexico where this plane was being stored and bought it on the spot for $650,000 cash. That's about 10% of the actual market value – pretty cool, huh?"

Frank started toward the front of the cabin and called back over his shoulder, "Anybody want anything to drink?"

When there was no answer from any of them, he turned back toward the three and asked, "Well?"

Tony looked back over his shoulder and said, "That depends, Frank. Normally I drink coffee this early in the morning, but it depends on what your phrase 'special circumstances surrounding this plane' means. Maybe I should be chugging those little bottles of whiskey instead."

Linda's face had gone white. "Frank, what's wrong with this airplane? And why didn't you tell us about this before we took off?"

Frank returned to his seat and smiled at his friends. "Look, guys, there's nothing wrong with this plane. It's been very well cared for since it left the factory ten years ago. And I had it checked out thoroughly, stem to stern before it ever left New Mexico. On top of that, the Fitzgeralds have gone over it with a fine-toothed comb. They've checked every system, every button and every gauge. There's absolutely nothing wrong with this plane – honest!"

"Then why was our government willing to practically give it away?" asked a tense Jim Barnes. "What aren't you telling us, Frank?"

"Nothing, Jim. Honest. This plane has a little history, that's all, and the government just wanted to make sure they knew where it was going to end up. They didn't want it to fall into the hands of a broker who might sell it to the wrong people. They wanted it in the hands of a U.S. citizen who would hang on to it for a while, that's all."

Frank started to get up again, but Tony gripped his shoulder and eased him back into the leather seat.

"Your long story is still a little too short, old buddy. I think we'd all like to know what you've gotten us into this time. Come on, spill it!"

"Okay, okay," agreed Frank, "but it's really no big deal. Like I said, our government confiscated this plane from a Central American drug smuggler. Well, it seems that this plane was on loan to this Rafael character by its real owner who purchased the plane brand new and would like very much to have it back."

"If the plane wasn't actually Rafael's wouldn't the government be obligated to return it to the rightful owner?" asked Jim, relieved that the plane's 'special circumstances' weren't mechanical in nature.

"Normally, yes," nodded Frank, "but in this case our government is taking special pleasure in withholding the property. In fact, if I hadn't offered to buy it, this plane was going to become a practice target on one of the Air Force's remote bombing ranges."

"Okay, so tell, us, Frank. Who did this plane belong to before the drug dealer got it?" demanded Linda.

Scanning the faces of his three friends, Frank finally gave in. "If I tell you, you have to promise me that you will never discuss this with anyone. This information is classified – literally.

"It seems that our friend Rafael traveled in some pretty exclusive circles. He had an enormous amount of cash at his disposal and he enjoyed the high life – and the sick life – available to only a select few in the world. In addition, he had access to large quantities of high-grade cocaine and other drugs, which made him an attractive playmate to some of the most screwed up people in the world. Apparently he coveted the private jets owned by many of his acquaintances but due to his status as an international drug dealer, no one would sell him a plane, and even if they had he wouldn't have been given permission to land it in most civilized countries. Instead he borrowed this plane, which was registered to a fictitious oil millionaire in the Middle East."

"Then who really owned the plane – who is it that wants it back so bad?" asked Tony, who also seemed unconcerned about the political history of the plane.

Lowering his voice, Frank said, "The plane actually belongs to a little-known Arab guy by the name Qusai. You've probably heard of his father – Saddam Hussein."

"Oh, my God, Frank!" cried Linda. "Do you know who this guy is? He's one of the most dangerous people in the world. He's in charge of Iraq's Republican Guard, their Secret Police and just about everything else evil or sinister in that country. And he's next in line to take over if anything happens to his father. Frank, if this guy wants his plane back bad enough, there's no safe place to hide!"

Glancing over his shoulder, Frank hissed, "Settle down, Linda. The government has given this plane a whole new identity, complete with a new tail number and a fictitious history of previous owners. Even the FAA couldn't trace it back to the real owner. The only person who knows that this plane fell into government hands is Rafael, and he'll be in prison for a long, long time. And I doubt if even he could identify it now that we've restored the trim colors to factory original and painted the NWIDI logo on the tail. It's just another Learjet."

As Linda was about to raise another objection, the cockpit door opened and Susan came down the aisle to where the four were seated.

"Am I interrupting something?" she asked politely.

Frank looked up and forced a smile. "No, no we were just talking about how great this plane is."

"And how lucky Frank was to get it," added Linda, glaring directly at Frank.

"I know! Isn't it incredible that Frank would be the only bidder at a private auction and get such a great price on it?" beamed Susan. "And just think, you're riding in a plane that was once owned by the richest man in the world! I understand that Bill Gates actually wrote his famous 'computer on every desk' speech in this very cabin."

Realizing that Frank had not shared the plane's true history with the Fitzgeralds, Linda had to turn her head toward the window and bite her lip to keep from speaking out.

"Anyway, I'd like to give you a quick update on where we are and the route we will be taking to Japan, so if you'll direct your attention forward, I'll use the Airshow map as a visual aid."

Susan opened a nearly concealed panel above the galley to reveal a built-in flat panel screen. After flipping some switches on a control box below the screen, a map of the northern part of North America came into view. A curving line extended from Seattle northwest to a point along the west coast of Canada.

"As you can see," she continued, "we are currently in Canadian airspace on a route that will take us up the coast to near Prince Rupert, where we'll turn west out over the Pacific. The numbers at the bottom of the screen indicate that we're traveling about 420 knots – that's about 450 miles per hour – and that we are cruising at an altitude of 41,000 feet.

"Out here, near the end of the Aleutian Islands, is our first stop. These letters, PADK, that you see displayed is the airport designation for Adak Island. It's almost exactly half way between Seattle and Tokyo as the crow, or in this case, as the Learjet, flies along this arc."

"Excuse me for sounding dumb," interrupted Tony, "but isn't Japan at about the same latitude as southern California? It seems like we're going north to get south."

"That's a good observation, Tony, and on a flat earth that would be very true. The map you see here is somewhat misleading because we're actually following the surface of a sphere. Our flight path follows what's called a Great Circle route and it actually represents the shortest path from Seattle to Tokyo. Fortunately for us, someone saw fit to put Adak Island almost exactly in the middle of our arc because otherwise that's about where we would run out of fuel."

The four sets of raised eyebrows prompted Susan to continue.

"You see, the distance from Seattle to Tokyo, along our arc, is about 4,800 miles and the Learjet only has a range of about 2,700 miles. If we don't make the stop in Adak, then, right about here," Susan pointed to a spot in the ocean just a little west of the tiny island, "we will go from being a very luxurious aircraft to a rather poorly designed submarine!"

"But we have plenty of fuel to get to Adak, right?" asked a nervous Jim. "Why don't we just stop in Anchorage or someplace and get more fuel?"

"Well, like I said, Adak is almost exactly half way and there's nothing between Adak and Tokyo except ocean. If we don't take on a full load of fuel there, we'll never make it the rest of the way. Besides, every aircraft has a slightly different cruising range, so this first leg will give us a chance to get familiar with the plane and see what she can do.

"Now when we land in Adak, we'll be taking a short break. It will take about thirty minutes to refuel and we need everyone off the plane while that's taking place. Fitz will monitor the refueling while I go inside and file the flight plan for the second leg of our trip. There's a small coffee shop inside the terminal building so I suggest we all meet there before reboarding.

"I need to get back up front now, so you all just relax and enjoy the trip. As you can see from the display, we should be landing in about three and a half hours."

As Susan opened the door to the cockpit, Sandstrom zipped through into the cabin, tail wagging wildly.

"Do you mind if I leave this door open for a while? I think he wants to get acquainted with you guys."

After some coffee and muffins from the galley, everyone settled in for the rest of the flight. Tony moved to one of the two rear seats, reclined it and was asleep in minutes. Linda took the other rear seat and she, too, was soon asleep.

Frank and Jim took up positions on opposite sides of the aircraft and made use of the pullout tables. Frank worked on the last of the permit paperwork that would allow the NWIDI team access to the underwater pyramid and Jim alternated between going over his Yonaguni notes and worrying about running out of fuel.

Later, Frank went aft to use the lavatory and chuckled when he saw Sandstrom sound asleep under Tony's outstretched legs. On his way back to his seat, the plane lurched violently and Frank was almost thrown into Linda's lap. The jolt startled everyone, momentarily waking Linda who was surprised to find Frank leaning over her clinging to the side of the plane.

"Sorry," he said with a smile as he regained his balance.

The plane bounced again and Linda put up her arms to help steady Frank and to keep him from falling onto her. Her eyes showed signs of panic setting in.

Although Tony hadn't stirred, Frank noticed that Sandstrom was no longer asleep on the floor. As he moved carefully back up the aisle, Frank spotted a furry tail disappearing into the cockpit. He settled into his rear-facing leather seat and heard the cockpit door close behind him.

The remainder of the flight was relatively smooth and even Jim succumbed to the hypnotic feeling of the aircraft and fell asleep. There were several more "bumps" and, while they weren't as violent as the first, Frank noticed that the plane seemed to change cruising altitudes after each one.

Frank had just dozed off for the first time when Susan's voice over the intercom startled everyone awake.

"I'm sorry to disturb you but we have begun our final descent into Adak. I need to ask you all to move to forward-facing seats and fasten your seat belts as quickly as possible because it appears that we may experience some turbulence on our way down."

Since Frank was the only one not already facing forward, he moved to the opposite side of the table and buckled in. Glancing around the cabin, he noticed looks of concern on the faces of both Jim and Linda.

"It's nothing to worry about," Frank assured them. "There's been some intermittent turbulence the whole flight and ..."

In mid-sentence, the plane suddenly felt like it was in an elevator with a broken cable. As quickly as it had started the terrible sensation stopped, but there was no doubt the Learjet had lost some altitude.

"Sorry about that, folks. We hit a wind shear and dropped a couple of hundred feet, but everything's fine." This time it was Fitz's voice on the intercom. "The rest of our descent into Adak should be a little more gradual but we would like to ask you all to stay seated until we land. Please stow the tables and secure any other items you may have taken out. We should be on the ground soon."

"What the hell does he mean by should be on the ground?" questioned Linda nervously. "Wouldn't a pilot know something like that?"

"Yes, but remember Susan's little submarine analogy earlier?" teased Tony from across the aisle. "Maybe he means that we should be on the ground but might end up in the ocean."

Another wind shear caught the plane and this time Linda screamed out loud.

"Steady back there," Fitz said over the intercom. "These conditions are actually quite common in the Aleutian Islands this time of year. We'll get you down."

"And by that he probably means we'll end up on the ground, one way or another," laughed Tony.

"Tony, you're not helping!" barked Frank.

To Frank and Tony the turbulence they were experiencing was nothing like some of the flights they had made in Viet Nam, but it was clear that Jim and Linda were feeling some serious stress.

Frank looked to Jim questioningly and Jim nodded slightly. He had taken his hands away from his mouth, so Frank assumed the feeling of nausea had passed but Jim was gripping the armrests so tight that his knuckles were white.

The plane pitched and rolled several times and finally assumed a nose-down angle that was so steep it even concerned Tony. When the plane didn't level out, Tony unbuckled his seat belt and made his way forward.

"Tony, where are you going?" yelled Linda. "Get back in your seat before you get killed!"

"Something's not right, and I'm going to find out what's going on," he replied as he gripped the seats to keep from being thrown down the aisle.

As Tony passed Frank's seat, Frank grabbed his arm and said, "Tell them to try an alternate airport!"

Tony reached the front of the cabin and pulled the cockpit door open slightly while bracing against the forward bulkhead. Frank could see several exchanges take place between Tony and the crew, but he couldn't hear any of the conversation over the sound of the now straining engines.

Finally Tony closed the door and made his way back "up hill" toward his seat.

"What's up?" asked Frank, as the plane lurched again.

"We're about ten miles out, but there's one hell of a storm going on out there. It came in real sudden, I guess."

"What about another airport?"

"Can't do it," replied Tony. He leaned over close to Frank's ear and continued, "They're not sure we even have enough fuel left to make Adak."

Chapter 7

Tony finally reached his seat and flopped down. Just as he secured his belt, the Learjet leveled off to nearly horizontal and the sound of the engines returned to normal. The four NWIDI team members in the cabin all breathed a deep sigh of relief, especially Linda and Jim. Seconds later, Susan's voice came over the intercom.

"I think we're through the worst of the weather, folks, and I apologize for the rough ride, but even the Air Force radar station on Adak didn't see this one coming! We'll be on the ground in just a few minutes and then Fitz will explain what we just went through. Until we land, though, please stay in your seats and keep your belts fastened. We expect a smooth landing, but with these freak weather systems, you never know."

Frank looked to his right across the aisle to see how Jim was doing.

"Are you okay?" Frank asked when he finally caught Jim's eye.

Jim nodded. "I think so. I've flown all over the western hemisphere and had some pretty wild moments, but that was scary."

"Roger that!" called Tony from the seat behind Jim. "I haven't been for a ride like that since 'Nam."

Ten minutes later the Learjet rolled to a stop in front of a single terminal building that could have been in any small city in the United States. Susan Fitzgerald came out of the cockpit, followed closely by a tail-wagging Sandstrom.

"Well, we made it," she smiled. "It's still raining pretty hard outside, so please be careful going down the steps. If you will make your way into the terminal as quickly as possible, Fitz and I will secure the plane and meet you in the coffee shop."

Inside, the NWIDI team brushed the rain from their clothes and gazed around. To the right was an empty baggage carousel. To the left was a small boarding area, but it was also empty. Directly ahead of them, on the other side of the building, a pair of double doors led to the parking lot, but there were no cars in sight. In fact, the place looked totally deserted.

"Come on in, folks!" called a deep voice from somewhere inside the building. "I understand you had quite a ride."

The four continued forward until they reached the main hallway that ran left and right the entire length of the terminal building. To their left they could just see the head and waving hand of a large black man leaning over an otherwise deserted lunch counter. As they approached, he smiled and indicated that they should make themselves comfortable on stools at the counter. The crackle of a two-way radio came from somewhere back in the kitchen area.

Checking his watch, the man said, "Afternoon, folks. My name is Henry. Can I get you some coffee or tea? I also have cold soft drinks and I think I still have a beer or two in the refrigerator."

Jim ordered tea, Tony got a beer, and Frank and Linda declined.

When the man came back with the drinks, Frank asked the obvious question. "So, where is everybody? This place looks deserted."

"Well, sir," smiled the black man, "it ain't too busy right now, I'll grant you that, but we had quite a crowd in here this morning – a bunch of government folks out of Juneau, I think – must've been 15 or 20 of them. But this airport doesn't see much traffic in the winter – not since the military pulled out in '96."

Frank looked down the long hallway toward the other end of the building. "But it looks like we're the only people in the terminal, Henry. How can anybody afford to keep this place open?"

"Well, the U.S. Government feels it's important to have a full-service landing field out here in the Aleutians for safety reasons and since this is the largest facility west of Kodiak, they provide all the necessary funding. Since I have to be here anyway, I moved most of my stuff down to this end of the building and I just hang out back here behind the counter." Laughing and rubbing his large stomach, he added, "I'm afraid moving my office into the kitchen hasn't done much for my waistline, though."

Drawn into the conversation, Linda asked, "What do you mean you have to be here anyway? Do you have other duties besides this counter?"

"Yes, ma'am. In fact, I have all the duties around here. As the Airport Manager, I do as much as I can and I contract locals for additional services as necessary. I talked your flight crew down through that nasty storm you ran into and I'll see to their fuel needs when they're ready. I also load and unload baggage, do some minor aircraft maintenance and at the end of the day I turn out the lights and lock the doors."

Now Tony's interest was also peaked. "Why in the world would anybody build a terminal like this out here in the first place?" he asked.

"Well, it wasn't always like this," sighed Henry in a friendly, grandfatherly voice. "Adak Island has had its share of booms and busts but as recently as ten years ago there were more than 5,000 people living here – mostly military personnel and their families. It was called Adak Naval Air Station back then and there were a dozen commercial flights a day in and out of here. I spent my last six years of active duty here on Adak and when they announced they were closing this facility back in 1996 I decided to retire and stay here on the island. I applied for the Manager's position at the airport and, well, I just sort of became the airport guy."

"Amazing," said Frank, shaking his head. "I'm curious, though, what made you decide to stay on a tiny island in the middle of the Bering Sea, half way between Alaska and Russia?"

"Well, I don't have much family down in the lower 48, and I enjoy the peace and quiet up here. Now that the Navy is gone, things move along at a nice comfortable pace and folks pretty much leave me alone. With my pension and the salary I get from my work here, I can live pretty well and if I start to get cabin fever I can always take off for the Orient. Japan's only four hours away, you know."

"Yeah, that's where we're headed, actually. How's the fishing up here?" asked Tony.

"My friend, you wouldn't believe it! I know I don't look like much of a sportsman, but I'd rather fish than eat and Adak is a fisherman's paradise. Do you like to fish?"

"A little," smiled Tony. "Maybe when I get back from Japan I'll look you up and you can show me some good spots."

The large man reached under the counter and brought out a business card that said simply, "Henry Jones" followed by a line that read "Adak Island, Alaska". Near the bottom of the card was a telephone number.

"We don't need street addresses anymore," smiled Henry, as he handed the card to Tony. "On Adak, everybody knows everybody. Just call me a few days before you fly in and I'll set up a trip that'll make you think you've never been fishing before."

Just then the radio crackled again and Henry turned to listen.

"It sounds like your flight crew is ready to fuel up. You folks wait right here and I'll go see to the plane. Help yourself to the coffee pot or the refrigerator. We'll settle up when I get back."

Henry disappeared into the kitchen and a couple of minutes later Frank noticed him near the far end of the terminal dressed in bright yellow rain slickers.

"What a character," he commented to no one in particular.

While the Learjet was being refueled, Frank decided to check to see if he had any voice-mail messages on his cell phone. When Jim saw Frank adjust the unit's cylindrical antenna, he shook his head.

"I doubt if there's any service up here, Frank."

"Actually, the phone thinks analog roaming service is available, but I'm using the satellite service to check my voice-mail. I've only used the satellite link a couple of times and I'm curious how it works up here."

Frank held up a finger to indicate he had a connection and put the phone to his ear. After a series of listening and button pushing exchanges, Frank clipped the phone back onto his belt.

"Damn!"

"What's the matter?" asked Linda, who had been chatting with Tony.

"Oh, that cop back in Seattle wants to ask us a bunch of questions about the murder and his message suggests that he wants us all back in Seattle ASAP."

"Do they know who the victim really was?" asked Tony. "I assume they've figured out by now that the dead man wasn't really a private detective from Las Vegas named Larry Schultz, right?"

"Yes, they came up with that info all by themselves a couple of days after Linda did," nodded Frank. "The last time I talked to the police they were still waiting for the results of a fingerprint search to come back from Washington D.C. Maybe they finally got the results and that's why Lt. Snyder wants to talk to us, but he didn't leave any clues in his message."

"So what are we going to do, Frank?" asked Linda. "Do we have to turn around and head back?"

Frank thought for a minute and then said, "You know what, screw him! I did agree that we'd return to Seattle if he needed us to, but it's Sunday and he's probably not in his office anyway. I'll call him tomorrow morning from Japan and see if we can give him whatever information he needs over the phone. Maybe the fact that we're so far away will discourage him from demanding a face-to-face meeting."

"Good plan," nodded Tony. "But now I'm curious. Even if they've identified the body, what could they want from us? We already told them we didn't know who the guy was."

"Who knows," agreed Frank, "unless ..."

"Unless what?" demanded Linda.

"Well, unless they've somehow linked the dead man to one of us."

Just then, Henry reappeared through the door at the far end of the terminal, followed by the Fitzgeralds. They were all wearing the same typical yellow rain gear and they looked soaked.

"It's been raining cats and dogs out there!" exclaimed Fitz as he shed his rain gear.

"Speaking of dogs ..." said Tony, half expecting to see Sandstrom trotting down the hallway dressed in yellow.

"Oh, he was smart enough to stay onboard where it's dry," laughed Susan Fitzgerald.

Henry was out of his rain gear and behind the counter pouring coffee for Fitz and Susan.

"You folks might want to consider laying over until tomorrow. This storm should be moving out of here soon, but that sky doesn't look very promising right now. There's a bed-and-breakfast type of place not far from here and they should be able to put you up for the night. I can give you a lift in the airport van."

Jim was nodding his head and Linda said, "I, for one, certainly don't look forward to taking off in this weather, especially if it's going to be anything like the landing. Maybe we should take Henry's advice, Frank."

"That would mean changing all of our reservations in Tokyo and beyond, but I guess we can do that if necessary. Personally, I'd rather go on to Japan today, but I'll leave the decision up to our crew. What do you think, Fitz?"

Fitz shrugged. "It doesn't really matter to me, Frank. Like Henry said, this storm should be just about past and we'll be above it ten minutes after we take off anyway. From a safety standpoint, I certainly don't think there's any danger now that the winds have died down. Maybe we should have lunch and then decide."

"Yeah, lunch sounds like a great idea – I'm starving," agreed Tony.

"I'm afraid I don't have much to offer here," apologized Henry with a frown. "There might be a few bags of chips around here, but otherwise the cupboards are bare. This place hasn't operated as a real lunch counter for almost five years."

"There are plenty of sandwiches on the plane," offered Susan. "I also packed some chips and pretzels but somebody has to volunteer to go out there and get them."

After some discussion, Frank volunteered Tony and himself to make the food run. Henry found them a plastic bag to protect the food and they dashed out the main door they had used when they originally entered the terminal.

About five minutes later they returned, followed by the Fitzgeralds' dog, Sandstrom. Neither the two men nor the dog appeared to be very wet.

"It's already looking better out there," said Frank as he put the bag down on the counter. It's just barely raining and the sky is beginning to lighten in the north."

Sandstrom was sitting quietly between Fitz and Susan.

"Who's your friend?" asked Henry, nodding his head toward the dog.

"This is Sandstrom," replied Susan. "Say 'Hello' to the nice man, Sandstrom."

The dog barked and wagged his tail wildly, which made the large man laugh.

During lunch, which they shared with Henry, they got a lesson in the history of Adak Island.

Henry told them about the island's original inhabitants, the Aleuts, who had occupied Adak for as many as 9,000 years. Russian traders first visited the island in the early 1740s and eventually relocated the Aleuts to neighboring islands and the Alaskan mainland.

Adak was sold to the United States as part of the Alaska Territory in 1867 and in 1913 it became part of the Alaska Maritime National Wildlife Refuge, a preserve and breeding ground for native birds and fur-bearing animals such as sea otters and seals.

By the spring of 1944, Adak had a population of more than 32,000 military personnel but the number dropped to less than 300 by 1953. The build-up began again in the early 60s, reaching a high of more than 5,000 by 1990.

"I see what you mean by booms and busts," commented Frank as Henry finished his monologue. "What did the Aleuts have to say about all this?"

"Not much. When the Russians moved them off the island there were only 193 of them here. I doubt if there's many more than that living here today although the island technically belongs to them – or at least to their Aleut Corporation."

"And this airport?" asked Tony. "Do they own this, too?"

"Technically, yes. It was built with federal funds back in the early 90s at a cost of about $30 million. It includes two 7,800 foot runways, several taxiways, a maintenance hangar, a control tower a fire station and, of course, this terminal building. I like to think of it as Henry International Airport." His broad grin showed white teeth.

During lunch, Frank gave Henry a little background on NWIDI and why they were headed for Japan. When Frank explained that they hoped to shed some light on the origin, or at least the purpose, of the Yonaguni Monument, Henry seemed unusually interested in the project.

"Sure wish I was going with you folks," said Henry, sadly. "Back when I first joined the Navy I went through SEAL training and I practically lived in the water for a couple of years after that. Of course, I was a lot thinner then," he smiled.

"What got you out of the water and into the aviation end of the Navy?" asked Tony.

"Well, back in '71 my unit was on a mission in the South China Sea when a fire started below decks near the compartment where I was sleeping. Before I could get into a breathing apparatus I was overcome by smoke and damn near died. Fortunately, one of my buddies found me and saved my life, but the smoke caused some permanent damage to my lungs and the Navy wouldn't let me dive any more. I've been trapped behind a desk ever since."

As former Special Ops soldiers themselves, Frank and Tony felt a special bond to Henry and the three swapped "war stories" for the next half-hour.

By the time everyone had finished eating the sky was looking much better and the decision was made to continue on to Japan. Henry accompanied the travelers to the boarding area door and they exchanged good-byes.

As they were going out the door, Henry put his hand on Tony's shoulder to stop him. "You hang on to that card I gave you and if you folks get into any trouble down there you call me, you hear? During my 28 years in the Navy I've developed quite a network of resources and I can get you pretty much anything you need – and in a hurry, too."

"Thanks, Henry, I'll remember that. You take care of yourself," replied Tony sincerely, as he shook the big man's hand.

The travelers crossed the apron to the Learjet while Henry made his way to the control tower. The NWIDI Learjet lifted off at 2:00 p.m. Seattle time (11:00 a.m. local Adak time) but it was already 6:00 a.m. the next morning in Tokyo.

***

Aya Yamato had arrived in Japan the day before on a non-stop United Airlines flight from Seattle. The eleven-hour flight had left her tired and cranky, but a night's rest in her favorite hotel had made a world of difference in her mood. The early-morning bustle of downtown Tokyo reminded her of how much she missed Japan and she asked herself, for the millionth time, why she continued to live in the United States. The answer, of course, was her father. Aya would never understand how the old fool could call a country home that had imprisoned his family and, indirectly, caused the death of his father. Because of the Japanese internment camps, Aya had never known her paternal grandfather.

Thankfully, Aya's mother had trained her daughter in the traditional Japanese ways. Aya had even attended the University of the Ryukyus, in Okinawa, until her mother had been diagnosed with cancer and Aya was forced to return to the U.S. to be with her mother during her last days. When Aya's mother passed away, her father was so distraught that Aya was afraid to leave him alone and he refused to return to Japan. They bought the martial arts school south of Seattle mostly so her father, Koji, would have something to do with his time but when her father's age would no longer let him teach, Aya felt obligated to take over as Sensei. She hated the school, she hated Seattle, and she hated the United States. On this cold, sunny January morning, she was very glad to be back in Japan.

As Aya settled into the back seat of the taxi, she reached into her jacket pocket and fingered the envelope containing the 3.25-inch *tsubute* she had "liberated" from her father's display case earlier in the week. She had no idea how the ancient artifact had fallen into the hands of the two men who had visited her father's store, but she knew that if word got out that the Genji clan was being revived, all hell would break loose.

The taxi dropped her at Kaminarimon Gate, one of several entrances to the famous Asakusa district. It is one of the oldest areas of Tokyo and the narrow streets lined with quaint shops were already packed with merchants and shoppers. Aya made her way down the pedestrian lane toward the Sensoji Temple until she reached a narrow alley named Kito Dori. She stopped on the corner and pretended to examine something in a shop window. Satisfied that she wasn't being followed, she made her way briskly down the alley and into a small used book store about mid-way down the block. Inside, she went directly to the rear of the store and through a curtained doorway into a small, dimly lit back room.

"Ohayoo gozaimasu," said a deep voice in the far corner of the room. Good morning.

"Ohayoo gozaimasu," returned Aya.

"Did you get it?" asked the man, switching to English and standing.

"Of course, Tanaka-san."

Aya placed the envelope containing the *tsubute* into the man's outstretched hand and stepped back, bowing slightly to the dark figure.

"And you're sure you weren't followed, Aya?"

"Quite sure. Have you discovered how the *tsubute* got to America yet?"

"Yes, one of our agents assigned to an ally in the mid-east apparently got careless but he has been dealt with. Thank you for your assistance. Wait out in the shop for ten minutes, select a book and then proceed on down the street in the direction you were originally headed. Be sure the bag containing the book is clearly visible as you leave the shop. If we need any more help you will be contacted."

Aya did exactly as the man instructed. After leaving the bookstore, she wandered in and out of several more shops on the block, giving the appearance that she was on a casual shopping trip. At the corner, another left turn took her to the main avenue where she hailed a taxi back to the prestigious Imperial Hotel in the Ginzu district.

The doorman who helped Aya out of the taxi greeted her in Japanese, something that always made her smile.

"Doomo," she replied. Thanks.

Inside, she made her way across the luxurious lobby to the Travel Desk where she booked reservations on JAL's 10:25 flight to Okinawa and Japan Transocean Air's connecting flight to Yonaguni. If everything went according to schedule, Aya would be at her great uncle's minshuku (similar to an American Bed & Breakfast) by mid-afternoon, in time to visit with her favorite relative before he retired for the evening. And at almost 100, the old man went to bed pretty early!

***

Frank, Tony, Jim and Linda all had their faces pressed against their windows as the NWIDI Learjet made its final approach into Tokyo's Haneda Airport. Unlike the first leg of their trip, the flight from Adak Island to Japan had been very smooth and the clear morning skies over Tokyo were providing them an incredible view.

"It's huge!" exclaimed Linda, as the plane circled out over the city to line up with runway 34L.

"More than 12 million people jammed into less than 800 square miles," commented Jim, holding up a tourists' guide he had been reading. "This book says it makes New York seem like a ghost town."

As the jet's wheels made their first gentle contact with the runway, Susan's voice came over the intercom.

"Folks, please don't forget that we have to clear customs here in Tokyo, so sit tight until they let us know where they want us to go."

Aya's JAL flight to Okinawa had pushed back from the gate right on time and as the new Boeing 737-400 came to a stop on the taxiway, she looked out the window to see what the holdup was. Directly in front of her plane, a private Learjet, with the letters NWIDI painted on its tail, was just touching down.

"More damned Americans coming over here to promote their western ways," she mumbled to herself.

As her plane finally started to move again, Aya had the feeling that she had seen that NWIDI acronym somewhere before.

On the Learjet, Frank was lost in thought, pondering what the Seattle police Lieutenant wanted to talk to them about. Tony, on the other hand, was worrying about the customs inspectors and how thoroughly would they search the aircraft.

Chapter 8

Following instructions from the control tower, Fitz taxied the Learjet to a spot near a small satellite terminal at Tokyo's Haneda Airport and shut down the engines.

"We're supposed to wait here for the Customs Agents," he announced as he opened the door between the cockpit and the cabin. "The tower said it would only be a few minutes so please pass your passports up to me."

Frank decided to make the best of the time by calling Lt. Snyder, of the Seattle Police Department.

"Might as well get this over with," he said to himself as he dialed the on-board telephone.

"Lt. Snyder here," said the voice that answered the phone at the other end of the line.

"Good morning, Lieutenant," greeted Frank, being as pleasant as possible. "You left me a voice mail and I'm returning your call."

"Yes, I left that message yesterday, Mr. Morton. And what do you mean, good morning? Where in the hell are you?"

"We just landed in Tokyo, Lieutenant, and this is the first chance I've had to call since I received your message. How can I help you?"

"Tokyo! I thought you weren't leaving for Japan until next week. Damn it! I need to talk to you and the other two who were at the hangar the day of the murder. When will you be back?"

"I'm afraid we won't be back for several days – maybe a week or more. Can't we answer your questions over the phone, Lieutenant?" asked Frank.

Overhearing Frank's side of the conversation, Tony slid into the seat facing Frank and made obscene gestures at the telephone handset.

"I knew I shouldn't have agreed to let you leave the country. I'm tempted to make you all come back to Seattle today."

"I'm afraid that won't be possible. You see, once we return to the US we won't be able to get another Visa to come back to Japan for at least six months," Frank lied, shrugging to Tony. "I take it you've identified the victim?"

"Yes, we have, and that's precisely why I want to talk to you ... and to Linda McBride and Tony Nicoletti. I'm damn curious what somebody like our victim was doing outside your hangar. This man was ... hold on a minute."

Frank could hear muffled sounds as if the other man was shouting with his hand over the mouthpiece. A few seconds later, Lieutenant Snyder came back on the line.

"Well, apparently I no longer need to ask you any questions, Mr. Morton. I was just informed that my murder case has been transferred to the U.S. Department of Justice. Give me the name of the place where you'll be staying in Japan so I can pass it on to the Feds."

Frank gave the policeman the name of the hotel where they had reservations on Yonaguni Island.

"What about the victim, Lieutenant? Who was he?"

"You'll have to ask the Feds – I'm sure they'll be contacting you very soon. Good night, Mr. Morton."

The line went dead and Frank replaced the air phone in the cradle next to his seat.

"Well, that was interesting," he said, scratching his head.

"What's going on," demanded Tony. "Do we have to go back to Seattle?"

Linda had moved to the seat facing Jim and they all hung on Frank's every word.

"I don't know yet. In the middle of the call Lieutenant Snyder was informed that the Justice Department had just taken the murder case away from the Seattle Police. Apparently a federal agent is supposed to be contacting us very soon."

"The Justice Department!" shouted Linda. "That guy who got shot must have done something pretty serious if the Feds are after him."

"Actually, they already have him, Linda," commented Tony, leaning his head back against the seat. "It's us they want now."

As the NWIDI team members contemplated the significance of Tony's statement, there was a loud knock on the aircraft's door that startled them all.

"Akero, kudasai!" shouted a voice from outside. Open, please.

Fitz came out of the cockpit, unsecured the door and lowered the stairs. Two Japanese customs agents entered the plane followed by a Caucasian man wearing sunglasses and a black trench coat. The two customs agents followed Fitz into the cockpit but the third man remained in the cabin.

"Mr. Morton, Mr. Nicoletti and Ms. McBride? Please come with me," said Trenchcoat, as he stepped back and motioned toward the stairs with his right arm.

Frank stood first and asked, "Who the hell are you?"

"I'm Agent Bryant, Mr. Morton. I'm with the U.S Government and I need to ask you and your friends some questions. Please get in the vehicle at the bottom of the stairs."

Tony started to object but the agent cut him off and pointed to two other similarly dressed men outside the aircraft.

"We can do this the easy way or the hard way, Mr. Nicoletti. We're quite familiar with your reputation."

Frank and Linda were already outside, so Tony let it go, but he couldn't help himself and as he passed the agent he turned his head so he was nose-to-nose with the other man and grinned broadly.

"Apparently you're not <u>that</u> familiar with my reputation, Agent Bryant, or there would be more than three of you."

As Bryant followed Tony down the steps, he said quietly, "There are three more agents on the other side of the aircraft, Mr. Nicoletti."

On the plane, Jim sat bewildered, wondering what had just happened. This trip was turning out to be a lot more cloak-and-dagger and a lot less archeology than he had bargained for, and his sabbatical leave was wasting away with no visible progress toward publishable material. He decided to remind Frank of that fact – if he ever saw him again!

Moments later, the customs agents came out of the cockpit, followed by Fitz, Susan and Sandstrom. One agent looked casually through several of the cupboards in the forward galley while the other one walked to the back of the plane and opened the lavatory door. They exchanged some words in Japanese, shook hands with both Fitz and Susan and then disappeared down the stairs.

Fitz closed the door to keep out the chilly January air and handed Jim his passport.

"Well, that was pretty painless. More of a formality than an inspection, I'd say. We have to stay put until the others come back, Jim, so you might as well make yourself comfortable. How about a fresh pot of coffee?"

Jim's head was still reeling from the Justice Department visit and he hardly heard what Fitz had said.

"Jim? Are you all right?"

"Uh, yes, of course. I was just a little surprised by the sudden departure of Frank, Tony and Linda. Any idea when they will be back?"

"No, that was a surprise to us, too. The tower told Susan that customs agents would be coming out to inspect the aircraft and check our documents, but they never said a word about the Americans. Either they didn't know or ..."

"Or they didn't want us to make a run for it," finished Jim. "What the hell is going on, Fitz? Do they really think one of us is mixed up with this guy that was killed at the hangar?"

"Oh, I'm sure it's all some big mix-up," consoled Susan. "The Japanese customs folks didn't seem too threatened by us. In fact, I got the feeling they were a little amused by the bravado of the American agents."

Frank, Tony and Linda were loaded into the Japanese version of a Volkswagen van and driven across the tarmac to the main terminal. A garage door opened and the minibus entered the "business" level of the airport. To the left, as far as the eye could see, conveyor belts carried baggage in every direction. On the right, a row of diagonal parking spaces separated the painted roadway from a series of office doors, each stenciled with Japanese letters. The vehicle pulled into a space about fifty feet down the row, directly in front of a door that included the words *U.S. Department of Justice, Anti-Terrorism Unit* along with a number of Japanese symbols.

"Anti-Terrorism Unit! What the hell is going on here," shouted Tony. "Do you idiots have any idea who we are? Frank and I both have Top Secret security clearances! I've been working for the Department of Defense for the past 24 years and Frank was a project engineer on the International Space Station until just recently."

The side door of the van slid open and a hand reached in to take Tony by the arm but he jerked away.

"Tony, let's just go get this straightened out and be on our way. These guys have obviously been drinking too much Sake. Don't cause a commotion, okay?"

Tony glared at Frank, but finally relented and climbed out of the minibus without saying another word. The three NWIDI members were escorted through the DOJ door and into an interrogation room. After they were fingerprinted, Bryant told them all to be seated at the table in the center of the room and then he and the other agents left, leaving Frank, Tony and Linda alone.

Linda was visibly shaken by the recent events and Frank guessed that the only thing keeping her from becoming hysterical was the fact that she was in a state of shock. She sat with her arms folded across her chest and stared straight ahead. Tony, who was sitting on the other side of Linda, started to say something to her, but Frank shook his head to stop him.

The room's only door finally opened and Agent Bryant entered carrying a manila routing envelope stamped with the word 'Secret' in large letters. He sat down on the opposite side of the six-foot folding table from Frank, Tony and Linda and smiled.

"Good afternoon, folks. As I told you on the plane, my name is Agent Charles Bryant. As you could tell by the sign on our door, I'm with the Department of Justice's Anti-Terrorism Unit. I've been asked to interview the three of you about a murder you all witnessed."

"Just a damn ...," began Tony before Agent Bryant interrupted him.

"Mr. Nicoletti, I know you're upset, and I don't blame you. I would be, too, in your position. But as they say, don't kill the messenger. I'm just doing my job and following orders. If you'll cooperate with us, I'll try to explain what this is all about and why the Justice Department got involved in a seemingly routine murder case."

The man's manner and apparent sincerity surprised Tony, and he nodded his acceptance.

"Okay, then, let's get started. Have any of you ever seen this man before?" he asked, taking a photograph out of an envelope and placing it on the table in front of Linda.

Frank and Tony scooted their chairs closer to Linda's and they all stared at the photo for a second before shaking their heads "No."

"Okay, then how about this man?" asked the agent as he laid another photo beside the first.

Again, the answer from all three was no.

This process was repeated three more times, each with a negative response from the three NWIDI team members.

The sixth photo was one taken by the police photographer during the initial investigation of the murder at the hanger. It showed the corpse lying in a pool of blood and Linda turned her head away as a sob escaped.

"Of course we recognize him," said Frank. "What's the point of all this?"

Bryant indicated the six photos spread out on the table and explained.

"Well, the point is that all of these pictures are of the same person. His name is, or was, James Maxwell Nasser. He is also known as Abdullah Mohamed Al-Nasser. He dropped off our radar screens about two years ago, when he apparently assumed the identity of a Las Vegas private investigator named Larry Schultz. Al-Nasser is suspected of terrorist activities in at least six countries, and we'd like to know just what he was doing at your hangar two weeks ago."

"Apparently, getting shot to death," said Tony sarcastically.

Bryant shot Tony a cold glance but said nothing.

"We have no idea," offered Frank. "He began shadowing me last fall, disappeared for a while, and then showed up again a couple of days before he was killed. I had him checked out and when I thought he was just a harmless private investigator, I chose to ignore him."

"Do you have any idea why he was interested in you, Mr. Morton?"

"No, of course not. I spent some time in Las Vegas last summer – in fact we all did – so I just assumed it had something to do with that. I came into quite a bit of money back in June so I also thought he might be a fortune hunter. Hell, for a while I even thought he might have been hired by a long, lost relative who wanted to share in my good fortune."

Indicating the pictures again, the agent said, "But he wasn't an investigator, Mr. Morton, he was a terrorist. And you'll have to admit that your activities of late look pretty suspicious. After coming into a great deal of money, you buy a Learjet, put together that state-of-the-art hangar out at Boeing Field and assemble a rather unique team of people. That could easily be construed as the activities of a newly activated terrorist cell even if Mr. Al-Nasser hadn't showed up. And when you add the fact that a known terrorist who has apparently been hiding underground for two years suddenly shows up at your facility with a bullet in his head, well, you can understand why we're interested, right?"

Frank slumped in his chair and nodded. "Well, given all that, I guess it might look a little suspicious. But I'm telling you, we had nothing to do with this Nasser character and we have nothing to do with terrorists or terrorism. Our work is purely scientific in nature. We investigate mysteries of archeology and anthropology for the pure enjoyment of finding some answers."

"Well, that certainly makes a good cover story, Mr. Morton. Why don't you explain to me what you're doing in Japan while we wait for your fingerprint checks to come back from the NSA."

So Frank did. He explained the recent discovery of the Yonaguni Monument and the apparent lack of interest on the part of the established archeology community. He touched on some of the prevailing theories about the origin of the structure and similar ones that had been found. He described the qualifications of each of the team members and how they complemented each other's skills. He even considered describing the team's *Tractrix* project of last summer but he decided that flying saucers and aliens and conspiracy theories were probably more than the straight-arrow agent would be able to deal with. Instead, Frank reminded Bryant again that all three of them had been granted Top Secret security clearances the past summer by the very government that was now accusing them of being a terrorist cell.

"Well, technically, those clearances aren't much more than an official gag order to keep you from disclosing some very specific Department of Defense information," replied Bryant, tapping the manila envelope to indicate that he was aware of the clearances. "I don't suppose you'd like to tell me about your involvement with the DOD, would you?"

"Sorry, we can't – there's a gag order, remember?" replied Frank.

"Very well, then why don't the three of you just sit tight while I go check on those finger prints?"

While Bryant was out of the room, Frank and Tony discussed the government's allegations and how ridiculous they were.

"The only reason we're in this room right now is because that Al-Nasser character decided to stop a bullet with his head in your parking lot," fumed Tony. "If we had a plausible explanation for why he was tailing you, we'd be out of here in a flash."

"I agree, but I actually thought he was just a two-bit private-eye named Larry Schultz until Linda discovered that the real Schultz had been dead for two years. I had no idea who he really was. But, still, there has to be some logical reason why he was interested in me."

Linda, who hadn't said a word throughout the entire interrogation process, finally spoke. "Could it have anything to do with the original owner of the Learjet?"

Frank and Tony looked at each other, their eyes wide.

"Of course!" they said at the same time.

Tony jumped up from the table and waved at the mirror that both he and Frank had correctly identified as a two-way glass. A couple of minutes later, Agent Bryant returned with several sheets of paper in his hand but before he could say a word, Frank was reciting the history of the Learjet, right back to it's original owner, Qusai Hussein.

"That's probably what brought Al-Nasser out of retirement," finished Frank. "Maybe Qusai is looking for his plane!"

Indicating the sheets of paper, Agent Bryant said, "Yes, we've come to the same conclusion, Mr. Morton. Your fingerprints check out okay. I just spoke to an Agent Edwards at the Department of Energy and it seems that your aircraft has quite a record. You might want to consider trading it in – I hear this Hussein family is a really nasty bunch. Let me fax all this info back to the States for their okay and then we'll try to get you out of here as soon as possible."

An hour after they had been ordered off the Learjet, Frank, Tony and Linda were back on board. Both Jim and Linda were very upset about the incident and Frank had the feeling that both of them were ready to return to Seattle on the next available flight. Only his promise of a quiet, peaceful stay on a small remote island kept them from jumping ship.

At exactly noon, Tokyo time, the Learjet began its 1,200-mile journey south to the mysterious island of Yonaguni.

***

The bump of the aircraft touching down awoke Aya from a light sleep. She glanced at her watch; it was noon and they were landing in Okinawa exactly on schedule. After a quick plane change, she would finally be on her way to Yonaguni Island – the place she always considered home, even though she had been born in Seattle, Washington.

Aya had made arrangements to stay in her great uncle's guesthouse and she was looking forward to spending the afternoon with him. Later, after he retired for the evening, Aya would slip out to meet with several of her old friends. When Aya was attending the University of the Ryukyus, in Okinawa, she had spent her holidays and long weekends on Yonaguni and she had made several lasting friendships – especially with Haruki Matsuki. They had enjoyed an on-again, off-again relationship for the past fifteen years and it was Haruki who had put Aya in contact with Tanaka when she had called him about the *tsubute* in her father's display case.

Haruki had been very angry when he learned that the *tsubute* had made its way to the United States and he had told her that it "must be returned to Yonaguni at all cost." Aya now suspected that her friend Haruki was somehow involved in the revival of the ancient Genji clan and tonight, in the intimacy of his bed, she intended to find out!

***

The NWIDI Learjet touched down on Yonaguni Island at 4:57 p.m., local time. Fitz had warned them when they began their descent that the runway was "a bit on the short side", so everyone in the cabin was pleasantly surprised when the aircraft made a smooth left turn off the active runway and rolled to a stop some distance from the small terminal building.

"Looks like you had plenty of runway, Captain," commented Tony when the Fitzgeralds and their dog came through the cockpit door.

"Yes, we did okay. I think we had a good nine or ten feet of pavement left."

A look of stress on Susan's face indicated that Fitz probably wasn't exaggerating.

Quickly changing the subject, Frank announced, "After we get our gear unloaded, Fitz and Susan are going to take the plane up to Okinawa and wait for our call. There's not really any place to tie it down here on the island and they have some friends they want to visit up there. That will also put them in a good position to round up extra equipment for us, if we need it."

Looking out the window at the deserted airfield, Linda asked, "Is somebody picking us up, Frank? I don't see a soul out there."

"Yes, the hotel is supposed to be sending a van over. We can unload our stuff into a pile and then, if necessary, I'll walk up to the terminal and call them."

Fitz opened the cabin door and lowered the plane's steps. A strong, hot breeze blew into the plane and Jim grabbed for a stack of papers on his tray before they blew away.

"Sorry about that," apologized Fitz. "I should have warned you that the wind blows 24 hours a day here. I'll go down and open the external baggage compartments. Be sure you take all your personal items so they don't end up in Okinawa with us."

"Okay, folks, this way out," smiled Frank, indicating the door. "Welcome to Yonaguni Island and the beginning of a new project!"

Jim and Linda made their way down the stairs, followed by Susan and Sandstrom, but Tony hung back and Frank gave him a questioning look.

"You go ahead, Frank, I'll be right there," explained Tony with a nod toward the lavatory.

"Oh, right. Take your time. I'll help Fitz with the baggage."

Once Frank was down the steps and out of sight, Tony went to work. He retrieved the small leather carry-on he had stored under the lavatory sink and took out a tool that looked similar to a screwdriver with an odd looking tip. Carefully, Tony removed a panel from the lavatory wall, exposing a compartment about one foot wide by two feet high by one foot deep. He removed the two boxes he had stashed back in Seattle and carefully placed them in his bag. He replaced the panel, tossed the tool back into the bag and zipped it shut. One of the advantages of traveling on a smuggler's airplane, he thought, as he walked the length of the cabin and down the steps to join the others.

Chapter 9

Fitz was still removing baggage from the aircraft when Tony joined Frank and Jim at the stack of offloaded items some distance away. Frank noticed the leather bag in Tony's hand and wrinkled his brow.

"Where'd you find that?"

"Oh, I almost left it behind when we were boarding back in Seattle. Fitz already had the exterior compartments secured so I stowed it under the sink in the lavatory. It's just some personal items that wouldn't fit in my suitcase," replied Tony, as casually as he could.

"Okay, well, toss it on the pile and give us a hand hauling stuff over here. I think I see our car up by the fence but I don't want to wave them over here until we have everything out of the plane." Frank pointed to a black sedan parked some distance away, on the other side of the chain link fence.

Fifteen minutes later, after saying their good byes to Fitz, Susan and Sandstrom, the NWIDI team was bouncing their way down the road that led from the airport to the Hotel Irifune. Their transportation turned out to be a mini-van from the hotel, not the black sedan Frank had pointed out earlier, and the driver, who spoke passable but broken English, filled the travelers in on the island's statistics.

Yonaguni is Japan's second southernmost island and lies in the East China Sea less than 75 miles from Taiwan. The 2.5-mile wide by 6-mile long island is home to about 1,200 people and hundreds of the odd-looking ponies they had spotted in a field near the airport. According to the driver, Yonaguni is the only island in the Okinawa chain that has these ponies and no one knows for sure how they got to the island or where they originally came from.

Frank asked if the island saw much tourist traffic and the driver laughed out loud.

"The Hotel Irifune is the only hotel on Yonaguni, Frank-san. There are also four *minshukus* (traditional Japanese guesthouses), but they are not popular with Westerners. Altogether, there are no more than 75 rooms available for rent on the entire island."

A few minutes later the driver stopped the van in front of a three-story concrete building and announced, "Welcome to the Hotel Irifune. Please allow me to bring your luggage inside. The reception is right through that door, Frank-san."

Each team member had brought a carry-on aboard the Learjet and they collected those from the back of the van rather than trusting them to the driver. Linda had her new laptop computer in a nylon travel bag. Jim carried his worn leather briefcase full of notes, CDs and his new laptop. Frank carried an aluminum briefcase containing the team's travel documents and data on the Monument they would soon visit and Tony clutched the leather carry-on he had retrieved from the Learjet's lavatory.

The hotel lobby was small and dated but well maintained. When a desk clerk appeared through a door at one end of the counter, Frank stepped forward and handed the young man a copy of the confirmation he had received by fax.

"Ah, Mr. Morton, welcome to Yonaguni," the desk clerk said in perfect English. "We have your rooms all prepared and I believe there is a message for you ... yes, here it is. Ms. Okada sends her apologies and says that she has been delayed in Okinawa and won't be arriving until the day after tomorrow. She suggests that you take this opportunity to see the beautiful island of Yonaguni."

Tony stepped forward and asked, "Who the hell is Ms. Okada, Frank?"

"Yukiko Okada – and I had no idea that was a woman's name – is our dive master. That's the same person who was supposed to make all the arrangements for our dives at the monument. I guess our investigation will have to wait until she gets here."

"Excuse me, sir, but are you referring to the underwater pyramid out at Iseki Point?" asked the desk clerk.

Frank nodded.

"I've been diving at that site several times and there are several local dive operators who would be happy to take you out there."

"I was told that because we are Americans we were required to use this government-approved operator from Okinawa," frowned Frank. "Is that not true?"

"Or maybe it's only a requirement for foreigners," said Tony.

"Oh, I'm not a Japanese citizen," replied the distinctly Japanese-looking clerk. "My name is Bill Ito and I'm from San Francisco. I'm here on a college program called Total Cultural Immersion. I live with a Japanese family for six months to better understand the subtleties of their customs and language. When I go back to the States next month I'll finish up my Masters Degree in Asian American Studies."

"Well, that explains the perfect English," nodded Tony, "but how did you manage to get stuck way down here, 1,200 miles from Tokyo?"

"Actually, I requested this area. Most of the rest of the country has been strongly influenced by Western culture ever since Japan opened its doors to the world in the mid-nineteenth century, but the southern islands still cling to the ancient traditions and the old ways. The language here is more pure, closer to the original Japanese of a thousand years ago."

The clerk was gazing out the window, almost talking to himself. He suddenly snapped out of his spell and returned to the present.

"Besides, I'm an avid diver and who wouldn't want to be here on Yonaguni, where there's actually something interesting to explore?"

Realizing that the college student might be a wealth of information, Frank made him a proposition.

"Listen, since it looks like our guide service is going to flake out on us, could we hire you as a temporary tour guide? You know, show us around the island, fill us in on the local history, stuff like that? We'd be willing to pay top dollar for your services."

"Well, I have to work here at the hotel until 6:00 p.m. tonight, but I'm off tomorrow and Wednesday and I can always use extra money. Besides, it's kind of cool to have someone to speak English with for a change. Sure, I'd be happy to show you around. I have to warn you, though, there's not a lot to see. Yonaguni isn't a very big place."

"Oh, I think we'll find plenty to see. We're especially interested in any unusual or historical sites you might know about. Even if they're just legends or folk tales and especially if they relate to the Yonaguni Monument. Do you follow me?"

The young man's eyes widened. "So I take it you're not just another American diving club out on a field trip, huh? I noticed that your company name is listed as NWIDI – what does that stand for?"

"We'll fill you in tonight over dinner. Let us get settled in and cleaned up and we'll meet you here in the lobby about 7:00 p.m. How does that sound?"

Later, as the five walked to a nearby restaurant, Bill Ito pointed out buildings and points of interest as if he'd lived on the tiny island all his life. He had taken his cultural emersion project very seriously and, because he spoke fluent Japanese, he had been able to collect a lot of interesting folklore from some of the older citizens of Yonaguni. He had carefully documented these stories and legends as part of his school project because he was considering doing his Masters thesis on the origin of the people of southern Japan.

"That sounds more like an anthropology thesis than it does Asian American Studies," commented Jim, as the group entered the small eating establishment.

"Well, actually anthropology is my minor, Mr. Barnes. Are you also interested in the field?"

The four NWIDI staffers were still chuckling at Bill's comment when the kimono-clad waitress seated them at a large round table in the back corner of the room. The table was shielded from the main part of the room by a shoji screen (a traditional Japanese paper room divider) and the waitress appeared to know Bill quite well.

Frank took the seat on Bill's left and patted him on the shoulder.

"Please excuse our rudeness, Bill, but that was the understatement of the day. I think it's time we told you a little about NWIDI and why we're here on Yonaguni. By the way, Jim over there is actually Professor Barnes, of the University of Washington's Department of Anthropology and I can assure you that he's very interested in the field."

An hour later, after several courses of local cuisine and some warm sake, Bill understood almost everything there was to know about the NWIDI team and its mission and he had shared much of his personal history with them.

Bill Ito's father was a second-generation Japanese-American engineer at Hitachi Corporation, in California's Silicon Valley. Hitachi had transferred Bill's grandfather from Tokyo to the U.S. when it opened its first facility back in 1959 and Bill was the first to break the family-company ties. His lack of interest in electronics had been a major disappointment to both his father and his grandfather but they were proud of Bill's intense interest in his heritage and, reluctantly, they allowed him to pursue those interests. When Bill graduated first in his class at San Jose State University with a Bachelor of Arts degree in Japanese, both elder Itos gave up all hope that Bill would follow in their footsteps and they encouraged him to accept a scholarship to San Francisco State University's prestigious graduate program in Asian American Studies which had, ultimately, taken Bill to Yonaguni.

Tony leaned back in his chair and rubbed his belly in satisfaction. "So, what do you actually do on this dot of an island, besides work at the hotel?"

"Oh, I manage to keep busy with a lot of volunteer work. I help out at the local library, which gives me access to the literature of the region, and I also spend some time each week at the island's only museum – for obvious reasons. If a teacher is ill, I fill in at the local elementary/junior high school and I also teach English to the few folks on the island who are interested in it. My work at the hotel covers the cost of my room and board at one of the local minshukus, but I really took the job because it provides me with some contact with outsiders. There are a number of variations of the Japanese language and it's interesting to hear the different dialects and accents."

"Yeah, that sounds real interesting," yawned Tony, "But what do you do for excitement, entertainment, adventure? Excuse the observation, but this place looks pretty boring to me."

"Well, I actually consider the library and the museum exiting places, but there's also the diving. There's nothing like a swim with a few dozen hammerhead sharks to get the old adrenalin flowing, if you know what I mean."

"So you've actually been in the water with them?" questioned Tony, suddenly interested.

"Oh, yes, several times. You have to pick your time of year, though. Right now, and for another few weeks, they're harmless because they're in some kind of fasting phase. But come spring, they suddenly turn into eating machines and they devour everything in sight. That's a pretty slow season for the local dive shop operators," smiled Bill.

"That wouldn't by any chance include a man named Aratake, would it?" asked Frank.

"As a matter of fact, yes. Kihachiro Aratake was the first to discover the pyramid, back in 1985, I think. For a while, his dive shop had a monopoly on tours out to the monument and, as a result, he now owns a lot of property on Yonaguni, including the hotel where you are staying. Do you know Aratake-san?"

"Only by reputation," replied Frank. He leaned closer to Bill and asked, "Do you suppose he would take us out to the site? I'd love to call those jerks in Okinawa and tell them to forget it."

"Perhaps. I'll inquire in the morning when the shop opens, but this is pretty short notice and I know he stays busy this time of year. But I can certainly ask."

"But Frank," interrupted Tony, "none of our gear is here yet. I shipped it over last week, but it's not due in by ferry until tomorrow, at the earliest."

"Then we'll rent gear from the dive shop! Now that we're here, I'm anxious to get a look at this place. If we have to use rental gear, then we won't take Linda on the dive. She can go later on an escorted dive if she feels up to it and if the conditions around the pyramid are safe. This first trip will just be our check-out dive."

"Agreed," said Tony. "Tomorrow we can get a quick read on the currents and bottom conditions."

"If you don't mind, I would like to join you," said Bill. "I'm an experienced diver and I know the site. Besides, there's something down there I'd like to show you."

Later, on the way back to the hotel, Bill took them on a walking tour of the rest of the small "downtown" area of Yonaguni. The night air was warm but breezy and the mood was upbeat. As they said good night to Bill at the hotel's main entrance, Tony noticed that the black sedan from the airport was parked directly across the street.

At 8:15 a.m. the next morning, Bill Ito called Frank's room to tell him that he had arranged a dive trip for that afternoon. Aratake's boats were all booked, but Bill had talked one of the other local dive shops into taking the group out at 2:30 p.m.

"Excellent work, my friend, you did well," complemented Frank. "Now, what do you suggest for this morning? Tony, Linda and Jim have already called me, anxious to do some exploring. Apparently your passion for Yonaguni is contagious!"

"I'm happy to hear that, Frank. There are no flights in or out of the airport until this afternoon, so I made arrangements to borrow the hotel's van for a few hours. How about a tour of the island and a short hike to a place I think you might find interesting?"

"Perfect," replied Frank. "We'll meet you in the lobby in fifteen minutes."

Bill started the tour by showing the NWIDI team where he lived. The *minshuku* was on a hill south of the hotel and provided a spectacular view of the island.

Pointing just slightly east of due south, Bill showed the team where the ruins were located.

"The land that juts out into the ocean over there is called Iseki Point and the ruins are just off the point. I brought you up here first to help you get oriented on the island. You are facing almost due south. Behind you, on the northern edge of the island, is the airport. Also behind you, at the bottom of this hill, is the main part of town.

"To your right, the tip of the island is the westernmost point in all of Japan. The island's port and ferry terminal are also located on the west end.

"To your left, the east end of the island is mostly deserted except for some wild ponies. An ancient cemetery is also in that direction and we'll go down there last."

Linda turned a full 360-degree circle to take in the entire view.

"It's beautiful, Bill. The dark green trees contrasted against the lighter green meadows remind me of Wisconsin, except that there's no ocean in Wisconsin."

Frank had brought along his camcorder and he shot a 360-degree panorama from the hilltop.

On their way down the hill they passed several large, grassy areas and grazing horses.

"There don't seem to be any fences around these fields, Bill. What keeps the animals from wandering off?" asked Frank.

"Nothing. These are wild ponies and this land is what we would call 'public land' back in the States. Neither the ponies nor the land belong to any one individual. They sort of belong to everybody. Cool, huh?"

As they approached the west end of the island, wood and concrete houses with traditional tile roofs began to appear along the road.

"I've noticed these hollowed out rocks in most of the yards. Some are being used as flowerpots; others are just sitting there. Do you know what they are," asked Jim.

"They are one of the many mysteries of Yonaguni, Jim. If you examine them closely, it's obvious that they are man-made, but no one has any idea how old they are, how they were made or what they were used for."

They stopped at the ferry dock and bought a supply of bottled water. While they were waiting for everyone to return to the van, a small ferry arrived and unloaded three cars, a small cargo van and about thirty foot passengers.

"That would be the daily ferry from Ishigaki," commented Bill. "Ishigaki is about four hours away by boat."

"Are there any ferries between here and Taiwan?" asked Frank. "It seems like I heard that it was only about 75 miles south of here."

"No, there's no transportation at all between here and Taiwan. The people of Yonaguni have never permitted the government to open a customs office here so anyone coming in from Taiwan has to go to Okinawa first. That's one of the things that keeps Yonaguni so pristine. This island is, quite literally, the end of the line as far as Japan goes."

"Sorry to hold everybody up," apologized Linda as she rejoined the rest of the group. "I had a hard time finding the bathroom – the damn signs are all in Japanese."

"Imagine that!" said Tony sarcastically. As they were climbing back into the van, he thought he spotted the black sedan from the hotel leaving the parking lot but the vehicle disappeared behind a hill before he could be sure.

From the port area, Bill followed the highway along the northern shore back around to the airport, through the main part of town and east into the countryside. Soon he turned into a gravel lot next to an unmarked concrete building and stopped the van.

"I think you'll find this interesting. This is a distillery that makes a type of sake called Awamori. It's based on a 500-year old recipe that uses special black yeast found only in the Okinawa islands. They claim that Awamori is so pure that it causes no hangover."

Inside, Bill exchanged a few words with an elderly man in a white lab coat who seamed to know him quite well. The man smiled broadly and motioned the others into the back room with his arm.

"*Dozo*," he said bowing to each visitor as they passed him.

After a brief tour of the plant, the four NWIDI team members and their guide, Bill Ito, were escorted back to the showroom where they were offered samples of the plant's product. They each bought several small bottles of sake before returning to the van.

"Bill, I get the feeling you know everybody on the island," commented Linda as they turned east back onto the highway.

"Almost," laughed Bill. "The older gentleman in the white coat who showed us around is one of my English students. He's also very interested in the history of the island and he has some unusual theories about the origin of the monument. I hope you don't mind, but I asked him to join us for dinner this evening so you can hear his ideas first hand."

About ten minutes later they came to a large cemetery. It was situated on a hill overlooking the sea and the place had an eerie but peaceful feeling about it. Intermingled among modern headstones were traditional tombs. Some of the older natural ones had been carved out of the surrounding bedrock. Others were made of a mixture of quarried rock and concrete but they all had a similar shape.

"Notice that all the tombs seem to have giant steps that run along one side," explained Bill. "They obviously weren't intended to be steps, because of their shear height, but they have that general appearance. I suggest you shoot some video of a couple of the older tombs for future reference."

Frank took up the task of videotaping while Jim examined the tombs close up. Linda and Tony wandered among the graves reading head stones, but all they could read were the dates on some of the newer ones.

After a few minutes, they all found their way back to a particularly old looking tomb that Jim had been studying on his hands and knees.

"Some of these appear to be very old," he said to Bill.

"They are. In fact, no one on the island, including the families who can trace their ancestors back hundreds of years, knows how old they are or who they belong to."

Shaking his head, Jim said, "This island is an anthropologist's dream. There seem to be mysteries everywhere"

"Oh, you haven't seen anything, yet," replied Bill with a smile. "The best is yet to come."

Chapter 10

On the drive back to the hotel, Jim sat in the front and continued to question Bill about the old tombs they had seen at the cemetery.

"Are there any theories about those step-like features on the sides of the tombs?"

"Well, yes and no," replied Bill. "I've never actually heard anybody offer any explanations, but I've run across a few references in the library that hint at a possibility. Have you ever heard of the Jomon culture?"

"Of course," nodded Jim. "They were an ancient maritime people who inhabited this part of the world about 2,000 years ago."

"Right, but some anthropologists think they may have been sailing around the China Sea as early as 12,000 years ago. They are also credited with being one of the world's first cultures to use pottery. In fact, back in the 70s, a research team from the Smithsonian found Jomon pottery clear across the Pacific in Ecuador."

"Wait a minute!" interrupted Frank. "Did these Jomon actually have boats capable of crossing the Pacific that long ago?"

"Not that we know of," continued Jim, "but the truth is, we don't know that much about these people. Remember, we're talking about a culture that may have flourished thousands of years before the Pharaohs of Egypt."

"I'm confused," said Tony, who had been staring out a back window of the van. "If anthropologists know that these Jomon people were here 12,000 years ago, why do they still maintain that the earliest civilizations developed in the mid-east? Don't they read their own findings?"

"Because," began Jim and Bill at the same time.

Jim motioned for Bill to continue the explanation.

"Because it has to do with the definition of the word 'civilization'. Most traditional anthropologists require more than just a group of people living together. There must be organization, specialization of labor, record-keeping and a number of other characteristics before a tribe or band can be considered 'civilized'."

"In other words," added Jim, "a bunch of folks running through the woods picking fruit off trees wouldn't be considered civilized, but when that same group evolves to the point where they plant fruit trees in an orchard and cultivate the crop in anticipation of a harvest, they have crossed the line and can be called civilized.

"A similar comparison can be made regarding dwellings. Popping up a few tents in the middle of a field is the work of a nomadic tribe but building permanent structures, laid out according to some organized plan is the work of a civilization."

Tony nodded in understanding, but then his brow wrinkled with a question.

"So wouldn't the building of a 100-foot high structure, like the one we're going to see this afternoon, require a lot of organization and specialization of labor?"

"Of course," nodded Jim.

"And if this monument really turns out to be 12,000 years old, wouldn't that mean that the earliest civilizations developed here, rather than in the mid-east somewhere?"

"Of course," said Jim again, only this time with a broad smile. "And now you understand why we're here. If we, or some other group, could prove that the Yonaguni Monument is actually 12,000 years old, the sciences of anthropology and archeology would be turned upside down. It would be no less revolutionary than when Galileo demonstrated, once and for all, that the earth really wasn't at the center of the universe."

"I love it!" beamed Tony. "Let's burst their bubble!"

"Before you get too excited about destroying science as we know it," laughed Frank, "you should probably know that Galileo died a pauper in prison as a reward for his ground-breaking work in astronomy. It seems that not everybody was thrilled to hear about his discoveries."

The group was chuckling at Frank's Tony-to-Galileo comparison when Bill suddenly and violently spun the steering wheel, forcing the van sharply to the left and then, just as sharply, back to the right to avoid driving off the road. Tony twisted in his seat and through the back window he watched a boulder the size of a beach ball roll off the pavement and into a ditch on the right side of the road.

"Where the hell did that come from?" asked Frank as Bill stabilized the vehicle and slowed to a stop.

Pointing off to the left, Jim replied, "It must have rolled down from that hill back there. Boy, that was a close one! If we had hit that rock we'd have done some serious damage to both the van and ourselves. Good reflexes, Bill."

Bill was visibly shaken and before he could reply, Tony had flung open the van's sliding door and was headed across the road and back toward the hill on a dead run.

Bill turned on the van's emergency flashers and then joined the rest of the occupants, who were now standing along side the road waiting for Tony's return.

"Maybe he saw something," commented Frank to no one in particular.

About five minutes later Tony rejoined the group. His shirt was completely unbuttoned and he was sweating profusely.

"What was that all about?" asked Linda.

"I could have sworn I saw a head poking up over the top of the hill when I looked back at the boulder," he said, wiping his brow with the back of his hand. "But I didn't see anybody, or even a trace of anybody, once I got up there."

Frank motioned everybody back into the van like a shepherd.

"It was probably just a freak incident," he said casually. "And the head you thought you saw was probably just another rock."

Climbing into the van, Tony shook his head.

"No, I don't think so. As a matter of fact, there weren't any other rocks, big or small on that hilltop. Just the one that rolled down at us."

Frank shot Tony a questioning look, but he just shrugged in reply. The ride back to the hotel was very quiet.

Bill brought the van to a stop beside the hotel at exactly 11:30 a.m.

"I need to go up to the *minshuku* and grab my gear, so you will have time for a light lunch before we head over to the dive shop. I suggest that you don't eat a lot, though, because this could turn out to be a strenuous dive. The currents around the Monument can be pretty wicked sometimes. I'll see you back here at 1:30 p.m."

Bill's comments brought a look of fear to Linda's face until Frank explained that she wouldn't be making the dive.

"We'll be using unfamiliar gear in unknown conditions so I think you should sit this dive out, Linda. If the site checks out, we'll get you down for a look as soon as our own gear gets here."

"That's fine with me," she said with a sigh of relief. "But I'd like to go along on the boat and watch. I promise that I'll stay out of the way."

After lunch in a restaurant across the street from the hotel, the four retired to their respective rooms for some rest before the afternoon dive trip. When they regrouped in the lobby, Frank and Tony were dressed in swim trunks and T-shirts and Tony was carrying the small bag he had stashed under the Learjet's lavatory sink. Linda had changed into shorts and a matching top, but Jim was still wearing his khaki pants and polo shirt and he was carrying his brief case.

"Aren't you going out with us, Jim?" asked Linda.

"No, I'm sorry, but bobbing around in the ocean like a cork just isn't my idea of a good time. I think I'll just walk over to the library and spend the afternoon there."

"Are you sure you want to miss this?" pressed Linda. "I'm not diving today, either, but I wouldn't miss this trip out to the Monument for anything."

"No, sorry, but I'd rather not. The truth is, I get motion sickness pretty easily. The Learjet is just about my limit and even the thought of being in a small boat makes me queasy."

"Okay, suit yourself, but you are going to miss a great opportunity," added Tony. "Here comes Bill now."

Bill was walking down the street toward them carrying a large dive bag over his shoulder. When he reached the NWIDI team members, he lowered the bag to the ground and they exchanged pleasantries. He also noticed Jim's attire and raised his eyebrows but before he could even ask, Jim explained his problem with boats and asked about the library.

"Sure, Jim," replied Bill. "As it turns out, the library is open this afternoon but you should know that there are virtually no English-language books in the place and the librarian doesn't speak very much English – only what she's learned since I've been working there."

"That's okay, smiled Jim, "I'll just look at the pictures - that will still be better than a boat trip!"

"Speaking of boat trips," interrupted Tony, "how are we getting to the boat? The hotel van seems to be missing."

"There's a JAL commuter flight due in from Okinawa at about 2:00 p.m., so the driver's probably already left for the airport. Our dive master said he would send somebody over to pick us up.

We're meeting our boat down by the ferry docks, where we were this morning."

Bill had no sooner finished his comment than a small Japanese truck screeched to a stop beside the hotel. It resembled a cross between a Volkswagen minibus and a flatbed truck and it had obviously seen better days.

Bill exchanged greetings with the driver and then turned to the team.

"Okay, everybody hop on. Takamura-san is not only our dive master but he's also our chauffer. I suggest you hang on to one of those stakes along the side."

Bill heaved his dive bag up onto the bed of the truck and secured it with a piece of rope that had one end nailed to the wooden truck bed.

"I'll ride up front and brief our guide," he smiled as he climbed into the cab.

A few minutes later, the truck slammed to a stop in front of a small concrete building on the waterfront. A faded sign over the door contained a number of Japanese symbols. Underneath, somebody had scrawled 'Hammer Diving Service' in white paint.

Frank, Tony and Linda were white-knuckled from clinging to the truck and they looked at each other as if to say, "What have we gotten ourselves into?"

"This is it," announced Bill as he climbed out of the cab and came around to untie his bag. "Takamura-san will get you set up with gear and then we can head out to the Point. Our guide says the waters are relatively calm today, so we should have a good dive."

"The Point?" asked Frank as he eased himself down off the truck bed.

"Iseki Point. That's where the Monument is. It's that place that juts out into the ocean that I showed you this morning from the hilltop, remember? Oh, and by the way, Takamura-san doesn't speak English, so I'll have to translate for you. Once we're below the surface he'll use the normal hand signals, so language shouldn't be an issue."

Frank motioned Bill aside and turned them so their backs were to the others.

"Listen, Bill, I know we pressed you to get us a trip out to the Monument on short notice, but are you sure about these guys?" Frank motioned toward the small building with his head. "Maybe we should wait until we can get space on another boat."

Bill's face showed his disappointment.

"Frank, if you expect to find a five-star PADI dive center on Yonaguni – like the kind of shop you'd find in a Caribbean resort – I'm afraid you're in for a big shock. This is Yonaguni, and this is as good as it gets. But, I promise you, the folks here are as competent as any dive masters you'd find in Maui or Cancun or Grand Cayman. Trust me on this, okay?"

Reluctantly, Frank agreed but he was very glad that Linda wasn't going diving today.

The inside of the dive shop wasn't much more appealing than the outside. The single room was cluttered with dive gear, fishing gear and miscellaneous boat parts. A small wooden table served as a desk and the room's only window was so dirty that the marina was barely visible through it.

Takamura motioned them over to the table and pointed to some papers that he laid out after clearing away the remnants of someone's lunch.

"He needs you to sign these waivers," translated Bill.

Frank picked up one of the forms and stared at it.

"This is in Japanese. I can't read a word of it," he complained.

"It's the typical release that you would sign at any dive shop, Frank. Just sign on that line at the bottom and we'll be on our way."

Even Linda was required to sign a form and while they were doing that the young Japanese dive master began rummaging through dive gear behind him.

Fifteen minutes later, the NWIDI team – minus Jim – was finally standing outside on the narrow boardwalk that separated the dive shop from the water. Takamura and Bill had gone down a ramp to the boat and Frank and Tony were each holding armloads of gear. Tony poked his index finger out through a one-inch hole in his wet suit and wiggled it. Both he and Frank burst into laughter, but Linda frowned.

"I don't know what you two think is so funny. There's no way I'd trust my life to the likes of this place! Back in the states, a suit like that would be in the trash, not draped over your arm."

"You're probably right, Linda, but the wet suit isn't the important part, the regulator is, and this one is a top-of-the-line Scuba-Pro," Frank said, indicating the black hose dangling from his left arm. "I'd trust my life to it – in fact I did, every time I jumped out of a helicopter in 'Nam. Bill was right. These guys know their stuff and they spend their money where it counts. Look, they're waving for us to come aboard. Let's go diving!"

The appearance of the boat was in keeping with the shop. It had probably been painted blue and white at some time in the distant past, but now it was so faded that it was hard to tell where the blue ended and the white began.

Frank, Tony and Linda climbed aboard the aging, 36-foot dive boat and sat side by side on one of the benches that ran down both sides. Bill was standing at the boat's controls, but Takamura was nowhere to be seen.

"Did we lose our guide already?" questioned Tony.

"He's below, making an adjustment," replied Bill, pointing to the small door that led down into the front of the boat.

Tony looked at Frank and rolled his eyes back as if to say "Now what!"

Suddenly the boat's twin diesels came to life with a roar and Bill scrambled to return the throttle to the idle position. The deep husky purr of the marine engines reinforced Frank's earlier statement – this operation spent their money where it counted.

After Bill helped Takamura untie the boat from the dock, he returned to brief the team.

He leaned casually against the row of air tanks and said, "I explained your interests to Takamura-san and he has offered to give us the 'deluxe' tour today. We'll be making an extra stop after we leave the Monument to see something he claims that only he knows about. Obviously, I've never been there either, so I can't tell you much about the place except that it's not very far from here.

"First, we're going to cruise around the southern side of the island to Iseki Point. That will take about 30 minutes. The currents at the Point are too strong to use an anchor, so I'll stay onboard to keep the boat from running aground while Takamura-san takes the two of you on a tour of the Monument. He'll show you as much as he can, but you're depth will vary from 10 to 30 meters, so you should limit your total dive time to about 20 minutes.

"After the first dive, we'll follow the coastline back to the site he wants to show you. Apparently we can anchor there, so I'll get to dive with you. That is if Linda doesn't mind staying aboard alone."

"Oh, no, I'll be fine," she smiled nervously. "Just don't get lost down there."

As they traveled along the southern side of the island toward Iseki Point, the coastline got more and more rugged and the

Point itself was a large, semi-circular portion of the island that jutted out into the ocean. It had high, shear cliffs on all sides, making land access to the area impossible.

Frank and Tony had begun preparing as soon as they left the dock and by the time the boat slowed to an idle they were ready to dive. Their guide did a final check of their gear and gave them the 'OK' sign before he stepped off the dive platform at the back of the boat. Frank and Tony waved to Linda and Bill before following Takamura into the water.

Bill eased the boat forward and then back out away from the point to get out of the worst of the currents. He would maintain the boat on a large, circular path near the dive site until the three divers reappeared.

As they dropped below the surface, Frank and Tony were amazed at the excellent visibility. They had entered the water just west of the main part of the monument and Takamura signaled for them to follow him down as he quickly descended to the bottom. The eastbound current was so strong that they only needed to kick their fins for steering and depth control.

Their guide led them around a corner and behind a perfectly smooth wall that provided some protection from the current. He touched his index and fore fingers to his mask and then circled his hand, indicating that Frank and Tony should take the opportunity to look around.

Everywhere they looked there were large, flat terraces of smooth rock with perfectly square edges. Some of the terraces were tall, with relatively small tops, and others were short with huge areas on top but they all had the distinctive square edges and corners. In several places there appeared to be a series of steps suitable for human use, but they often ended halfway up a shear rock face, leading to nowhere.

After giving them time to take in the astounding sight, Takamura motioned for the other two to follow him again. He crossed the small plaza they were on and swam directly into a 4-foot high tunnel on the opposite side. When they exited the short tunnel they were face-to-face with twin stone pillars that had somehow been fashioned from a giant vertical slab that had been cut straight down the middle for most of its length. The pillars were close to the shore and their tops extended up, ending just below the surface. Frank and Tony later learned that many locals think the pillars represent the symbolic gate to the Monument. Leaving the pillars, the divers circled left and directly into the current. Only constant and vigorous kicking kept the three from being pulled backwards. A left turn took them behind another part of the structure and brought temporary relief from the force of the sea. Takamura swam up close to a wall and signaled for Frank and Tony to move in closer. Using the knife he had strapped to his leg, the dive master scraped away a fine coating of algae to reveal what appeared to be a glyph. Using his finger, Takamura indicated that there were more such symbols on the rock face.

Takamura checked his watch and indicated to Frank and Tony that they had five minutes left in their dive. He led them back out into the current, but this time they turned right and drifted with the flow, observing the structure's northern side as they gradually made their way to the surface. Suddenly Frank realized that, from this side, the Monument looked remarkably similar to a giant version of the tombs they had seen earlier in the cemetery. He drew an outline of the monument in the water with his finger and Tony nodded his understanding.

As they reached one of the top levels of the Monument, their guide pointed to the flat rock surface below them, then to his watch and then he held up 3 fingers. Frank and Tony understood this to mean that this was their 3-minute safety stop to prevent the 'bends'. When they had both responded with an okay, Takamura pointed out two large circular holes side by side on the other side of the plateau. Each hole was about 7 feet deep and they looked like they could have been cisterns.

When it was time to surface, Takamura patted the top of his head, pointed to his eyes and then pointed up to remind Frank and Tony to look up as they ascended so they wouldn't hit the bottom of a boat. As it turned out, the dive boat was some distance away when they broke the surface but Linda quickly spotted them and they were soon climbing up the ladder she had lowered for them.

As the dive boat powered away from the site, Frank and Tony were talking a mile a minute about their experience. Their animated descriptions included a great deal of hand waving and unfinished sentences and pretty soon Bill was reliving his first visit to the Monument with the same excitement. When they finally settled down, Linda handed them each a bottle of water from a cooler.

"So when can I see this place?" she asked while they were all drinking and unable to talk.

"Wow, I don't know about that, Linda," said Frank, shaking his head. The currents are everything we've heard and more and that's definitely no place for a beginner."

"Oh, come on, Frank! I didn't come all the way to Japan just to go for a boat ride. You have to let me see this place, you just have to!"

Tony held up his finger to interrupt.

"Frank, maybe if we put in on the west side and just did a shallow drift dive, she'd be okay. We could even tether her to us, if you think that's necessary. At least then she'd be able to see the structure for herself."

"I'll think about it, but I'm not sure it's such a good idea. Too many things can go wrong down there."

After reminding him that it was his idea for her to get her scuba certification, Linda finally convinced Frank that he owed it to her to let her try the drift dive the next day.

The boat slowed and Takamura turned into a small inlet with high, shear sides, similar to the terrain near the Monument. Even the end of the inlet was blunt and high. Because of the angle of the inlet, the water was unusually calm and when the engines finally stopped, Frank could see the bottom.

"It can't be more than 20 or 30 feet deep right here," he said, pointing to the sandy bottom.

Takamura tossed an anchor off the bow of the boat and set it in the sand while Bill scrambled into his dive suit. Frank and Tony watched in amusement as the young diver attached one device after another to his like-new BCD. Finally, Tony couldn't take it any more and burst into laughter.

"Bill, we're not diving the Marianis Trench, here. You can probably leave that side-scanning sonar unit, or what ever the hell it is, here on the boat."

Just then, Takamura walked by and said, "Good com-put-a. Me sell."

"So you do speak English, you little faker!" shouted Tony, shaking his finger at the dive master. "I thought there was more to you than met the ear."

Laughing, Frank and Tony helped each other back into their BCDs, checked each other's main air valves and headed for the back of the boat. Takamura and Bill were already in the water, so Frank turned to make sure Linda was okay.

"We'll be back in a few minutes. Don't sail off and leave us, you hear?"

Linda gave Frank a thumbs-up and shouted, "Have fun."

The four divers made their way along the sandy inlet bottom toward the end. Soon they detected a slight current flowing against them and out toward the ocean.

Frank spotted the opening before Takamura even had a chance to point it out. At the very end of the inlet, in the face of the rock cliff that formed the island's edge, was a perfectly round hole about two feet in diameter!

Frank's first thought was that it was the end of a storm drain, or worse, a sewer pipe but as he examined the opening more closely it was obvious that the hole was bored right into the rock. The water rushing out of the opening was very cold and Frank suspected that it was also fresh. It could be the outflow from an underground stream, but why would the opening be so perfectly round? It really looked more man-made than natural.

Takamura waved the other three divers closer and used his knife to scrape an area on the tube's wall just inside the opening. Soon he had exposed a symbol identical to the one he had shown Frank and Tony back at the Monument.

Suddenly, Takamura cocked his head like he was listening for something and then he shook it negative. The regulators from four divers in close proximity to each other could make some pretty strange sounds.

On the way back to the boat, the four divers spread out and enjoyed a leisurely swim along the bottom, looking for sea-life. When they reached the anchor line, they used it to make their way slowly, hand over hand, to the surface.

Frank was the first one to the top and when he swam around to the back of the boat he was surprised to find that Linda hadn't swung down the dive ladder. He struggled up onto the dive platform and lowered the ladder for the others. Once inside the boat he slipped out of his BCD and its attached tank. Linda wasn't in sight, so he assumed she was below deck using the portable toilet. He called to her and, when there was no answer, he stuck his head into the hole that led down into the bow of the boat and called again. There was still no answer so he crawled down into the small space to look around.

When he reemerged, Tony and Bill were already onboard and Tony noticed the expression on Frank's face.

"What's wrong?

Suddenly, Frank spotted something in the distance and pointed to the entrance of the inlet, where a dark-colored boat was just making its turn into open water, and shouted, "They've got Linda!"

Chapter 11

Tony scrambled to where he had been sitting before the dive and pulled his bag out from under the bench. He unzipped the bag, rummaged around with his hand and pulled out a Beretta M9 semi-automatic pistol, which he handed to Frank. He then took out a second one for himself, along with an ammo clip for each weapon.

In response to Frank's look of surprise, he said, "What'd you think I had in here, my lunch? I figured we might need some firepower so I brought along a few of our friends from 'Nam. Now let's get going – those bastards have already got a big head start on us."

By this time Bill Ito, the Japanese-American student who had become the unofficial fifth member of the NWIDI team, and Takamura, their dive master, had joined Frank and Tony. The dive master was babbling frantically in Japanese and pointing at the hand guns Frank and Tony were now holding.

"Tony, he says handguns are illegal in Japan and that we could all go to prison for a long time just for being near them," translated Bill.

"Shut him up and tell him to get this bucket of bolts underway," yelled Tony. "Now!"

Bill pushed Takamura toward the wheel while trying to explain to him that somebody had just kidnapped Linda. Suddenly the young Japanese diver got the picture and flew into action. He jumped out onto the front of the boat and cut the anchor rope with a single pull of the knife strapped to his leg. Leaping back to the controls, he fired up the engines and slammed the throttles forward, knocking Bill to the floor as the boat spun and headed for the open end of the cove in pursuit of the mysterious speedboat.

Frank helped Bill to his feet and they joined Tony, who had taken up a lookout position next to their captain. By the time the dive boat rounded the bend into open water it was flying over the surface faster than any 36-foot sport boat should be able to go. In the distance, they could just make out the fleeing boat and they didn't seem to be getting any closer.

Takamura reached under the instrument panel and pulled out a small walkie-talkie radio. While he was shouting into the unit,

Tony leaned closer to Frank, so he could be heard above the roar of the engines, and said, "This guy is full of surprises, isn't he?"

They were headed east, back toward the Monument and away from the marina where the trip had originally begun. When Takamura finally put the radio down, Bill turned to Frank and Tony.

"I assume he called the police," said Tony.

"No, local law enforcement isn't equipped or trained for something like this. Eventually we'll have to contact the Japanese authorities, but they can't help us right now."

"So who did he call?" demanded Tony

"He called his other dive boat for help but they're coming from Sonai Marina, on the north side of the island. If the guys we're chasing follow the shoreline and head north, we've got 'em trapped. However, if they head into open water off the east end of Yonaguni, we'll never catch them. The next closest island is about 40 miles east of here and we won't be able to maintain this speed out in the open sea."

Frank nodded. "Ask him if he knows the boat we're chasing."

Bill translated the question to Takamura, who shook his head and then offered some further explanation.

Bill translated the response for Frank and Tony. "He's never seen it before, but he said that new boats come and go all the time. There are seven inhabited islands in this immediate area and he says it's even possible that a boat like that may have traveled all the way down from Okinawa or even further north, from the big island of Japan."

"What about the other directions?" shouted Tony.

Bill shook his head. "North of Yonaguni there's nothing but the East China Sea and south is the Pacific Ocean. Taiwan is only about 80 miles to the west but that's a different country, with customs and all that."

"Bill, these guys are kidnappers! I doubt if they'd be too worried about a little paperwork. What's beyond Taiwan?"

"Well, China, but ..."

The boat swerved to the right, causing Frank, Tony and Bill to grab for a handhold and cutting off Bill's answer.

The captain shouted something over his shoulder and Bill translated.

"He has to swing wide to avoid the area directly over the Monument and any divers that might be in the water."

Along with the handguns, Tony's bag had also produced a pair of large, military-issue binoculars. He and Frank took turns peering into the distance at the speedboat, hoping to see Linda, but it was clear that the distance between the two boats was increasing with time.

"We're losing them!" shouted Tony, handing the binoculars back to Frank. "Can't we go any faster?"

As if to answer, the captain slapped the throttles with the heel of his hand to indicate that they were fully advanced and then he punched the instrument panel in frustration. The only hope of overtaking the faster boat was if it slowed down.

Off the left side of the boat the rugged coastline of Yonaguni was racing by. High cliffs that dropped directly into the surf didn't seem to offer any likely destinations for the boat carrying Linda. As the chase continued, Frank cursed himself for getting Linda involved in this reckless endeavor. Earlier she had almost been shot in a bizarre incident in front of the hangar and now she had been kidnapped right out from under his nose. He would never forgive himself if anything happened to her, and he knew Donna would never forgive him either. What was Linda – or any of them, for that matter – doing half way around the world looking for the builders of an ancient monument? Frank knew he didn't have an answer that would satisfy himself, let alone his dear Donna, who had died little more than a year ago.

The eastern-most tip of Yonaguni Island is an area known as Agarizaki Point – a narrow, rocky peninsula about a quarter of a mile wide and a third of a mile long that juts out into the sea like a giant finger. Its rounded end terminates in the same high cliffs they had been seeing for the past 15 minutes.

All eyes were on the small dot up ahead because the captain had explained, and Bill had translated, that very soon the speedboat would either break right to the east, where it would be lost in the open water, or it would break left and disappear around Agarizaki Point – and right into the path of Takamura's other boat.

As the point came into view, Frank held his breath. He didn't know how he was going to get Linda back yet, but he knew the job would be a lot easier if she remained on the tiny island of Yonaguni. If the fleeing speedboat headed for open water, his task would become a thousand times harder.

Suddenly the Japanese dive master let out a yell and threw his fist into the air. He had been able to detect the boat turning an instant before it disappeared behind the point. Linda's captors were not heading for open water but were, instead, following the coastline back toward the west, along the north side of the island!

Takamura grabbed the radio and began yelling to his other boat. He kept repeating a phrase in Japanese that means "Do you see them?" but the answer was always "*Iie*" – "No".

In what seemed like an hour, but was actually only a couple of minutes, the dive boat carrying Frank, Tony and Bill rounded the point and headed northwest. They followed the shoreline, staying just far enough out to avoid the large rocks that dotted the shallower water. Frank pointed out a boat in the distance, but they quickly realized that it was coming toward them, not going away. As the two boats got closer to each other, Takamura again pounded his fist on the instrument panel and pulled the throttles back to half speed. It was his boat from Sonai Marina!

The two boats pulled along side each other and Takamura began shouting angrily at the occupants of the other boat. Bill tried to translate as much as he could for Frank, but the conversation quickly grew heated and everyone was talking at once.

Standing behind Frank and Bill, Tony soon understood enough of the translation to realize that the speedboat had disappeared sometime after it rounded the point and before it had come into view of the other boat. Only a small section of coastline, where the peninsula joined the main part of the island, would make this possible.

Frank heard a loud splash and turned to see Tony, now back into his dive gear, slipping below the surface. Frank yelled, but Tony was already too deep to hear and he probably wouldn't have come back anyway.

Frank quickly gathered up his own gear and started putting it on, but Bill grabbed his arm to stop him.

"Frank, you can't go after him. These waters are infested with Hammerhead sharks."

"Bullshit! He's an idiot for going alone, but he's my best friend and I'm going after him. Now help me with this tank, and stop wasting my time!"

Frank turned so Bill could tighten the straps securing his tank and found himself staring into the hairy chest of a huge Japanese man.

"No bullshit, Amerika-jin. Too many hammas. You stay, Mito go," said the man, tapping his fist on his chest. He was wearing swimming trunks, swim fins, a mask and a snorkel, but no other diving gear except for a huge knife in a sheath strapped to his leg. The big man yanked the knife out, stepped up onto the bench seat and stepped off into the water in almost exactly the same spot where Tony had submerged only a minute earlier.

Angry and worried, Frank stared into the water. He started to step up on the bench but by now several others from the second boat had crossed into Takamura's and one of them pulled him down off the seat roughly.

Takamura said something to Bill, who translated for Frank.

"He says that one kidnapping and one suicide is all he is permitted on a single dive trip. You will have to wait until tomorrow to kill yourself, Frank."

The other men were laughing, but Frank didn't see anything funny about the situation and he let them know it. By the time Bill finished translating Frank's remarks, nobody was laughing.

In a hastily held strategy meeting, it was decided that the second boat, with its complement of 6 young locals, would stay and wait for some sign of Tony and Mito while Frank and Bill would go west to Sonai with Takamura and contact the authorities. Frank hated the idea of leaving the area where both Linda and Tony could be in serious trouble, but he finally agreed that only he possessed the information necessary to report the kidnapping and he knew he would need Bill's help with translation.

On the way back to the northern marina, Frank learned that the second boat was Hammer Diving Service's only other vessel. It was stationed at Sonai and used to access dive sites on the north and east sides of the island. The boat they were on was normally stationed at Kubura Marina and used primarily for trips to the Monument and a few other southern sites. The seven men who had arrived on the second boat turned out to be the entire staff of Hammer, except for Takamura, who owned the operation.

Takamura radioed ahead and when they arrived at Sonai, the equivalent of the local Sheriff was waiting to escort them to his office a block from the dock. He was actually attached to the Yaeyama Islands Police Department, which had jurisdiction over all 11 islands in the chain, including Yonaguni.

While Frank and Bill were filling out the police reports, Takamura walked down to the wharf and borrowed an old jeep-like vehicle from a fishery. When the reports were finally completed and signed, he took Frank and Bill back to the hotel where Jim was anxiously waiting to hear about the dive trip to the Monument. The story he heard was not at all the one he expected. By the time Frank and Bill had finished relating the events of the afternoon, Jim was visibly shaken.

"Kidnapped? How could Linda have been kidnapped, Frank?" he said, shaking his head and wringing his hands. "This just can't be happening to us! What do we do now?"

Takamura's radio crackled and he ran outside for better reception. When he stuck his head back into the lobby door, he was waving his hands and yelling.

"They've found something," translated Bill. "I couldn't understand exactly what, but they want us out on the point immediately."

With Takamura at the wheel, Frank, Bill and a reluctant Jim raced for the east end of the island. They passed the Damatu Burial Grounds, where they had examined the burial vaults that very morning, and continued east as fast as the road and the aging vehicle would allow. As they flew past a large pasture, where a small herd of Yonaguni Ponies was grazing, Takamura explained that the other boat had recovered Mito, bleeding but still alive, from a small island of rock that stuck out of the surf near the shore.

When Frank asked about Tony, the driver shook his head and said "No yet."

Eventually they came to an unmarked intersection and Takamura made a hard left turn onto a gravel road and headed north. When the jeep finally slid to a stop at the end of the road, they were on a high cliff overlooking the ocean.

Takamura grabbed his radio and jumped out of the car without saying a word to the other three occupants. As he headed for the edge of the cliff, he was yelling into the radio again.

"I guess we're here," Frank observed as they piled out of the car and followed their driver.

Takamura pointed to the boat bobbing around in the heavy surf directly below them without interrupting his conversation on the radio. Bill tried to listen to what was going on, but he was having trouble with the Okinawan dialect that Takamura and his friends had lapsed into.

Finally, Takamura lowered the radio and turned to offer Bill an explanation in conventional Japanese. Bill translated for Frank and Jim.

"He says that the boat needs to take Mito back to the hospital immediately because he is badly wounded. They are concerned about leaving without Tony, so we are going to stand watch here until they can return. When they come back they're going to bring both boats and some dive gear back so they can search a larger area for Tony."

Frank nodded reluctantly. Takamura keyed the radio and simply said *"Hai!"* – "Yes." They heard the boat's engines change pitch and watched it quickly disappear behind a small point of land. Frank's thoughts returned to the fate of his two friends, Linda and Tony. Linda, at least, was probably still alive but how could Tony survive where the experienced Japanese diver had failed? Realizing that the big man had risked his life to help a total stranger, Frank felt suddenly embarrassed.

"Please express my gratitude to Takamura and ask him how serious Mito's shark bite is."

Bill translated Frank's question and as the other man responded, Bill's face clouded with question.

"Frank, he says Mito wasn't bitten by a shark – he was shot with a spear gun! Apparently the spear went completely through his leg and when the others found him he was trying to pull it out so he could continue his search for Tony. The others wouldn't let him back in the water, of course, because he was bleeding badly and the sharks … well, you get the picture."

Frank nodded, trying to look compassionate, but his mind was spinning with activity. He wasn't sure how Tony would fare against a school of Hammerhead sharks, but if the danger below the surface were merely other humans, Tony's chances of survival were greatly improved. He pitied the poor bastard who would dare to point a spear at his friend!

"The guys on the boat are all experienced divers and trained in first aid," continued Bill, "so they managed to get the bleeding under control but Mito had already lost a lot of blood and he was lapsing in and out of consciousness."

"Right," mumbled Frank, half listening. "Tell him I will take care of all the medical expenses. And then get over here and help me with this. Jim, give us a hand, will you?"

Frank ran back to the vehicle and examined the winch mounted on the front. It was old and rusty but it looked serviceable. The question was, would the cable reach the 75 feet or more to the rocks at the bottom of the cliff?

"Frank, what are you doing?" asked Jim, who was still in shock over the recent events.

"I'm going down to help Tony, what do you think I'm doing? Grab that rope out of the back and bring it around to me. Quickly, Jim, quickly!"

Seeing what Frank was up to, Takamura returned to the vehicle, set the brake, put the gear shift in neutral and started the engine. Barking something to Bill, he joined Frank at the winch.

"He says to watch your fingers, Frank!"

Manipulating a small lever on the side of the winch, Takamura released the tension enough to allow him to free the hook on the end of the cable. He indicated that Frank should pull on the hook and he activated the lever again, allowing a short piece of cable to unwind. Satisfied, Takamura gave Frank the thumbs up sign and spoke to Bill.

"He thinks the winch still works, but he doubts if the cable is long enough to reach to the bottom of the cliff, Frank."

"That's what this is for," replied Frank, taking the bundle from Jim. The rope that he had seen in the back looked like the kind used for water skiing or other marine purposes. Frank tied a loop in one end and placed it over the hook on the winch. He secured the other end around his waist using a bowline knot he remembered from his Boy Scout days and then made his way to the edge.

"The three of you grab the rope and lower me down slowly. When we run out of rope, start unwinding the winch cable until I'm at the bottom, got it?"

Jim was still trying his best to talk Frank out of the descent, but to no avail. Frank laid on his stomach with his feet out over the edge and waited for the others to take the slack out of the rope. With a slight nod of his head, he pushed back and off the lip of the cliff.

The slope wasn't quite as vertical as it had appeared from the boat and Frank was able to lean back against the rope and keep his feet against the cliff face in a slow, belaying type of descent. About half way down he heard someone yell "stop" from up above and he guessed that they had come to the end of the rope. Soon he heard "go" and he started to descend again, this time more smoothly, as the winch played out the cable.

The cliff had become steeper as he descended and he was hanging vertically about 25 feet above the rocky shoreline when he felt something let go. As he fell away from the dangling end of the rope, Frank remembered another detail from his scouting days – bowline knots sometimes come loose!

Chapter 12

Standing on a narrow patch of sand with her hands on her hips, Linda watched the dive boat disappear and fumed! If those guys thought this were some kind of smart-ass, macho practical joke, they had another think coming!

Bored with sitting on the boat, Linda had decided to try her hand at snorkeling in the quiet waters of the inlet while Frank, Tony and Bill were off looking at some underwater mystery with their guide, Takamura. She had been exploring an area along the rugged shoreline when she had heard the sound of a powerful boat approaching from the open end of the inlet. As the long, pointed craft got closer, Linda had scrambled out of the water and behind a large rock to avoid being hit.

The speedboat had slowed as it approached Takamura's dive boat and the sound of the engines changed to a low rumble. When one of the men in the speedboat stood up to get a better look at the other craft, Linda had seen that he had been holding some sort of pistol in his right hand. Afraid that she would be spotted, she had crouched down behind the rock to collect her thoughts. Her hands trembled with fear as she agonized about her friends who were still below the surface somewhere in the inlet. Minutes had gone by while she tried to calm herself down.

Suddenly, she had heard a familiar voice in the distance. It sounded like Frank, and it sounded like he had shouted, "We've got Linda!" Slowly, hands and legs still trembling, she had raised herself up so she could see around the rock just as the dive boat's engines roared to life and thrust the boat through a hard turn and toward the open end of the inlet. They had left without her!

Alone in the now quiet inlet, tears trickled down Linda's cheeks. She was so mad all she could do was stomp her feet and yell, "Damn you, damn you!" How could her friends do this to her? They knew she had been anxious about this whole trip to Japan and especially about dive boats and open water. And now they had left her stranded on a narrow strip of sand, trapped by high, rugged cliffs on three sides and by the ocean on the other. As the water gently lapped at her feet, she realized that the rising tide would soon make her small buffer of rocks and sand around the perimeter of the inlet disappear.

Linda sat down on a flat rock and let her feet dangle into the rising water, wondering how long this cruel trick would go on. As she calmed down, she began to realize that Frank and Tony wouldn't have left her here, in the middle of nowhere, as a practical joke. As she replayed the events of the last few minutes, she recalled Frank's yell from the boat and it suddenly occurred to her that he must have said, *"They've got Linda!"* The guys must have thought that the gun-wielding men on the speedboat had taken her!

"Oh, no!" she cried out loud as she realized her real dilemma – since no one knew she was still here, no one would be coming back for her. She would have to find a way out of this inlet or she might die here!

Linda heard a noise behind her that sounded like a small rock rolling. Startled, she spun around and listened, but the only sound was that of the surf against the rocky shoreline. Fighting to keep the feeling of panic from returning, she scanned the base of the cliff for any signs of life.

"Who's there?" she shouted. And then, more timidly, "Hello? Is anybody here?"

Off to her left, just inside her field of view, Linda saw something move. She pressed back against the boulder and held her breath as a small dark creature darted between rocks, apparently oblivious to her presence.

When the animal momentarily moved into the open, it appeared to be a cross between a small rabbit and a rat. Linda would later learn that the furry creature was a young Amami Hare, also know as the Ryukyu Rabbit, but her immediate thought was how did this little guy get down here on the rocks without being killed by the fall from above?

The animal made its way past Linda's position and along the shore, stopping frequently to nibble on bits of seaweed that had been snagged by the rocks. Linda realized that the creature couldn't survive on the shoreline without fresh water and protection from the rising tide so she followed it at a distance, hoping to discover some hidden pathway up the face of the cliff to the meadow above. She tried to quietly pick her way among the rocks along the waterline, but a loose stone caused her to stumble and, in the instant it took her to regain her balance, the small animal disappeared.

Linda made her way to the place in the rocks where she had last seen the rabbit-with-mouse-ears and began a frantic search.

Looking back over her shoulder, she realized that she was now at the end of the inlet farthest away from the opening to the sea and trapped by the rising water. As she approached a 20-foot high boulder, she felt a short blast of cool air. Squeezing between the huge rock and the face of the cliff, she found herself standing in the entrance of a large cave that was completely obscured by the boulder. The cave seemed to extend back into the darkness forever and in the distance she thought she could hear the sound of running water.

Carefully, Linda made her way into the cavern a few feet to investigate. She discovered that the floor of the cave sloped up and away from the sea and that it was covered in soft, dry sand. At least she could wait out the high tide, she thought, and then maybe she could make her way back out to the entrance of the inlet to flag down a passing boat.

Linda ventured into the cave to the point where the bright sunlight from the outside turned to darkness and sat down on the sand with a feeling of relief. It looked like she was going to be okay after all. Of course, she hadn't given any consideration to what – or who – might be lurking in the shadows behind her.

***

The instant Frank felt the knot slip in the rope around his waist, his survival instincts kicked in. He had been an Air Force Pararescueman in Viet Nam and many of his parachute jumps had ended in less than perfect landings. Mentally, he prepared himself for the bone-shattering jolt that awaited his legs if he landed on the rocks directly beneath him. At the same time, he tried to will his body ahead and to the right, where he could see a small patch of sand. An instant before he hit the ground a strong blast of wind caught him by surprise and knocked him off balance. The act of flaying his arms, combined with the force of the wind, got him to the sand, but at an odd angle. Frank's feet slammed into the sand and broke his fall, but he fell backwards onto his butt so hard that the landing knocked the wind out of him.

He lay back onto the sand, gasping for breath. Above him, he could see Jim and Bill peering over the edge and waving their arms wildly.

"Yeah, I'm alright," he hissed through clenched teeth. He tried to lift an arm to signal back, but forcing air into his lungs was taking every ounce of his strength. Now the two up on the cliff were pointing toward the ocean, so Frank tilted his head back as far as it would go. He was barely hanging on to consciousness and he felt the shadow before he saw the large figure in scuba gear looming over him with a spear gun in one hand. Frank desperately wanted to get to his feet to defend himself but he was still too winded to move.

"Nice of you to drop in, old man," laughed Tony as he brushed the swim mask off his face with his free hand and pointed to the rope still dangling from the cliff. And then, kneeling beside Frank, he asked, "Do you think you broke anything important?"

Frank shook his head slowly, and whispered, "Where'd you get the spear gun?"

"Oh, this? Some dumb shit made the mistake of pointing it at me out there in the surf so I took it away from him and cut his regulator hoses. The last time I saw him he was shooting to the surface like a cork. Are you sure you're okay?"

"Yes, I just had the wind knocked out of me, I think. Help me sit up, will you?"

Tony helped Frank get positioned against a nearby rock and waited for him to regain control of his breathing. He signaled up to Jim and the dive master with the finger-to-thumb "OK" sign and then gave them a thumb's up. While he waited for Frank, he kept a watchful eye on the surf just offshore.

Finally, Frank could talk again. "What the hell happened out there?" he asked.

"Well, you guys sounded like you were lapsing into a debate about who's fault it was that we had lost the trail of the speedboat so I decided to go look before the trail got any colder."

"No, I mean with the spear gun. Somebody shot Mito in the leg and Takamura's men had to take him to the hospital to keep him from bleeding to death," puffed Frank.

"Mito? Who's Mito?"

"One of Takamura's guys. He went in after you when you jumped off the boat. He was afraid you'd run into a school of hammerhead sharks and he went in to help you."

"I never saw him, Frank. The only other person I saw was the guy I took this spear gun away from, and he wasn't bleeding the last time I saw him."

"Well maybe the guy you ran into had already shot Mito before you caught up with him. But why? Why would he attack Mito and then come after you? Did you see anything down there worth protecting with deadly force?" asked Frank as he tried to get to his feet and failed. "Damn it, I think I hurt my knee!"

"Easy, old man," said Tony as he helped Frank back down against the rock. "We'll have to get a boat out here to get you back to a doctor. I hope Jim and our young Japanese friend haven't run off yet."

Frank explained that Takamura's staff would be returning soon with dive gear to continue the search for Tony.

"Frank, I'm disappointed! What made you think I would need a bunch of Japanese guys looking out for me? By the sounds of it, I should have been looking out for this Mito guy instead of the other way around."

"Yeah, it looks that way now. So what about this guy you disarmed?"

"It doesn't make sense, Frank. I was cruising along the bottom, heading for a section of the shoreline that seemed to be a likely hiding spot for the speedboat when this guy came at me from out of nowhere. The bottom along this coast looks pretty much like the shoreline – lots of big rocks everywhere – and as I circled around one of them, there he was. I don't think he was expecting to see me any more than I was expecting to see him. He got off one spear, which I managed to dodge, and then I overtook him while he was reloading. That's all I know."

"Did you ever find the speedboat, or any sign of it? Or of Linda?" Frank asked, shifting his position in the sand and wincing as he did so.

"No, but to be honest with you, I was a little concerned about bumping into more spear-wielding divers, so I didn't cover much ground after my run-in with the first one. I found the entrance to a cave a little east of here that looked promising, but by then I was almost out of air and I had to surface. That was just about the time you dropped off the end of that rope, so I swam over here to see what you were up to."

"A cave, huh? As soon as that dive boat gets back here we need to check that spot out. Every minute we delay is another minute Linda is in danger."

"We? Frank, I don't think you'll be doing any diving for a few days. You stay on the boat and coordinate and I'll look for Linda. With the help of a couple of Takamura's divers we should be able to cover this whole area in an hour or two. After all, how many places could a boat that big hide?"

Up on the top of the cliff, Jim had finally recognized Tony as the spear gun toting diver who had come ashore near Frank and he breathed a sigh of relief.

"You know, I've had just about all the adventure I can stand! I'll be very glad when this trip is over and I'm back in my 12x12 office at the University," he said to Bill as they watched Takamura rewind the cable onto the winch. As soon as the cable was secure, he tossed the rope into the back of the rig and climbed into the driver's seat.

"I guess we're leaving," shrugged Jim, feeling completely out of control of his life at the moment.

Bill exchanged some words in Japanese with Takamura and then nodded.

"Yup! He wants to get back to the marina as fast as possible to check on Mito, his diver. He also wants to be there in time to get on the boat before they come back out here to pick up Frank and Tony."

"Whatever," mumbled Jim as he climbed into the back seat. His stomach was starting to feel a little funny and he just wanted to rest for a minute. He was terribly concerned about Linda and the worrying was upsetting his whole system.

Takamura drove like a madman back down the dirt road that led away from the cliff. At the intersection, he managed to get two wheels of the high-centered rig off the ground negotiating the corner and Jim was sure they were going to tip over. He hung on as long as he could but when he was sure he was going to be sick he yelled, "Stop!" at the top of his lungs.

Jim's yell startled both men in the front seats and Takamura slid the vehicle to a stop. Jim jumped out and barely made it to the side of the road before he threw up. Takamura was chattering frantically at Bill, who felt caught in the middle.

"Jim, he really wants to get back. Jump in, will you?"

"Go!" shouted Jim, still bent over along side the road.

"What? We can't leave you out here! Just get in – you'll be okay."

As if to prove his point, Jim threw up again.

"Go! Get him back to the marina and then you can come back out to get me. If I have to ride another meter with that lunatic I'll have a heart attack! Now, go!" shouted Jim, waving his arm.

Bill translated and before the last words were out of his mouth Takamura was spinning tires in the gravel. Jim sat down on the grass at the side of the road and watched the rig disappear, leaving a rooster-tail of dust behind.

As he sat waiting for his stomach to calm down, Jim reflected on how beautiful the tiny island of Yonaguni really was.

Under different circumstances, and perhaps with different travel mates, he could really learn to like this place. The view, across the lush green meadow that ended at the edge of the ocean, was very tranquil. A few minutes later, Jim was feeling much better.

Now in a more relaxed frame of mind, he decided to begin walking slowly back toward town. The exercise would be good for him and it would shorten the distance Bill would have to drive back to meet him. Jim hadn't taken more than ten steps when he noticed another dust trail just ahead on the opposite side of the road. As he watched, he realized that a black sedan of some kind was speeding down a side road that joined the road he was walking on. He considered flagging the driver down for a ride back to town, but before he could raise his arm, the car disappeared over a small rise and was gone.

Jim walked on and as he approached the side road where the car had been he realized that it was the entrance to the cemetery where they had seen the ancient tombs earlier that same day.

Jim crossed to the other side of the road and stood gazing at the cemetery, which was only a hundred feet down the driveway. He's had enough adventure to last him a long time, but his scientific curiosity finally got the better of him and he decided to take this opportunity to examine the tombs more closely, without the constant chatter of the others. He hung his sport jacket over a small, faded sign where the driveway met the road, assuming that Bill would see it and figure out where he had gone.

Unbuttoning his shirt and smiling, Jim hiked the short distance to the gate happier than he'd been since leaving Seattle. As he walked, he reviewed what he had learned about this area during his preparation for this trip.

Most archeologists believe that the islands south of Japan were first inhabited by a race of people called the Jomon, who date back to at least 8,000 B.C., but there are popular legends about a mythical place called Mu, or Lemuria, which is supposed to have existed about the same time as Atlantis. As an anthropologist, Jim found the stories of Atlantis and Lemuria comical, but the discovery of the underwater ruins here in Yonaguni, and elsewhere, was causing many in his field to reconsider their theories about man's ancient past. As he passed between the stone gateposts of the cemetery, Jim reminded himself to keep an open mind and not let what he thought he knew affect what he might be able to learn.

Of all the tombs in the cemetery, one held particular interest for Jim. He had discovered it that morning, but its obvious age deserved a more patient review. He wandered among the gravesites until he found the one he was looking for. He had noticed some markings around the base that morning, but he had left his notepad back at the hotel and hadn't been able to record any of them. This afternoon, while the rest of the team had been out diving, Jim had spent some time in the small local library. Kneeling beside the tomb, he pulled a sheet of paper out of his pocket and compared the drawings on it with those on the stone.

"Ah, hah!" he said out loud. His memory had served him well and one of the symbols he had traced back at the library matched one on the base of the tomb almost exactly. On his hands and knees, he inched slowly along the side of the tomb looking for more matches. The end of the stone block had no markings at all, and as he made the turn and started up the other side, the one with the step-like feature, he noticed that the grass was trampled and that the dirt near the base was disturbed. As a trained archeologist he knew he had not disturbed the "dig" during his morning examination, so who …?

The black sedan! He had spotted it leaving the cemetery in a hurry earlier. But what would the sedan's occupants have been doing here? Bill had said that no one even knew who was buried in most of these older tombs.

From his vantage point on the ground, Jim noticed that a thin black line marked the interface where the slab met the side of the tomb as if the slab had been moved recently. Jumping to his feet, he faced the tomb and lifted the small overhanging lip of the slab. To his great surprise, it moved with little resistance. Opening it like the lid of a giant stone trunk, Jim soon had the slab standing vertically, exposing a deep hole that extended down as far as he could see. A series of steep irregularly shaped stone steps led downward from the right end of the tomb into the darkness below and cool, damp air drifted up out of the hole.

Jim was in shock and he just stood there, staring down into the pit. The steps were cut from single blocks of stone and the edges had been worn smooth from use. They could be hundreds, or even thousands, of years old but the hinge and the hydraulic cylinder that secured the back edge of the slab to the tomb was obviously much newer.

"Holy crap!" he shouted out loud. "What is this?"

He put his hands on the side and leaned over the edge hoping to see or hear something – anything – but the ancient vault offered no clues about what lay below. Jim felt his stomach start to turn again but he fought back the feeling and steeled his nerves. This was too important a find to let his many fears and phobias get in the way and he forced his foot up onto the step feature on the outside of the tomb before his common sense could stop him.

Facing the steps the way one would climb a ladder, Jim eased down the steep stairway until his head was just below ground level. From here he could see that the tomb simply covered a hole in the top of a large, underground cavern. Below the surface the steps weren't blocks but were, instead, cut out of the solid stone wall of a large chamber. The small amount of light coming down from the opening above diminished quickly as he descended and Jim had absolutely no intention of exploring in the dark, but he was fascinated by the structure and he thought he could get down another two or three steps before he would be in total darkness. As his foot touched the next step, Jim heard a click from above and he looked up. To his horror, he saw the stone slab closing and before he could move a muscle he was sealed into the tomb, in absolute, total darkness!

Chapter 13

What Linda hadn't realized when she had so proudly plopped down on the sand just inside the cave was that low tide was more than six hours away and by then it would be nearly 11:00 p.m. At dawn it would be high tide again, so she wouldn't be able to make her way out to where the inlet joined the sea until the next low tide, in the late morning. By then she would be dehydrated and <u>very</u> hungry!

The inlet was located on the southern side of the island, not too far from the west end and the marina they had departed from earlier that afternoon. It opened to the sea in a generally southwest direction, so Linda had the benefit of direct sunlight right up until the orange globe disappeared into the sea. In the minutes just before the sun actually set, the terminator – the line between daylight and darkness – actually retreated up into the cave several yards, allowing Linda to explore more of her temporary shelter.

The soft sand on the floor of the cave extended all the way to the back, indicating that the sea probably filled the cave during the unusually high seas that accompanied typhoons and other bad storms. Linda examined the back wall, where it met the sand, looking for the furry rabbit's escape route. As the light in the cave was beginning to fade, Linda found an opening in the wall just above the floor. The circular hole wasn't much wider than her shoulders, but the sound of running water was unmistakable. She got down on her hands and knees and poked her head inside to ponder her next move but some sand under her gave way and made the decision for her.

Linda soon discovered that the hole was the end of a tunnel that sloped steeply down, away from the cave and the sea. The shifting sand had dumped her headfirst into the tunnel and she tumbled several times before coming to a stop on her back, head pointing downhill, in total darkness. As she lay there listening to the sound of water somewhere below her, she rubbed a bump on her head and mentally assessed her situation. Her left knee hurt and she was sure she was bleeding from a small cut on her hand, but nothing seemed to be broken.

From below, Linda thought she heard something like a man's voice. Terrified, she quietly rolled over and got to her hands and knees again, ready to scramble back up the tunnel and out into the now dark cave. She listened carefully, but there was only the sound of water. Maybe her imagination was playing tricks on her. She had been on the verge of hysteria ever since the appearance of the speedboat and now maybe she was starting to hear things.

There it was again! She couldn't make out the words, but she was sure she could hear a deep voice coming from somewhere down the tunnel. The words sounded like short phrases, as if someone were giving commands to another.

Slowly, and very quietly, Linda raised herself into a standing position and pressed her hands against one side of the dark tunnel. She was surprised by the smooth, featureless rock surface and realized that this was no natural subterranean shaft. This tunnel certainly hadn't been dug out of the solid rock by natural forces!

Inching along the wall, she worked her way down the tunnel in the direction of the sounds. The further she went, the cooler the air became and the skimpy two-piece swim suit she had bought for the trip offered very little protection from the elements. As she navigated a bend in the passage, she spotted a faint glow in the distance. The artificial light confirmed what the sound of a voice had already implied – someone else was down here with her!

In the dark it was hard to judge distance, but Linda guessed she must have traveled nearly 100 feet from the point where she had entered the tunnel to where she finally reached the source of the light. The tunnel ended at a heavy wooden door and small cracks between the planks allowed slivers of light to filter through from whatever was on the other side. She hadn't heard the mysterious voice for several minutes so she knelt down and put her eye to the largest of the cracks. The thick vertical planks constrained her field of view to a narrow strip directly in front of the door, but she could see that the room on the other side was a large cavern with rock walls. The light was coming from a large industrial fixture that appeared to be hanging down from a ceiling she couldn't see. Directly in front of the door, and about half way across the room, she could see a large, rustic table with benches along two sides. A wisp of smoke drifted up from an ashtray on the table, but there was no one in sight and the only sound was that of running water, which seemed to be coming from the other side of the door.

Linda stood up and shivered from the cold. Bill hadn't mentioned any underground caverns on Yonaguni, so it was likely that the room on the other side of the door wasn't common knowledge among the locals. It was probably being used for some secret, and possibly illegal, activity. Her years of work as a researcher for the Seattle newspaper had sharpened her investigative instincts and she automatically began a mental review of the facts.

Yonaguni was a tiny island far from the provincial government in Okinawa and even further from the national authorities in Tokyo. It was, however, relatively close to mainland China and Taiwan. Its position would make it an ideal location for a drug smuggling operation, especially if the smugglers could come and go without being noticed. They could use the island as a manufacturing, storage or transfer point without the knowledge of the small native population.

Linda knew she should turn and flee back up the tunnel as fast as she could. If drug traffickers really were using this cave, they would be dangerous people and they would probably kill her if they found out that she had discovered their secret hideout. She knew all this, and still she operated the metal latch and slowly pushed the large door open.

**

Takamura had raced back to the small village like a madman, arriving just in time to catch his crew before the boat started back to the east end of the island to continue the search for Tony. He tossed the keys to the borrowed vehicle to Bill and shouted, in Japanese, "Go get your friend and meet me back here as soon as possible."

Bill watched the dive boat speed out of the small harbor and listened until he could no longer hear the powerful engines. He hoped Tony was okay and that Linda would be found soon, because sunset was only a few hours away. And they had left poor Jim on the side of the road heaving his guts out!

Bill hopped into the Japanese mini-SUV and headed back toward the east end of the island. Not long after he left the village, he was almost forced off the road by a black sedan traveling at a high rate of speed in the opposite direction. Cursing in both English and Japanese, he made a mental note to find out who owned the car as soon as he got back to town.

Bill wasn't exactly sure where they had left Jim, so he slowed down just before reaching the cemetery they had visited earlier that morning. As he crested a small hill he thought he spotted Jim beside the road but as he got closer he could see that it was just Jim's sport jacket hanging over a signpost. He stopped to retrieve the jacket and scanned the countryside for the ailing professor but the man was nowhere to be seen. Bill returned to the vehicle and honked the horn several times but there was no response from the frail man. It was obvious that Jim had made it this far west, so Bill turned the vehicle around in the cemetery driveway and started slowly back toward town. As he drove, he honked the horn at regular intervals and carefully checked both sides of the road for any sign of his new friend.

"Great!" he thought. "First Linda gets kidnapped, then Tony dives into shark infested waters and now I've lost Jim!"

***

Frank and Tony heard Takamura's boat before it appeared on the horizon.

"Man, I'd like to have a peek at those engines, someday," remarked Tony. "That thing sounds like a whole fleet of Detroit muscle cars."

With Tony's help, Frank had managed to get to his feet and lean against a rock, but he couldn't put his full weight on his right leg due to the injury to his knee.

"This should be fun," he frowned. "We've lost our translator and I'll bet none of them speaks a word of English."

Whoever was piloting the boat brought it in as far as possible without risking a collision with the giant boulders that stuck out of the water. Others on the boat lowered anchors from both the front and back and moments later two divers were in the water and headed for the beach. Tony walked out into the surf to meet them, leaving Frank leaning against the rock. After the traditional bowing and introductions, the divers removed their masks and fins and followed Tony back to Frank's position on the rocky beach. Tony was chatting and smiling broadly.

"We're in luck, Frank! Takamura brought along another translator, and this one is a lot cuter than Bill." Putting his arm around the smaller diver's shoulder, Tony continued. "This is Riko and she's one of Takamura's dive masters. I forget the guy's name. Riko suggests that we put my buoyancy vest on you, minus the tank of course, inflate it from one of their tanks, and then float you out to the boat like a pudgy white air mattress."

Frank laughed at Tony's analogy and then introduced himself to the two Japanese divers. The second diver's name was Hisaki and he was also a dive master working for Hammer Diving Service. He didn't speak English, but it was clear from the way he interacted with the female diver that the petite girl/woman was his superior.

Once Frank had the buoyancy vest secured and inflated, Tony and the male diver made a seat with their interlocked fingers and carried him out into the water until it was waist deep. With Frank floating on his back, the divers each took one of his hands and began to pull him toward the boat. Tony brought up the rear, so to speak, by pushing on Frank's extended good leg.

About half way out to the boat, Tony spotted something wedged between two exposed rocks and yelled for the divers to stop. He swam over and dislodged what appeared to be a buoyancy vest. When he returned to the group, he tossed it up onto Frank's chest and waved the divers forward.

"It's the vest I cut the hoses on," shouted Tony as he grabbed on to Frank's foot and began pushing again. "Maybe we can get some identifying marks from it."

When Frank was onboard and his knee had been wrapped with an elastic ACE bandage, Tony related their recent experiences to Riko, who translated for the other crewmembers. Tony ended his tale by suggesting that several of them don dive gear and search the coastline for the underwater cave he had seen earlier.

A nod and the single word "*Hai*" from Takamura resulted in a flurry of activity at the rear of the boat. Tony strapped a fresh air tank to the vest he had removed from Frank and reattached his regulator. Within minutes the boat had been repositioned several hundred yards to the east and eight divers were in the water. Takamura had ordered one of his crewmen to stay aboard to handle the boat and to look after Frank, but every other soul on the boat, including Tony, was involved in the search. As the divers entered the water two-by-two, Frank noticed with a smile that Tony had paired himself with Riko, the only female member of the crew.

Facing backwards on the port side of the boat, Frank sat with his right leg stretched out on the bench seat that ran the length of the deck and his back against the cabin. It was killing him not to be a part of the search, but he was obviously in no condition to swim. As he considered the possibility that this morning's dive might have been his only glimpse of the famous Yonaguni Monument, his eyes scanned the interior of the boat. Suddenly he spotted Tony's bag under the seat on the opposite side of the vessel. It was sandwiched between dive bags and gear and had, apparently, gone unnoticed.

Frank started to get up, with the intention of hopping across the boat, but the crewman wagged his finger and motioned for him to remain where he was. After several minutes of pointing and gesturing, Frank finally conveyed his message to the crewman, who retrieved Tony's bag and handed it to Frank. During a moment when the crewman was preoccupied with the boat's constantly changing position, Frank unzipped the bag to check the contents. To his great relief, the two semi-automatic handguns and several clips of ammunition were still safe inside. If they fell into the wrong hands, especially those of the authorities, the NWIDI team would be spending the next few years in a Japanese prison! As angry as he had been when he had first learned of the risk Tony had taken, he now felt considerably more secure as he stuffed the bag down between his injured leg and the side of the boat

***

Jim was mortified! Frozen with fear, he had watched as the lid of the tomb closed in a quick, smooth action, plunging him into total darkness. Clinging to the stone stairway for dear life with no idea what he would do next, he heard a second click.

Suddenly, the cavern burst into light and when he jerked his head around to see what was happening he almost lost his balance and fell. The light had caused his eyes to slam shut, and as he slowly opened them again, he scanned his surroundings.

He was only a few feet below the ceiling of a high domed cavern. The tomb in the cemetery above only covered the stairway and gave no indication of the vast size of the chamber below. The stairway was made of solid rock and clung to the side of the cavern as if it had been glued in place. Below him were several crude, wooden workbenches and what appeared to be a small forge at one end of the long room. At the opposite end, a heavy wooden door sealed an arched opening.

Jim carefully listened for any sound of activity, but the room was silent. He inched his way slowly down the steep staircase as if it were a ladder. At the bottom, he listened again. Satisfied that he was alone, he began a quick examination of the cavern. The walls and floor appeared to be solid rock, indicating that the cavity had probably been formed naturally and modified for use as a workshop. The floor had obviously been leveled and smoothed, whereas the walls retained their original irregular surface. Electricity for the hanging light fixtures and several outlet boxes was provided by surface-mounted conduits that all seemed to converge in a small electrical box on the wall near the door. A large flashlight stood on end on top of the box.

Jim walked to the nearest workbench. Along with a number of wooden mallets and some other odd looking tools, he found a small, eight-sided piece of metal that seemed to be in some intermediate phase of manufacture. Tiny dimple marks covered the surface where it had been worked with a mallet and a square hole had been punched in the center.

On the next bench he found a similar object, except that the dimples had been transformed into a smooth surface and three of the eight sides had been sharpened to a razor's edge.

Moving to the last workbench, Jim found several sealed vials, each containing a different colored liquid, along with a number of small paintbrushes. "The finishing touches," he thought. Whatever was being crafted in this room involved a lot of hand labor and attention to detail.

He worked his way around the chamber until he came to the door. The wood was rough and it appeared to be very old. A sliding metal latch resembling an ancient deadbolt secured the door on one side and equally ancient looking hinges held it to the rock on the other side. Jim put his ear to the door and listened.

In the distance he thought he could hear the sound of the ocean crashing against rocks. Jim remembered that the cemetery was situated on top of a small hill that sloped away toward the rugged cliffs that defined the northern shoreline of Yonaguni. Although trees and vegetation had hidden the ocean from view up on the road, he deduced that the cave he was now standing in must be part of a larger complex that eventually opened to the sea.

Jim glanced back over his shoulder and considered his situation. Unless he could find the secret to opening the tomb at the top of the stairs, his only way out was through the door. And what if the occupants of the black sedan came back while he was trying to find the switch? No, he really had no choice. Grabbing the flashlight, he dashed back to the first workbench, pocketed the strange, dimpled metal disk and let himself out through the wooden door. As he quietly eased the heavy door shut, he heard the sound of another click and froze in his tracks. Was that the lights going off inside or was it the tomb lid opening? As the familiar feeling of panic began to consume him, he snapped on the flashlight and fled across a large cavern toward an opening on the other side. As he passed through a series of interconnected caves, he slowed only to listen for the sound of the waves, which he hoped would lead him to the ocean – and safety.

***

Meanwhile, Bill was beside himself. He had traveled back and forth along the road in the general area where Jim should have been several times and there had been no sign of the man except for the jacket he had found hanging on a signpost. Finally, Bill decided that maybe Jim had become disoriented and wandered back toward the east end of the island where they had left Frank and Tony. He followed the road until it ended at Agarizaki Point, a scenic viewpoint perched on a cliff at the northeastern tip of the island. He rested his elbows on the stone wall and gazed down into the surf, pondering his next move. It would be dark soon, and Jim wasn't prepared, physically or mentally, for a night in the outdoors by himself.

Out of the corner of his eye, Bill spotted something moving far below him in the water. As he squinted, he realized that it was the speedboat they had chased half way around the island! Somehow they had ducked in behind a huge rock as they had rounded the tip of the island, momentarily shielded from Takamura's view. That's why the second boat hadn't seen them!

Both the front and back of the boat appeared to be securely tied to anchor points set into nearby rocks, indicating that this hiding spot was used frequently. The boat was empty and there was no sign of its former occupants.

Bill raced back to the SUV, sped back down the road to the intersection and turned right toward the point where he had left Frank and Tony on the beach. If he could attract the attention of someone in the dive boat, maybe he could direct them around to the spot where he had spotted the speedboat.

Just after he turned off the main road and headed for the ocean, Bill thought he saw a movement in his rear view mirror. Had that been a car speeding toward the viewpoint? Seconds later he saw a large black sedan back up, turn and follow him down the dirt road. With one eye on the road and one eye on his mirror, he accelerated, knowing that in a matter of minutes the road would end at the edge of a cliff!

Chapter 14

Linda quickly slipped through the heavy wooden door and eased it shut. She found herself in a small, damp room that appeared to have been hand hewn from the solid rock that surrounded it. In one corner a metal ladder had been attached to the wall and it led up to a round opening that reminded her of the hatch in a submarine. The table she had seen through the crack in the door was bare, except for the ashtray and its smoldering cigarette. She snubbed the butt out and fanned the smoke away with her hand.

"This is certainly no cave," she thought. "This has the look of a man-made hideout."

The sound of running water that had originally lured her down the shaft and into her current situation was louder than ever. It seemed to be coming from below her and she soon discovered a metal grate, similar to the storm drains back in Seattle. Linda peered between the rough bars, but it was too dark below to make anything out. The sound of the water and the cool draft coming up through the grate made her shiver violently.

Turning her attention back to the room, she spotted a small crate in the opposite corner. Circling the table, she knelt next to the wooden box and studied its exterior. There were identifying marks on two sides as well as on the lid, but they were written in what looked like Chinese and she couldn't understand the message. She tested the lid, and it yielded easily. Inside, she found an odd mixture of objects: several tall candles, a box of stick matches, several cans of something also labeled in Chinese and a journal or ledger, all carefully arranged on top of a folded woolen blanket.

A blanket! Dumping the other items into the bottom of the crate, Linda yanked the blanket out and wrapped herself in it. She rubbed her arms vigorously and huddled inside the blanket until her swimsuit-clad body returned to a more comfortable temperature.

Once she was warm, Linda examined the remaining contents of the crate more closely. The cans appeared to contain food – at least they were sealed at both ends like a can of fruit would be in the United States. The cans themselves were painted flat gray and stenciled in black – were they military food rations?

Linda removed the journal, replaced the crate's lid and moved to the table where the light was better. She couldn't read the journal's entries, but they appeared to be transactions of some sort. The leftmost column contained what she guessed was a date. Next, a wide column stretched most of the way across the page – possibly a description. The two right-hand columns seemed to be pluses and minuses or debits and credits because each row had symbols in one column or the other but never in both. The two columns appeared to be totaled at the bottom of each page and the totals were carried over to the first line of the following page.

As she sat, casually flipping through the cryptic pages of the journal, Linda was jolted back to reality by the sound of the voice she had heard earlier. It seemed to be coming up through the grate from somewhere below her. She froze and listened as the voice barked, as if keeping a cadence. The words changed but the voice was monotone and the rhythm even. He's counting! Somewhere below her, someone was counting out loud!

Sitting in the center of the room under the light fixture, Linda felt suddenly exposed and vulnerable. She clutched the blanket tighter around her shoulders and barely breathed. When the counting finally stopped, there was a brief exchange between Counting Man and another male and then she heard what sounded like the crackle of a two-way radio. This was followed by the sound of a heavy metal door closing and then silence.

She considered fleeing back out the door and up the tunnel to the cave at the end of the inlet, but she knew it would be dark by now, and it was probably high tide, as well. Being trapped in the cave wasn't any better than being trapped in this room, so she eyed the ladder and its round hatch. She had no idea who or what was on the other side, but it appealed to her more than the darkness of the cave and a night in the cold. Tucking the journal into the waistband of her swimsuit, she tossed the blanket over her shoulder and climbed the ladder. At the hatch, she listened for a moment and then operated the lever and pushed up.

Keeping one hand on the lever, Linda slowly eased her head up through the opening, ready to retreat and slam the lid shut at the slightest sound. The room above had concrete walls and a concrete floor. It was almost entirely filled with a huge piece of machinery that was connected to two large pipes – one that disappeared down through the floor and another that exited through the ceiling. Behind the machinery, a stairway led to a floor above.

She crawled out of the hole, closed the hatch and rotated a handle on the top of the round door that seemed to latch it shut. She wrapped the blanket round herself again, clutched the journal in her left hand and started for the stairway. Just as her bare foot touched the first step, the machinery behind her burst into action and, in a panic, she bolted up the stairs to the floor above. She stopped just long enough to notice that she was in a service area along with a number of mops, brooms and other janitorial supplies. The stairs continued up, away from the loud machinery, and so did Linda.

The ground floor of the building was deserted and dark, except for an exit light over the door and one florescent tube left on for security. Linda had passed two small offices after exiting the stairway and the main area she now stood in appeared to be some sort of control room. Two office chairs were neatly positioned at a semi-circular console that held several large gauges. A row of lighted push buttons stared back at her through the dim light. The machinery two floors below still hummed and created a low frequency vibration in the floor.

She moved to the door and looked for any sign of an alarm system. She didn't know if there was any connection between the building she now stood in and the voice she had heard far below, but she didn't want to take any chances – especially since she had "liberated" the journal.

Satisfied that the building wasn't wired, Linda pushed on the door's horizontal bar and stepped into the warm Yonaguni evening. She checked the door to make sure it had locked behind her and crossed the small gravel parking lot toward a driveway that led away from the building. Glancing back over her shoulder, she saw a large metal tank standing behind the building and guessed that the facility and its machinery might be a pumping station constructed to provide fresh water to the neighboring area from a well or some other underground source.

The short driveway connected to a secondary gravel road that apparently connected to a main road off to her right, because she could hear the occasional sound of tires on pavement. Sticking to the extreme side of the road so the sharp gravel wouldn't cut her bare feet, Linda headed off toward the sound of civilization.

***

After an hour in the water, Tony and the Japanese divers had finally returned to the boat. While the crew stowed the gear, Tony briefed Frank on the results of the search.

"Well, there's a cave down there, alright!" exclaimed Tony as he slipped off his air tank. "And it's a big one, too, but there were no signs of the speedboat or Linda and the opening to the cave is completely underwater, so the boat couldn't have gotten in anyway."

Frank shook his head. "Damn it! We must have lost them on the way over here. Otherwise, Takamura's other boat would have spotted them. We're going to have to search every inch of the coastline on this end of the island, but that will take time and Linda …"

"Frank, I'm worried about her, too, but it's going to be dark soon and we need to get this boat and its crew back to town. Once Riko explained to the other divers that we were looking for a female comrade, they all volunteered to help and Takamura has offered unlimited use of his boats, but we can't do anything until daylight tomorrow. These waters are just too dangerous for us to be out here in the dark."

"I know, I know, but Linda …"

Frank's words were interrupted by shouts from a diver working at the rear of the boat. He was pointing up at the top of the cliff Frank had descended earlier.

"There's somebody up there waving at us," shouted Tony. "Can you make out who it is?"

Frank pulled Tony's bag up from behind his injured leg and offered it to the other man. "Are your binoculars still in here?"

Shocked at the sight of the bag, Tony replied, "Shit! In all the excitement I'd completely forgotten about that. Did anybody else …"

"No, it was under the bench over there, hidden between dive bags. I don't think anybody got into it, but you do know what would happen if we got caught with this stuff, right?"

"Yeah, and I'm sorry about that. It won't happen again."

Tony took the bag and, with his back to the others, he removed the binoculars and handed the bag back to Frank.

"Maybe you should hang on to this for now," he smiled. Raising the binoculars to his eyes, he scanned the cliff top. "It's Bill, and he seems to be pretty excited about something. It looks like he's pointing back toward the east end of the island."

"Maybe he's found Linda!" shouted Frank as he started to get up. His knee was feeling better but the effort to stand reminded him that his injury was serious and the return of the pain forced him back to the bench.

Still staring through the binoculars, Tony thought he saw a dark figure appear behind Bill and then the young man vanished. Tony lowered the glasses and scratched his head.

"What is it?" demanded Frank. "What's going on up there?"

"I don't know. One second he was jumping up and down like a crazy man and the next second he was gone. I'm pretty sure I saw someone come up behind him just before he disappeared, but it's hard to tell in this light."

"That was probably Jim. Didn't Riko tell us that Takamura sent Bill back out to pick up our poor sick professor?"

"Maybe," mumbled Tony as he scanned the cliff top again, "but this person looked bigger than Jim."

"Probably just the light," shouted Frank as the boat's high performance engines roared to life and pushed the bow up out of the water.

As the boat picked up speed, Tony handed the binoculars to Frank and turned his attentions to his new friend, Riko. Frank shifted his position, wincing at the pain in his knee, and raised the binoculars to his eyes, hoping to spot something – anything – that would provide a clue to Linda's whereabouts.

In the fading daylight, Takamura kept the boat as close to the coastline as he could without running the risk of hitting one of the many rocks that reached up through the water. He had the boat throttled back to a moderate speed and two of his crewmembers were positioned on the bow to help scan for obstacles. The rest of the crew had settled onto the bench seats that ran the length of each side of the rear portion of the boat.

Suddenly, Frank yelled, "Stop! Stop the boat!" and began pointing to a small beach that had just come into sight. "There's somebody over there and they're waving at us!"

Riko relayed the order to Takamura, who immediately slowed the boat and changed course toward the beach. Tony and Riko joined Frank on the port side of the boat and the rest of the crew leaned over the starboard side. All eyes were on the beach, but no one could see Frank's mysterious waver and Tony suggested that maybe Frank was just imagining things.

"No, damn it, I know I saw someone on the beach flagging us down. Keep looking – it could be Linda!"

A shout from one of the men on the bow brought the engines to an idle and Frank felt the boat shift into reverse to stop their forward motion. He looked to Riko for an explanation.

"The water's too shallow. We can't go any closer. Shinji will swim in to look."

The words had no sooner left her mouth than there was a splash on the other side of the boat and a swimmer began moving smoothly toward the shore.

Frank and Tony took turns watching through the binoculars, but the sun had set and it was difficult to make out much detail on the beach.

During one of Tony's turns with the binoculars he suddenly handed them back to Frank and said, "By God, you're right! I see someone, too," and without another word he was in the water and swimming like an Olympic athlete toward the shore.

Smiling at a surprised Riko, Frank said, "He's got to stop doing that."

Minutes later, Tony and the diver named Shinji had helped a tired and wet, but otherwise healthy, Jim Barnes aboard the boat. Apparently, in his excitement at seeing the boat, he had tripped over something on the beach and knocked the wind out of himself. Now fully recovered, he was babbling something about a tomb, a strange underground workshop and a network of caves that had led him to the beach.

One of the divers offered Jim a large towel, which he used to dry his head and then drape over his shoulders.

"Slow down, Jim. One thing at a time. First of all, where is Bill? We thought we saw the two of you back at the cliff just a few minutes ago."

"Nope, it wasn't me. I haven't seen Bill since he and your crazy captain left me along side the road earlier this afternoon."

"Didn't he come back for you?" asked Tony, haunted by the image of Bill standing at the edge of the cliff with a dark figure behind him.

"Well, he might have," smiled Jim sheepishly, "but I'm afraid I strayed away from the road a bit."

On the way back to the marina, Jim described his afternoon adventure, beginning with the tomb in the cemetery and ending with his rescue from the beach. He wasn't used to being the center of attention and he enjoyed watching the crewmembers hang on every word as Riko translated his narrative.

Jim finished his story with the question of the day: "Any word on Linda?"

Frank shook his head sadly. "No, nothing. Nobody's seen her since we jumped into the water for our dive in the inlet. They must have had her down in the cabin when we were chasing the speedboat, because Tony had his binoculars on them a couple of times and there was no sign of Linda. We're going to pick up the search near the cliff at first light tomorrow. Takamura has offered both his boats and the entire crew to help us find her."

"Well, count me in, too," said Jim. "I'm not much of an outdoorsman, but at least I can be another set of eyes and ears. But what about your leg? Shouldn't you see a doctor before you go out tomorrow?"

"It's my knee, actually, and it will have to wait until we find Linda. I probably won't be doing much hiking, but you and I can shadow the coastline in one of the boats and direct the others toward likely spots to search."

"Sure, I'll do anything I can to help," nodded Jim.

When the boat slid up to the wharf at Sonai Marina, Frank noticed the hotel van parked nearby. As the crew threw lines to tie up the boat, the van drove out on the wharf and stopped right beside the boat.

"Boss call hotel for you," explained Riko. "We go visit Mito now and meet here in morning." And then to Tony, she said "One hour."

As she disappeared over the side and up the wharf, Frank and Jim looked at Tony.

"What?" he said, louder than necessary. "Mito is her cousin and she's really worried about him."

"Tony, she's half your age, for God's sake. What's going on in an hour?" asked Frank in a disapproving tone.

"Oh, that! Riko has offered to take me back to the cliff where I saw Bill. I'm afraid that if we wait until tomorrow morning any trail will have gone cold. I'm sure I saw someone up there with him and it obviously wasn't Jim."

"What do you expect to find in the dark?" pressed Frank.

"Riko suggested taking along some high-powered underwater dive lights so I can have a quick look around. If I don't see anything, we'll look again in the morning but I can't just sit here in the hotel and do nothing with both Linda and Bill out there somewhere," huffed Tony in frustration.

"Okay, sorry. I understand how you feel. This has been one hell of a day for all of us and I'm really sorry I got us into this mess. Let's get back to the hotel and rustle up some food. Then we can work out a plan for tomorrow."

Frank's knee actually was feeling a little better, but it still wouldn't support his weight so when they arrived at the hotel Jim and Tony put his arms over their shoulders and helped him hop though the main entrance.

As they entered the lobby, Frank was saying, for the tenth time, "They'd better not hurt ... LINDA!"

Frank's eyes lit up and then started to tear as he saw Linda, dressed in a bright print sundress, sitting on a loveseat opposite the door.

"How did you ... what the ... are you all right?" stammered Frank.

Tony's jaw dropped and Jim left Frank leaning against Tony on his good leg and raced to give Linda a big hug.

"My God, woman, we thought you had been kidnapped! Where have you been?" he asked as she broke free and grabbed Frank's dangling right arm to keep him from falling.

"Stranded on a beach, thanks to these two idiots," she replied in mock anger. "Why the hell did you guys take off and leave me on the shore this afternoon? You won't believe what I had to go through to get back here!"

Tony and Linda moved Frank to the love seat and eased him down onto the cushions. Because of the elastic wrap he couldn't bend his knee, so they propped his foot up on a small table. Linda sat next to him and the other two dragged chairs to the opposite side of the table. Almost as if on cue, they all started to talk at once.

Laughing, Frank held up his hand. "Hold it, hold it. Let Linda talk first and then we'll go around the table. But I need some food and a good stiff drink. Tony, can you see what the desk clerk can do for us? I don't feel like hopping down the street to a restaurant."

While Tony made arrangements for food, Jim dashed up to his room to change into dry clothes. When he returned to the lobby, he was dressed in khaki shorts and a t-shirt – much more casual attire then any of them had ever seen him wear.

By the time Linda had finished her story, the van driver had returned carrying a large tray with an assortment of local dishes. They had been prepared "*Amerika-jin*" style, he promised, and Frank hoped that meant that the fish was cooked, not raw. The driver also had a one-liter bottle of Sake and four tiny cups.

Grateful, Frank reached for his wallet, but the driver waved his finger and said, "No, no. Hotel pay for food. You enjoy."

As the driver walked away, Frank pulled a soggy $100 bill out of his wallet and held it up. "I guess this money has been sufficiently laundered."

"So where is this journal you found," asked Jim, bringing the conversation back to the events of the day.

"I have it locked in my suitcase upstairs. Do you want me to get it?" she replied, starting to get up.

"No, leave it for now," said Frank. "None of us can read it anyway, and it's safer where it is. If it's really a journal of drug deals, like you think, we'll need to be very careful whom we show it to until we find out just who it belongs to. Tomorrow, after we locate Bill, I'd like to pay this pumping station a little visit."

While they ate, Jim described his discovery at the cemetery and the adventure that resulted. When he produced the eight-sided, rough disk, Frank's and Tony's eyes widened.

"That's a *tsubute*," whispered Tony. "Or at least it will be, when it's finished. Just like the one we found in front of the hangar back home. Put that away before somebody sees it!"

Jim and Linda knew about the discovery of the *tsubute*, of course, but they had never seen it because it had been given to old Mr. Yamato the same day it had been found. Yamato had also told them that a secret Ninja sect called the Genji had made the *tsubute* in the 12th century right here on Yonaguni.

Frank laid his head back against the back of the loveseat. "Does anybody else think it's just a little strange that both Jim and Linda would stumble across underground caves and hidden rooms on the very same day at opposite ends of this island? Is it possible that Yonaguni has a secret it's trying to hide?"

"Do you mean something other than a 9,000-year old sunken monument and a bunch of Ninja warriors that were supposedly exterminated 900 years ago? Hell, I'd say this place is the very definition of secret," laughed Tony sarcastically.

The speculation was interrupted by the appearance of Riko in the hotel's doorway. She looked visibly shaken.

"What's the matter, Riko?" asked Tony, standing to offer his chair. "Has something happened to Mito?"

"No, it's Bill. Some teenagers found him near the viewpoint at the east end of the island. Tony … he's dead!" she said, bursting into tears.

Chapter 15

"Dead?" questioned Tony. "What do you mean he's dead? What happened?"

Riko was sobbing uncontrollably and Tony put his arm around her shoulder to comfort her. He led her to the other side of the lobby and let her cry.

Frank was in shock. Only a couple of hours ago Bill had been standing on a bluff at the east end of the island, waving to him.

"My God," he said, shaking his head. "He had his whole life ahead of him." He laid his head back on the couch and put his forearm over his eyes.

Stunned, Jim put his elbows on his knees and rested his head in his hands. Linda just starred at the floor, remembering how their new friend had always seemed so full of positive energy.

When Tony rejoined the group, they all looked up and realized that Riko was gone.

"Does she know what happened?" asked Frank, finally breaking a long silence.

"Not exactly. She's devastated and embarrassed that you all saw her cry and she asked that you excuse her. That must be a cultural thing. Anyway, all she knows is that some local teenagers went out to Agarizaki observation point just before sunset and when they peered over the wall, they saw a body on the rocks below. They raced back to town and notified the authorities, who are attempting to recover the body right now. Apparently a volunteer firefighter who was lowered down from the observation point wall knew Bill personally and he radioed up a positive ID.

"And that's not all. It seems that Bill and Riko had been secretly dating for several months. She was one of his English students but she knew her family wouldn't approve of her relationship with an "off-islander", so they kept the whole thing a secret. She's heartbroken, obviously."

"Of course," sniffed Linda. "I'm so sorry for her. Is there anything we can do?"

"Not at the moment, but I took the liberty of offering her anything we might be able to provide. I hope that was all right …"

Frank dismissed Tony's question with a hand gesture. "Of course, Tony. Anything we can do. Where is this Agarizaki place, do you know?

"Riko told me it's at the very tip of the island, not far from the cliff where you hurt your knee and where we saw Bill waving to us. Obviously, Riko and I won't be going out there tonight, but I want to be out there tomorrow morning at first light to look around because I still think I saw somebody behind Bill just before I lost sight of him."

"Tony, what are you suggesting?" asked Jim in disbelief. "When you said he was found on the rocks, I just assumed he had fallen."

"Well, apparently that's what the authorities are assuming, too, Jim. At least that's what they told Riko."

"And we shouldn't say anything to the contrary," warned Frank. "Not based on a figure you may or may not have seen. This is a very small community and a rumor like that would spread over the entire island in an hour. If Bill's death were the result of foul play, of course we'll notify the appropriate people. Until then, we need to keep this to ourselves, agreed?"

"Sure, Frank, but I still want to go to there and check it out for myself. These local lawmen wouldn't know a crime scene if it bit them on the butt."

"Fine, Tony. All I'm asking is that you keep your suspicions to yourself until you have some hard facts. Since Takamura was willing to put his entire operation at our disposal to look for Linda tomorrow, maybe we can charter one of his boats for the day under the guise of searching for that mysterious speedboat we chased. That would give you a reason for being down near this Agarizaki place. I think I'll stay here in town and see if I can talk to the Sheriff, or whatever he's called. Maybe I can learn more about what happened from him. I'm also going to call Fitz and Susan and have them bring the plane back down here."

Looking at Jim and Linda, he added, "What do you two want to do?"

Without the slightest hesitation, Jim said, "I'm going with Tony. After what I saw in those caves today, I think there's a lot more to this place than meets the eye."

In response to Tony's glare, he added, "I'll stay out of the way, I promise."

"What about you Linda" asked Frank.

"I've had enough of the outdoors for a while. I think I'll stay with you, Frank. Besides, you're going to need a nurse for the next day or two."

Linda's comment lightened the group's mood momentarily, and Frank suggested they all retire for the evening to recover from the events of the day. Frank's room was on the second floor but with the help of both Tony and Jim he was able to make it up the stairs. On the way past the hotel desk he stopped to thank the clerk who had secured their dinner and insisted that he accept a substantial, if not damp, tip even though he knew tipping was not normally done in Japan.

The next morning Tony and Jim left the hotel early and were long gone by 8:30 a.m. when Linda knocked on Frank's door.

"Come in," he shouted from the bathroom. "It's unlocked."

Linda pushed the door open and entered the room. Frank had asked for an extra large room (the hotel called it a "suite") with a small table and chairs in case the four wanted to have private meetings. Linda could see from the tray on the table that Frank had already had breakfast.

"Have you been up long?" she asked.

Frank opened the door and hobbled out of the bathroom.

"Yeah, since about 5:00 a.m., I guess. I met with Tony for a few minutes before he and Jim took off." Indicating the table, he said, "Tony brought up some coffee and pastry from downstairs. Help yourself if you want. There's a clean cup over there somewhere and I think there's still a couple of rolls in the basket."

"Thanks. How's your knee this morning?"

Frank was wearing khaki walking shorts and his leg was wrapped in the Ace bandage again.

'Oh, it's still pretty tender, but I can get around if I take it easy. There's some discoloration, so I think it's just a bad sprain. Last night I was afraid I'd torn the ACL, but it feels better this morning, so I don't think it's that serious. I would like to find a pair of crutches, or at least a cane, though. We have an appointment with the local police chief at 9:30 a.m. and the hotel is going to run us over there in the van, but maybe after that we can find a clinic or local doctor. And the plane should be here about noon.

"How about you? Did you sleep well after your big adventure yesterday?"

Linda sat down at the table and poured a cup of coffee.

"No, not really. I was plenty tired, but I was – and still am – so upset about poor Bill that I didn't sleep very well. I can't help feeling that we are somehow responsible for what happened. He was out there looking for Jim and if Jim hadn't wandered into that cemetery, maybe ..."

"It's not Jim's fault, Linda. If it's anybody's fault, it's mine. The only reason Jim was out there alone in the first place was because he, Bill and Takamura were racing back to town to check on Takamura's injured diver and Jim got sick. If I hadn't foolishly rappelled down that cliff, I would have been with Jim and none of this would have happened."

"But if Tony hadn't leaped into the water, the Japanese diver wouldn't have gone after him and he wouldn't have gotten injured in the first place. There's plenty of blame to go around, so don't be too hard on yourself, either."

"Yeah, I guess you're right, but ultimately it's my responsibility. I'm the one who talked you all into coming over here in the first place and I'm the one who recruited Bill to help us. Damn it!"

Linda helped Frank into a chair at the table and then, standing behind him, she massaged his tense shoulders.

"I'm sure some good will come from all this, Frank."

The meeting with the local police chief was interesting, to say the least. The middle-aged man, who was actually a member of the Yaeyama Islands Police Bureau, spoke passable English as a result of being educated on the main island of Okinawa.

Frank explained why he and the NWIDI team happened to be on Yonaguni and how they had met Bill. He told the Chief that they had been diving that morning and that Bill had driven back out to the point to check out something they had seen on their way back to the marina. He chose not to mention the separate underground facilities Jim and Linda had discovered or the cave that Tony and the other divers had found just north of the point.

The chief acknowledged that Bill Ito's body had been recovered from the rocky shoreline below Agarizaki Point the night before and that, for now, the death was being ruled accidental.

"The young people who first discovered the body thought he had fallen out of the boat, but the injuries to the body clearly indicate that Mr. Ito fell from the observation area up on the cliff. He was well liked here on Yonaguni, and he will be missed."

Frank nodded and then did a double take.

"Wait a minute. What did you say about a boat?"

"Well, the young man who first reported the body told me there was a boat in the water not too far from where the body was found. He just assumed that the body on the rocks had been the victim of a boating accident."

"What kind of boat? Was it still there when Bill's body was recovered?"

"I'm afraid I don't know, Mr. Morton. Our first concern was with a rescue and then, once we knew the victim was deceased, our efforts were concentrated on recovering the body. By then it was too dark to see any boat, but to be honest, we really didn't look once it was determined that Mr. Ito had fallen from above."

"Listen, Chief, it's really important that I find out what that boat looked like. How soon can you get a description from the witness?"

"I'm afraid that won't be so easy, Mr. Morton. The young man told me he had plans to be on the morning ferry for Ishigaki and asked if it was still okay to go. I felt that I had all the information I needed, so I gave him permission to travel. The ferry left at 8:00 a.m. and it won't arrive in Ishigaki until nearly noon. Why is this boat so important to you?"

Admitting that he had left out a few details, Frank described the chase of the previous day, when they thought Linda had been kidnapped, and the mysterious disappearance of the boat somewhere near the east end of the island.

"So that's what Mr. Ito really went out there to look for, wasn't it? But since there wasn't actually any kidnapping, I don't see why that boat should be of any interest to you now," said an impatient chief. "However, if there's a chance that the occupants of this boat saw anything that would shed light on Mr. Ito's death, I'll have one of my associates on Ishigaki meet the young man at the ferry dock and get a description."

"I'd really appreciate that, Chief. And, of course, if any of the folks in my group can be of assistance, please don't hesitate to call. We'll be at the hotel a couple more days, at least. We only knew Bill for a short time, but we felt like he was a part of our team."

Frank asked if any arrangements had been made to transport Bill's body back to the U.S, and the Chief shook his head.

"We haven't been able to contact his family yet, but the body will have to go back to Okinawa first, if it is to be transported back to the U.S. We don't have the proper type of shipping containers here on the island and it would have to go there anyway, to meet a connecting flight to the U.S."

"Our plane will be arriving this afternoon, Chief, and I'd like to make it available for the transfer to Okinawa. That's the least we can do. I'd offer to transport the body all the way back to the States, but our little jet doesn't have enough fuel capacity for a direct flight. Here's my cell phone number – please call me when you're ready to make the move and I'll put the plane at your disposal."

The Chief accepted the paper and thanked Frank and Linda. Pointing to Frank's leg, he told them about a local doctor whose office was just a few doors down the street.

When the doctor opened his door and saw Frank leaning on Linda with his leg wrapped in a bandage, he waved them into his small house and offered them seats in his combination living room/exam room. As he carefully unwrapped Frank's knee, he babbled away in Japanese. Frank and Linda looked at each other and laughed – the Chief had neglected to mention that the doctor didn't speak English!

Fifteen minutes later, after much gesturing and nodding of heads, Frank and Linda left the doctor's house with the understanding that the injury wasn't too serious and would not require any further medical treatment. Frank also had a pair of old, well-worn crutches that the doctor had produced from a closet. They were too short for Frank's 6'2" body, but they were better than nothing and at least he could get around without assistance. The doctor had left the ACE bandage off the knee so Frank could bend it to manage the crutches.

As they moved slowly down the side street toward the hotel, Linda reflected on her experience of the previous day.

"What do you suppose is up with that water pumping station I discovered yesterday, Frank? Whoever works there must know about the hatch that leads down to the room where I found the journal. The thing wasn't even locked, for God's sake!"

"I've been wondering about that myself. If your suspicions about drug trafficking are correct, somebody here on the island must be involved. It's hard to believe that any secrets could survive in a place this small, but something's going on, that's for sure."

"And I'll bet that boat you guys chased yesterday is involved, too," added Linda. "I didn't mention it back at the police station, but the man who seemed to be in charge was holding a gun – a pistol of some kind – and barking orders to the others. They seemed to be interested in what Takamura's boat was doing in the inlet and then all of a sudden they turned tail and shot out of the inlet like a rocket. By the time I realized you guys were out of the water, Takamura had started the engine on that monster boat of his and you guys couldn't hear me yelling from the shore."

"Yeah, sorry about that, but when I couldn't find you onboard, I assumed they had grabbed you and all our attentions were focused on catching them. They probably saw our bubbles, or maybe even us, returning to the boat and decided to get out of there."

"You never did tell me what Takamura wanted to show you in that inlet. Did it have to do with the Monument?"

"In a way, yes. During our dive at the Monument, Takamura pointed out some symbols, like hieroglyphics, on a rock. They were covered with green algae and weren't visible until he scraped a spot bare.

Later, he showed us the exact same markings on the inside of a hole in the rock wall that makes up the cliff face at the end of the inlet. With all the excitement that followed the dive, I never got around to asking him why he thought the markings were so significant."

"A hole? You mean like the entrance to a cave? Maybe the cave under that room I discovered?"

"Well this hole was only about two feet in diameter, so I wouldn't call it an entrance, but I'm sure it connected to something inside because there was cold, and probably fresh, water streaming out into the inlet. My guess is that it's the end of an underground stream or something."

"Of course!" shouted Linda. "That's the running water that I heard down there! And that explains the pumping station up above – its source of water is that stream."

"Possibly, but that still doesn't explain the voices you heard. If you were in a semi-secret room, two stories below the pumping station, why would anybody have been even further down in a cave. And how did they get in there? They obviously didn't gain access through the pumping station, or you would have seen them leave."

"Strange, huh? We need to get somebody to translate that journal. It may provide a lot of answers. And what about the underground workroom Jim found below the old tomb in the cemetery? Do you think they're connected?"

"If by 'connected' you mean physically attached, I doubt it. It's quite a distance from where you were to the cemetery, and

Mt. Urbu is right between the two. But if you mean logically connected, well that certainly seems possible."

"Mt. Urbu?" asked Linda, almost laughing. "Is that what they call that little hill?"

"Hey, I didn't name it, but that's what it's called. Tony and I noticed it when we were studying a map this morning. It's the highest point on the island – a whopping 231 feet above sea level! Another interesting thing that we noticed is that the mountain is exactly due north of the underwater Monument."

"Or the Monument is due south of the mountain," mumbled Linda as they reached the hotel. "So what's next, boss? I'm guessing that a 10k run is out of the question, right?"

"It is for today, smart-ass. And so is diving, at least for me. I'd like to know more about that cave system that Jim discovered, but I'm in no shape to be crawling around on the rocks. Jim told us that once he left the workroom he ran as fast as he could toward the sound of the ocean, but he indicated that there were lots of side tunnels. I'd like to know how extensive that system is and who's using it. It's too risky to go down through the tomb entrance again, but if Takamura would be willing to take Tony and Jim back out to the beach, maybe they could back-track and do a little reconnaissance."

"Frank, let me go with Tony," pleaded Linda. "After my adventure yesterday, I'm dying to find out what's going on out there and I'm in better shape than Jim is. The two of you can make arrangements for Bill and see what you can find out about the pumping station."

"Well, I'll leave that up to Tony, but I'm guessing he'd rather have you as a companion than Jim – I know I would," laughed Frank as they entered the hotel lobby.

Tony and Jim were sitting in the same place where they had discovered Linda only last night. Tony laughed when he saw Frank's too-short crutches, but quickly wiped the smile off his face when he caught Frank's glare.

Frank eased into a chair across from Tony and asked, "So what did you two find?"

"Nothing," answered Tony. "Absolutely nothing. No signs of a struggle, no torn pieces of clothing, nothing. We checked the observation area, where Bill's body was found, and the other point, where we last saw him from the boat, but there was nothing out of the ordinary in either place."

"Well, I guess we may have to resign ourselves to the fact that he actually fell, like the local police think. Did you see any sign of a boat near the observation point? Apparently one of the kids who spotted the body on the rocks reported that there was a boat not too far away."

"Boat? What kind of boat?" Tony's eyes got big. "That would be just about where we lost those guys yesterday, wouldn't it?"

"That's what I thought, too, but our friendly police chief failed to get a description of the boat before he let the kid leave the island. He's trying to remedy that oversight as we speak."

Frank told Tony and Jim about the morning visit to the police station and his idea about investigating the cave complex that Jim had discovered. As he expected, Jim insisted on being part of the "away team" and finally won when he convinced the other three that he was the only one with any first-hand knowledge of the caves.

Frank suggested that the four of them retire to the table in his room to discuss strategy where they wouldn't be overheard. While Tony and Jim helped Frank up the stairs, Linda ran ahead to fetch the journal from her room.

When they were all together again, Frank and Tony studied a map of the northern shoreline while Linda showed Jim the journal.

"Can you read it?" she asked after a couple of minutes.

"No, but I'm pretty sure it's not Japanese. It's not Korean, either. It could be Chinese but I'm out of my league there."

Frank looked up from the map and asked, "Didn't these islands have their own language before they were absorbed by Japan?"

"Yes, that's absolutely right!" replied Jim. "And I think it was derived from the early Chinese dialects. Everything from the island of Okinawa south was originally called the Ryukyu Islands and was independent from Japan several different times. In fact, the Americans controlled this area from just after World War II until the early 70s."

"Jim, the journal?" reminded Frank.

"Oh, yes. Well, it's possible that this is ancient Okinawan, all right but I'm not sure how we can verify that without tipping our hand. I assume we're not supposed to have this, right?"

"Jim, you're beginning to catch on to our methods," laughed Tony. "I don't think we should ask Riko, at least not for a few days, and our only other ally on the island is Takamura. Unfortunately, he doesn't speak enough English to be much help."

"He might fool you," cautioned Frank. "A couple of times on the boat yesterday I had the impression he understood a lot more than he was letting on. But that said, I'm not ready to share this with him either."

"What we really need is a way to get this analyzed off the island by someone who wouldn't associate it with either us or Yonaguni," suggested Jim.

"I offered to transport Bill's body back to Okinawa on our plane, so maybe we could send the journal back at the same time and have somebody look at it there. Jim, do you have any contacts in this part of the world?"

"Not that I know of, but if I can make a call back to Seattle, maybe I can get one of my colleagues at the University to track down a local expert."

Frank picked up his satellite phone and just as he was handing it to Jim, it rang. Frank answered the call, but he said very little during the course of the conversation. When the call ended, he handed the phone to Jim and said, "Crap!"

Looking at the other three, Frank explained his frustration.

"That was our local police chief. He says he now has evidence that Bill was murdered and that we're all confined to the island until further notice."

Chapter 16

"What kind of evidence?" Tony asked.

Frank shook his head. "He didn't go into details, but he said something about a medical examination, so I assume it has to do with bruises on the body or some such thing. I'll try to find out more this afternoon, but he also wants us all in his office at 9:00 a.m. tomorrow morning for questioning."

"Well, I guess that rules out taking the journal to Okinawa," frowned Jim, handing the satellite phone back to Frank.

"Not necessarily. Go ahead and make your call, Jim. Although he has confined the four of us to the island, the Chief has also accepted my offer to fly Bill's body back to Okinawa, so he must not be extending his travel restrictions to Fitz and Susan. I can slip the journal to them and they can get it into the necessary hands."

Jim moved across the room to make his call while the other three discussed the plan to explore the cave system that led from the ancient tomb to the beach on the north side of the island.

Tony leaned back in his chair. "Frank, I could cover a lot more ground without Jim and Linda and I wouldn't have to worry about baby-sitting them, either. I think I should go in alone."

"Not a chance, mister," objected Linda. "You guys didn't let me go on the dives yesterday, and I'll be damned if you're going to make me sit this out. I'm going, and that's that!"

Frank nodded his agreement. "And Jim has first-hand knowledge of the caves. Besides, Tony, six eyes are better than two. Just be careful and stay together. I'll hang out here in town and see what I can turn up. You three can help me back downstairs and when the plane gets here I'll make the necessary transportation arrangements with the Chief."

When Jim was off the phone he wrote a name and telephone number on a piece of paper and handed it to Frank.

"This is a professor at the University of the Ryukyus in Okinawa. He's a good friend of one of my associates back at the University of Washington and he can be trusted to keep quiet about the journal. He'll be expecting the call from Fitz."

"Thanks, Jim, I'll pass this on to our pilots when they land. Now I think you three should head down to Takamura's place before he changes his mind about making his boat available. I suggest swim wear for the trip ashore – they can't get the boat very close to the beach because of the rocks."

An hour later, Frank's satellite phone rang. Fitz and Susan had arrived with the Learjet and were waiting at the airport. Frank brought them up to date on the events of the past few days and apologized for offering their services to fly Bill's body back to Okinawa that same afternoon.

"Sorry about the short turn-around, but I promise that when you get back we'll show you around the island. I'll see if the hotel van can come out and get you right now."

Frank convinced the desk clerk to rent him the hotel van and its driver for the rest of the day on the condition that both could be recalled if needed for other hotel business. With the driver's help, Frank climbed into the front seat and they headed for the airport to pick up Fitz and Susan.

The NWIDI Learjet was parked on the tarmac near the small Yonaguni terminal building and Fitz waved from the open cabin door as the van carrying Frank pulled up next to the plane. Frank managed to get out of the van by himself and hobbled over to the steps leading up into the plane with a small backpack slung over one shoulder. Seeing Frank's condition, Fitz rushed down the stairs to help, but Frank waved him off and passed him the backpack.

In a low voice, so as not to be overheard by the van driver, Frank said, "There's a journal in this bag that needs to go back to Okinawa with you and it's very important that nobody knows you have it on board. I'll tell you more later, but for now just trust me and hide it somewhere."

Without saying a word, Fitz nodded and dashed back up the stairs and into the plane. A second later, Susan came down to join Frank, followed closely by the couple's dog and constant companion, Sandstrom.

"How are you feeling?" asked Susan with a look of concern. "Fitz said you fell over a cliff."

"Well, not quite, but there was a cliff involved and I did take a fall, that's for sure. I'll tell you all about it over lunch," laughed Frank, indicating Fitz coming down the stairs. "We'll eat before we go see the local police chief and discuss your unpleasant task for this afternoon."

Frank asked the driver to take them to a restaurant where the three could talk privately and he recommended a place near Nanta Beach that had an outdoor patio and was popular with western tourists. When they arrived at the restaurant, the driver introduced Frank and his party to the host, who happened to be a distant relative, and then excused himself to refuel the van, promising to return in 45 minutes.

During lunch, Frank explained the need for secrecy regarding the journal Linda had found and detailed her adventure in the underground room.

"So you think this thing may document drug transactions, huh?" asked Fitz, checking over his shoulder to make sure no one was close enough to hear.

"Well, it certainly seems possible. Linda found it in a small wooden crate along with a blanket, some cans – possibly food – and some candles and matches."

"It almost sounds like a crude disaster preparedness kit," suggested Susan as she slipped Sandstrom a piece of chicken under the table.

"Yes, or a camping box," nodded Fitz. "Maybe that room Linda found is somebody's hideout. That would explain the door and tunnel leading in from the beach of a secluded inlet."

"True," agreed Frank, "but what about the ladder leading up to the pumping station? Unless, ..."

Frank stopped in mid-sentence as the waiter brought the check to the table and cleared away the remaining dirty dishes. When they were alone again, he continued.

"Unless the pumping station provides a way to get off the island secretly."

Susan shook her head and indicated the view from the patio with a wave of her arm. "Why in the world would anybody want to sneak away from a paradise like this?"

"Well, I don't know, but there's something strange about this place, and I've felt it ever since I first set foot on the island. And I'm not the only one, either. This morning Tony told me that he thinks we've being shadowed by someone in a black Mercedes sedan. Apparently he's seen it in the distance almost every place we've gone."

"Of course he did! A car that big would be visible from everywhere on this little dot of land," laughed Fitz. "Is that our driver over there?"

Frank glanced in the direction Fitz was looking and nodded. "I guess it must be time to go. Don't discuss anything about the caves or the journal in front of him, okay? We're trying to keep this to ourselves for now."

As Fitz was helping Frank into the van, he suddenly froze and pointed to a small parking lot across the street.

"Ah, Frank, is that the sedan you were talking about?"

Frank looked up just in time to see a black S-class Mercedes with tinted windows disappear around the corner. He considered asking the driver to follow the car but a glance at his watch reminded him that the police chief would be waiting for them.

When Frank, Fitz, Susan and Sandstrom arrived at the small police station, the chief was on the telephone with someone but he waved them into his office and motioned for them to have seats in front of his desk. As he replaced the receiver, he bowed slightly to Fitz and Susan and took a seat behind his wooden desk.

To Fitz, the chief said, "I assume you are the pilot that has agreed to transport the body of poor Mr. Ito over to Okinawa."

Fitz nodded. "Actually, my wife and I are both licensed pilots and we will be making the trip together, but yes, we'll be handling the transportation at the request of our employer, Frank Morton."

Susan showed just a hint of a smile as she listened to her husband openly challenge the Japanese man's chauvinistic perceptions.

"Ah, yes, well, be that as it may, I'm afraid I must insist that one of my officers accompany you and the body since the death has now been ruled a murder rather than an accident. I assume you have no objections to that arrangement?"

"Of course not, as long as it's okay with Frank. After all, it's his aircraft."

The chief looked to Frank as if challenging him to deny the request.

"I have no objections, chief. As I told you this morning, my team and I are willing to do anything we can to help. But I'm curious about what made you change your mind. Last night you thought Bill's death was an accident. What makes you think he was murdered?"

The chief leaned back in his chair and said smugly, "I'm afraid I can't discuss evidence in an ongoing murder investigation, Mr. Morton."

Frank shrugged. "How about a description of the boat you promised to get for me? Have you managed to catch up with the young man who now appears to be a material witness in a murder investigation or is he still running loose with your blessing?"

The chief glared at Frank. "As a matter of fact, I do have a description of the boat, but as I said, I can't ..."

"Yeah, I know, you can't discuss evidence with me. Well let me guess what the boy told you. The boat was a high-powered inboard capable of inter-island travel. It had a dark colored hull, possibly blue or green, with a light colored deck and interior. It was between 28 and 30 feet – about 9 meters – long with a closed bow and a ship-to-shore or CB antenna mounted on the right side, just forward of the windshield. How am I doing so far, chief?"

The other man just grunted, but Frank could tell by the expression on his face that the boat seen in the water near Bill's body was the same one they had chased half way around Yonaguni the day before.

"And I'll let you in on another little secret, my friend," continued Frank. "I have an eye witness who can testify that the men who were using that boat yesterday were carrying handguns. I believe that's illegal in Japan, isn't it?"

The chief's eyes widened slightly and leaned forward. "Mr. Morton, I'm quite aware of Japanese law and I don't need you to ..."

Frank was losing his patience. "I think you do, chief, and I think you need our help, too. There's something wrong on this island and I think you know it. And now you have a corpse on your hands – an American corpse that's sure to result in an investigation at the highest levels of both your government and mine. Now, we can work together and figure this out before those investigators get here or you can face them alone with no more information than you have now. It's your call."

The chief slumped back into his chair and closed his eyes. Not until Frank stood to leave did the tired man speak.

"All right, Mr. Morton, perhaps you're right. I'm a simple man with limited training and I've just been trying to get by until the end of the year when I can apply for my government pension. I took this assignment two years ago because nothing more serious than the occasional drunk-and-disorderly ever happens on this island of 1,200 souls. When my superiors learn that there has been a murder here, they'll come swarming to Yonaguni and they'll have a lot of questions – questions for which I don't currently have any answers."

Frank eased himself back into the chair and tried to put on his most sympathetic face.

"In that case, chief, I propose that we work together. Now, what can you tell me about a large black Mercedes sedan that we've seen around the island?"

***

"Damn it, Jim, I told you to stop wandering off!" shouted Tony as he retraced his steps to look for the anthropologist again. The other man had wandered off for the third time since they entered the caverns.

Takamura's crew had dropped Tony, Jim and Linda off on the same beach where they had found Jim after his discovery of the secret room beneath the ancient tomb. They each carried a small backpack and Tony had borrowed three underwater flashlights from the boat. The lights had the brightness and reach of an automobile headlamp, making navigation through the vast underground complex relatively simple – when they stayed together.

"Jim!" shouted Tony again. Where are you?"

"I'm down here. You guys have got to see this!" Jim's voice came from far down one of the dozens of side tunnels they had encountered.

Tony turned to Linda. "I want you to stay right here and do not wander off, do you understand? If we get separated in these tunnels we'll never find each other again. I'll go fetch Jim and be right back. If you hear me calling, just call back so we can keep our bearings. Do not follow me, okay?"

"Yeah, yeah, yeah, I get it Tony. Geez, you're really a crab when you're underground."

"Well, I think Frank would be pissed if I lost one of you down here, although I can't for the life of me see why. Here, take care of my bag – I'll be right back."

Tony had traveled about a hundred feet down the winding tunnel before he spotted Jim's light playing back and forth on the rock. He opened his mouth to scold Jim again, but before he got a word out he saw what Jim was studying so intently. A portion of the tunnel wall had been smoothed flat and Jim was running his fingers over a series of about three dozen Chinese-looking characters that were carved into the wall.

"What the hell ..." uttered Tony. "Where did all this come from?"

"I'm not sure," whispered Jim. "Do any of these look familiar to you?"

Tony stepped closer and used his own light to illuminate the entire grouping.

"No, should they?" he asked.

"I think this is the same style of writing we saw in Linda's journal last night," replied Jim, almost to himself.

"I suppose it could be, but this stuff all looks the same to me. I have a digital camera in my backpack, but I left that with Linda. You stay right here and I'll go back … Oh, shit!"

Tony turned to start back down the tunnel and ran right into Linda.

"Damn it! You scared the crap out of me, Linda! I thought I told you to stay back in the main tunnel so we could find our way out of here!"

"Give me a break, Tony. You three guys are always running off and leaving me behind. From now on, I'm going where the action is. And by the looks of this wall, I'd say this is the place. Here's your pack – let's get some photos."

While Tony retrieved the camera and photographed the wall from several angles, Linda joined Jim, who was examining one of the characters near the floor with a jeweler's loupe.

"What are you looking for?" she asked in a whisper.

"I'm trying to figure out what kind of tool or implement was used to inscribe the rock," he replied. "Sometimes you can date this kind of find by knowing what type of tool was used to create it."

"So what's the verdict, Professor?"

"Well, I don't have one, yet. All the characters I've looked at so far seem to be almost too perfect. See, look here Linda. The curved portion of this line appears to be perfectly smooth rather than the series of small straight lines you'd expect from something cut with a chisel. And look over here! The tiny groove that makes up this line is exactly the same depth, from the top to the bottom. This doesn't look like it was done by hand at all."

"Could it have been done with something like a metal stamp and a hammer?" asked Tony as he joined the other two. "You know, like the kind used in leather working."

"Sure, I guess that's possible, but it would have been quite a project because there are so many unique characters in the message."

"And I suppose there's no way to date it, is there?" asked Linda as she stood back and rubbed her arms with her hands. "Brr, it's cold in here."

"No, but if Tony's theory is correct, it would mean this wasn't put here until metal working was commonplace, so that might help narrow down the timeframe. When we get back to town, I'll do a little research and see if ..."

"Shhh," hissed Tony, pointing back down the tunnel the way they had come. He quickly turned off all three lights, leaving them in total darkness and holding their collective breath.

They all listened intently for a minute and then Tony turned his light back on and relaxed. "Sorry, I thought I heard a noise, but it must have been my imagination. Let's get back to the main shaft and continue on the way we were headed. We're supposed to be looking for an entrance into Jim's room below the cemetery, and we know it's not in this direction."

"Tony, can I just have a few minutes?" protested Jim as he switched his own light back on and pointed it at the floor. "The reason I started down this branch in the first place was because the floor here seems to be well worn, indicating a lot of foot traffic. That pattern continues on, so let's follow it just a bit farther and see if we find another one of these murals. The more of this writing we record, the more likely we will be able to decipher it later."

Tony started to shake his head, but Linda joined the protest and soon the trio was heading farther into the complex and away from the cavern that opened onto the beach.

The floor remained smooth, but the ceiling gradually got lower and after about five minutes they came to a "Y" in the tunnel. Tony, the tallest of the three, could no longer stand upright and he decided he had had enough.

"Okay, that's it! We haven't found anything else of interest in this direction and this is as far as we go. Let's make our way back to the main tunnel and see if we can find that room with the *tsubute* factory in it."

Jim started to protest again, but Tony would have none of it, turning Jim around by the shoulders and prodding him back in the direction they had come.

"If you would like to mount a scientific expedition to explore the caves of Yonaguni, be my guest, but that's not our task for today. Now move it!"

Grumbling and shuffling his feet like a scolded child, Jim started back down the shaft, followed by Linda, with Tony bringing up the rear. When they reached the spot where Jim had discovered the glyphs on the wall, he stopped for a last look and Tony held his tongue, knowing that it was difficult for the anthropologist to pass up the opportunity to explore this place.

Sympathetically, Linda patted Jim on the shoulder and said, "Maybe Tony has a good idea, Jim. Maybe the exploration of these caves could be your research project for this year and satisfy your obligation to the University. I'll even offer to be part of your team, if you'll have me."

The prospect of returning to explore the caves when and where he wanted lifted Jim's spirits and he and Linda chatted away until the shaft rejoined the main cavern that led to the beach.

Up ahead, Tony spotted what looked like a brightly colored cloth on the sandy floor of the chamber. "It looks like you dropped something, Linda."

When she reached the object, Linda picked it up and examined it.

"It's a scarf, Tony, but it's definitely not mine. I guess you did hear something earlier, after all. Apparently we're not the only ones interested in this place."

Linda handed the scarf to Tony, indicating a small label in the corner.

"And it's from the U.S., too. I recognize this brand."

"Okay, we have to assume we're not alone in here, so let's move very slowly and very quietly," cautioned Tony in a whisper. "And stay together!"

As the other two moved forward, Tony partially unzipped his pack and withdrew his Beretta automatic. After checking the safety, he slipped the handgun into his waistband and covered it with his loose shirt.

***

"Oh, crap!" exclaimed Aya Yamato as she and her companion approached the heavy wooden door that led into the underground workroom. "I had a scarf tied around my hat and I must have dropped it back there somewhere. "

"We can pick it up on our way out, Aya-san," replied the large man as he opened the door. "This way please."

Inside the large cold room, Aya shivered and squinted from the bright light that had come on automatically as they passed through the door. The room was bigger than she had imagined and when she saw the steep stone stairway climbing up one wall, she pointed to it and asked, "Where does that go?"

"It opens into Yonaguni's oldest cemetery, Aya-san, but it's too risky to use during the day. Especially now, with these Americans snooping around."

"I agree, of course," nodded Aya. "The secrets of this ancient place must be protected at all cost. Now show me these amazing rubies I've heard so much about."

Chapter 17

Once the local police chief, whose family name turned out to be Sato, accepted Frank as an ally, information flowed like water. Frank and his flight crew soon learned that the doctor who had examined Bill's body the night before and officially pronounced him dead had discovered a tiny cut at the base of the skull. Further testing this morning had confirmed that Bill had been killed by the deadly poison *bufo marinus*, probably introduced into his body by whatever created the slit on the back of his neck. The doctor speculated that Bill was already dead before his body was thrown over the cliff at Agarizaki Point.

Frank wrinkled his brow. "I learned a little about Asian poisons when I was in 'Nam, but I've never heard of this *bufo marinus*, Chief. What is it?"

"The *bufo marinus* is a large toad found only here in the southern islands of Japan. The poison is made from a fluid extracted from just behind the creature's eyes. Death is almost instantaneous, even from a tiny amount of the poison, and it was a favorite of the ancient Ninja warriors. They often applied it to darts, arrows and throwing stars."

"And *tsubutes*?" questioned Frank.

The chief's eyes widened in surprise. "Well, yes, I suppose so," he stammered, "but how is it that you know about such a thing?"

Frank told the chief about the murder outside the Seattle hanger and the subsequent discovery of the *tsubute*. When he got to the part about it being stolen from the display case at Aya Yamato's martial arts studio, the chief's jaw dropped.

"She's here, you know," he blurted out. "Aya Yamato arrived on yesterday's flight from Okinawa."

"Really! Now that's a coincidence, isn't it? Do you have any idea where she's staying while she's on the island?"

He nodded. "I assume that she'll stay at her uncle's house on Mt. Inbi. It's a large estate on the other side of the island. Yamato-san is a powerful man on this island and he owns most of the land between Mt. Inbi and Mt. Yonaguni."

Frank rubbed his chin and tried to recall the map of the island that he and Tony had studied.

"That wouldn't by any chance include the water pumping station up on the hill behind town, would it?"

"Yes, of course. Yamato-san built that facility to provide fresh water to the island many years ago. The people of Yonaguni owe him a great debt."

"Yes, I'm sure they do. Listen, Chief, I'd like to discuss the Yamato family with you some more, but how about if we get the plane headed back to Okinawa first, so Fitz and Susan can hand off the casket before dark?"

"Of course. I'll call the doctor and ask him to meet us at the airport. The three of you can ride with me, if you like."

By the time they reached the airport, dark clouds were visible on the northern horizon and the air was hot and humid.

"Looks like a storm is brewing," commented Fitz, as they climbed out of the chief's small car. "We may not make it back tonight, Frank."

"That's up to you, obviously, but once you get to Okinawa, give me a call on the satellite phone and let me now what your plans are. And please don't forget my package."

The doctor and a uniformed policeman were waiting at the Learjet in a small minivan. As soon as they saw the Chief's car pull up, they began unloading the casket containing Bill's body. Fitz opened the Learjet's door and lowered the stairs. With some effort, the five men were able to position the casket in the aisle between the seats and anchor it in place with rope so it wouldn't slide if the plane pitched steeply up or down.

Once Fitz was satisfied that the cargo was secure, he helped the policeman settle into the seat nearest the cabin door while Frank, the Chief and the doctor returned to the tarmac. When the cabin door was latched, the three men returned to their vehicles and moved out of the way.

"I take it this is the first time your assistant has been in a private jet," smiled Frank, remembering the look of utter surprise on the man's face as he sunk into the supple leather seat of the Learjet.

"It was my first time, too, Mr. Morton. It's a very impressive aircraft – and very expensive, I would imagine."

"Normally, yes, but I was able to acquire that baby at a greatly reduced price thanks to a friend who works for the government – the U.S. Government, that is. Someday I'll tell you all about it over a cup of Sake but right now I'd like to hear more about your Mr. Yamato. Would you mind driving by his place on our way back to your office?"

As the chief drove, he explained that the Yamato family had been on Yonaguni for as long as records had been kept – and probably much longer.

"There's a cemetery on the road out to the point where Bill's body was found that contains many very old tombs and the oldest one of all belongs to the Yamato family. You're aware of the significance of the family's name, are you not?" asked the chief.

Frank shook his head, so the chief explained.

"The word 'Yamato' has been around as long as Japan has – in fact it was Japan's original name. The Yamato peninsula is located on the southwestern tip of Honshu – that's Japan's big island – and it was in this area that cultural influences from the mainland first came to Japan about 200 A.D. The earliest known Japanese state was ruled by Yamato kings around 500 A.D. and their court was based on a Korean aristocracy model that emphasized military supremacy."

Frank raised his eyebrows.

"But Yonaguni is a long way from the main island of Japan and 500 A.D. was a long time ago. You're not suggesting that there's a connection between your local resident and the kings of ancient Japan, are you?"

"No, of course not, but the Yamato family did control this entire island as recently as 100 years ago and the current patriarch is still treated like nobility by many of the island's elders."

Chief Sato slowed his car and pointed to a small structure about a hundred yards down a lane that joined the road to his left. The concrete single-story building was capped with the traditional red tile roof common on the island and it sat on the crest of a small hill. A high iron gate stretched across the lane from the gatehouse to a stone column on the other side of the road.

"That's all of the Yamato estate that can be seen from the road. The rest of the structures are on the other side of the hill and are only visible from the sea. I've never been past the gatehouse but I hear the view is magnificent."

"Yes, I'm sure it is. You're not originally from Yonaguni, Chief, so how do you feel about the Yamato family and their hold over the people of this island? Does anything about it strike you as out of the ordinary?"

"I'm not sure what you mean, Mr. Morton. Out of the ordinary in what way?" The Chief glanced in his mirror and eased the slow moving car closer to the side of the road.

"I think you know exactly what I mean. From the moment we first landed on this island, my comrades and I have sensed something dark, maybe even sinister. No specifics, just a gut feeling. Is there something going on here that you're not telling me about?"

The Chief glanced in his mirror again and his expression changed to one of concern. Just then a black Mercedes sedan roared past and disappeared over a small hill ahead. Visibly shaken, the Chief slowly brought his car back up to speed.

"Let's start with who owns that car and why you're so obviously afraid of them," demanded Frank.

***

Tony, Jim and Linda rounded a bend in the wide tunnel and Jim spotted the heavy wooden door up ahead. He almost shouted out his excitement at finding the entrance to the workroom he had discovered the day before. In fact, he probably would have shouted out except that Tony had also spotted the door and in the same instant that he saw Jim's arm rise to point, he instinctively clamped his hand over the other man's mouth from behind. The quick movement startled Linda, but, thankfully, she remained silent. Tony turned Jim so the two were nearly nose to nose and, holding the index finger of his free hand to his lips, he slowly released his grip on the other man's mouth. Using simple hand signals, Tony made his two companions understand that they were to follow him and remain absolutely quiet.

As they approached the door, they could hear at least two voices engaged in what sounded like an argument. Tony guided Jim and Linda back behind a large bolder and signaled for them to stay put. As Tony inched closer to the door, he could make out some of the conversation coming from the other side.

"I don't care what Tanaka-san told you! Matsuki-san is in charge now and I'm telling you to give me one of those stones." It was a female voice.

"But Tanaka-san was very specific. He said none of them were to leave this room until more is learned about them. He said they could be very dangerous!" the male voice insisted.

Tony crept as close to the thick door as he dared and listened.

"Tanaka doesn't support your family, my uncle does, and I want to examine the stone from one of those ancient *tsubutes*. Now be quick about it or you'll be answering to Haruki Matsuki and the other Genjis."

There were noises from inside the room that sounded like something heavy being moved and then a long period of silence. Tony made his way back to the spot where he'd left Jim and Linda and signaled for them to be quiet and follow him. Once they were back around the bend in the tunnel, Tony answered his two companions' questioning looks in a whisper.

"It sounds like two people, a man and a woman. They were arguing over some sort of stones that has been ... removed, I think they said ... from ancient *tsubutes*. The woman wanted to take one with her and the man was trying to convince her that it was too dangerous."

Jim started to speak, but Tony held up his hand to stop him.

"Sorry, Jim, but we need to find a place to hide until they leave that room. Once they're gone, we'll do a little exploring of our own. Very quietly, move a few yards down that side tunnel behind you and stay down. I'm going to find a hiding spot out here where I can get a visual on them when they come by and as soon as the coast is clear, I'll come and get you."

After he was sure that Jim and Linda were out sight, Tony carefully climbed up onto a large boulder at the side of the main shaft and found a vantage point that would allow him to see the man and woman just after they passed his position. The line of sight was such that they would have to turn and look back in his direction in order to see him.

A few minutes later Tony heard the large wooden door bang shut and the sound of talking as the two approached. Tony tensed his muscles, ready to spring into action if it became necessary. As the pair passed his position, he raised his head just enough to see the sides of their faces. The man's head was in a partial shadow, but Tony mentally noted as many features as he could. Asian male, about 5' 10", lean build, all black clothing and carrying a stout bamboo staff in his right hand. Tony's eyes darted to the woman and he almost gasped out loud. It was Aya, the daughter of the old man back in Seattle who had identified the *tsubute* found near the NWIDI hanger! Tony had only seen her once, as she was getting out of her convertible in the parking lot of the martial arts school, but there was no mistake – it was definitely Aya Yamato.

Tony held his position for a couple of minutes after he could no longer hear the voices of the retreating pair and then he retrieved his companions. As they made their way back toward the large door, Tony related his observations to Jim and Linda.

"What would she be doing here?" asked a surprised Linda. "What on Earth are the chances of that?"

Remembering the conversation with the old man, Tony snapped his fingers and said, "Of course! The man we met in Seattle is Aya's father and he told us he was born on Yonaguni. She must have relatives here."

As they approached the door, Tony signaled for silence again. He examined the door and the wall surrounding it for signs of an alarm system or booby traps but he didn't find anything suspicious.

He looked back over his shoulder at his two charges and whispered, "Ready?"

Jim and Linda both nodded and Tony carefully slid back the heavy metal latch that appeared to be the only mechanism securing the door. Tony gave the door a pull and the ancient metal hinges let out a creak that sounded deafening in the relative quiet of the Yonaguni underground. They all froze in their tracks for a moment, heads cocked, listening for any sign that Aya and her companion might be returning.

Satisfied that they were still alone, Tony stepped through the threshold and was nearly blinded by the bright ceiling lights that flashed on.

Following Tony through the doorway, Jim said, "Oh, yes, I should have warned you about that. I think the lights are on some sort of sensor." Pointing to the steep stone staircase to his right, he continued. "When I came in from up there, the lights clicked on about the third step down and scared me so bad I almost fell off the stairs."

"Where do they go again?" asked Linda, looking at the staircase Jim had pointed out.

"There's a trap door at the top that's actually the lid of an old tomb in the cemetery where Bill took us our first day here. I discovered it quite by accident and once I started down those steps it closed automatically. My only way out of here was the door we just came through and from there I ran until I stumbled out onto the beach where Frank and Tony picked me up."

Tony was searching the room, carefully inspecting the few objects that it contained.

"What are you looking for?" asked Jim.

"After the woman demanded the stone, I heard what sounded like a heavy object being moved. I'm trying to find their secret cache."

"Everything looks exactly like it did when I was here before," mumbled Jim, as he scanned the room.

To his left, lined up down the long wall, were the three rough, wooden workbenches where he had seen metal disks – *tsubutes*, he now knew – in various states of manufacture. The far end of the room was almost entirely consumed by a large fireplace that apparently served as a makeshift forge and the wall to his right held the stairs leading up to the cemetery above. The staircase seemed to be chiseled out of the solid rock that made up the wall, rather than being attached to it.

"The only thing that's changed is that the flashlight is gone, and that's because I grabbed it just before I ran out the door and down the tunnel. It was on top of that electrical box."

Jim pointed to an electrical panel attached to the wall just to the right of the door.

Tony stood up and looked at Jim. "Did you say 'flashlight'? With all the lights they've installed in here, why would they need a flashlight? Unless …"

"Unless there's another chamber!" finished Jim. "The sound you heard must have been a door opening – maybe a stone door."

Without any further discussion, the three began carefully inspecting the walls of the room. Running their hands over every square inch of the surface, they searched for secret panels, hidden actuator buttons and even hairline cracks in the surface that might indicate a doorway. After about ten minutes, Tony finally called a halt to the search.

"Folks, we're getting nowhere fast but there has to be a simple solution to this because I heard that scraping sound not ten seconds after the woman demanded the stone. Jim, you said the flashlight was on this electrical panel, right?" asked Tony as he approached the one-foot square metal box attached to the wall. Three electrical conduits entered the top of the box and Tony visually followed one of them back up the wall and across the ceiling to the light fixtures. Another went directly up to and through the ceiling, presumably a connection to power from the outside, and still another ran along the wall beside the stone staircase and up to the tomb lid. That left one final piece, which exited the bottom of the box, ran straight down the stone wall and disappeared into the floor.

Pointing to the last conduit, Tony smiled and said, "I think what we're looking for may be below us."

Feeling along both sides of the box, Tony located a latch, and then gently pulled on the right side of the box until the hinged front panel swung open. Inside, amidst a tangle of colored electrical wires, Tony found a push-button switch heavily wrapped in black electrical tape to keep its connections from coming in contact with the metal box.

Glancing over his shoulder, he said, "Watch your feet, folks," and motioned for Jim and Linda to move back against the wall. He pushed the button and turned to see an eight foot long by six foot wide portion of the floor rotating on its long center axis. Tony recognized the sound as the same one he had heard earlier. When the rectangular slab of rock was perpendicular to the floor, it stopped moving and the room was once again silent.

Slowly, the three moved forward and peered down into the black hole that had opened in the floor. Tony retrieved one of the borrowed underwater lights from his backpack and shined it into the abyss to the right of the vertical stone slab that now split the hole.

"A stairway!" shouted Jim, digging in his pack for his own light. "Let's check it out!"

"Hold on there, Indiana Jones. We're already a long ways behind enemy lines and we have no idea when Aya and her friend might be back. One of us should stay up here as a look-out."

Tony looked from Jim to Linda, waiting for a volunteer.

"Don't look at me," said Jim. "If there are any more writings on the walls, I'm the only one qualified to identify them."

"And I've already told you that I'm not going to be left behind again," declared Linda. "If you want a look-out, Tony, I guess it's going to be you."

"Right! With the track record you two have for getting lost in caves, I'm sure as hell not letting you go down there alone. Okay, we'll all go, but take it slow and don't get ahead of me. We have no idea what we're getting into."

Jim started down first, followed closely by Linda. Tony held back to take a long look around the workshop.

From below, Jim shouted, "Oh my God, you guys! Look at this!"

Tony hurried down the stone steps and as soon as his head dropped below the level of the floor, the bright lights in the workshop clicked off, plunging the room above into total darkness.

"What was that!" cried out Linda from the bottom of the stairs.

"The lights seem to be on some kind of automatic circuit that turns them off whenever the room is vacant," replied Tony. "I really think you should wait up there and let Jim and I check this out. What if ..."

Before Tony could finish, the heavy door started rotating and the lower edge of the slab forced him to jump out of the way to avoid being struck.

As the slab clanged into its closed position, sealing the three into the chamber, Tony continued.

"As I was saying, what if this door is also on an automatic switch and it traps us down here!"

Chapter 18

It was just after 4:00 p.m. when the NWIDI Learjet rolled to a stop on the tarmac at Naha International Airport on the island of Okinawa. The storm Fitz and Susan had monitored on their flight from Yonaguni was now no more than a few minutes west of Okinawa and it was promising to be a bad one. The clouds were taking on an evil black color that reminded Susan of her childhood in Oklahoma's "tornado alley" and the air was warm, heavy and moist.

"I assume we're not going back tonight?" she asked her husband as he finished up the last of the post-flight checks.

Fitz looked up at the sky through the Learjet's cockpit windshield and shook his head. "Nope! In fact, I think we should see if we can rent hanger space for the night and get this bird out of the weather. I don't know much about Asian storms, but back home a sky like this would deliver large hail stones – or worse."

The Fitzgerald's dog, Sandstrom, had been asleep in his bed behind Fitz's seat when he suddenly jumped up and started barking, something he rarely did. An instant later, there was a knock on the cabin door.

Susan started to get out of the right pilot's seat, but Fitz put his hand on her arm and said, "I'll get it. You stay here with Sandstrom and see if ground control can arrange that hangar space."

As he left the cockpit, he closed the door and checked to make sure it had latched. Having a dead body, even Bill Ito's, inside the plane was giving him the creeps and he laughed at himself for being such a wimp.

Fitz nodded to the Japanese police officer in the seat next to the door. He didn't bother speaking because he was pretty sure the man didn't speak English and Fitz only knew a few words in Japanese. There was another knock on the cabin door just as Fitz turned the latch. As he started to open the door, it was ripped out of his hands and flung in violently. Two uniformed men stormed into the cabin and almost knocked Fitz to the floor. Behind the two men, a ferocious wind scattered loose papers all over the cabin.

Using his entire weight, Fitz pushed the cabin door shut and latched it. As he turned, his two visitors bowed deeply and then looked up in embarrassment.

"Please excuse our entrance!" apologized one of them in a heavy accent. "There is a storm approaching."

Smiling, Fitz nodded. "Yes, I can see that. I assume you're here to pick up the body?" he asked, pointing to Bill's casket roped into the Learjet's center aisle.

"That is correct, but I don't think we can safely move it until the wind decreases. We will ..."

His sentence was interrupted by a sudden jerk of the plane. At first Fitz thought the wind had caught a wing and an image of the Learjet lying flat on its back flashed through his mind, but he quickly realized that they were taxiing. The look of terror on the faces of his three Japanese visitors told him they hadn't figured that out yet.

Holding up his finger to indicate the number one, he said, "I'll be back in just one minute."

Inside the cockpit, he bent down to look out the front window. "I take it you found us a parking space with a roof?"

Susan nodded. "Yeah, sorry about not giving you any warning, but when I heard you close the door, I decided to make a run for it. The tower said we have about ten minutes to get to shelter and then this area is going to get pounded. They've closed the runway, so we got in just under the wire. How's our passenger doing?"

"Passengers – there's now three of them, and they were all a little surprised when you decided to go joy riding! Where are we headed?"

"It should be just ahead. The hanger is supposed to have a number six ... there! I see it just to the left."

As they approached the hangar, a large door swung out and up, exposing an empty bay. It had already started to rain hard and a short man in orange coveralls was waving wildly at them.

Susan aligned the nose wheel with a yellow stripe that was barely visible through the standing water outside the hangar and kept her eyes on the orange man as she eased the 43-foot wide aircraft into the hangar. When he held up his arm and made a fist, she hit the brakes hard and shut down the engines. Almost immediately, they heard the sound of the big door closing behind them.

"Nicely done, my dear," remarked Fitz. "Can you parallel park it, too?"

The three Japanese men were more than a little surprised when they saw a woman and a dog follow Fitz back into the main cabin.

Noticing their reaction, Fitz smiled and nodded at Susan. "Oh, don't worry, she wasn't driving." He pointed casually to Sandstrom, who was staying close to his side, and continued, "The dog was."

Fitz's attempt at humor was apparently lost on the men, because the one with the accent just nodded and said, "Of Course." Looking out the window, he wrinkled his brow and asked, "What is this place?"

Fitz explained the rapidly worsening situation outside and the arrangements Susan had made for temporary shelter. The man with the accent translated for the other two, who nodded their approval silently.

"So we should remain here?" asked the English-speaking man as he looked nervously back and forth from the casket to the door.

"For the time being, yes. I need to take my dog out into the hangar before he has an accident, but I'll be right back. While I'm gone, maybe Susan could offer you some refreshments from the humble supplies we have on board and we'll just wait out the storm. When things settle down, we can unload the casket and you can be on your way."

Fitz opened the cabin door and lowered the stairs to the cement floor. Sandstrom was eager to get out of the plane, so Fitz let him run on ahead before the poor dog's kidneys burst.

While Sandstrom was taking care of business, Fitz did his normal post-flight inspection of the aircraft. He felt very fortunate to have landed the flight crew job with Frank Morton and his friends. There was always enough money to keep the plane in top-notch condition and Frank was a generous employer. In return, Fitz cared for the Learjet like it was his own.

The hangar was a dozen feet wider than the Learjet, maybe more, but as Fitz walked toward the rear of the craft he saw that the door opening was somewhat narrower. His eyeball guess was that there had been no more than a foot between the wingtips and the door frame when Susan had taxied in. His shock was quickly replaced with a deep sense of pride in his wife. She was one hell of a pilot!

Sandstrom returned from a dark corner of the hangar and Fitz headed back to the stairs leading into the cabin. As he poked his head through the door, Susan turned from where she had been rummaging for food in the small refrigerator.

"What's this doing in here?" she asked as she held up the journal Frank had secretly given Fitz to deliver.

The policeman who had made the trip over from Yonaguni let out a loud gasp and then uttered the phrase – *kindan no shomotsu* – the Forbidden Book!

***

Meanwhile, back on Yonaguni, Frank pressed Chief Sato about the identity of the occupants of the black Mercedes sedan that had just disappeared over the hill.

"Come on, Chief, what's going on? Who's in that car and why are you so eager to stay out of their way? If you want my cooperation on the Bill Ito murder, you've got to help me in return. That car has been shadowing my friends and me since we first arrived here, and I want to know who's in it!"

The Chief glanced in his rear-view mirror and then spoke softly, as if he might be overheard.

"The car belongs to Yamato-san, but he only uses it when he is entertaining very important guests."

"And who might he be entertaining today? Who's so important that Yamato would get his fancy German car all dusty?"

The Chief was silent for a moment, and then he whispered, "*Chugoku-jin*. The Chinaman."

"The what? Did you say the Chinaman?"

Chief Sato nodded. "About twice a year he journeys here from his home on the Chinese mainland and spends several days with Yamato-san. We always know when these visits are about to take place because Yamato-san becomes very demanding just before his guest arrives and he is disagreeable for days after his guest leaves. Then he goes back to being the withdrawn nobleman we all know until it's time for the next visit."

"Interesting," replied Frank. "Any idea who this Chinaman is, or why he has such a negative effect on Yamato?"

"All I know is that his name is Hao Zhuo and that he arrives here by private jet from Fu-Chow, China. He has diplomatic papers that permit him to travel directly from China to Yonaguni without having to go through customs in Okinawa but I haven't been able to find out any more about the man. He arrived the day before you did and, if he follows his normal pattern, he should be leaving tomorrow or the next day."

As the Chief turned northeast back toward the airport and the main village, Frank spotted the black sedan parked in the lot at the Kubura Marina, where Bill Ito had first introduced Frank, Tony and Linda to Takamura's Hammerhead Diving operation.

"There they are, in the parking lot. Who do you suppose they're waiting for?" asked Frank, looking back over his shoulder to see if the sedan would follow. It didn't.

The Chief glanced at his watch and replied, "It's about time for the afternoon ferry from Ishigaki Island to arrive. Maybe they're meeting someone."

He retrieved a small, cell-phone sized walkie-talkie from the center console of his car. After several exchanges with another man, he returned it to the console and frowned.

"The Harbor Master is going to keep an eye on the car and let me know if it picks up any passengers. That's the best I can do, since my assistant is traveling to Okinawa on your jet."

On the way back to the Chief's office, Frank directed the conversation back to the subject of Bill Ito's murder.

"So, tell me, Chief, do you have any theories about Bill's death? Any suspects yet?"

"No, I'm afraid not. For the most part, the people of Yonaguni are hard working, honest folks who have a strong sense of right and wrong, but Yonaguni is a small island that keeps its secrets very well. I've made some informal inquiries of people I know and trust but many of the older citizens still see me as an outsider and I'm certainly not part of the inner circle of elders. Still, there's a chance someone might hear something – maybe just a whisper – and pass it on to me. In the mean time, we'll pursue the traditional methods of crime scene investigation in the hopes that a clue will turn up. Any assistance you and your team can provide will be greatly appreciated."

Frank thought he detected a small crack in the Chief's attitude and he decided to jump on it.

"Well, as you probably know, we're not without our resources – both financial and physical. I assume that by now you've made some inquiries and know that Tony and I served together in a Special Ops unit in Viet-Nam. Linda is a first-rate investigative researcher, so I'll put her on the trail of the mysterious Hao Zhuo and see what she can turn up. And Jim – well, Jim seems to have a knack for discovering things that he wasn't even looking for. In fact, he's with Tony and Linda on a little field trip right now. How much do you know about the Damatu Burial Grounds?"

"You mean that old cemetery along the road to Agarizaki Point, where we found Bill's body? As I told you earlier, the oldest grave sites on the island are located out there and one of the oldest belongs to the Yamato family. But, from what I understand, that place hasn't been used in years. Most Japanese now prefer cremation and the remains are typically cared for by the family rather than being placed in a tomb. Why do you ask?"

Frank decided it was time to see just how far the other man's cooperation would go.

"Chief, rather than stopping at your office, let's drive out to the cemetery. Jim discovered something yesterday that you might find very interesting."

The local police chief wrinkled his brow questioningly but otherwise seemed unaffected by the request.

"Of course, if you wish, but I must ask what your associate was doing at the cemetery yesterday. That places him unpleasantly close to the scene of the crime, you know."

"I know," Frank nodded, "and that's one reason why I didn't mention this earlier. But I hope I can impose on you to hear me out. As you'll soon see, Jim couldn't have been at the crime scene."

Minutes later, as the chief's car climbed the hill where the cemetery was located, Frank turned in his seat so he could watch the road behind them.

"If you see any vehicles approaching us from either direction, continue on past the cemetery and don't turn in," cautioned Frank. "I have a feeling Yamato wouldn't want us poking around out here."

"I'm sure he considers it sacred ground, Frank-san, but it is a public cemetery, after all."

"Oh, I think it's more than that, Chief – a lot more."

Frank instructed the Chief to park his car on the opposite side of the cemetery from the Yamato tomb, in a spot where a clump of bushes would make it difficult to see from the road. As the two men were climbing out of the car, the Chief's walkie-talkie beeped and he answered it. When the conversation was over he slipped the device into his pants pocket and addressed Frank's unasked question.

"That was the Harbor Master. A man he didn't recognize got off the ferry, accepted a small bag from someone inside the

Mercedes and then got right back on the boat. The car has left, headed in the direction of the Yamato estate, and the ferry is just clearing the dock on its way back to Ishigaki. I asked him to call ahead and have the man followed when he gets off the ferry but I must tell you that I don't feel right spying on Yamato-san."

"Well, let me see if I can change that feeling," said Frank, waving his arm. "Follow me, Chief."

As Frank led the way through the grave markers, it was apparent that he knew exactly where he was going.

"I take it you've been here before," commented the Chief as Frank circled the large Yamato tombstone examining its sides.

"Yes, once, the morning we arrived on Yonaguni. When Bill found out we were interested in ancient mysteries, he brought all four of us up here to show us some of the older grave sites, including this one. But I'm pretty sure he didn't know anything about what I'm going to show you. Jim discovered this yesterday completely by accident."

Frank slipped his fingers under the lip of the stone lid and lifted. As the huge slab on stone swung up into the vertical position, the Chief nearly fainted.

"You must not disturb the dead!" shouted the policeman. "Please close that tomb – we must leave this place immediately!"

Frank swung his leg over the edge of the rectangular, box-like opening and placed his foot on the top step of the stairway that lead down into the secret workshop Jim had discovered the previous day.

"Trust me, Chief; there haven't been any dead bodies in this tomb for a long, long time. Follow me and I'll prove it to you."

Terrified, the Chief crept closer to the opening and just as he had summoned enough courage to peer over the side, Frank's descent down the stone staircase triggered the automatic light switch and the blackness below was replaced with the view of a brightly lit room that was obviously not a tomb.

"Hurry!" called Frank, as he continued down the stairs. "According to Jim, that lid closes automatically and I don't know how to open it from down here."

Reluctantly, the Japanese man followed Frank over the edge of the fake tomb and down the stairs backwards. He nearly fell when, about a third of the way down, the lid above started moving."

"Hold on!" called Frank. "Take it slow and don't look down. That's right, one step at a time."

As much as the man was out of his element on the staircase, he was immediately into it the second his feet were safely on the floor of the room. He carefully examined everything in sight without touching a single object.

"These are *tsubutes*!" he shouted with excitement as he approached the first workbench. "Or at least they will be when they're finished."

After examining the room, he joined Frank, near the door that led to the ocean, placed his hands on his hips and scowled.

"What's the meaning of all this? Why would Yamato-san allow something like this to be done to his family's ancient burial site?"

"I'm afraid you'll have to ask him yourself, Chief, but, like I said up above, I don't think this place has been a tomb for a long, long time. This large door opens into a network of connecting caverns that eventually lead to a beach on the north side of the island. That seems like a pretty odd thing to build into a tomb, wouldn't you agree?"

"Yes, of course, but … but I don't understand. What is going on here?" he stammered, indicating the workbenches with a sweep of his arm.

Frank took a long look around the room and then walked to the workbench on the far side of the room. It held a nearly complete *tsubute* surrounded by a number of tiny brushes and several glass beakers sealed with matching glass stoppers. All but one contained colored fluids that matched the colors on the *tsubute*. The last beaker contained a yellowish-orange fluid that reminded Frank of a urine sample.

Noticing Frank's interest in the last workbench, the Chief joined him.

Frank pointed to the last beaker. "I'd be willing to bet that this is that frog-eye poison you mentioned earlier. I'd also be willing to bet that Bill Ito was killed by a *tsubute* that was made right here in this room."

"But that's impossible!" exclaimed the Chief. "That would mean that Yamato-san is involved in …"

The Japanese man couldn't make himself finish the statement, so Frank did it for him.

"… in a murder. I'm afraid it's beginning to look that way. When Jim described this place to me it was obvious that Yamato was into something unusual, but when you described the wound on Bill's neck, the pieces started falling together. I wish we could take a sample of this fluid back for testing, but if it's as dangerous as you say, I'm not sure I even want to touch the container."

"Oh, no, Frank-san, you must not handle it! If it truly is *bufo marinus*, then it's very dangerous and even a single drop could prove fatal if it entered your bloodstream. No, we must leave here immediately and return to my office for help. I will call my supervisor on Ishigaki and ask him to alert the federal police. I'm afraid this investigation is out of my hands now."

"Well there's just one problem, Chief. Jim never figured out how to reopen the tomb's lid at the top of the staircase. Instead, he fled out the door and through the caverns to the beach where, by some stroke of good fortune, we happened to spot him while we were searching the coastline for Linda. If we make our way to the beach now, we may not be spotted for days."

The Chief started to protest but he was interrupted by a loud grinding noise. Both men spun toward the door and were shocked to see a portion of the floor moving. A large rectangular portion rotated on its central axis until it was standing vertical, half above the surface and half below. The Chief started to make a run for the door, but Frank grabbed him by the jacket and pulled him back, realizing that he would have to pass directly over the newly formed opening in the floor. Frank pulled him down behind the workbench and the two men tried to hide as best they could. They were trapped!

"Frank, is that you?" came a loud echoing voice from the hole. "We're coming up, so if you have a gun, please don't shoot us."

Peering around the end of the workbench, Frank watched as Tony's head slowly and deliberately emerged from the opening in the floor. He tensed, ready to spring into action in case it wasn't really Tony or in case Tony was being forced to emerge by some unseen enemy.

When his shoulders were above the surface of the floor, Tony slowly raised his arms over his head, joined his hands together and made a sign with his fingers that he and Frank had learned back in Special Ops training. A pair of signals was used to let comrades know whether or not you were being forced to act against your will.

When Tony gave the "OK" sign, Frank slowly stood and waited for Tony to completely exit the hole and scan the room. As the two men made eye contact, Tony's broad grin told Frank that everything was, indeed, okay.

"Man have we got something to show you!" shouted Tony, as he helped first Linda and then Jim off the last step and onto the floor's surface.

Chapter 19

As Tony, Jim and Linda moved away from the opening to the chamber below, the slab of concrete began rotating back into place. Frank started to shout, but Tony interrupted him.

"Don't worry, we know how to operate this one," he smiled. "I take it you decided to let the Chief in on Jim's accidental discovery, here."

Frank nodded. "Yes, he's beginning to realize that all is not as it appears on Yonaguni. Now, what's your big discovery?"

Tony started to answer, but Jim was bubbling over with excitement and couldn't contain himself any longer.

"It's amazing, Frank! There's even more glyphs down there than we saw on the way in, and we found this natural depression in the rock wall that has eleven ancient *tsubutes* arranged in three neat rows of four each. And the rubies are incredible, Frank, just incredible!" babbled Jim.

"Hold on, Jim", laughed Frank. "What glyphs on the way in? What rubies? And you said eleven *tsubutes* – wouldn't three rows of four be twelve?"

"It would," interjected Tony, "except one seems to be missing, and we think we know who has it. After we made our way here from the beach, reversing Jim's escape route of yesterday, we discovered that this room was already occupied so we hid just outside the door and waited. I overheard a woman demanding that she be allowed to remove a 'stone' of some kind. A male voice was trying to convince the woman that the stones could be dangerous, but she finally pulled rank and got her way. And you're not going to believe who that woman turned out to be!"

"Aya Yamato," the Chief whispered, mostly to himself. "I thought it was strange that she would arrive to visit her Uncle while the Chinaman was here, but maybe it wasn't a coincidence after all. Can you show me these *tsubutes* that you found?"

Tony looked to Frank for approval and when Frank nodded, Tony toggled the switch in the electrical panel. When the slab of rock had rotated back into its vertical position, they made their way down the narrow steps one at a time. Jim eagerly led the way, followed by the Chief and Linda. Tony motioned Frank aside and turned his back to the others.

"What Chinaman?" he asked with a shrug of his shoulders.

"I'll tell you the long version later, but apparently Yamato – that's Aya's uncle – receives a visit from a mysterious Chinese national about twice a year and the otherwise mellow Yamato becomes rather grumpy just prior to these visits. As it turns out, the Chinaman arrived on Yonaguni the day before we did and should be leaving in the next couple of days. Apparently he's the one that's been shadowing us around in the Mercedes."

"Hey, you two better get down here before that door closes on you," called Linda from the bottom of the staircase.

The stairs descended about twelve feet and ended in a small area about eight feet square. All the surfaces – floor, ceiling and walls – appeared to be made of solid rock and there was a musty smell to the place. The only light came from the flashlights carried by Tony, Jim and Linda.

A loud groaning sound from above startled everybody, especially the Japanese police chief, until Tony pointed his light up toward the closing slab at the top of the stairs.

"It's okay," he laughed. "We know how to open it from down here, too, thanks to Linda. Look over here, Frank. Jim found more of this on the wall of one of the side tunnels back toward the beach and he thinks there may be more all throughout the system of passages."

Frank followed Tony's light beam to the wall directly opposite the stairs and was shocked to see row after row of intricately carved glyphs, each about an inch tall and filling an area of more than four square feet.

"Wow!" exclaimed Frank, as he approached the wall and ran a finger over the engraved characters. "This is amazing! Any idea what it says, Jim?"

"Not yet, but I'll get started on a detailed examination as soon as we get back to the hotel. We've made digital photos of both this one and the one we found earlier and I'm sure they're not identical, so I've got plenty of material to work with. The local library has a number of books on the early history of the island and I should be able to come up with something on the origin."

"But this is just the beginning," added Tony. "Look what we found down this way."

Tony led the group down a narrow passage to the left about a hundred feet, where it made a "T" with another passage. Turning left, he looked back over his shoulder to make sure everybody was following. Frank was behind him, then Jim and the police chief, with Linda bringing up the rear. Somehow they had managed to arrange themselves so that every other person had a flashlight, so the path was well lit.

"There's a low doorway up ahead, so watch your heads," called Tony as he illuminated the arched top of an opening.

The passageway wasn't wide enough to allow the others to pass, so he went through and then pointed his light straight up at the arch, creating an eerie jack-o-lantern effect for those behind him.

The doorway opened into a low-ceilinged room. When Linda passed through, Tony resumed his role as tour guide.

Shining his light on the left, back and right walls, he pointed out the large symbols painted on each with some sort of reddish dye.

"This is a tomb!" exclaimed the police chief with noticeable fear in his voice.

"Maybe it was, but there's nothing in here now except this," replied Tony.

He turned his light to the wall behind him on the left side of the doorway. A rectangular depression in the wall created a crude display case which held the 11 *tsubutes* that Jim had mentioned upstairs. The reddish-brown eight-sided objects were about four inches wide and covered with glyphs and symbols. Even at a casual glance they appeared to be ancient artifacts, but their most striking feature was the square red stone that filled the hole normally found in the center of a *tsubute*. The stones reflected the light from the flashlights and glowed brightly. The left-most position on the top row was empty – the missing twelfth *tsubute*.

Tony reached out to retrieve one of the objects, but Frank grabbed his arm and shouted, "Don't touch that! It could be coated with a deadly poison!"

Frank quickly related the doctor's theory that Bill Ito had been killed by a deadly poison, possibly administered by a small knife blade or the edge of a *tsubute*.

"Now you tell me!" replied Tony, as he once again reached out. Selecting the *tsubute* in the second position of the top row, Tony picked it up between his thumb and index finger and turned to show it to the group.

"All three of us handled this one for several minutes and nothing's happened to us yet," he said. "And if you look closely, you'll see that while this looks like a *tsubute*, it doesn't actually have any sharp edges. And it's so light that it's unlikely it was used as a throwing weapon, either. Maybe these are just ceremonial replicas, made in the image of the real Ninja weapon – or vice-versa."

Being careful not to touch the object in Tony's fingers, Frank borrowed Jim's light and examined it closely. Not only were the eight sides not sharp, they didn't even have square edges. Instead, the edges were rounded and the overall thickness was two or three times that of the only other *tsubute* Frank had ever seen – the one he and Tony had found outside their Seattle hangar the day after the murder of the man posing as private detective Larry Schultz.

"What do you think it's made of?" he asked as he stood up and handed the light back to Jim.

"I don't know. It seems too light to be stone, unless it's sandstone or some kind of pumice, but then how do you account for the smooth, engraved surface? And it's too light to be made of metal unless it's one of those modern exotic alloys, like titanium or beryllium."

Jim stepped closer and shined his light on the very edge of the mysterious object.

"How about volcanic glass?" he asked. "I've seen some samples that are very light, smooth and strong. It just depends on what minerals were subjected to the extreme temperatures and pressures inside the volcano."

Everybody nodded in agreement, accepting Jim's theory as the most reasonable explanation. Tony carefully placed the pseudo-*tsubute* back in its place and wiped his fingers on his pants.

Jim swung his light around the room for effect and asked, "Frank, what does this remind you of?"

Frank's eyes followed the light until it came back to rest on the collection of *tsubutes*. He thought for a minute, and then it dawned on him.

"The secret cave Alfredo took us to in Loltun! The one where we found the last Mayan sphere! Jim, are you suggesting that …"

Frank was referring to a pivotal point in the NWIDI team's previous adventure where he had made a startling discovery in a cave deep in the heart of Mexico's Yucatan Peninsula.

"I know, I know, but you have to admit that there are some pretty bizarre similarities. We're in an underground chamber, these *tsubutes* are in a crude storage unit carved out of the rock wall and they're even on the same side of the room's entrance!"

"Jim, this has to be a coincidence. It just has to be. There's absolutely no reason to believe that these things, whatever they are, are in any way related to the spheres of Loltun. Isn't that true?"

Jim was lost in his own thoughts, almost trance-like, and didn't answer immediately.

"Jim?" repeated Frank.

"Yes, of course. I mean, no, there's no evidence that these artifacts have any connection to the spheres." Then, as if a light bulb had come on in his head, Jim returned to his normal, animated self. "Listen, Frank, there're some things I'd really like to check out right away. Can we get out of here and head back to town?"

"Of course. The longer we stay down here, the greater the chance that we'll be discovered and this is, after all, private property. Besides, we know how to find our way back in, if necessary."

"Let's take one of these with us," said Tony as he started to reach for the *tsubute*.

"Not yet, Tony. Right now nobody knows we've discovered this secret and that gives us the advantage. I'm sure Jim would like to have one to take back to the University of Washington, but let's wait until we get to the bottom of Bill's murder before we start stirring up the locals, okay? If one of these things turns up missing we'll become the hunted rather than the hunter."

"Then how about some close-up photos so Jim can analyze the inscriptions?"

"Okay, but be careful handling those things. I'm still concerned about this poison the doctor found in Bill's blood sample."

While Tony and Jim shot digital photos of the artifacts, Frank examined the symbols painted on the walls of the room.

"Chief, you immediately recognized this room as a tomb by these markings. What do they mean?"

The Japanese man, who had appeared nervous and on edge since entering the room, shook his head.

"I don't know what they mean, exactly. They're just symbols I've seen inside several old tombs I've been in during my career. They aren't Japanese characters, or any other language, as far as I know. They're just symbols. Are we leaving soon?"

"Yes, soon. You're obviously uncomfortable in here, Chief. Would you rather wait out in the passageway while they finish up the pictures?"

Sheepishly, the policeman nodded.

Linda was helping Tony and Jim with the photos, so Frank borrowed her light and escorted the Chief out through the low archway and into the narrow passageway.

"I assume this discovery will remain our little secret for a while, right Chief?" asked Frank, once they were out of the actual tomb chamber.

"Of course! If Yamato-san learned that I had been here it would mean my job – and my pension – at the very least. I should not have asked you to bring me down here in the first place, but my curiosity got the best of me. And now that I've seen this, and the room above, I'm afraid I may have to confront Yamato-san about it."

Frank could see the concern on the chief's face, even in the indirect rays of the flashlight beam.

"Chief, don't do anything hasty. My team has broad shoulders and maybe we can find a way to assume the role of accuser so that task doesn't fall directly to you."

Frank's offer surprised the Chief. "You'd do that for me?"

Before Frank could answer, Tony ducked through the archway and asked, "What have you volunteered us for now, Boss?"

"Nothing. You guys done in there?"

"Yep! We have front and back photos of all eleven and we also shot those symbols on the wall, too. I think Jim is starting to get a little freaked out, though. As we were taking the artifact pictures, he reminded me that he had done the same thing with the spheres at the bottom of the Yucca Mountain shaft."

"These spheres you keep mentioning," asked the Chief, "what are they? Are they also here on Yonaguni?"

"No, Chief, they're half a world away from Yonaguni, and it's a long story, better told another day," Frank laughed. He called into the chamber to Jim and Linda, "Come on you two, let's get out of here!"

The five retraced their steps back down the passageway, with Tony in the lead. When they came to the "T" junction, Tony turned right, back toward the stairway that led up to the workshop.

"What's down this way?" asked Frank as he brought up the rear of the column.

Linda, who was immediately ahead of Frank, replied, "We don't know. We walked down there a hundred yards or so earlier but we never came to anything – it just seemed to keep going so we turned around and came back. Tony said he thought it angled slightly down as it led away from here, but I sure couldn't feel it."

"Well, it must go somewhere. These passages appear to be cut through solid rock and nobody would have expended the energy to cut one unless it went somewhere – somewhere important, I'm guessing. We need to come back here when we're better equipped and do some serious exploring."

"Count me in," said Linda.

"Me, too," came Jim's voice from up ahead. "This could be the archeological discovery of the century!"

Tony had reached the small area at the foot of the stairs first and while he waited for the others to exit the passageway, he re-examined the strange mural on the wall. Suddenly his head cocked and his body instinctively froze. Had he heard a noise from above? He listened carefully and just as Frank joined the group he heard it again. It was the distinctive groan of the slab at the top of the stairway starting to open. Without a second's hesitation, Tony shined his flashlight on his own face, held his finger up to his lips for silence and motioned the others to follow him. He then turned and dashed down the passageway to the right of the stairs, opposite from the way they had just come. If whoever was opening that door was interested in the *tsubute* collection, he intended to be as far away as possible when they reached the bottom of the stairs.

The other four chased Tony, single file, down the passage until it, too, ended at a "T" junction. Forced to go either left or right, Tony chose right, taking his human chain in the same general direction they had gone to reach the *tsubute* chamber, except that they were now two hundred feet away, on the opposite side of the stairway.

Tony stopped as soon as Frank cleared the junction and once again held his finger up to his lips. He turned off his light and Jim and Frank followed suit. In the darkness, they could just barely make out the sound of human voices. Even with the natural amplification of the rock walls, the voices were too faint to be understood but it didn't sound like the speakers were trying to hide their presence, so they probably weren't aware that they had company.

In a low whisper, Tony spoke to the others in the darkness.

"We'll have to wait here and hope we hear them leave. After they've had time to get far away, we'll move back down to the stairway. That's where it'll get tricky, because we won't be able to know for sure if they've left the workshop above when we cycle the slab covering the stairs. We'll just have to …"

Tony's explanation was interrupted by a high-pitched sound.

"What was that?" hissed Linda.

"It sounded like a woman's scream," replied Frank. "Did they find something that one of us left behind?"

"No, they probably found something that we didn't leave behind," whispered Jim. "I'm sorry guys, but I just couldn't risk the possibility that we might not get back here."

Jim turned his flashlight on and shined it on his shirt pocket as he slowly eased one of the *tsubutes* out with his other hand.

"Damn it, Jim!" scolded Frank in a too-loud voice. "You may have put us all in serious danger. That's why ..."

"Shhh!" warned Tony in a whisper. "All right, everybody, on your feet. We obviously can't go back there so let's see if we can find another way out of here before we get caught red-handed. All lights off, except mine, and no talking. Frank, if anybody slows down, drag them if you have to. Let's go!"

Before anybody had time to react, Tony was moving swiftly down the passageway and the others had to run to keep up. So far the floors they had encountered in the underground complex had been perfectly smooth, but Frank worried that if one of them tripped and fell at this pace they would be seriously hurt so he periodically switched his light on and right back off taking just enough time to confirm the path ahead. At the head of the column, he could see Tony's beam swinging back and forth and up and down so he assumed his former Special Ops comrade had recognized the same danger.

After they had traveled like this for about five minutes, they encountered another "T" junction.

Tony stopped the group and whispered the single word, "Wait!" He took off to the left while the others stood motionless in the passage. Less than a minute later he returned and shook his head.

"Dead end! Interesting, but still a dead end. Let's try the other way."

He took off to the right and the others followed him. It was possible that they were trapped, and they all knew it. In addition to the anxiety shared by all of them, the short Japanese police chief was beginning to tire.

The next intersection they encountered was a four-way, the first they had seen.

"Too many choices!" exclaimed Tony. "Frank, you go right, Linda, you continue on straight ahead and I'll go to the left. Stop and come back to this spot after five hundred paces or if you come to a dead end. Do not deviate from the tunnel you start off in, understand?"

"What about us?" protested Jim.

"Well, the Chief looks like he could use a breather, and I want you to stand with your nose against the wall and whisper 'I will never steal again' one thousand times. Okay, move out!"

Ten minutes later, when Tony returned to the intersection, Frank and Linda were already there and Frank had his light standing on end so that it illuminated the ceiling.

"How'd you do? He asked as he squatted down to catch his breath.

"There's another "T" about two hundred paces straight ahead," offered Linda, "We'd either have to go right or left and there's nothing visible in either direction as far as my light would reach."

Tony nodded and turned to Frank who was holding his knee and seemed to be in some pain.

"There's another four-way intersection like this one three hundred and ninety paces out. Each short branch leads into a chamber like the one we found the *tsubutes* in except that there's no *tsubutes* and no symbols on the walls. Just bare, low-ceilinged rooms."

"Okay," replied Tony, "then I guess we go left. There's nothing this direction except passageway and if my mental compass is still working this leads in the general direction of the ocean. I'm hoping we'll either find a way out onto the beach or a way back to that original cavern that Jim, Linda and I were in earlier today – the one that leads from the beach to the workshop."

Frank bent over to retrieve his flashlight and grimaced noticeably as he stood up.

"The knee bothering you?" asked Tony.

"Yes, this little jog is definitely <u>not</u> what the doctor ordered, I can tell you that." Glaring at Jim, he added, "The stairs would have been a lot easier!"

Jim started to apologize, but Tony cut him off.

"There'll be time for explanations later. We've been here more than ten minutes, so I think it's safe to assume that we're not being followed. If we were, they would have caught up with us already."

Tony unzipped his backpack and handed Frank a bottle of water and a small paper packet containing two pills. Frank raised his eyebrows, but Tony just nodded.

"Everyone grab a drink and then let's get moving. We'll take it a little slower, for Frank's sake, but no talking in case there are others in these tunnels."

Linda shared her water bottle with the Chief and helped him to his feet. He forced a smile but it was obvious that the close quarters and the fear of being lost in the labyrinth of tunnels were wearing on him.

She patted him on the shoulder, forced her own smile and said, "Don't worry, Tony will get us out of here."

When they started off down the passageway again, she made sure to get in line behind the Chief in case he needed help. Tony led, followed by the Chief, Linda, Jim and then Frank, who had apparently assumed permanent custody of Jim's flashlight.

After they had walked for about ten minutes, Tony stopped the group.

"This is about where I got when I came down here earlier and I'm pretty sure we're on a slight upward incline. I thought so earlier, too, but I was running and my built-in altimeter works better when I'm moving slower. The workshop was slightly above sea level but the stairway took us down about twelve vertical feet. I estimate we've gained half that back, which means we could be only another ten minutes or so from the beach. How's everybody doing?"

They all grunted or moaned, which Tony took as an "okay" from everybody except Frank.

"How's that knee, big guy?"

From the back of the line Frank returned, "Don't worry about me. The pills will kick in soon. Let's just keep going and get the hell out of here."

"You heard the man," said Tony. "Move it out!"

Five minutes later, they came to another "T" junction and were once again faced with a right or left decision.

"Damn it!" exclaimed Tony. "I was hoping this would take us straight out onto the beach. We can't afford to head off in the wrong direction with Frank's knee acting up, so Linda, you take the left and I'll take the right. Same deal as before – no more than five hundred paces and then come right back here. Jim, you stay here with the Chief and Frank. Neither one looks like they're doing too well, so keep an eye on them."

When Tony and Linda had gone their separate ways, Frank eased himself down the wall and stretched his right leg out. Jim kneeled beside him and handed him a water bottle.

"Frank, I'm really sorry! I know I shouldn't have taken the artifact but after the disappointment with the spheres, I just couldn't let another opportunity slip by. Believe me, if I could undo this, I would – in a heartbeat."

Frank smiled and handed the bottle back. "I know, Jim, and it's not your fault that my leg is screwed up. I did that by acting like a kid up on that cliff. If I had ..."

Frank looked up to see Linda standing over him.

"No luck, huh?" he asked.

"Nope. Another one of those rooms just a few dozen yards down. Except this one has a mural on the back wall. What do you guys make of all this?"

Frank shrugged and deferred to Jim.

"You're the expert, Jim. What do you think?"

"Well, it's obviously a very highly organized complex, that's for sure. And these tunnels! I can't imagine how they were cut through this rock. They almost remind me of the small air shafts that have been discovered in the Great Pyramid in Egypt. Very regular shape, straight as an arrow, and somehow constructed into solid rock."

Jim's speculation was interrupted by Tony's return.

"Let's go," he puffed. "I think I've found a way out. About a hundred yards from here this passageway makes a bend – and there's daylight around that bend!"

Tony and Jim helped Frank to his feet and the five adventurers headed off with Tony once again in the lead. Linda let out a small cry of relief as she rounded the bend and spotted the proverbial light at the end of the tunnel.

The passageway widened as the light grew closer and Tony fell back to lend Frank a shoulder. The tunnel opened into the back of a huge cave, which opened onto a beach. By the time they reached the mouth of the cave, they were five abreast and totally unprepared for the semi-circle of armed men that awaited them.

Chapter 20

Frank, Tony, Jim, Linda and the Chief of the Yonaguni Police Detachment stood on the beach squinting at the four armed men facing them. The men were dressed in light-weight black trousers and long sleeved black shirts cinched at the ankles and cuffs. They all appeared to be Asian, but probably not Japanese. And they were all pointing small black submachine guns at the expanded NWIDI team.

Mentally, Frank and Tony went into defensive mode, calling on the Special Ops training they had received before their tour in Southeast Asia in the early 70s.

"Two for you and two for me," whispered Tony in Cambodian.

"Risk of collateral damage too high," replied Frank in Laotian. He indicated the three other captives to his right. "Do not engage."

"Shut up, you two," yelled the man closest to Frank and Tony. "Where's the *tsubute* you took from the crypt?"

"The what?" asked Frank, pretending not to understand what the man was saying.

Without moving a muscle, the man fired his weapon. The bullet hit the sand directly between Frank's feet.

The man raised the barrel of the gun just slightly and repeated, "Where's the *tsubute*?"

Before Frank could reply, Jim blurted out "I have it!" and pulled the stolen object from his shirt pocket. He held it out in front of himself in an open palm and one of the other gunmen stepped forward and snatched it away. Before he stepped back, he slammed the butt of his gun into Jim's mid-section, knocking the wind out of him and causing him to collapse onto the sand with a gasp.

Instinctively, Frank and Tony started to move in to help but the apparent leader of the group, the one who had fired the shot at Frank, yelled, "Don't move or I'll kill him!"

The sudden twisting motion caused Frank's bad knee to buckle, and Tony grabbed him to keep him from falling.

"Check out the boat down the beach to your right," whispered Frank when their heads were close together and his face was turned away from the gunman.

Tony helped Frank stand upright and they faced their captors defiantly.

Tony glanced to his right and spotted the blue speedboat they had chased the day before. It was anchored a little ways out from the beach and a small four-man inflatable was pulled up on the sand nearby.

"What do you know about the death of Bill Ito?" asked Frank angrily. "Your boat was seen near the place where he fell last night."

"Do you mean the American who was pretending to be an Asian?" laughed the leader. "I hear he's headed back to the U.S. in a box!"

Tony started to make a move toward the man, but Frank grabbed his sleeve and pulled him back.

"Don't be a fool, Tony," said Frank loud enough for everyone to hear.

As Tony stepped back, Frank added, in a voice that only Tony could hear, "Check out the water just this side of the boat."

Pretending to squint from the sun that was dropping into the ocean in front of him, Tony studied the water for several seconds before he spotted what Frank had seen. Only a trained eye could have spotted the tell-tale bubbles of divers occasionally breaking the surface!

Returning an angry stare to the leader of the band, Tony shouted, "If I find out that you had anything to do with Bill's death, I'll personally hunt you down and cut you wide and deep!"

The other man laughed again.

"You and your friends are going to be fish bait long before you have a chance to find out much of anything, Yankee, but just so you have something to think about on your way out to visit the sharks, I'll let you in on a little secret. Your friend, Mr. Ito, didn't fall, as your buddy seems to think. I personally tossed him down onto those rocks after administering a healthy dose of frog juice. Bill Ito couldn't keep his nose out of Island affairs and he was getting too close to some information that my superiors prefer be keep secret. When he took the four of you out to the burial grounds the day you arrived, he sealed his own fate. And he sealed the fate of all of you at the same time. Now, slowly, move down the beach to the dingy. It's time you all saw Yonaguni's famous hammerhead sharks up close."

Just as the four armed men turned toward the boat, two divers stood up in waist deep water and fired spear guns. They disappeared back into the water before the stunned men could react and the middle two gunmen crumpled to the sand with spears protruding through their backs. Tony lunged at the gunman on the far right and hit him from behind, smashing him into the sand, face first. In a quick, fluid motion Tony grabbed the man's head and twisted until his neck broke.

Frank charged for the leader, but his knee gave way and he fell. The leader raised his gun and pulled the trigger, but the police chief lunged between the gunman and Frank and took the bullet in his side, just above his waist.

Before Tony could react, the surviving gunman grabbed Linda by the hair and pressed the barrel of the weapon to her neck.

"Back off or I'll shoot her right here!"

Linda screamed and Tony froze, holding up his hand.

"Okay, take it easy, dude. Let the woman go and we can settle this right here – just you and me."

Dragging Linda by the head, with his hand over her mouth, the gunman slowly backed away from Frank, who was lying in the sand under the fallen police chief, and inched back toward the cave that connected to the underground tunnel system. The divers emerged from the water with their spear guns reloaded, but there was no way to get a clear shot at the gunman without risking Linda's life.

"If any of you follow me, I swear I'll kill her just as sure as I killed your friend Bill Ito."

The gunman, with Linda in tow, backed through the cave and disappeared into the small, black rectangle that was the entrance to the tunnel system. As soon as he was out of sight, Tony dropped on one knee to ease the Chief off Frank's bad leg and tend to the gunshot wound. Jim had recovered from his blow enough to retrieve the *tsubute* from the sand next to one of the dead gunmen and move to Frank's side. Seconds later they were joined by the mysterious divers. When they removed their masks Tony was surprised to see Takamura and the slender Riko, who had each delivered a lethal shot that probably saved the lives of the NWIDI team.

"How is he?" asked Frank as he held his leg and winced.

Tony was busy tending to the Chief and didn't answer immediately. He had torn the man's shirt open and was trying to stop the bleeding with a bandage made from his own t-shirt.

"He's lost a lot of blood and we need to get him to a hospital soon or we're going to lose him." Looking up at Riko, he asked, "How far away is your boat?"

"On the other side of those rocks, but the water here is too shallow to get close to the beach."

"We'll take their boat," announced Takamura in almost perfect English.

Frank and Tony looked at the young man in shock.

"Sometimes it's better to listen than to talk," he smiled. "Come, Riko, help me drag the inflatable down here."

The two divers ran down the beach to fetch the small craft while Jim helped Frank to his hands and knees. The Chief was drifting in and out of consciousness and Tony was trying to secure the bandage so they could move the man into the raft when it arrived. He picked up his pack from where he had dropped it when they first encountered the gunmen and rummaged around in the bottom. He produced two more packets of pills, which he tossed to Jim, along with a partially full bottle of water.

"Give them each one packet," he ordered.

When Takamura and Riko arrived with the inflatable, Tony and Jim loaded the chief and Frank in and then carried it down the beach and closer to the speedboat using its built-in rope handles. Jim climbed in between the injured men and the two divers hauled the raft off the beach and started to swim it out to the boat while Tony ran back down the beach for the three backpacks. Just as he reached his, the sound of a gun shot came from deep inside the cave.

Tony froze and listened, then quickly retrieved his 9mm Beretta from his pack.

He yelled to the others, who had also heard the shot.

"Go! Get the old man to the hospital and then come back for me. I'm going after Linda. Go! Go!"

Tony scooped up the other two backpacks, consolidated the useful contents into his own and dashed through the cave and into the tunnel entrance.

***

The ferocious storm that had come on Okinawa so quickly was over almost as fast, and Fitz deplaned to look for someone who could tow the Learjet out of the temporary shelter that his wife, Susan, had so skillfully taxied it into just 30 minutes earlier. As he walked the length of the plane, Fitz recalled the words of the Yonaguni policeman who had spotted the journal – *kindan no shomotsu*. One of the other men had translated the words as "forbidden book" before Fitz could grab it away from Susan and secure it in the cockpit. When Frank had given him the book, back on Yonaguni, Fitz had neglected to mention its hiding place to Susan, so she was naturally surprised at finding it in the Learjet's small galley refrigerator. Frank had made it clear that no one was to know about the book and Fitz was worried that he had betrayed his employer's trust. All he could do now was deliver it to the professor at the University of the Ryukus and hope the policeman would forget about it.

An hour later, the Learjet was secured on the tarmac and Bill Ito's body had been transferred to the custody of the Okinawa Prefecture officials. The Yonaguni policeman had been met by relatives at the airport so Sandstrom was fed and left to guard the Learjet. The Fitzgeralds hailed a taxi and headed to the University to deliver the journal that Linda had found in the chamber below the Yonaguni pumping station owned by the island's patriarch, the elder Yamato.

When the taxi stopped in front of a large glass and concrete building that could have been on any American campus, Fitz expressed his surprise.

"Somehow, I expected it to look more … well, oriental, I guess. I hope we're at the right place."

When they had gotten into the cab back at the Naha Airport, Fitz had simply handed the driver Jim's hand-written note with a name and address on it, assuming that the driver probably didn't speak English, so he was surprised when the driver turned in his seat and spoke to him.

"This is the right place. It's the Department of Sciences building." Smiling, the driver glanced at the note before handing it back to Fitz. "Someone in the lobby should be able to direct you to Professor Barac."

Fitz paid the driver in American dollars and he and Susan made their way into the building. Just as the taxi driver had predicted, a small circular counter stood in the middle of the lobby and a sign in English said, "Information." When Fitz inquired about Professor Barac, the Japanese student behind the counter nodded, picked up a telephone handset and dialed.

A few seconds later, she hung up and pointed to several sets of elevator doors across the lobby. "The Professor will be right down. I'm sorry, but visitors are not allowed on the floor where his office is located."

Fitz turned for the elevators, but Susan asked, "Does everybody on Okinawa speak such good English? First our taxi driver surprised us and then you. I was afraid we were going to have a much harder time with the language here."

The girl smiled back and replied, "There have been times when there were almost as many American GIs on Okinawa as Japanese. When so much of the island's economy depends on English, you must learn it to survive. Of course, in my case I had another reason."

The girl nodded toward a tall, lean man exiting one of the elevators and said, "That's Professor Barac – my father."

Susan laughed at the girl's cleverness and joined her husband.

"Dear, this is Professor Barac. And the young lady we just…"

"Is his daughter, I know. I'm very pleased to meet you Professor Barac," said Susan as she extended her hand.

"Oh, please, call me Don. Even my students don't call me Professor anymore. I understand you have something that you would like me to take a look at. Let's walk over to the Student Center for a cup of coffee and you can show me this mysterious book of yours."

"Actually, Professor…uh sorry, Don, I think it might be better if you looked at this in a more private setting. My employer insisted that we not share this with anyone except you."

Don wrinkled his brow but then shrugged it off and nodded. "Okay, there's a small conference room down the hall here where we won't be disturbed. Follow me, please."

Fitz and Susan remained silent while the Professor slowly read through a dozen pages of the book. When he finally closed it and looked up, Fitz broke the silence.

"So, what do you think?"

"I think whoever owns this book is going to be very unhappy when they find out that it's missing. I believe your Professor Barnes said he thought it was a journal written in some early form of Chinese, and he may be right on both counts."

"You said Jim was right on both counts, so I take it you think it's a journal. Any idea what kind of journal?" asked Susan.

"Uh, well, to properly answer that question I would need to study this book for several hours, Susan. All I can tell you at this point is that it appears to be a list of dated transactions."

Professor Barac opened the book and indicated various portions of the page as he continued. "The first column is clearly the transaction date. The first entry is smudged, but I think it's sometime in September, 1977. The second one is clearly November, 15, 1977, then August 12, 1978, and so on."

Flipping to the last entry in the book, he continued. "And this last one is about six months ago – July 18, 2001, to be exact."

Fitz stared at the book intently. "What about the rest of the line?"

"The next part of each line seems to be an individual's name, but it will take some time to translate them. Then there's this odd column, which is clearly a relatively small number."

Flipping back to the first page, he ran his finger down the column and read aloud, "52, 13, 24, and so on. The last two columns are probably amounts – like debits and credits or something."

"Maybe that third column is a quantity and the last two are charges and payments, like you said," guessed Fitz.

"Yes, that's possible, I suppose, but also just speculation. If I could have some time with this…when are you planning to return to Yonaguni?"

Fitz glanced at his watch. "Well, we were hoping to get back this evening, but a storm has already delayed us longer than we expected, so I think we'll lay over here in Okinawa and fly out early tomorrow morning. But I don't think Jim expected any instant answers, Don."

"Maybe not, but now this thing's got my curiosity up and if I can determine the correct dialect I might be able to send you back with both the journal and a translation guide. That way, Professor Barnes could unravel his own mystery. None of us anthropologists like to take another's word when it comes to something so subjective, you know."

"I'm sure Jim would appreciate that, Professor. If you can recommend a hotel near the Airport, we'll meet you back here in the morning before we head back to Yonaguni."

"You'll do nothing of the sort! My daughter and I insist that you be our guests for the night. We have a large house, by Japanese standards, and Yoko loves to show off her Japanese cooking skills.

After supper, she can show you some of the sights and I'll work on this book."

"Oh, we couldn't inconvenience you like that," stammered Susan. "And besides, we have our dog with us and we can't leave him on the plane by himself all night."

"Bring him along!" replied the Professor as he closed the book and stood up. "Since we lost my wife, we rarely have company any more and it will do us both good. If you'll wait right here, I'll run up to my office, grab a few texts and be right back."

After the Professor had left the room, Susan shrugged and smiled. "Well, I guess that's settled. I hope Sandstrom behaves himself."

"Yes, me too! We'll have to get the daughter – Yoko, I think it is – to run us back to the airport but it will be a great chance to see the island with a native guide."

A few minutes later the Professor and his daughter returned and the four walked several blocks to a local restaurant recommended by the Professor. The dinner conversation covered a wide range of topics from the early history of Okinawa to Yoko's studies at the University.

"I'm very proud of Yoko," beamed Don Barac, embarrassing his daughter, "and I know her mother would be proud of her, too. Because of her mixed ethnic background, she's taken a real interest in cultural anthropology, whereas my background is primarily linguistics – hence the call from the University of Washington"

As the two men continued to chat, Susan struck up a side conversation with Yoko.

"So tell me about this cultural anthropology – what is it, anyway?"

"Well, it's the comparative study of different societies accomplished by analyzing their respective cultures. We look at the norms, values, and standards transmitted from one generation to the next and study human behavior within a community. Then we interpret that behavior by comparing it to similar studies in other communities. I know that sounds like a text book answer, but it really is what we do. I'm particularly interested in the similarities and differences between early Asian civilizations and those of ancient Eastern Europe. I find it fascinating that my great grandmother, who immigrated to Japan from Korea, spoke a language derived from the same Ural-Altaic languages of my father's ancestors in Yugoslavia. I'm convinced that the two cultures share other common characteristics, too, and I hope to focus my graduate studies on that theory."

"So your mother was Japanese with Korean roots and your father is an American with Eastern European roots – that's quite a mix," smiled Susan.

"Yes, and I was born here on Okinawa. I guess I was destined to be an anthropologist, huh?"

After dinner, Yoko drove Fitz and Susan back down the island to the Naha Airport to retrieve their overnight bags and Sandstrom. She intentionally stayed to the side streets and secondary roads whenever possible to give the flight crew as much local flavor as possible. It was obvious that Yoko loved Okinawa and enjoyed sharing her passion with others. She was also intensely loyal to her birthplace.

"You know many people don't even consider Okinawa and the rest of the southwest islands part of the 'real Japan'. It really bugs me that Frommers, one of the leading publishers of travel books, completely ignores Okinawa in its 600-page book on Japan. Even the national government in Tokyo treats us islanders like second-class citizens. Sometimes I think the Ryukyu and Yaeyama Islands should secede from Japan and form an independent country. We have more in common with the Taiwanese down south than we do with those on the big island up north!"

In the back seat, Fitz and Susan glanced at each other with raised eye brows.

"Is that a common sentiment on the islands, Yoko?" asked Fitz. "I mean, do a lot of the folks here resent being under the control of a government so far away?"

"Oh, it's a lot more than the distance, Mr. Fitzgerald. The big island of Honshu, along with its adjacent sister islands of Hokkaido and Kyushu, contain more than 99% of Japan's total population and make up 98% of the land area. On top of that, there's a basic cultural difference. The people of the southwest islands – that's the Ryukyu and Yaeyama chains – are direct descendents of the *Jōmon*, the original inhabitants of this area. The natives of the big islands, on the other hand, are a mixture of prehistoric Japanese aborigines and various invaders, including Koreans and Chinese. Even our languages have different roots, although the islanders have been forced to speak Japanese since the early 1900s. When you add the fact that the southwest islands have been brutalized by the big islands since the first invasion in1609, you begin to understand why a lot of the locals dislike being controlled by Tokyo."

Fitz could sense an anger creeping into Yoko's voice, but he pursued his original question anyway.

"With less than 1% of Japan's population, nothing will ever come of the islanders' discontent, right? I mean, what could they ever hope to accomplish?"

"Nothing, by themselves. But there are others in the world who would love to interfere in Japan's internal affairs and who wouldn't hesitate to use the islands as a stick with which to poke Tokyo in the eye. At the University I hear of small groups that ..."

Yoko's comment was interrupted by the wail of a small Okinawan police car traveling in the other direction with its lights flashing. She veered to the side of the road to allow the vehicle to pass and when she pulled back out into the flow of traffic her mood, and the subject matter, had obviously changed so Fitz dropped the subject that obviously upset their host.

A few minutes later, Yoko turned down a tree-lined residential street and brought the small Nissan sedan to a stop in front of a large, single-story house made of concrete and covered with a traditional red tile roof. The house was surrounded by a high coral-block wall to protect it from typhoons and the grounds were immaculate.

As they made their way up the manicured sidewalk toward the house, Yoko indicated the property with a wave of her arm and explained.

"This actually belongs to the University, who leases it to my father at a very reasonable rate because of his position as head of the Anthropology Department. The house itself, or most of it anyway, is over a hundred years old and it's a historical building. When my father finally retires, it will probably become a museum or something."

When the trio reached the door, they were met by an obviously excited Professor Barac.

"Finally! I thought you had decided not to return after all. Please come in! I have some very interesting news for you."

While Yoko showed Fitz, Susan and Sandstrom to the living room area, the professor trotted off in the other direction. He soon returned carrying several text books and the journal Linda had found in the chamber beneath the water pumping facility back on Yonaguni.

The professor plopped the texts down on a large glass coffee table and pulled up a chair directly across from Fitz and

Susan. He indicated that Yoko should join them and then began his explanation.

"It didn't take me as long to decipher this book of yours as I thought it would, due to some research I'm currently working on. Once I had a few minutes to study the characters, I realized that this is written in an early Chinese dialect that probably originated somewhere south of Shánghǎi. The names were the hard part, because they turned out to be Japanese surnames and they don't translate very well, but here are some of them."

The professor handed Fitz a piece of paper, and he and Susan scanned it together.

"I can't even pronounce most of these names," laughed Fitz. "Should they mean anything to us?"

The professor shook his head. "No, probably not. The list didn't make any sense to me, either, until I spotted one name in particular and started back-tracking. But I bet Yoko recognizes many of them – show her the list."

As Yoko's eyes scanned her father's list, her eyes got wider and wider. When she finished, she handed the paper back to her father and locked her eyes with his.

"Are you absolutely sure about this?" she asked softly.

"I'm afraid so, my dear. I don't know what quirk of fate brought this list to us, but there it is."

The professor reached out to take his daughter's hand, but she pulled away and quickly left the room.

"Please forgive her rudeness, but, like me, she recognized some of the names on this list as those of Japanese citizens who have disappeared over the past twenty-five years – allegedly kidnapped and taken to North Korea."

"But why would such a list be found in Japan?" asked Susan. "You would expect to find this somewhere over in North Korea. Is that what upset Yoko?"

"No, what upset her was this name right here, dated January 17, 1991. It's her mother's name and that's the last time we ever saw her."

Chapter 21

Tony had been searching the tunnels under the east end of Yonaguni Island for fifteen minutes and there was still no sign of Linda or the armed man who had taken her hostage on the beach. He cursed himself for not pursuing the man sooner, but he had stayed behind to administer first aid to the wounded police chief so he wouldn't bleed to death. By the time the Chief was stabilized and on his way to a doctor, Linda and her kidnapper had a ten minute head start on Tony and he had no idea which way they had gone once inside the labyrinth of tunnels.

While still on the beach, Tony had heard the sound of a single gunshot come from inside the cave. The kidnapper had already admitted to being a cold-blooded killer, so Tony had no doubt that the man would dispose of Linda the instant he had no further use for her. The longer it took him to find her, the less likely she was to be alive.

For what seemed like the hundredth time, Tony stopped, held his breath and listened intently. He didn't believe Linda would allow herself to be carried off without a fight, so the continued silence might mean that she was unconscious – or worse.

Allowing himself a quick breather, Tony slid down the smooth wall of the tunnel and retrieved a canteen from his backpack. While he rested, he tried to put aside his fear for Linda's safety and concentrate on the situation at hand.

He had stayed to the main shaft that opened onto the beach and, after going around a slight bend to the right, the cave-like characteristics of the shaft had given way to the smooth-walled rectangular features they had seen earlier near the mysterious *tsubute* room. At each point where a side tunnel joined his, he had stopped and listened for any sound of the others but he had always continued on to avoid the possibility of getting hopelessly lost or traveling in circles. After fifteen minutes, he estimated that he must be at least half a mile from the beach and his mental compass told him he was heading due west. Recalling the map he and Frank had studied, Tony wondered if the tunnel continued on, all the way into town. If it did, that would mean another two miles, at least. Was that where Linda was being taken, or had the kidnapper dashed down one of the side passages Tony had already passed?

Tony stood and prepared to continue his search deeper into Yonaguni's underground but as he bent over to pick up his backpack, he heard a sound from down the tunnel in the direction he had just come. The sound was faint and impossible to decipher, but it was the first sound he'd heard since leaving the beach. With his flashlight in his left hand and his 9mm Beretta in his right hand, he trotted back down the tunnel toward the entrance. Since he had just traveled this same passageway in the opposite direction, he knew the tunnel was straight and that the floor was free of obstacles, so he used his light sparingly, flicking it on and off just long enough to spot approaching side tunnels. At each one he stopped, listened and then moved on. As he approached the fifth tunnel, he thought he heard another sound. He stopped and stood perfectly still for a second and then moved slowly forward until he was at the edge of an opening on his right. In a single fluid motion, he stepped into the opening and spun to his right to face the adjoining tunnel but before his thumb could press the flashlight switch he was hit by something and knocked backwards, off his feet and flat onto his back. On his way down, Tony managed to get the light on just in time to see the barrel of a submachine gun aimed at his head and the face of the person holding the weapon.

"Linda, wait! It's me!" he yelled as he tried to slap the gun barrel away from his face.

"Tony! Oh, my God! I almost shot you!" cried Linda. She tossed the weapon down and fell on Tony in relief and happiness.

Tony helped Linda to her feet and, after scanning her for injuries, he asked the obvious.

"So, what happened? Are you okay?"

Still gasping for breath, she pointed down the side tunnel and tried to explain.

"Yes ... down there ... he fell ... dead, I think ... must show you."

"Hold on, there! Catch your breath and then try that again," Tony laughed.

While Linda caught her breath, Tony handed her a canteen from his pack and picked up the kidnapper's submachine gun that she had tossed aside. He recognized it immediately as a Russian Kedr because he had seen many of them in the hands of the Vietcong back in 'Nam. Slinging the weapon over his shoulder by its strap, he turned back to Linda, who seemed to be breathing easier.

"Okay, now what did you say?"

"The guy who grabbed me is down there," she said, pointing down the side tunnel. "He fell into some kind of hole or pit in the dark and I think he's dead. I was afraid to move, afraid the same thing would happen to me, but I finally realized I couldn't stay there forever, so I crawled, literally, back to here. When I heard you coming, I thought you were one of his buddies, so I jumped you. You came within a nanosecond of getting shot, you know."

Tony shined his light on the 9mm pistol he still held in his right hand and replied, "So did you, my dear! And speaking of shots, I heard one not long after he dragged you in here. What was that all about?"

Linda smiled. "He had his hand over my mouth and he was dragging me by my neck so I couldn't put up much of a fight but I did get in one good kick to his crotch. I guess it must have hurt, because he flinched and accidentally squeezed off a shot. After that, he tightened his grip around my throat and I passed out. When I came to, he was dragging me by my arm and just a few seconds later I heard him yell. He released my arm and dropped the gun while he was trying to recover his balance, but I heard him fall and hit bottom. It was pitch black, so I couldn't see anything, but the impact sounded pretty final. Come on, I'll show you."

After assuring himself that Linda wasn't injured or in shock, Tony took the lead down the narrow passageway. He scanned the floor, walls and ceiling of the tunnel with his light as they moved slowly forward. They passed several glyph-covered murals like those Jim had discovered that morning but they seemed unimportant now. Eventually his light picked up a blackness ahead that spanned the full width of the passage and he stopped. He retrieved a second flashlight from his backpack and handed it to Linda.

"You wait right here and let me check this out. If anything funny happens, I want you to go back the way we just came until you come to the main shaft, turn right and then run as hard as you can until you come to the beach. Do you understand?"

"Yes, but ..."

"No buts, Linda! Nobody has a clue where we are, including us, and if we both get into trouble down here we'll never be found. At least not until after we died of thirst or starvation. Now stay here and don't move. I'm just going to see what this is and verify that your playmate from the beach is out of commission. I'll be right back."

Tony inched forward until he reached the edge of the opening. He dropped to one knee and aimed the light into the pit but a thick layer of condensation, almost like fog, obscured the bottom. He noticed that the edges of the hole were uncharacteristically rough and jagged, indicating that it might be the work of nature rather than something created by whomever had constructed the smooth-walled, rectangular tunnel around him.

"It looks like a sink-hole," he called back over his shoulder. "That would explain why your friend didn't expect it to be here."

"Is he in there? Is he dead?"

"I can't tell. The bottom is covered with steam or something. The whole inside of this island seems to be very porous. It's as if ... hold on! I think I've spotted something!"

Tony's light had picked up something flat and reflective down inside the sinkhole opposite his position. He turned to tell Linda what he was seeing and was almost startled into the hole by her face, only inches from his.

"Damn it, woman, stop sneaking up on me like that! I thought I told you to wait back there!"

Ignoring the scolding, Linda stared intently across the eight-foot gap in the floor at the spot on the other side of the hole.

"What do you think it is?" she asked.

Turning back to the sinkhole, Tony slowly moved his light over the flat patch and around its perimeter.

"Well, if you ask me, it looks like a spot on an old stucco building where the plaster has been knocked off and the wooden lathing is showing through. Except that what's showing through isn't wood. It looks more like ..."

"Like the gold on the dome of the capitol building back home," finished Linda, her voice trailing off in thought.

"Yeah, like that," nodded Tony. "I wish I had some way to get over there, but I'm not about to jump into a hole that I can't see the bottom of and there's no place to tie off a rope, even if I had one."

"But you still have the camera from this morning, right? Let's get some photos, at least. Maybe Jim will have some idea what it is."

"Okay, but then we need to get the hell out of here. The fact that the floor of this tunnel has already collapsed once may mean that this whole area is unstable. Besides, it's getting dark out on the beach and Takamura should be back by now."

With Tony holding securely on to the waistband of her jeans, Linda took several pictures of the sinkhole and the unusual area on its far side. Satisfied that they had captured all the information they could, Tony strapped on the backpack and Linda zipped the camera inside. She helped him get the submachine gun strap over his left shoulder and, with flashlights in hand, they prepared to move out. Linda turned to take one last look into the hole and, as she did, she felt the ground giving way beneath her.

She screamed and Tony spun to see her falling forward as a large chunk of the floor was breaking away. He lunged forward and grabbed for her ankle just as the upper portion of her body was dropping below the plane of the floor.

***

Meanwhile, back at the small Yonaguni emergency room, the doctor had done all he could for the local police chief. The man was stable, but he had lost a lot of blood and he was still very weak. On the table next to the chief, Frank had watched the young Japanese doctor skillfully remove the bullet and suture the wound as if he'd done it a hundred times. When the doctor finished and stripped off his surgical gloves, Frank complimented him on the procedure.

"Nice work, Doc. I haven't seen sewing like that since the field hospitals of Viet Nam. Where'd you study medicine?"

"At UCLA Medical Center in Los Angeles," replied the doctor, smiling. "I trained as a trauma surgeon under Dr. John Hennessey who was, in fact, an Army doctor in Viet Nam. He used to tell us that the faster we worked the more lives we would be able to save. I never really understood what he meant until the 1995 Kobe earthquake. I was an intern at Kobe General that day and I treated more than 300 patients in the first twelve hours after the 'quake. Now let's have a look at that knee."

After a quick examination, the doctor scribbled some notes to a nurse and shook his finger at Frank.

"I don't think you've damaged the joint yet, but there will be no more strenuous activity for you, my friend. I've ordered you a cortisone injection and we're going to wrap your knee, but you have to stay off it for a few days. If you don't, you're going to do some permanent damage – is that clear?"

"Yes, doc, I understand, but I can't just sit around, either. I have two friends who are, uh, lost somewhere down on the east end of the island. I need to ..."

"You need to give that knee some rest!" admonished the doctor, nodding at Jim and Takamura. "These two can go look for your friends, but you are going to stay off that knee!"

Frank was still fuming when Jim pushed his wheelchair out of the medical center and into the late-afternoon sun.

"I thought he was actually going to tape Frank into the chair," laughed Jim as Takamura opened the sliding door of his dive company's van.

"Me, too! That guy is way cool," agreed The Japanese dive master.

"Okay, wise guys, help me into the van and give it a rest!" shouted Frank. "We need to get back down to that beach where we left Tony and Linda, so step on it, will you?"

Jim and Takamura hoisted Frank back into his wheel chair when they arrived at the dive shop, but they refused to help him onto the boat.

Takamura shook his head. "I'm sorry, Frank-san, but I'm the captain, and I'm responsible for the safety of my passengers. Out there, you would be a liability, at best, and a casualty at worst. You can wait here in my office and we'll keep you updated on the radio. Riko will be here in a few minutes and she'll stay with you until we get back. Let's go Jim, before it gets dark."

As the deep, throaty engines eased Takamura's boat away from the dock, Frank turned and rolled his wheelchair into the small wooden structure that served as Hammerhead Diving's headquarters.

Frank had retrieved his satellite phone from the hotel so he decided to try to contact Fitz and Susan while he waited for the first report from the boat. As a charter pilot, Fitz carried an international pager and Frank hoped it would work in Okinawa.

The pager number was programmed into his phone, but when he dialed it, all he got was a busy signal. After adjusting the special satellite antenna several times he finally heard the faint triple beep signal from the paging service. Frank quickly entered the telephone number of the dive shop and pressed the pound key, trying not to move the antenna in the process. He was studying a nautical map of the island when the telephone on the counter rang and startled him. He answered it, hoping it would be Fitz or Susan and not a customer expecting someone who could speak Japanese.

"Frank is that you?" asked Fitz on the other end of the line.

"Yes, it's me. I wasn't sure I had gotten through to your service or that you would recognize this as a Japanese number. How are things going over there?"

"Well, interesting, to say the least," replied Fitz. He explained that he and Susan were planning to stay at the Professor's house for the night and return to Yonaguni in the morning and then he told Frank what they had learned about the journal so far.

When Fitz had finished his news, Frank told him about the encounter with the gunmen on the beach, the shooting of the Chief and the kidnapping of Linda. When he repeated what the group's leader had said about killing Bill Ito in cold blood, he heard a gasp behind him and turned to see Riko standing in the doorway. She put her hand over her mouth and ran out onto the dock in front of the building.

"Fitz, I've got to go. You guys get back here as soon as you can in the morning, okay? With Tony and Linda currently AWOL and me confined to a wheelchair, we need all the help we can muster."

Frank ended the call and wheeled his chair over to the door. "Riko?"

"Frank-san!" she said, as she turned and wiped tears from her eyes. "What has happened to you?"

"Oh, nothing serious, I just re-injured my knee. Listen, I'm sorry you had to hear that. I had no idea you were behind me."

"What has happened to this man who killed Bill? Is he dead, too?"

"I don't know. He was the one who grabbed Linda at gunpoint and ducked back into the cave, and Tony went in after him. You guys brought me back here, so I don't know what's happened to Tony, Linda or the killer. Speaking of Takamura, would you try to call him on the radio? He promised to call in, but I haven't heard a thing.

Riko adjusted some dials on the radio, keyed the microphone and spoke. After a few seconds, Frank heard Takamura's voice, but of course the conversation was in Japanese and Frank only understood the last sentence, which was obviously said in English for his benefit.

"And tell Frank-san to stay in that wheelchair!"

Frank smiled and nodded. "So, what was the rest of that about?"

"He said that they had just arrived and that there was no sign of Tony or Linda on the beach. He and Jim are just about to go ashore and will call back later. He asked me to call the coast guard and then wait here in case they need to contact us."

"With three bodies on the beach I guess we need to be calling somebody, but why the coast guard?" asked Frank.

Riko shrugged. "Didn't you say that Chief Sato was injured?"

"Oh, right! Well, you make that call and then I'd like you to explain this coastal chart to me. There's something I don't understand about it."

Riko called the coast guard station on neighboring Ishigaki Island and then made a pot of tea for the two of them on a hot-plate in the back room.

When she set his cup of tea down on the table where Frank had spread out the chart, he took her hand comfortingly.

"Riko, I'm truly sorry about Bill. I can't help thinking that if my friends and I hadn't come to Yonaguni, none of this would have ever happened."

Riko bowed her head and sniffed back a tear. Withdrawing her hand, she shook her head and said, "No, Frank-san, Bill discovered something several weeks ago that upset him very much. He never shared any of the details with me, but at times he acted very strange."

"And he never told you what this secret was?"

"No. I begged him to talk to me about it, but whenever I brought the subject up he insisted that I was just imagining things."

"Riko, think back to when you first noticed this behavior in Bill. Can you remember what he had been doing that day? Where he'd been or who he'd been with?"

"Yes, of course, because I was with him earlier that day. I had taken a group of tourists from Tokyo out to dive the Monument and Bill had come along for the ride. He kept me company during the trip out to the dive site, but remained aboard with Kogi, the captain, while I took the others below. When the dive was over I returned to the boat, he seemed disturbed about something, but he wouldn't say what. I thought he'd had an argument with Kogi, but he claimed that Bill had hardly said a word to him. Apparently, Bill had been studying something along the coastline through his binoculars. When we left the dive site and started home, Bill insisted on being dropped off at the first small inlet west of the Monument. He took his mask, fins and snorkel and jumped overboard 50 meters from the shore. All he would say was that he wanted to check something out and that he'd walk back to town. I didn't see him again for two days!"

Frank shook his head. "And he never told you what this was all about?"

"No. When he finally called me, I was frantic but he just laughed it off. All he said about it was, 'There's something very strange on your island.' Except, …"

"Except what, Riko?"

"Well, I remember laughing because he sometimes made mistakes with his Japanese and what he had actually said was, 'There's something very strange under your island.' I corrected him and we laughed about it, but he was never the same Bill after he returned. He always seemed preoccupied and very intense."

"My team and I have noticed something unusual about Yonaguni, too, Riko. Nobody's been able to put their finger on it, but it's as if there's some dark secret that nobody wants to talk about. And then there's this black Mercedes that keeps turning up wherever we go. Chief Sato told me it belongs to this Yamato character that seems to be so influential around here but apparently it's been at the disposal of some guy from China for the past few days."

"China? Do you mean Hau Zhuo is here again? You and your friends must avoid him at all cost, Frank-san!"

Riko was visibly upset at the news. She got up from the table and paced back and forth the width of the office several times before Frank spoke.

"Riko, what is it? Do you know this man?"

"No," she said, returning to the table. This time it was Riko that took Frank's hand.

"But please don't interfere with him, Frank-san. Every time he visits this island another …"

Riko's plea was interrupted by Takamura's voice on the two-way radio. As before, he spoke in English for Frank's benefit.

"We've got them! Just as we were about to give up, Tony and Linda stumble out onto the beach and we're heading back right now."

Riko asked something in Japanese, but Takamura answered in English.

"The gunman fell into some kind of sink-hole and Tony thinks the guy is dead. Linda was almost lost in a secondary collapse but Tony grabbed her at the last second. I don't have all the facts yet, but they think they've made the discovery of the century and Jim is wild with excitement. See you soon. Over and out."

Chapter 22

Frank and Riko were studying a nautical chart when they heard the engines of Takamura's boat approaching the harbor.

"They're here!" shouted Frank. "Help me outside!"

Riko wheeled Frank out onto the dock and they waited for the boat to ease into its berth in front of the Hammer Diving Service office. Dusk was turning to night by the time the boat was tied up and its occupants had disembarked. Linda was the first off, followed by Jim and Tony. Linda's hair was a mess and her khaki pants were coated with dirt but she broke into a run when she saw Frank in the wheel chair.

"My God, Frank, what's happened to you <u>now</u>?" she cried as she approached.

"I think I should be asking you the same question, my dear," laughed Frank. "I hear you did a little unexpected cave exploring. Are you guys okay?"

"Yes, thanks to Tony. He quite literally saved my life and the whole tunnel collapsed just as we hit the beach, but I'll tell you about that later. The big news is what we found inside the sinkhole I almost fell into. If Jim's right, science is in for a big shock!"

Jim had been explaining something to Tony ever since they had stepped off the boat and only stopped when Tony clamped his hand over the other man's mouth to inquire about Frank.

"Are you doing okay?"

Frank nodded and Tony released Jim with a warning.

"He's going to talk non-stop, so prepare yourself."

"Frank, you won't believe what we, well actually <u>they</u>, have discovered! This island isn't at all what it appears to be. It's ..."

Frank glanced both way up and down the dock and interrupted Jim's explanation.

"Jim, let's not broadcast your discovery to the whole island, okay? We need to go someplace a little more private to discuss this because Riko and I have made some interesting observations ourselves. Let's go back to the hotel so Tony and Linda can get cleaned up and then we'll all compare notes. I'll bet our cave explorers are starving, so maybe we'll go back to that place where we ate with Bill the first night we were on the island."

Assuming that she was being excused for the evening, Riko had started back toward the office door when she overheard Frank's comment.

"No, Frank-san, you should not go there! There are too many ears and they would not like what you are suggesting about Yonaguni."

"So, you know this restaurant?" asked Tony.

"It belongs to her parents," offered Takamura, as he joined the group. "And she's right – many of the island's elders gather there and they won't like Jim's theory either."

All eyes were now on Riko and Linda smiled broadly.

"But Bill seemed to be well liked by the staff there. Did they know …"

"No," smiled Riko sheepishly. "My mother used to talk about the cute Japanese-American who came into the restaurant almost every night, but she never knew that Bill and I were in love. I think Bill thought that if he got to know my family well enough, they might someday approve of our relationship, but it would never have happened. My parents are very old-fashioned and now Bill is …"

Linda put her arm around the other woman's shoulder and hugged her. "I'm so sorry for you, Riko."

Takamura cleared his throat to break the awkward silence. "I would be happy to offer my humble home. It's not large, but it's very private and you're welcome to stay as long as you wish."

"That's very generous, my friend," said Frank. "And if I haven't mentioned it, I would like you and Riko to join us. Your knowledge of the island will be invaluable and, besides, we owe you our lives. If you two hadn't speared those two thugs on the beach this morning, I'm afraid we'd be fish bait by now! And we don't even know your first name!"

"I only have one name, you know, like your Sting or Cher," smiled the young Japanese man. "But sometimes my friends call me Tani. And speaking of the beach, the Coast Guard wants to talk to all of us tomorrow about the bodies we left out there, but for tonight they have agreed to leave us alone and conduct their own investigation."

After a quick stop at the hotel, and another at Riko's family restaurant for some take-out, the NWIDI team – plus two – convened at Takamura's small, one-story home. The cement building was perched high on a cliff at the northwestern end of the island, overlooking a small beach far below. The gravel road that connected to the main highway continued past Takamura's and eventually wound its way down to the beach.

"My God, this is beautiful!" exclaimed Linda, as she stepped out onto the cement slab that formed a patio overlooking the East China Sea.

"Thank you," bowed Takamura. "This house has been in my family for as long as anyone can remember. Someday I'll enlarge and modernize it, but for now, I live alone and it meets my needs."

Linda noticed Takamura's stolen glance at Riko and wondered if they had been a couple before Bill Ito arrived on the island.

"Well, it certainly is breath-taking. And those lights in the distance – are those ships at sea?"

The rest of the team had joined them on the patio as Linda was pointing to some tiny dots of light in the distance.

"No, the lights you see over there are actually huge halogen lights in the shipyards of the city of Taipei. Taiwan is only about 80 miles from here."

"Really!" exclaimed Tony. "Bill mentioned that, but I had no idea you could actually see Taiwan from here. It's amazing that there's no trade between two islands that are so close."

"Well, no legal trade, anyway," smiled Takamura. "Let's go back inside and eat before the food gets cold."

The conversation during dinner was limited because everyone turned out to be hungrier that they had thought. Linda recapped her kidnapping incident and described how Tony had saved her from falling into the cavern below the passageway, but she stayed away from the subject of their discovery, saving that for Jim.

When everyone had finished, Riko cleared the containers and sake glasses away. Linda offered to help, but Riko politely refused her assistance.

"Please rest, Linda. You are a guest here."

Once the large coffee table was cleared, the six gathered their chairs around it and Frank nodded to Jim.

"Okay, Jim, it's your show. What's this big discovery you've made?"

Jim took a deep breath and exhaled as if he were about to begin a long, boring scientific dissertation. The five others were blown away by what actually came out.

"This island is a fake!" he shouted. "It's nothing more than a clever disguise."

"What?" everyone said in unison.

Jim spread out a map of Yonaguni Island that he had picked up at the hotel.

"Look!" he said pointing. "Here's the underwater monument where you guys went diving. Just to the north is Mt Urabu – elevation 231 feet above sea level. Further north and east, right about here, is where Linda had her near miss today. And she and Tony discovered something inside the sink-hole that I believe is the flat, sloping side of another pyramid!"

"You think there's a pyramid buried under Mt. Urabu?" asked a shocked Takamura.

"Not quite. I think Mt. Urabu is a pyramid. And I'd be willing to bet that the other three high points on this island – Mt. Inbi, Mt Kubura, and even Mt. Yonaguni itself, are also pyramids. I think …"

"Whoa, hoss!" interrupted Tony. "You've obviously had way too much sake tonight. Where did you ever come up with a hare-brained idea like that?"

"Let him finish, Tony. Jim, you were saying?"

"I was saying that I think the passageways we encountered when we fled the *tsubute* room, and the ones where we saw the murals when we retraced my path from the workshop to the beach, are all part of an intricate underground complex built to connect the pyramids together. I think this island was inhabited long before Tani's relatives settled here. And I mean long before!"

The room was silent for several long seconds before Riko suddenly gasped.

"That must be what Bill discovered when he went missing that time! He must have spotted something from the dive boat that made him curious enough to swim ashore and wander the southern coastline for nearly two days."

In response to Jim's puzzled look, Riko related her story of Bill's disappearance and strange behavior to the others.

"This place where Bill went ashore wasn't by any chance near the Yamato estate was it?" asked Frank.

"It would have been pretty close, I guess. Why?"

"I have a hunch that nothing happens on this island without Yamato's knowledge. If there is a pyramid – or four – under this island, I'd be willing to bet our Mr. Yamato knows about it."

"Wait a minute," objected Tony. "You're not accepting this whacko theory of Jim's are you? Give me a break, guys! There have been people on this island for hundreds of years. Surely somebody would have discovered the beach entrance that we've already used twice in just two days. Jump in here, Takamura! Haven't you ever been to that beach before?"

The dive master thought for a minute and then shook his head.

"No, I don't think I have. The only way in and out of there is by boat and there are too many other beaches with easier access. But I see your point. It does seem like somebody, at some point in Yonaguni's history, would have discovered the cave at the back of the beach and the cavern that leads to the passageway entrance. Unless ..."

Takamura looked at Riko and she apparently read his thoughts.

"Of course!" she shouted. "We had a minor earthquake about two months ago. It was just a little one, not like the ones they have up north, but they are so rare here that it really upset a lot of the older people. Anyway, maybe that caused the cavern to be exposed."

"And the floor of the passageway to cave in," added Linda. "Tony even said he thought it looked like a recent fracture."

"Was that quake before or after Bill's discovery?" asked Frank.

"Um, before, I think. Yes, I'm sure it was before because it happened on the night of Bill's birthday and we were ... ah, celebrating at the time. It was later that he started acting weird."

Riko blushed and looked away from the others, especially Takamura.

"But what about the other entrance?" argued Tony. "The one that leads to the workshop. There's at least one of those mysterious passageways that opens into it, too. Are you telling me that nobody ever found it, or the workshop itself, for that matter?"

"Well that's something I do know about," said Takamura. "We often take dive groups to the area just off that beach when the water's too rough on the south side of the island. Again, the only way to access it is by boat – or by falling off the cliff, like Frank did – but I'm sure that beach has been well explored over the years."

"However," countered Jim, "that workshop entrance is a long ways back in there and that would reduce the possible visitors substantially. And that heavy wooden door would stop the rest, if it were locked."

Tony shook his head. "That doesn't explain the passageway entrance. Are you proposing a 'shifting sands' theory here, too?"

"It's possible," nodded Jim. "Especially if the passageway entrances were intentionally hidden with sand in the first place. And that's exactly my point! I believe this whole island – at least the part we walk about on – is nothing more than camouflage designed to cover up the pyramids and the connecting passageways."

"But why?" asked an unbelieving Linda.

"And by whom?" asked an even more unconvinced Tony. "Transporting enough earth to burry a 200 foot tall pyramid from – well, from who knows where – would be an incredible task, even today. And you're suggesting that this was done before the island was inhabited by its current population, so that's what – hundreds of years ago, maybe a thousand years ago?"

"Actually, I was thinking more along the lines of ten thousand years ago, Tony. I believe the pyramids, along with the monument, were buried before the oceans rose. The rising water eventually washed away the soil used to disguise the monument, but it also covered it, so it wasn't discovered until a few years ago. The rest of the complex has remained buried."

"That's ridiculous!" shouted Tony, as he leaned back in his chair and folded his arms over his chest. "How you came to a conclusion like that based on what we saw in that hole is beyond me!"

"It's not just what we saw there, Tony," explained Jim. "It's the whole island. The workshop, the passageways below it, the *tsubute* room and the *tsubutes* themselves – none of this makes any sense. You've seen those passageways – do those smooth walls and perfectly rectangular shapes look like the work of nature? And what about the cave-in that almost got Linda? Below the passageway you guys were in, the island appears to be almost hollow. The pictures you showed me prove that!"

Tony's face softened a bit as he listened to Jim.

"Well, I'll admit that there are some odd things about this place, but none of them are as odd as your claim! We already know that some guys think there was an ancient civilization here a long time ago. That's why we came to Yonaguni in the first place – to explore the origin of the monument. Couldn't the passageways, and whatever they connected, have been buried in a tidal wave or tsunami? What makes you think they were intentionally camouflaged?"

Frank stood up and approached the low table. "Maybe I can help there."

He unfolded the nautical chart he had brought from the dive shop and smoothed it out on top of Jim's map.

"I'm not saying I buy your idea either, Jim, but what do you make of this?"

The chart had ocean depths marked at 10-meter increments at various points around the island and depths of equal value were connected together, much like altitude lines on a topographical map.

"The depth of the water drops off very dramatically everywhere around this island except over here by the monument. And it drops off fast once you get out past the monument, see?"

"Sure," nodded Tony, "but all that proves is that the monument was probably a part of the island, back when the ocean was lower. We already know that, Frank."

"Right, but now check this out." Frank flipped the chart over and pointed to the same features of several neighboring islands. "If these islands are the tops of mountains that stick up from the ocean floor, you'd expect them to be shaped something like a cone – pointed at the top and gradually spreading out as you descended from the peak. That would result in a more gradual increase in water depth as you move away from the island, such as you see here, and here."

Frank pointed to the charts for Ishigaki and Iriomote, the two largest islands in the Yaeyama chain.

Jim studied the map for a minute and then nodded.

"I see your point. It's almost as if Yonaguni sits atop a column rather than a cone. But there are other islands surrounded by very deep water, Frank. One of the deepest places on earth is the Cayman Trench just south of Grand Cayman Island."

"Well, maybe we'll go poke around down there after we're done here, because I'm telling you, Yonaguni doesn't fit the pattern of the other islands in this area. I don't know about buried pyramids, but there's something very strange under this island."

"That's exactly what Bill said to me!" cried Riko. Putting a hand over her mouth to stifle a cry, she ran out onto the patio and sobbed. A minute later Takamura joined her, but only Linda noticed. The others were embroiled in a debate about what lay below the surface of the tiny island of Yonaguni.

The next morning, the NWIDI team met in Frank's hotel room at 8:00 a.m. for breakfast. Takamura and Riko both had morning dive charters scheduled, but they had promised to call as soon as they returned to help with the investigation in any way they could. Frank had sworn them to secrecy before the meeting at Takamura's house had adjourned and he hoped they would keep their word because if what they knew got out, it would endanger everybody.

Jim's wild theories aside, they still had one of the *tsubutes* in their possession, and that put the entire team at risk. And then there was the matter of the Japanese Coast Guard and how to explain the three bodies on the beach and the wounded police chief. And on top of that, there was the journal of kidnapped Japanese nationals that was on its way back from Okinawa with Fitz and Susan!

They hadn't left Takamura's until just after midnight and Frank had been up since 4:00 a.m. worrying about these issues. Apparently, it showed.

"Are you okay, Frank?" Linda asked as she sat down at the small round table in his room. "You look terrible!"

"Thanks!" he replied through a forced smile. "Let's get started, okay? We need to come up with a story and make sure everybody has it straight before we meet with the Coast Guard this afternoon. And one of us should be at the airport by 9:00 a.m. to meet Fitz and Susan."

"I'll take care of that," offered Tony. "Our friendly desk clerk has offered the hotel van and driver for the morning – for a fee, of course."

"Of course," nodded Frank. "Pay him whatever he wants. We need Fitz and Susan back here in time to get caught up on our cover story. Now here's how I think we should handle this."

Over the course of the next 45 minutes, Frank laid out the plan he'd been developing since the early hours of the morning and, after a little haggling, the story they finally agreed on was this:

Give the Coast Guard everything they knew about the journal. This would include the story of how Linda ended up on the beach and found the journal, the boat chase after the "kidnappers", Frank's suspicion that the same boat had been spotted at the scene of Bill Ito's murder and the fact that Takamura and Riko had found the same boat tied up near the beach where the NWIDI team was ambushed. They would describe the attack on the beach exactly as it happened except that they would not mention the stolen *tsubute* or the trip through the underground passageways that took them there. With that tunnel now collapsed, there was little chance of it being discovered, so if they were asked what they were doing on the beach, they would simply say "exploring." They would also pass on the information about the contents of the journal that had been translated by Professor Barac. Frank hoped that the story, which was mostly true, would explain the bodies and that the journal would keep the authorities busy for months. Since the room Linda discovered on the south side of the island and Jim's *tsubute* workshop on the north side of the island were more than 3 miles apart, there was a good chance no one would ever make the connection.

As for the *tsubutes*, passageways and pyramids, they would remain a secret for now. Frank suspected that once the bodies on the beach were identified, they would lead directly to Yamato and, if they didn't, the connection between the room where the journal was found and Yamato's water utility would. Either way, the patriarch of Yonaguni was going to have some explaining to do.

In the mean time, the NWIDI team would explore the mystery under the island by accessing the passageways through the workshop Jim had discovered. Once they had enough information to form a credible theory, they would turn it all over to the press and let the chips fall where they may. Jim would finally get to publish his research – and probably become famous – and the team would fly back to Seattle to look for another "project."

"Okay, that's it then!" Frank slapped his open palm down on the table to close the debate. "If everybody sticks to the plan, we can make this work. We'll bring some bad guys down and we'll shake up the scientific community in the process – I love it!"

Just then the phone rang and Frank glanced at his watch.

"Oh, crap! It's 9:15 – I'll bet that's Fitz calling from the airport! Tony, go. I'll tell him you're on the way."

Frank wheeled over to the phone and picked up the receiver as Tony flew out the door.

"Hello?"

A deep, soft-spoken voice on the other end said, "You're dead – all of you – and everybody you've been associated with since your arrival on Yonaguni."

The line went dead and Frank stared into the receiver.

Chapter 23

Frank dropped the telephone receiver into the cradle and looked at the others without speaking.

Linda could see the concern on his face. "What is it, Frank? Are Fitz and Susan okay?"

"That wasn't Fitz. That was a death threat – against the four of us and everybody we've been associated with since arriving here." Frank slammed his fist down on the arm of the wheelchair. "We've got to notify Takamura and Riko! They're out in the ocean somewhere, completely unprotected. And we need to alert Tony and the flight crew."

Frank tossed his satellite phone to Linda. "The last call I placed was to Fitz's cell phone. Hit 'Star Redial' on the keypad and see if you can contact him. I'm going to alert the Coast Guard and have them radio a warning to the dive boats."

Linda's call went through almost immediately and she explained the situation to Fitz, who was just easing the Learjet into a parking spot at the Yonaguni airport. Using the phone in the room, Frank had asked the desk clerk to connect him with the Coast Guard but the nearest station was on the neighboring island of Iriomote and the connection was so bad that Frank couldn't hear the person on the other end of the line.

Using the satellite phone, Frank called Fitz's phone again but this time it was Susan who answered.

"Is Tony there yet?"

"Yes, Frank, he just pulled up in a van. Hold on and I'll get him."

A minute later, Tony came on the line.

"What's up?"

"Listen, Tony, I can't reach the Coast Guard and I think we need to alert Takamura and Riko. Will you stop by the dive shop on your way back here and get somebody to contact them on the radio? And do you have your gun with you?"

"Yes to both questions. Do you still have yours?"

"I do, and I think everybody in our little circle of friends should stay close to either you or me until we get to the bottom of this threat. When you talk to Takamura, have him contact the Coast

Guard on his marine radio and ask them to get some help over here ASAP! There must be a patrol boat or something in the area and we need some fire power at the emergency room to protect the Chief until we figure out how serious this thing really is. Oh, and tell him we'll meet him at his place."

"Will do, Frank. What about the plane? Susan is asking if we should move it off the island for now."

"Negative. It's our only way out of here right now and this may all turn out to be a hoax. It wouldn't hurt to see if you can find a local who'd be willing to keep an eye on it, though, in exchange for some good old Yankee dollars."

"Okay, I'll see what I can do. See you soon."

Frank ended the call and summarized the situation for Jim and Linda.

"Tony's just picking up Fitz and Susan at the airport and he's going to try to contact our diver friends on his way back here. I need you two to go back to your rooms and pack whatever you need for a couple of days. Be sure to leave enough behind so it looks like you're coming back. Then get back here as fast as you can. As soon as Tony arrives with the Fitzgeralds, we're moving out to Takamura's place where we can set up a more defendable perimeter."

While Jim and Linda were busy, Frank called the desk clerk again and asked to be connected to the emergency room. After some language difficulties, he finally reached the doctor who had operated on the Chief the day before.

"Doc, this is Frank Morton. I'm the guy who came in with the local police chief yesterday. Listen, we've just received an unusual phone call and I'd like you to keep an eye on the Chief until I can get someone over there. His life may be in danger."

"I'm afraid it's not, Mr. Morton. I was going to call you as soon as I had a free minute to let you know that Chief Sato died about an hour ago. He seemed to be improving throughout the night and I actually thought he'd be well enough to transport to a larger facility today, but he started to fade about 7:00 a.m. and we couldn't turn things around. I'm very sorry."

"Yeah, me, too. He was a good man. Thanks, Doc."

Frank was still sitting by the phone when Linda knocked once and opened the door without waiting for a reply.

"Now what's happened?" she asked when she saw his expression.

"The Chief died earlier this morning. And the bastard who killed him is the same guy who killed Bill. It's too bad he fell into that hole, because I'd sure like to have a few minutes with him. Damn it, I wish we'd never come to Yonaguni!"

Frank's face was red and his fists were clenched into tight balls. Linda had never seen him so angry. She poured him a fresh cup of coffee and tried to change the subject.

"I didn't get to know him very well, but he seemed like a nice man. I'm sorry, Frank. Let me help you get your things packed."

When Jim knocked on the door, Linda opened it and stepped out into the hall to tell him about the Chief's death. Frank was still sitting at the small table in his room staring into his coffee cup.

By the time Tony arrived, thirty minutes later, Frank had shaken off the news of the Chief's death enough to get back to business.

"Were you able to contact Takamura and Riko?" he asked as soon as Tony appeared in the doorway.

"Yes and no, in that order," replied Tony. "But Takamura was able to contact a Coast Guard patrol boat that was only about 3 miles away from the site where she was supposed to be diving and they're headed that way now."

When Frank frowned, Tony held up a large, military-style walkie-talkie. "Takamura promised to call me as soon as he hears anything."

Seeing Jim and Linda's bags beside the door, he added, "Are we going somewhere?"

"Yes, but with as little fanfare as possible. We're too closed in here at the hotel, so we're moving in with Takamura for a while. His place is protected by high cliffs on two sides and there's enough open space in the other directions to prevent anyone from sneaking up on us."

Fitz and Susan, who was holding Sandstrom, finally squeezed into the room and Frank greeted them with a nod.

"Good work, you two. Sorry you've had to spend almost this entire trip in the air, but the info you gathered about Linda's journal is going to make the Japanese authorities very happy."

"Thanks," acknowledged Fitz. He handed the journal to Jim and added, "It was all we could do to keep Professor Barac off the plane, Jim. He expects a full report before you leave for the states."

Frank brought the conversation back to the business at hand.

"Alright, now I'd like as few people as possible to know we've left the hotel and it's really important that <u>nobody</u> knows where we're headed. Anybody have any ideas?"

"Well, the Fitzgeralds' bags are down in the van, but that's still six people, a dog and a lot of baggage to sneak past the desk clerk," said Tony. "And, even then, the driver would know where he took us. To pull this off, we need a vehicle of our own, or at least one we can keep while we're on the island. What about a rental car agency?"

"There aren't any, I already checked that out. What we need is the use of a private car, one that … wait a minute, I've got it! Yesterday, when the Chief and I found you guys in the *tsubute* workshop, we went in through the tomb entrance that Jim had discovered in the cemetery. But we ended up fleeing through the passageways, out onto the beach and into the ambush, remember?"

"Of course I remember, but how does that help us now?"

"The Chief's car is still in the cemetery, right where we left it! And he certainly won't be using it any more. Get the bags out of the van and have the driver take you out there. Tell him you're retrieving the car as a favor, or whatever sounds good at the time, but let him know he's no longer needed today. In the mean time, we'll check Fitz and Susan into the hotel, as if they were going to stay here tonight, and then we'll figure out how to sneak out of here when you get back. Leave that walkie-talkie with me and give Linda your room key so she can pack your stuff while you're gone."

"Speaking of keys, what about car keys?" asked Tony, as he slipped on his sun glasses and started for the door.

"Oh, I'm sure you'll think of something," Frank grinned.

Once Tony was on his way, Frank called down to the front desk and made arrangements for a room for the Fitzgeralds. He'd been paying for the team's lodging in cash each morning, so he sent Jim down with a $100 bill to cover the extra room.

"Tell him to keep the change," he instructed. "We want to keep him happy – and quiet. And tell him we'll get the bags in a few minutes."

Linda left to do Tony's packing and Frank waved Fitz and Susan into vacated chairs at the small table.

"So, how's the leg doing?" asked Fitz as he poured coffee for his wife.

"It's been better, that's for sure, but this damn cast is a bigger pain than the injury. I think the doctor put it on just to tick me off! Are you guys doing okay?"

"Actually, yes," replied Susan. "Jim's friend, Professor Barac, was quite an interesting fellow, to say the least. And his daughter, too. I don't know if Fitz mentioned it on the phone last night, but her mother's name was in that journal."

"Really!" exclaimed Frank. "The poor kid."

"She was pretty upset, of course, and earlier in the evening she had hinted to Fitz and me that there was a pretty strong anti-Tokyo movement down here in the southern islands. Have you run into any of that?"

"You know, we've noticed some kind of dark undercurrent on this island ever since we first arrived, but it could be due to a number of things. Apparently the defacto patriarch of Yonaguni has a guest from China and this guy's regular visits are of some concern to the locals. And then there's the journal and whatever it points to as well as this underground mystery Jim has discovered. It sure seems like a lot of secrets for such a small island."

"While we're waiting, tell us more about these passageways," prodded Fitz. "It sounds like the biggest archeological discovery of all time!"

Frank had only hit the high points when he had talked to Fitz the night before, so he brought the flight crew up to date. While he was talking, both Jim and Linda returned from their tasks and added their own thoughts.

When Frank was done, both Fitz and Susan were stunned.

"My God, Frank, what do you think this all means?" asked Susan.

"Well, I've been thinking about that very thing since early this morning. It could be an archeological discovery, like you say, but Tony makes a good argument against that when he asks how primitive people could have moved enough earth to cover the structure – or structures – on this island. That only leaves two other choices. Either what Tony and Linda photographed wasn't really part of a structure or, well, that dirt wasn't moved by ancient people."

Fitz scratched his head. "I don't get it. If the ancients didn't bury the pyramid, or whatever it is, then who did?"

"You and Susan weren't with us on our first outing, but we uncovered some evidence that the Maya of Mexico's Yucatan may have been influenced by an off-world intelligence. What if that same intelligence was responsible for the construction and subsequent burial of whatever's under this island?"

"Get out of here!" exclaimed Susan. "Are you saying you think this island was once inhabited by little green men from outer space?"

Frank shrugged his shoulders and leaned back in his chair.

Jim picked up the explanation for the disbelieving Fitzgeralds.

"Anthropologists have always wondered how the Maya came to have such an advanced knowledge of astronomy and yet never learned to make metal tools. It turns out that the Maya probably learned their astronomy from a group called the Olmec, about which very little is known. A reliable source within our own government has suggested that the Olmec may have traveled to Earth from somewhere else in the Universe."

"I don't believe I'm hearing this!" said Fitz. "You're all educated people, and Jim, you're a scientist! Do you guys really buy this?"

"We saw the evidence," added Linda. "All four of us physically touched one or more metallic spheres that almost certainly came from somewhere other than Earth. But Frank, I don't understand how this relates to Yonaguni? We haven't found any spheres or ... oh, my God! The *tsubutes*! Do you think the *tsubutes* we found in that chamber below Mt. Urabu are alien?"

"Wait a minute," interrupted Fitz with waving hands. "What the hell are *tsubutes*?"

"They're ancient eight-sided Ninja throwing disks," answered Jim. He fished the stolen *tsubute* out of his buttoned shirt pocket and handed it to Fitz. "Like this one, except they don't normally have that red stone in the center."

Fitz examined the object carefully and then handed it to Susan, who also inspected it.

"This red stone – is it a ruby?" she finally asked.

"No, but that's a good guess, especially since the ruby figures prominently in the ancient folklore of this part of the world. But check this out!"

Jim retrieved a flashlight from his pack by the door and shined it on the *tsubute*. The square red stone in the center of the *tsubute* glowed bright, as if from an internal light source. When Jim switched off the light, the glow quickly dimmed away. He repeated the on-off sequence several times to make his point.

"I played with this thing a little last night," he continued. "It seems to respond to almost any kind of light, either man-made or natural, except for fire light. When I illuminated it with light from a match, I got nothing. But the flashlight, the fluorescent light in my bathroom and even a narrow beam of sunlight this morning all create the same glowing response. I think you'll agree that's not the kind of behavior you'd expect from a ruby."

Jim's explanation was interrupted by the crackle of the walkie-talkie and Frank almost tipped his wheelchair over reaching for it.

" ... found ... everyone ... Riko ... over," was the broken transmission.

Frank pushed the talk button and said, "Please repeat, over."

"Coast Guard ... found boat ... everyone fine ... Riko ... ashore ... over."

Frank tried in vain several more times to reach Takamura, but the reception had degraded to just scratchy sounds and clicks.

He threw the portable radio onto his bed and swore.

"Damn it, I think I heard him say that the Coast Guard had found the boat and everybody was okay but that Riko had gone ashore. Did anyone else get that?"

Everyone agreed, except that Susan thought she had heard the word "near" after "ashore" and Jim thought he heard Takamura say "my house" in one of the latter transmissions.

Just then, Tony burst into the room and shouted, "Okay, let's go! The car is in an alley beside the hotel but it's hot-wired, so I had to leave it running. We can get out through a side door but we're going to have to make at least two trips, because the car is too small for all of us."

Frank brought Tony up to date on the radio message but they both agreed that they should get the group moved before they tried to deal with anything else. They decided that Tony would take Frank, Fitz, Susan and Sandstrom on the first trip, so Fitz could help carry Frank when necessary. Tony would then return for Jim, Linda and the bags. Before they left, Frank stuffed the walkie-talkie, his satellite phone and his 9mm Beretta pistol into a small carry-on.

"Okay, let's do this!" he said, as Tony helped him out of the wheelchair and onto his good leg.

An hour later, the group of six people and one dog were reassembled at Takamura's house. Frank and Tony were out on the patio trying to contact Takamura on the walkie-talkie, but they both realized that the chances were slim, now that they had moved to the far western end of the island. Jim was still trying to explain to Fitz and Susan why he thought the *tsubutes* found under Mt. Urabu were alien, and Linda was in the kitchen trying to put together some sort of brunch from the meager contents of Takamura's cupboards.

A noise in the distance grew louder until it became the unmistakable roar of a helicopter. Tony helped Frank inside and ordered everyone to stay away from the windows until he could determine if the approaching aircraft was friend or foe. As the sound outside became almost deafening, Tony tried to spot the aircraft but it had approached from the east and there were no windows on that side of the building. He was about to dash outside for a quick recon when there was a loud thump that shook the entire house.

Tony fingered the safety on his Beretta and signaled for everyone to take cover as he yelled, "They're on the roof!"

Seconds later, a rope dropped down from above and banged against the windows on the side of the house. Tony tensed and prepared to fire at the first commando to slide into sight. Instead, a dive bag full of gear dropped past the low window, followed by Takamura's smiling, waving body sliding down the rope. He waved to someone above and the helicopter immediately lifted off and disappeared down over the cliff in front of the house.

Seeing Tony's drawn handgun through the window, Takamura's smile quickly turned to an expression of some concern.

"Don't shoot! It's me! I live here, remember?"

Tony lowered his gun and reengaged the safety as Takamura picked up his dive bag and made his way around to the open patio doors.

"Nice entrance, man," commented Tony, as he tucked his Beretta into the waistband of his pants. "You almost got shot, you know!"

"Well, it _is_ my house," smiled Takamura. "And I didn't expect an armed welcome. You do know that handguns are illegal in Japan, don't you?"

"Only if you get caught," quipped Tony. "What's with the rooftop landing? You scared the hell out of us!"

"Oh, that. Well, I hitched a ride home with some of my Coast Guard buddies. They picked me up off my boat and flew me directly here to save some time. Once the dive was over and all the tourists were back on board, there was no need for me to hang around and I wanted to get back here and see what the big emergency was all about."

"Do you do this often?" asked Frank, pointing to the roof.

"Often enough so that it's a Coast Guard approved heliport, if that's what you mean. When your leg is better I'll take you up and show you the big white circle with the letter 'H' in it. I probably should have mentioned this earlier, but I'm sort of a consultant to the Coast Guard. I spent six years on active duty as a rescue diver and I still get called out now and then for odd jobs."

"Covert odd jobs, I'll bet," grinned Tony. "And that explains the power plants in your dive boat!"

"Ah, yes, my boat. I overheard you lusting over it several times, Tony." On the outside it looks like a typical dive operator's rig, but I can assure you there's nothing ordinary about it below decks. It's the fastest boat in the China Sea."

"Then why couldn't you catch that speedboat the day we thought Linda had been kidnapped?" demanded a puzzled Frank.

"I could have, Frank, but I'm not supposed to blow my boat's cover unless it's a Coast Guard emergency and I was sure that my other boat would nab them when they rounded the end of the island. I miscalculated – sorry."

"What about Riko?" asked Frank. "I couldn't understand most of your radio transmission. Is she okay?"

"Well, that's actually why I had my buddies fly me over here. What I tried to tell you on the radio was that the Coast Guard located her boat not long after it left the dive site. All the tourists were back on board but she had talked the captain into dropping her off near Higawahama Beach. Apparently she swam ashore with just her fins, mask, snorkel and a spear gun. The boat arrived at our satellite office over by the ferry dock about fifteen minutes ago."

Listening from the kitchen doorway, Linda said, "I'll bet this beach is close to the Yamato Estate, isn't it?

"Yes, it's directly below it, in fact. How would you know that?" asked Takamura.

"Because that's where Bill went ashore that time he disappeared for two days. Riko told me the whole story last night."

"That's right," agreed Frank. "She told me the same thing while we were waiting for you guys at the dock last night. Damn her! And you can bet that spear gun isn't intended for fish!"

Tony and Takamura exchanged a quick glance and nodded to each other.

"We can take the boat that's at the ferry dock," said Takamura. "Give me a minute to grab a couple of things and I'll meet you at the car."

He hurdled over the luggage piled in the middle of his living room and disappeared into his bedroom while Tony began rummaging through his leather carry-on. He tossed Frank the walkie-talkie and an extra clip for his gun.

"Hey, wait a minute," protested Frank. "Let's talk about this first."

"You talk, Frank, and let us know what you decide. Meanwhile, we're going after Riko before she kills somebody – or gets killed herself!

"You did the right thing by moving everybody out here. Now it's up to you to take care of them until we get back. See you soon, Gimp!" smiled Tony.

Frank tried to object, but Takamura reappeared carrying a canvas bag.

He tossed a key to Frank and jerked his thumb in the direction of his bedroom. "That large armoire in the back is actually a well-stocked armory – help yourself if you have any trouble."

Without another word, he picked up his dive bag and dashed out the door with Tony close behind.

As the Chief's small car came to life, Frank called, "Good luck!" knowing that neither one of them could hear him.

Chapter 24

Outside, Takamura headed directly for the driver's side of the Chief's car, so Tony climbed into the passenger's seat while the other man piled his dive bag and the canvas bag onto the back seat. When Takamura was behind the wheel, Tony leaned over and touched the two wires that hung down below the dashboard and the engine came to life. Without a word, Takamura slammed the gearshift into reverse and spun the tires in the gravel as he raced the car backwards down his short driveway and onto the road toward town. He was clearly a man on a mission and twice Tony had to remind him that they wouldn't be much help to Riko if they were killed in an automobile accident on the way to rescue her.

At the ferry dock, Takamura parked the Chief's car behind the small satellite dive shop, grabbed the two bags from behind his seat and unlocked the back door of the shop. Looking over his shoulder, he scanned the area carefully to make sure they weren't being watched and then nodded to Tony, who climbed out of the small car, grabbed his own bag and made his way quickly to the door.

Once they were inside and the door was locked, Takamura spoke for the first time since leaving his house.

"Grab whatever you need for dive gear and meet me at the boat. I'll go down and make sure we have some full air tanks onboard."

Tony nodded and set about rounding up the necessary equipment: a wet suit, fins, a mask and snorkel, a regulator and a BCD to carry the tank. He also grabbed a strap-on scuba knife and a large underwater dive light. On his way out, he twisted the button in the knob and locked the door that led out to the dock.

Takamura had the engine running when Tony reached the boat, so he threw his gear aboard and untied the rear mooring line. Takamura took his position behind the wheel and gave Tony the thumbs up to release the front line. Within seconds, they were headed for open water with the throttle of the 48-foot dive boat wide open.

Tony climbed up onto the small flying bridge beside Takamura and stared straight out over the bow.

"We'll find her, my friend."

Takamura nodded and hit the throttle lever with the heel of his hand.

"Damn it, I wish we had my other boat down here! We ended up switching them around after the chase the other day and this one will take twice as long to get around to Higawahama Beach."

"Yes, but on the bright side, they won't be able to hear you coming from miles away," smiled Tony, trying to get Takamura to relax a bit. Tony knew from his Special Forces training thirty years ago that too much stress caused a soldier to forget his training and become a danger to himself and his companions.

Takamura tried to smile. "That brings up another problem. We can't take the boat right up to the beach or we'll be spotted from the Yamato estate. There are only two places where we can safely anchor without risking the loss of the boat and the best one is the inlet where I showed you and Frank the glyphs on that mysterious pipe – the place where we accidentally stranded Linda. The problem with that location is that it's apparently frequented by our friends in the speed boat. If they're involved in this, there's a chance our boat will be spotted and we'll lose our element of surprise."

"So what about the second place?" asked Tony.

"Ubamahama Beach. But it's just beyond our target, and we'll have to pass the estate to get there."

Tony scanned the boat deck and then asked, "Do you have any fishing gear onboard?"

"There might be something down below, why?"

"I'll set up on the back of the boat like a tourist on a private fishing trip and you can ease by as if we're supposed to be there. That will give us a chance to check out the beach and any obvious security so we don't storm into a trap."

"I like it!" replied Takamura. He pointed to the compass and indicated that Tony should take the wheel. "I'll go see what I can find. Just keep us on this heading until I get back."

By the time the boat had reached the opening to the bay that formed Higawahama Beach, Tony had learned a great deal about Takamura. The Japanese man had started diving as a youngster and had joined the Coast Guard soon after he graduated from the equivalent of American high school. His diving skills had helped him advance through the ranks quickly and he had soon become an instructor in the Coast Guard's elite Search and Rescue group. One day, about six years after his enlistment, Takamura's commanding officer called him into his office and made him an offer he couldn't refuse.

The CO explained that the government was becoming increasingly concerned about the amount of illegal trafficking that went on between Taiwan and its neighboring islands in southern Japan, especially Yonaguni. The Coast Guard offered to set Takamura up with a complete dive operation, including a specially equipped boat that could overtake smugglers in the open waters between the islands. The daily dive charters would provide the opportunity to monitor the area undetected and report suspicious activity to Coast Guard ships stationed in the area.

For Takamura, it was a dream come true. Publicly, he left the Coast Guard and returned to his family's home on Yonaguni with a cover story that a long-lost relative in Okinawa had died and left him a substantial amount of money. Secretly, he became a paid civilian agent for the Japanese government, who actually supplied the start-up cash for the dive operation. His six year hitch in the Coast Guard provided a reasonable explanation for his periodic meetings with "buddies" still in the Guard and the best part of the deal was that he got to dive almost every day!

Tony also learned a little about the history between Takamura and Riko that Linda had picked up on. The two had known each other all their lives and had been inseparable through their school years. Their families were very close and had negotiated a traditional arranged marriage between the two. The marriage was to take place when Riko, who was two years younger than Takamura, finished school.

Just a few weeks after he graduated, Takamura's parents were killed in an automobile accident while visiting relatives in Okinawa. The accident left Takamura devastated and alone on Yonaguni with nearly two years to wait before his marriage to Riko so he joined the Coast Guard to fill the void and soon discovered that he loved the adventure and challenges provided by the Guard. When his initial two-year enlistment was over, he surprised everyone, especially Riko, by signing up for another hitch. She was heart-broken, and felt left at the alter, while her parents were publicly and privately humiliated. When Takamura finally returned from the Guard, four years later, he tried to patch things up with Riko, but she was no longer interested and her family wouldn't have anything to do with him. By the time she took the job as dive master with Takamura's Hammer Diving Service, she was secretly involved with Bill Ito and head over heels in love.

"So what happens now?" asked Tony when Takamura finished his story.

"I don't know," he replied sadly. "Before, I just always knew we would be married some day and I never really thought about it. It was all arranged. While I was away on active duty, especially the last couple of years, I realized that I had real feelings for Riko, but by then it was too late. We grew up together and we've become friends again, but I'm afraid it will never be anything more than that.

"Anyway, that's enough of my sad story. We're almost to the estate, so you'd better get into your tourist outfit. I put some gear back on the stern. We must have found that hat after a charter but it's totally you."

The hat Takamura was referring to was one of those Budweiser caps with beer cans attached to each side and plastic tubing to sip from.

"Perfect!" he said to himself as he pressed the hat down so the noon-day breeze wouldn't blow it overboard. He took off his tee-shirt and tilted back in the deck chair before casting the large lure over the back of the boat. He flashed a thumbs-up to Takamura, who eased the boat past the entrance of the bay and into the view of the estate.

As they slowly crossed in front of the Yamato estate, both men scanned the beach for signs of surveillance equipment or guards.

Takamura called down to Tony, "I think I see someone sunbathing on the beach just in front of that large tree. Otherwise, the place looks deserted."

Takamura sounded the loud horn on the dive boat and the startled sunbather sat up in surprise.

"Oh, crap! I think that's Aya Yamato!" shouted Tony as he looked away so she wouldn't recognize him.

"I don't know who she is," laughed Takamura, "but I believe she's topless. And judging by those hand signals, I think she's pretty upset about being disturbed!"

"So much for our element of surprise!" shouted Tony. "Can we just go, please?"

Takamura eased the throttle forward and waved a friendly "Good by" to the woman on the beach who was now clutching her beach towel with one hand and shaking a fist with the other.

Just past the jut of land that formed the east side of the bay was a slight indentation in the shoreline and the area known as

Ubamahama Beach. The narrow arc of sand was backed by a high rock cliff that ran east all the way down to the Yonaguni Monument dive site. Only a steep, grassy slope on the west end of the beach offered any hope of getting from the beach to the upper portion of the island.

Pointing to the narrow passage, Tony said, "That's going to be a tough climb, Mr. T, especially with our gear."

"Oh, no, we're not going up through there. I've got a little surprise for you. I discovered an interesting natural feature last year when I had a dive group over here. I often use this area for the second dive when I take groups out to the Monument because the bottom here is pretty flat and there are lots of boulders on the bottom that have fallen from the cliffs up above. They make an interesting but easy second dive after the rigors of the currents over at the Monument."

Takamura secured the boat with anchors both forward and aft and then joined Tony in the small cabin below the main deck. Tony had donned his wet suit and was organizing the gear he had selected at the shop. Takamura opened his dive bag and pulled out his black dive suit and other gear. When both men were ready, they went back up on the main deck, secured a tank to each of their BCD vests and were in the water in a matter of minutes.

The boat was anchored in about fifty feet of water and Takamura signaled Tony to descend to the sandy bottom. Once there, they took a minute to acclimate before Takamura gave the "follow me" signal. The two divers skimmed along a few feet off the bottom directly toward the point of land that separated their beach from the one in front of the Yamato estate. Bringing up the rear, Tony kept thinking that any minute they would turn toward open water to navigate around the point, but Takamura pressed on, heading directly toward the outcropping of rock that was the point.

Finally, just a few feet from a shear rock wall, Takamura stopped and settled to the bottom on his knees. Tony followed suit and pointed to the rock wall in front of them with a shrug. The Japanese diver pointed to his mask and then his chest, the signal for "watch me". He gathered the loose hoses and other hanging gear close to his body as if hugging a baby, swam up over the top of a boulder near the wall, and disappeared!

Realizing that Takamura must have discovered an underwater tunnel, Tony quickly followed. He hoped the other man was aware of the difference in their respective sizes. Tony was several inches wider in the shoulders and hips and had a brief mental picture of being stuck in the shaft, arms and legs flailing wildly.

Fortunately, the opening was at least four feet across, leaving Tony more than a foot on each side. What he wasn't prepared for was the total blackness of the shaft. He tried to locate the small dive light he had clipped to his BCD without losing sight of the other diver, but he finally decided to quit fooling around and just follow the dim circle of light from Takamura's light.

For the next ten minutes the shaft made several bends and after one such turn the water ahead brightened considerably. The shaft seemed to join a small, perfectly rectangular room and the wall to the left was open to the bay. Takamura waited in the room area until Tony emerged from the shaft and then pointed to the bay and gave the signal to surface. Recognizing the rectangular passageway from his explorations beneath the *tsubute* workshop, Tony waved him off and pointed straight ahead, where the passageway continued on through the rock. As he started to swim toward the other side of the room, Takamura grabbed him by the arm and gave the "out of air" signal. Pointing to his air gauge, he gave the sign again and swam through the opening into the bay.

Realizing that something must have gone wrong with the other diver's equipment, Tony followed and when he caught up with Takamura, he offered his spare regulator. Takamura pulled his own regulator out of his mouth and took a long breath on Tony's spare, slowing his ascent as his lungs filled with air. While they hovered 15 feet below the surface for the routine decompression stop, they held on to each other's BCD. Tony reached down and checked Takamura's air gauge but it showed that his tank still had more than 2,000 psi – nearly two-thirds of a tank. Takamura shrugged to indicate he didn't know what the problem was. When his watch indicated that they had completed the three minute safety stop, Takamura held his finger up to his lips to indicate the need for silence on the surface and then moved slowly up. Tony let him go ahead so only one of them would break the surface at a time. When Tony's head poked up into the air, Takamura was studying the shoreline for signs of movement. Both divers added air to their BCDs so that just their heads were above the surface and then moved slowly to their right and into the shadows against the cliff that formed the east side of the bay.

"I don't see anybody on the beach," whispered Tony.

"Yeah, me neither. I guess our sunbather went inside. See that doorway in the hillside over there? It must provide access to the house up on the hill."

"It's probably similar to the passageway we just came out of. Not the tunnel you brought us through, but the rectangular one that continued on. My team and I have discovered a whole network of them on the other side of the island. They lead to a workshop of some kind that can be accessed through a fake tomb in the old cemetery."

"What?" asked Takamura a little too loud. Then more quietly he added, "Are you kidding me?"

"I'll tell you all about it another time. There's something very strange about this island of yours, Mr. T, but right now let's focus on finding Riko. Did she know about that tunnel you just brought me through?"

"She knew of its existence, but not its exact location. I'm sure I mentioned it to everybody on my crew at one time or another, because it was something of a local oddity."

"What about Bill? Did he know about it?"

"Bill Ito? I guess it's possible. We used to include it in the pre-dive briefing if we stopped there. Why? What are you getting at?"

"Maybe Bill found a similar feature somewhere around here and that's where he spent his two missing days that Riko told us about."

"It's possible," nodded Takamura. "And in her grief, Riko somehow thought retracing Bill's steps would help explain why he was murdered."

"It makes sense to me. I'm guessing she doesn't make it a habit of asking her captain to leave her behind after finishing a dive trip. And if she didn't know about the shaft, she would have had to come in right through the bay. It would have been easy for somebody up there," he indicated the huge house on the hillside above them, "to spot her and be waiting."

The two men made their way along the wall, staying in the shadows until they reached the sand on the extreme east end of the beach. Using rocks and low bushes as cover, they removed their dive gear. As Tony pushed his fins out of site under a bush, he saw something yellow move.

"Look at this!" he whispered to Takamura as he held up a yellow and black swim fin.

Turning the fin over, Takamura pointed to the name written on the bottom in black marker. "It's Riko's!" he replied.

"Well, that probably means she's still here," frowned Tony. "And now that we're here, what's your plan? You do have a plan, don't you?"

Takamura glanced at his watch. "Of course, my friend, but we have to sit tight for another eleven minutes. I have a little surprise planned for the Yamato clan, but I miscalculated our arrival time by a few minutes. While we're waiting, how about filling me in on this fake tomb and the workshop you mentioned. Did you say you found a whole network of tunnels?"

Tony summarized everything they had learned about the passageways and their mysterious murals of intricate glyphs. He was just about to describe the cave-in incident, where he and Linda had discovered what Jim now believed to be the side of a pyramid, when they heard the unmistakable sound of a military helicopter in the distance. Suddenly a Japanese Coast Guard helicopter zoomed around the cliffs at the entrance to the bay and headed straight for the hilltop above their position.

"They're going to land on the other side of the main house," yelled Takamura over the roar of the helicopter. "As soon as they drop out of site, we're going to run for that doorway in the hillside as fast as we can. They will all be preoccupied with their unexpected guests and we can slip in before they realize it."

On Takamura's signal, the two men raced from their position on the east end of the beach to an ornate Japanese doorway built into the hillside about midway down the beach. Fortunately, the door was unlocked because it turned out to be solid steel rather than the aged wood it had appeared to be from the beach.

Inside, a short hallway lead to a steep flight of stairs which led to another hallway that ended at an elevator door.

The two men looked at each other and Tony said, "What the hell!" as he pressed the single button on the metal plate beside the door and they waited for the elevator to make its way down to their location. They tensed as the door began to open and waited an instant after the doors opened in case there was anyone inside. The elevator car appeared to be empty, so they dashed in and punched the button to begin their ascent. When the door had closed, Tony flashed Takamura a "thumbs up" sign just as a cloud of white gas started pouring in through a vent in the ceiling.

As he began to lose consciousness, Tony slid helplessly down the smooth metal wall of the elevator car. He smiled across at

Takamura, who was also collapsing, and called, "So, what's your plan B?"

Chapter 25

Back at Takamura's house, Frank set about accomplishing the task that had been his underlying reason for moving to the house in the first place – to get his team to a place they could defend. After the telephoned death threat, he had decided that the hotel in downtown Yonaguni was too dangerous and far too exposed. Takamura's house sat on a bluff overlooking the East China Sea. Only the west and south sides of the house were approachable, and the lack of trees on the bluff would make a sneak attack virtually impossible.

The seaward sides of the one-story structure had lots of windows but the large master bedroom, in the back of the house, was a different matter. Its windowless, solid concrete walls gave it a bunker-like appearance and the room's steel door completed the fortress effect. What ever this room's original purpose had been, it was now NWIDI's temporary headquarters.

After a light lunch that Linda and Susan had scrapped together from the limited provisions in Takamura's cupboards, Frank had his team secure the living room area as well as they could. Curtains were drawn and both the patio door and the main entrance were locked. After a quick once-over from his wheel chair, Frank moved the group into the bedroom.

Linda turned on a small television on Takamura's dresser, but it only received two channels and they were both in Japanese, so she soon flicked it off. Fitz spotted a commercial-grade marine radio on the nightstand and pointed it out to Frank.

"Looks like our friend still stays in touch with his coast guard buddies," commented the pilot as he tapped the microphone clipped to one side of the radio.

Frank wheeled over to the armoire in the corner and unlocked it with the key Takamura had left him. The armoire was nothing more than a cleverly disguised weapons vault and it contained an impressive cache of weapons.

Frank whistled as he swung open the door and gazed inside.

"Either he's still working for the government, in some undercover capacity, or he's a one-man terrorist group. I bet every weapon in here is illegal in Japan!"

The rest of the team huddled around the vault and Frank pointed out the pieces he recognized. During the "tour" of Takamura's private weapons cache, Sandstrom had barked several times from the bedroom doorway, so Frank handed Jim a small walkie-talkie from the armoire and stuffed the matching unit into his shirt pocket.

"Fitz and I are going outside to take a look around and walk the dog. You guys sit tight in here until we get back." Tapping his shirt pocket, he continued, "If anything comes up, I'll call Jim."

Frank removed a military-issue M-16 rifle and an ammunition clip from the armoire and handed it to Fitz.

"Ever use one of those?" he asked.

"A long time ago, but I'm a hand-gun person myself. I'd rather have that Glock," replied Fitz, indicating a 9mm Glock automatic on a shelf.

Fitz handed the rifle back to Frank, accepted the pistol and shoved it into his belt. Frank replaced the rifle, secured the armoire and retrieved his Beretta from the bag slung over the back of his wheelchair. With a nod from Frank, Fitz pushed the wheel chair through the bedroom door and down the hall to the living room. Sandstrom trotted along behind, eager to get outside.

While Sandstrom explored the few shrubs near the house, Frank and Fitz discussed the current situation.

"Frank, do you think they'll find the girl? Before she gets into trouble, I mean?"

Frank shook his head. "I don't know, but the chances are a lot better with Tony out there. And it appears that our friend Takamura has had some serious military training, too. Between the two of them, they will be a formidable force."

From a distant bush, Sandstrom barked loudly. Fitz started to shush him when he noticed that the dog's attention was focused on the driveway that led from the road to Takamura's house.

Easing the pistol out of his belt, he said, "We may have visitors."

Fitz knelt down and signaled Sandstrom to return to him. The dog hesitated for a second, looking back and forth between his owner and the driveway, but reluctantly started for the house. He had almost reached Fitz when the sound of tires on gravel broke the silence and, with a loud bark, Sandstrom made a dash for the line of bushes that separated Takamura's lot from the road beyond.

Fitz stood up and called once, but his attention was diverted by the grill and characteristic hood ornament of a Mercedes sedan as it turned off the road and into the driveway. As the vehicle made its way slowly toward the house, Frank rested his gun in his lap under the edge of his shirt and Fitz stood with his hands behind him, his finger on the trigger. As subtly as possible, Frank touched his shirt pocket and keyed the talk button on the walkie-talkie. He instructed Jim to secure the bedroom door and stay inside until further notice and as soon as he was done speaking he flicked the radio off so any reply from Jim wouldn't give away the presence of the radio.

"I thought so!" said Frank. "This vehicle has been shadowing us since we first arrived on the island. Not a word about the others inside. This might just be a social call."

"Yeah, right," mumbled Fitz.

The sedan continued up the driveway and turned so the passenger side of the vehicle was no more than six feet in front of Frank and Fitz. The tinted windows completely masked the identity of the occupants but Frank had spotted two Asian men through the windshield. There was no movement from either side for several seconds. Finally the front window slid down about half way, revealing the face of a thin, middle-aged Asian man.

"Please place your weapons on the ground in front of you, gentlemen," said the monotone voice.

When neither Frank nor Fitz complied, the man smiled.

"I didn't think it would be that easy," he said. "Maybe this will change your mind."

The back window slid part way down, revealing Tony's face. The end of a pistol barrel was being pressed against his left temple by someone Frank couldn't see.

"Hi, Frank," greeted Tony with a grin of embarrassment. "I think he's pretty serious about that 'drop your weapons' thing."

"Tony! Where's Takamura? Did you find Riko?"

"Mr. T is here with me but we didn't catch up with Riko. I'm sorry, Frank."

"That's enough of the pleasantries, Mr. Morton. Place your weapons on the ground or my associate will terminate him right now!"

"That's going to make quite a mess in Yamato-san's expensive car, isn't it?" replied Frank without expression.

The Asian smiled again and then, without warning, raised a pistol and fired. The bullet struck the left side of Frank's chair right where the wheel connected, causing it to fly off and topple the chair. Frank groaned as he hit the gravel, dropping his Berretta.

"I'm quite good with this, you know," smiled the Asian.

With his gun still pointing at Frank, he looked to Fitz and said without emotion, "Put it down or your friend dies right there on the ground."

Without moving his arms, Fitz let the gun fall at his heels and then stepped back so the man in the car could see that the Glock was on the ground.

"Good. Now kick it away from you and then go do the same with your friend's gun. And then help him up – I hate to shoot someone when he's down."

Once Frank was up and holding on to Fitz's shoulder for support, the man in the car uttered a few words and the back door on the far side of the Mercedes opened. A young man with a gun got out, followed by Takamura. The gunman motioned Takamura around the car with a wave of his gun barrel and followed close behind. The pair took up a position near the front tire and, with his pistol firmly against Takamura's head, he nodded to the man in the front seat, who slowly opened his door and got out of the car.

Without taking his eyes or his aim off Frank, he uttered several more words and then, in English, he said, "Open the door very slowly, Mr. Nicoletti, and put both hands on your head before you get out. I'm aware of your background, so be very careful. Mr. Morton's life is in your hands."

Tony did as he was told and was followed by another slim Asian whose gun barrel never left contact with Tony's temple.

Frank took a quick inventory: three armed men outside the car and at least one – the driver – still inside. Normally these wouldn't be impossible odds for Frank and Tony, but Frank's right leg was in a cast and the three gunmen weren't just common street thugs. Their handling of their prisoners indicated that they had done this sort of thing before.

With his hands clasped on top of his head, Tony flashed Frank a finger signal: "Attack?"

Frank adjusted his grip on Fitz's shoulder to hide his reply: "Abort!"

He waited for Tony's acknowledgement before addressing the Asian who appeared to be in charge.

"I take it you're the one who called my hotel room this morning."

"That's correct. You and your nosey friends are becoming a threat to the security of my operation and I can't allow that. Did you really think that moving out here would make you any safer? You've actually made my job easier, because the waters right off this bluff are famous for their schools of hungry hammerhead sharks. Ask your diver friend here."

The man guarding Takamura poked him in the head with his gun barrel and the Japanese man nodded.

"It's true, Frank. This time of the year there are hundreds of them just off the point out there."

Frank shook his head. "I don't get it. What have my team and I done to threaten you? We came here to investigate the Monument and its origin, like so many other curious westerners before us. How does that pose a threat to you and whatever you're into?"

The gunman called through his open window to the driver, who emerged from behind the wheel on the other side of the car.

"Do either of you recognize this man?" the gunman asked.

"The policeman we took to Okinawa!" shouted Fitz. "You're the one that recognized the journal!"

"Very good," grinned the gunman. "And before we're finished here today, I intend to have that journal back. Now do you understand why I can't let you and your team leave Yonaguni, Mr. Morton?"

"Things are starting to come together, yes," nodded Frank. "But tell me something. The Japanese citizens listed in that journal are thought to have been taken to North Korea. What's your connection to all this. You don't look Korean to me, and I'm damn sure you're not speaking Korean – or anything even close – so what's the connection?"

"Very perceptive, Mr. Morton. Your years in Southeast Asia taught you much. The dialect is called Min and since this is your last day in this life, I'll tell you what my connection is. Maybe it will give you something to think about in the after-life.

"My name is actually Hao Zhuo but I understand that I'm known around here as *Chugoku-jin* – the Chinaman. I live in a city not too far from here called Fu-Chow. It's on the Chinese mainland just the other side of the northern tip of Taiwan.

"I operate a small but lucrative business providing selected individuals to my friends in North Korea. When I receive an order for a specific type of individual, I contact my network of suppliers in Japan and the bidding begins."

"The bidding?" interrupted Fitz.

"Yes. A specifications sheet is transmitted and the supplier who provides the most qualified individual at the lowest price becomes the successful bidder. The selected subject is then acquired and delivered here to Yonaguni. Once the financial transaction is complete, the individual is transferred to me in Fu-Chow, where I arrange for transportation up the Chinese mainland to the Shandong Peninsula. There, he or she is put aboard a freighter for the short trip across the Yellow Sea to North Korea. It's a simple plan, I know, but it's one that works quite well. And it's become a rather brisk business now that the Japanese government is keeping such close tabs on the North Koreans. They spend so much time patrolling the waters between their big island of Honshu and the Korean Peninsula that they never bother to look at the traffic headed south. And every once in a while we get lucky and find the right individual in Okinawa or the other southern islands and that reduces the delivery expense, which reduces our cost and increases our profit."

"You bastard!" shouted Takamura as he lunged for the Chinaman. "You talk as if these people were sacks of rice!"

Before Takamura had completed his first step, his guard hammered him at the base of his skull with his gun and Takamura dropped to the ground.

Frank started to move, but the Chinaman's gun swung back toward him and Frank could see the other man's finger tensing on the trigger.

"Please don't do anything foolish, Mr. Morton. Your turn will come, to be sure, but I'd prefer to save you for last so you can watch the demise of your comrades. You brought them here and it's only fitting that you have a chance to watch them leave.

"Now, back to my journal. Please tell my driver where it is so he can retrieve it."

"Sorry, but we no longer have it," replied Frank, knowing full well that the journal was tucked away in Jim's backpack just inside Takamura's house.

"Really? We know your flight crew delivered it to a Professor Barac in Okinawa but we've, ah, *questioned* the Professor and his daughter and we're convinced they no longer have it. That would imply that your crew brought it back here to you."

"Damn you," muttered Fitz. "If you hurt them ..."

"Listen, I said we don't have it!" interrupted Frank. "We've already turned it over to the Coast Guard, along with Professor Barac's interpretation of its contents. You're too late, and killing us will accomplish nothing."

"I don't think you've had time to turn it over to anyone, Mr. Morton. My host has been keeping pretty close tabs on you and your people and he assures me that you haven't spoken with the authorities."

"Your host – would that be Yamato?" asked Frank in a calmer voice.

The Chinaman nodded.

"So he's involved in this kidnapping ring of yours, too?" pressed Frank.

"Yes, but not willingly. He provides us with our southern transfer point in exchange for my silence about his archeological discoveries. You might say we have a business relationship, but nothing more."

"So the room where the journal was found – the one below Yamato's water pumping station – is the transfer point you keep talking about!" exclaimed Frank. "That explains the box of survival supplies that Linda found. But why would anyone leave something as important as a detailed list of transactions down there?"

"A careless error, I assure you, and one that won't be made again. The individual responsible has already joined the sharks, Mr. Morton, as you soon will."

"So Yamato knows about the pyramids?" asked an unusually quiet Tony.

"The what? I don't know anything about pyramids, but the old man is obsessed with these ancient Ninja trinkets his men found in a cave a few years ago. He thinks they link his family to nobility, or some such crap, and now he's convinced that the rubies in the center of these things have some magical power. All I know is that he's so wrapped up in this fantasy of his that he'll do anything to protect the secret. He'd have a stroke if he knew that his very own niece – the lovely Aya – was the one who brought his weakness to my attention. She's very involved in this anti-Tokyo movement, you know. A weakness we exploited to our benefit.

"I pay the old man a personal visit a couple of times a year to make sure he hasn't forgotten about our deal and, as a little bonus for my trouble, I usually take back a free sample or two, if you get my drift. This time, your young friend Riko will be accompanying me back to China. Her value as a technician isn't very high, but the North Koreans are always looking for Japanese breeding stock and my investment is negligible, so I'll do okay."

The Chinaman's face broke into an evil grin as he added, "And who knows – I may even keep her for myself."

R.J. Archer

On the ground, Takamura moaned and started to roll over but his guard pressed the side of his face into the gravel with his foot and hissed, "Don't move!"

"Alright, enough talk!" shouted the Chinaman. "I'll give you five seconds to tell me where that journal is before I start killing your associates. And I'll start with this one – I believe he's an old friend."

The Chinaman moved to Tony, turned him sidewise and pressed the end of his gun barrel to Tony's forehead. The man who had been guarding Tony helped the other guard pull Takamura to his feet and dragged him over to join Fitz and Frank.

"Don't tell him anything," said Tony sternly. "He's going to kill us all anyway – let him squirm!"

The Chinaman began counting backwards from five.

"Five ... four ... I'm not kidding, Mr. Morton. Where's that journal?"

Near the back of the car, to his left, Frank spotted a slight movement and it took all his special ops training to not turn his head and look.

"Three ... two ..."

Fitz let out an ear-piercing whistle and before the Chinaman could say "One" Sandstrom darted around the Mercedes and latched on to the back of the man's leg.

Tony saw the small dog coming and smashed the gun away from his forehead just before it went off as the Chinaman flinched from being bitten.

Fitz took out the guard next to him with an elbow to the throat and grabbed the man's gun before it hit the ground. In one smooth, rolling motion, he fired one shot into the thigh of the other guard before the man knew what was happening. He went down with a howl.

Meanwhile, Tony had wrestled the Chinaman to the ground and disarmed him. Sandstrom released his grip but he had opened a three-inch gash in the man's leg. The Chinaman screamed as blood spurted from the severed artery.

From his position on the ground, Tony felt the sedan starting to move. He grabbed the Chinaman's handgun and tossed it to Frank, who was struggling to stand without the support of Fitz.

"Frank! The driver!" yelled Tony.

Frank caught the gun but lost his balance in the process. He knew he was going down face first but he managed to get off one good shot before he crashed into the gravel. The bullet passed

Page 241

through the open window on the passenger's side of the car and hit the driver in the right shoulder. The car sped up and then crashed into a large boulder Takamura had used to line his driveway.

Fitz raced to the car. He yanked the driver from behind the wheel and turned off the ignition. The driver was seriously wounded, but he would live. Fitz dragged him back to join his injured comrades. The Chinaman was losing a lot of blood and Fitz indicated the stricken man with a nod.

"Shall we try to save him or just let him bleed to death?" he asked Tony, who was still holding the man down.

"Save him if you can, but don't worry about it if you can't. Nice shooting, Frank. Are you okay?"

"I'm fine, but I can't get up with this damn cast on. Give me a hand, will you?"

Takamura had regained full consciousness during the fight and was now holding the two guards at gunpoint.

"This one's going to need some doctoring, too," he said, pointing at the guard Fitz had shot in the leg. "What's your dog doing over by the car?"

Sandstrom was standing on his hind legs barking at the trunk of the black Mercedes.

"It looks like your mutt has found something. Toss me the keys and I'll check it out while you play Florence Nightingale."

"Be nice to him, my friend – he just saved your life," laughed Fitz as he tossed the keys.

"Yeah, I guess he did, at that," Tony frowned. "Now I'm indebted to a dog!"

As Tony approached, Sandstrom got down off the car and ran to meet him, barking and tail wagging. Tony bent down to pet the animal, but he ran back to the car, still barking.

"Okay, Lassie, show me what's wrong," grumbled Tony.

As he inserted the key, Sandstrom stood up against the bumper again and barked even louder.

Tony raised the lid and peered into the trunk not knowing what to expect. There, securely bound and gagged, was Riko!

Two hours later, the Japanese Coast Guard finally left. There would be more questions, to be sure, but they were satisfied for now. The Chinaman and his three accomplices had been airlifted out by helicopter and were now under heavy guard at the clinic. The Chinaman was in danger of losing his leg and one guard probably wouldn't speak again, thanks to Fitz's elbow, but they would all live and that was more than they deserved.

In Takamura's living room, the mood was one of guarded optimism. Other than a little rough handling, Riko hadn't been hurt but there was serious concern for the safety of the Professor and his daughter. The Coast Guard had dispatched a team to check on them and they had promised to call as soon as they knew anything.

Frank and the team had stuck to their original plan, telling the investigators everything they knew about the journal, including what the Chinaman had added when he thought they weren't going to live to repeat the information. They implicated the elder Yamato but they also made sure the Coast Guard understood that his participation was forced. They neglected to mention the *tsubutes*, the ancient passageways and Jim's theories about the pyramids.

Takamura passed around a tray of Sake and proposed a toast. "To Yonaguni – whatever it is!"

"Here, here!" added Frank. "I guess we should think about returning to the States once we get the lose ends tied up here. What about it, gang?"

"Not me," announced Jim. "I'm staying on for a while to gather more information about those tunnels and the inscriptions in them. This could be a major discovery and I'm not letting it slip through my fingers, like I did with the Maya spheres!"

Frank had expected Jim's response, because he had mentioned further research several times since they had discovered the passageways, but Linda's response came as a complete surprise.

"I think I'll stay for a while, too," she said, draping her arm over Jim's shoulder. "He's going to need somebody to keep him out of trouble and I'm fascinated by those *tsubutes*."

"Well, now there's a team of misfits if I ever saw one," laughed Tony. "And who's going to keep you out of trouble while you're keeping Jim out of trouble?"

"We will!" shouted Takamura. "Riko and I, and the whole Hammer Diving Service staff would be happy to help in any way we can, if they'll have us."

"Perfect!" beamed Jim. "I'd like to do a detailed survey of the entire Yonaguni coastline and your boat would be a big help. Maybe you can even teach me to dive before I go home."

"What about you, Frank?" asked Riko, who was lounging comfortably on the arm of Takamura's chair.

"Well, I need to give my leg a few days to mend and then I guess I'll head back to Seattle. It's going to be pretty lonely though, if you're all staying here."

"Hey, I never said I was staying," cried Tony. "I've got a young lady waiting for me in the Caribbean who's still pissed that I came over here in the first place. Besides, the nightlife here sucks!"

Frank raised his sake cup again. "Well, I guess everybody has a plan. Here's to successes and safe travels!"

Just then, the island of Yonaguni was jolted by the worst earthquake in recent times.

"The gods are restless," whispered Riko as she clutched Takamura's arm.

"Or the aliens," added Jim.

THE END

Epilogue

Frank closed the manila folder he'd been reading and leaned back in his plush leather desk chair. The rest of the NWIDI team had left for the day and the hangar was quiet. The sun had just set on another unusually warm September day and the metal roof of the building was popping as it cooled. Frank closed his eyes and smiled. It was hard to believe it had been six months since their trip to the mysterious island of Yonaguni, in southern Japan.

When he and Tony had returned on the Learjet piloted by Fitz and Susan Fitzgerald, Jim and Linda had remained behind to investigate the underground passageways of Yonaguni. Within a month, Jim had deciphered enough of the passageway writings to change the entire history of ancient Japan. Based on star maps and other information that had been found, the writings appeared to be at least 14,000 years old and described a rich cultural history that probably dated back another 2,000 years. The theories of Graham Hancock and others had been substantiated overnight and mainstream anthropology was being forced to rethink the entire timeline of human civilization.

Best of all, Jim was receiving credit for his discoveries and he was a rising star. When the team had first discussed the trip to Japan, back in early February, Jim had been reluctant to go because he was being pressured to publish by the University of Washington, where he was a professor. Now the University was begging him not to accept any of the dozens of prestigious positions he'd been offered.

Linda had stayed, too, but her interest was with the ancient *tsubutes* that had been found in a tomb deep under Mt. Urabu. It had been decided that her work would not be made public until it was better understood but Frank knew it was just a matter of time before the rest of the world learned what he and his team already knew – that the red stones in the center of each of the twelve ceremonial *tsubutes* were some sort of alien technology that had been fashioned into the objects by the same ancients Jim had discovered.

Because of Jim's work, NWIDI had received a lot of publicity and Frank found himself bombarded with research grant offers and proposed scientific partnerships but the most unusual request to date was the one he'd just finished reading. The file had come to him through a friend at the Department of Energy, in Las Vegas, but it had been approved at the highest levels of the U.S. government. And that's what made Frank nervous.

The file described a remarkable discovery that had been made a year earlier by a Canadian underwater exploration company called Advanced Digital Communications. While doing some salvage work for the Cuban government, ADC accidentally discovered what appears to be an entire sunken city just off the western tip of Cuba, at a depth of about 2,200 feet. The complex covers nearly eight square miles and appears to contain many pyramids, roads and buildings. Tests that had been completed only two months earlier concluded that the megalithic structures are made of granite but the nearest source of granite is more than 1,000 miles from the site. And geologists estimated that the land mass containing the complex probably sank between 15,000 and 50,000 years ago. The press was already hinting that this could be the location of the mythical lost city of Atlantis described by Plato in 350 B.C. And to make matters worse, Castro was prohibiting exploration by all American companies in retaliation for the US trade embargo. National Geographic had offered to fund a large-scale expedition to the site, but it had been refused. Now NWIDI had received a request from "the highest levels" to learn all it could about the site, with or without the consent of the Cuban government. And Frank knew he wouldn't be able to decline. Not because of where the request had originated but because, well, what if it is Atlantis? That would be an incredible discovery! Or what if this new site were somehow related to the alien spheres his team had discovered in the hands of the Maya or the alien rubies they had found on Yonaguni? What if this much larger and older site had been the aliens' capitol? What if it still is?

R.J. Archer

Watch for the next Seeds of Civilization adventure
Triangle
in early 2007

Books previously published in this series:

Tractrix, Book 1 in the Seeds Of Civilization series

www.ingramcontent.com/pod-product-compliance
Lightning Source LLC
Chambersburg PA
CBHW050509260626
47157CB00004B/1253